SMALL MAGICS

ILONA ANDREWS

Small Magics
Copyright © 2015 by Ilona Andrews
Ebook ISBN: 9781943772254
KDP Print ISBN:9798425724236
IS Print ISBN: 9781641971973

Cover and interior illustrations by Luisa Preisler
Magic Tests was originally published in the anthology, An Apple for the Creature. Copyright © 2012 by Ilona Andrews
A Questionable Client was originally published in the anthology, Dark and Stormy Knights. Copyright © 2010 by Ilona Andrews
Retribution Clause was originally published in the anthology, Hex Appeal. Copyright © 2012 by Ilona Andrews
Of Swine and Roses was originally published as a short story. Copyright © 2011 by Ilona Andrews
Grace of Small Magics was originally published in The Mammoth Book of Paranormal Romance. Copyright © 2009 by Ilona Andrews
Curran's Point of View
Copyright © 2013, 2019 by Ilona Andrews
Jim's Point of View
Copyright © 2013, 2019 by Ilona Andrews

NYLA Publishing
121 W 27th St., Suite 1201, NY 10001, New York.
http://www.nyliterary.com"

MAGIC TESTS

Sometimes being a kid is very difficult. The adults are supposed to feed you and keep you safe, but they want you to deal with the world according to their views and not your own. They encourage you to have opinions, and if you express them, they will listen but they won't hear. And when they give you a choice, it's a selection of handpicked possibilities they have prescreened. No matter what you decide, the core choice has already been made, and you weren't involved in it.

That's how Kate and I ended up in the office of the director of Seven Star Academy. I said I didn't want to go to school. She gave me a list of ten schools and said to pick one. I wrote the names of the schools on little bits of paper, pinned them to the corkboard, and threw my knife at them for a while. After half an hour, Seven Stars was the only name I could still read. Choice made.

Now we were sitting in soft chairs in a nice office, waiting for the school director, and Kate was exercising her willpower. Before I met Kate, I had heard people say it, but I didn't know what it meant. Now I knew. Kate was the Beast Lord's mate, which meant that Curran and she were in charge of Atlanta's giant shapeshifter pack. It was so huge, people actually called it the Pack. Shapeshifters were kind of like bombs: things frequently set them off and they exploded with violent force. To keep from exploding, they made up elaborate rules and Kate had to exercise her willpower a lot.

She was doing it now; from outside she looked very calm and composed, but I could tell she was doing it by the way she sat. When Kate was relaxed, she fidgeted. She'd shift in her chair, throw one leg over the other, lean to the side, then lean back. She was very still now, legs in jeans together, holding Slayer, her magic saber, on her lap, one hand on the hilt, the other on the scabbard. Her face was relaxed, almost serene. I could totally picture her leaping straight onto the table from the chair and slicing the director's head off with her saber.

Kate usually dealt with things by talking, and when that didn't work, chopping obstacles into tiny pieces and frying them with magic so they didn't get back up. The sword was her talisman, because she believed in it. She held it like some people held crosses or the star-and-crescent. Her philosophy was, if it had a pulse, it could be killed. I didn't really have a philosophy, but I could see how talking with the school director would be difficult for her. If he said something she didn't like, chopping him to tiny pieces wouldn't exactly help me get into the school.

"What if when the director comes in, I take my underwear off, put them on my head, and dance around? Do you think it would help?"

Kate looked at me. It was her hard-ass stare. Kate could be really scary.

"That doesn't work on me," I told her. "I know you won't hurt me."

"If you want to prance around with panties on your head, I won't stop you," she said. "It's your basic human right to make a fool of yourself."

"I don't want to go to school." Spending all my time in a

place where I was the poor rat adopted by a merc and a shapeshifter, while spoiled little rich girls jeered when I walked by and stuck-up teachers put me in remedial courses? No thanks.

Kate exercised her will some more. "You need an education, Julie."

"You can teach me."

"I do and I'll continue to do so. But you need to know other things, besides the ones I can teach. You need a well-rounded education."

"I don't like education. I like working at the office. I want to do what you and Andrea do."

Kate and Andrea ran Cutting Edge, a small firm that helped people with their magic hazmat issues. It was a dangerous job, but I liked it. Besides, I was pretty messed up. Normal things like going to school and getting a regular job didn't hold any interest for me. I couldn't even picture myself doing that.

"Andrea went to the Order's Academy for six years and I've trained since I could walk."

"I'm willing to train."

My body tensed, as if an invisible hand had squeezed my insides into a clump. I held my breath…

Magic flooded the world in an invisible wave. The phantom hand let go, and the world shimmered with hues of every color as my sensate vision kicked in. Magic came and went as it pleased. Some older people still remembered the time when technology was always in control and magic didn't exist. But that was long ago. Now magic and technology kept trading places, like two toddlers playing musical chairs. Sometimes magic ruled, and cars and guns didn't work. Sometimes technology was in charge, and magic spells fizzled out. I preferred the magic myself, because unlike ninety-nine point nine-nine-nine-whatever percent of people I could see it.

I looked at Kate, using a tiny drop of my power. It was kind of like flexing a muscle, a conscious effort to look the right way at something. One moment Kate sat there, all normal, or as normal as Kate could be, the next she was wrapped in a translucent glow. Most people's magic glowed in one color. Humans radiated blue, shapeshifters green, vampires gave off a purple-red... Kate's magic shifted colors. It was blue and deep purple, and pale pearl-like gold streaked through with tendrils of red. It was the weirdest thing I had ever seen. The first time I saw it, it freaked me out.

"You have to keep going to school," freaky Kate said.

I leaned back and hung my head over the chair's back. "Why?"

"Because I can't teach you everything, and shapeshifters shouldn't be your only source of education. You may not always want to be affiliated with shapeshifters. Down the road, you may want to make your own choices."

I pushed against the floor with my feet, rocking a little in my chair.

"I'm trying to make my own choice, but you won't let me."

"That's right," Kate said. "I'm older, wiser, and I know better. Deal with it."

Parenting, kick-ass Kate Daniels's style. Do what I say. There wasn't even an *or* attached to it. *Or* didn't exist.

I rocked back and forth some more. "Do you think I'm your punishment from God?"

"No. I'd like to think that God, if he exists, is kind, not vengeful."

The door of the office opened and a man walked in. He was older than Kate, bald, with Asian features, dark eyes, and a big smile. "It's a view I share."

I sat up straight. Kate got up and offered her hand. "Mr. Dargye?"

The man shook her hand. "Please call me Gendun. I much prefer it."

They shook and sat down. Adult rituals. My history teacher from the old school once told us that shaking hands was a gesture of peace—it demonstrated that you had no weapon. Since now we had magic, shaking hands was more a leap of faith. Do I shake this weirdo's hand and run the risk that he will infect me with a magic plague or shoot lightning into my skin or do I step back and be rude? Hmm. Maybe handshakes would go away in the future.

Gendun was looking at me. He had sucker eyes. Back when I lived on the street, we used to mob people like him, because they were kind and soft-hearted and you could always count on some sort of handout. They weren't naive bleeding hearts—they knew that while you cried in front of them and clutched your tummy, your friends were stealing their wallets, but they would feed you anyway. That's just the way they moved through the world.

I squinted, bringing the color of his magic into focus. Pale blue, almost silver. Divine magic, born of faith. Mister Gendun was a priest of some sort.

"What god do you believe in?" I asked. When you're a kid, they let you get away with being direct.

"I'm a Buddhist." Gendun smiled. "I believe in human potential for understanding and compassion. The existence of an omnipotent God is possible, but so far I have seen no evidence that he exists. What god do you believe in?"

"None." I met a goddess once. It didn't turn out well for everyone involved. Gods used faith the way a car used gas; it was the supply from which they drew their power. I refused to fuel any of their motors.

Gendun smiled. "Thank you for responding to my request so promptly."

Request? What request?

"Two of the Pack's children attend your school," Kate said.

5

"The Pack will do everything in our power to offer you assistance."

Huh? Wait a minute. I thought this was about me. Nobody said anything about the school requesting our assistance.

"This is Ms. Olsen," Kate said.

I smiled at Gendun. "Please call me Julie. I much prefer it." Technically my name was now Julie Lennart-Daniels-Olsen, which was silly. If Kate and Curran got married, I'd be down to Lennart-Olsen. Until then, I decided Olsen was good enough.

"It is nice to meet you, Julie." Gendun smiled and nodded at me. He had this really strange calming thing about him. He was very…balanced somehow. Reminded me of the Pack's medmage, Dr. Doolittle.

"There are many schools in the city for the children of exceptional parents," Gendun said. "Seven Stars is a school for exceptional children. Our methods are unorthodox and our students are unique."

Woo, a school of special snowflakes. Or monster children. Depending on how you chose to look at it.

Magic didn't affect just our environment. All sorts of people who once had been normal and ordinary were discovering new and sometimes unwelcome things about themselves. Some could freeze things. Some grew claws and fur. And some saw magic.

"Discretion is of utmost importance to us," Gendun said.

"Despite her age, Ms. Olsen is an experienced operative," Kate said.

I am?

"She understands the need for discretion."

I do?

"She has a particular talent that will make her very effective in this case," Kate said.

Gendun opened a folder, took out a picture, and slid it across the table to me. A girl. She had a pretty heart-shaped face framed by spirals of red hair. Her eyes were green and her long eyelashes curled out until they almost touched her eyebrows. She looked so pretty, like a little doll.

"This is Ashlyn," Gendun said. "She is a freshman at this school. A very good student. Two days ago she disappeared. The location spell indicates she is alive and that she hasn't left the grounds. We've attempted to notify her parents, but they are traveling at the moment and are out of reach, as are her emergency contacts. You have twenty-four hours to find her."

"What happens after twenty-four hours?"

"We will have to notify the authorities," Gendun said. "Her parents had given us a lot of latitude in regard to Ashlyn. She is a sensitive child and her behavior is often driven by that sensitivity. But in this case our hands are tied. If a student is missing, we are legally bound to report it after seventy-two hours."

Report it to Paranormal Activity Division of Atlanta's police force, no doubt. PAD was about as subtle as a runaway bulldozer. They would take this school apart and grill all of their special snowflakes until they melted into goo in their interrogation rooms. How many would fold and confess to something they had not done?

I looked at Kate.

She arched an eyebrow at me. "Interested?"

"We would give you a visitor pass," Gendun said. "I will speak to the teachers, so you can conduct your investigation quietly. We have guest students who tour the school before attending, so you wouldn't draw any attention and the disruption to the other children will be minimal."

This was some sort of Kate trick of getting me into this school. I looked at the picture again. Trick or not, a girl was hiding somewhere. She could be hiding because she was playing some sort of a joke, but it was highly unlikely. Mostly people hid because they were scared. I could relate. I'd been scared before. It wasn't fun.

Someone had to find her. Someone had to care about what happened.

I pulled the picture closer. "I'll do it."

My student guide was a tall dark-haired girl named Brook. She had skinny legs, bony arms, and wore round glasses that constantly slid down her nose. She kept pushing them up with her middle finger, so it looked as if she was shooting the bird at the entire world every five minutes. Her magic was a strong simple blue, the color of human abilities. We met in the front office, where they outfitted me with a white armband. Apparently they marked their visitors. If there was any trouble, we'd be easy to shoot.

"Okay, you follow me and don't touch things," Brook informed me. "Stuff here is randomly warded. Also Barka has been leaving little tiny charges of magic all around the school. You touch it, it zaps you. Then your fingers hurt for an hour."

"Is Barka a student?"

"Barka is a pisshead," Brook told me and pushed her glasses up. "Come on."

We walked up the stairs. The bell rang and the staircase filled with kids.

"Four floors," Brook told me. "The school is a big square, with the garden slash courtyard in the center. All the fields, like for soccer and football, are outside of the square. First floor is the gymnasium, pool, dance studio, auditorium, and cafeteria. Second floor, humanities: literature, history, sociology, anthropology, Latin—"

"Did you know Ashlyn?" I asked.

Brook paused, momentarily knocked off her course by the interruption. "She did not take Latin."

"But did you know her?"

"Yes."

"What kind of a student was she?"

Brook shrugged. "Quiet. We have an algebra class together, fourth period. I thought she might be competition at first. You have to watch out for the quiet ones."

"Was she?"

"Naaah." Brook grimaced. "Progress reports came out last week. Her math grade was seventeen. One seven. She only does well in one class, botany. You could give her a broom and she'll stick it in the ground and grow you an apple tree. I took botany last semester and she beat my grade by two points. She has a perfect hundred. There's got to be a trick to it." Brook squared her shoulders. "That's okay. I am taking AP botany next year. I'll take her down."

"You're a little bit crazy, you know that?"

Brook shrugged and pushed her glasses up at me. "Third floor, magic: alchemy, magic theory—"

"Did Ashlyn seem upset over the seventeen in math?" Maybe she was hiding because of her grades.

Brook paused. "No."

"She wasn't worried about her parents?" When I got a bad grade in my old boarding school, Kate would make a trip to the school to chew me out. When I got homesick, I'd flunk a grade on purpose. Sometimes she came by herself. Sometimes with other people. Boy kind of people. Of whom I promised myself I wouldn't be thinking about, because they were idiots.

"I met her parents on family day. I was in charge of Hospitality Committee. They are really into nurture and all that," Brook said. "They wouldn't be upset with her. Fourth floor: science and technology—"

"Do you have lockers?"

"No. We have storage in our desks in the homerooms."

"Can we go to see Ashlyn's homeroom?"

Brook stared at me. "Look you, I'm assigned to do this stupid tour with you. I can't do the tour if you keep interrupting."

"How many tours have you done so far?"

Brook peered at me. "Eleven."

"Aren't you tired of doing them?"

"That's irrelevant. It's good for my record."

Right. "If you don't do the tour this time, I won't tell anyone."

Brook frowned. That line of thought obviously stumped her. I worked my iron while it was hot. "I'm here undercover investigating Ashlyn's disappearance. If you help me, I'll mention it to Gendun."

Brook puzzled it over.

Come on, Brook. You know you want to.

"Fine," she said. "But you'll tell Master Gendun that I helped."

"Invaluable assistance," I said.

Brook nodded. "Come on. Ashlyn's homeroom is on the second floor."

ASHLYN'S HOMEROOM WAS IN THE GEOGRAPHY CLASS. MAPS HUNG on the walls: world, Americas, U.S., and the biggest map of all, the new magic-screwed-up map of Atlanta, complete with all the new additions and warped, dangerous neighborhoods.

A few people occupied the classroom, milling in little clumps. I took a second to look around and closed my eyes. Nine people in all, two girls to my right, three boys farther on, a girl sitting by herself by the window, two guys discussing something, and a blond kid sitting by himself at the back of the class. I opened my eyes. Missed the dark-haired boy in the corner. Oh well, at least I was getting better at it.

Brook stopped by a wooden desk. It was nice, large and polished, the sealed wood stained the color of amber. Pretty. None of the places I ever studied at were this nice.

"This is her desk," Brook said.

I sat down into Ashlyn's chair. The desk had one wide

drawer running the entire length of it. I tried it gently. Locked. No big. I pulled a lockpick out of the leather bracelet on my left wrist and slid it into the lock.

The blond kid from the back sauntered over and leaned on the desk. His magic was dark, intense indigo. Probably an elemental mage. He had sharp features and blue eyes that said he was up to no good. My kind of people.

"Hi. What are you doing?"

"Go away, Barka," Brook said.

"I wasn't talking to you." The kid looked at me. "Whatcha doing?"

"I'm dancing," I told him. Ask a dumb question…

"You're breaking into Ashlyn's desk."

"See, I knew you were smart and you'd figure it out." I winked at him.

Barka made big eyes at Brook. "And what if I tell Walton you're doing that? That would be a spot on your perfect record."

"Mind your own business," Brook snapped.

"He won't," I told her. "He wants to see what's inside the desk."

Barka grinned.

The lock clicked and the drawer slid open. Rows of apples filled it. Large Red Delicious, Golden Delicious, green Granny Smith and every color and shape in between, each with a tiny sticker announcing its name. Even a handful of red crab apples the size of large cherries, stuck between Cortland and Crimson Gold. I had no idea so many varieties of apple even existed. None of them showed any signs of rotting either. They looked crisp and fresh.

I concentrated. My sensate vision kicked in. The apples glowed with bright green. Now that was a first. A healthy hunter green usually meant a shapeshifter. Human magic came in various shades of blue. Animal magic was typically too weak to be picked up by any of the machines, but I saw it just fine—it was yellow. Together blue and yellow made green. This particular green had too much yellow to belong to a regular shapeshifter.

Most shapeshifters were infected with Lyc-V virus, which let them turn into animals. Sometimes it happened the other way and animals turned into humans. The human-weres were really rare, but I've met one, and the color wasn't right for them either. Human-weres were a drab olive, but this, this was a vivid spring green.

"What kind of magic did Ashlyn have?"

Brook and Barka looked at each other. "I don't know," Barka said. "I never asked."

Whatever she was, she didn't advertise it. Totally understandable. Seeing the color of magic was an invaluable tool for law enforcement, for mages, basically for anyone who dealt with it, so much so that people actually made a magic machine, called an m-scanner, to imitate it. My magic wasn't just rare, it was exceptional. I was a hundred times more precise than any existing m-scanner. But in a fight, being a sensate didn't do me any good at all. If I walked around telling everyone about it, sooner or later someone would try to use me and I had to use other means than my sensate ability to protect myself. It was easier to just keep my mouth shut.

Ashlyn could be that kind of magic user, something rare but not useful in combat.

Still didn't explain her obsession with apples, though. Maybe she was using them to bribe her teachers. But then her grades would be better.

The shorter of the three girls to our left glared at me. Her magic, a solid indigo when I came in, now developed streaks of pale celery green. Normally the magic signature didn't change. Ever. Except for Kate.

Hello, clue.

I pretended to look at the apples. "Did Ashlyn have any enemies?"

Barka picked up a pen and rolled it between his fingers. "Not that I noticed. She was quiet. A looker, but no personality."

Brook pushed her glasses up at him. "Pervert."

The girl took a step toward us. "What are you doing?"

"Dancing!" Barka said.

Brook didn't even look in her direction. "Mind your own business, Lisa."

Lisa skewed her mouth into a disapproving thin line, which was quite a fit because she had one of those pouty-lip mouths. Eyebrows plucked into two narrow lines, unnaturally straight hair, carefully parted, pink shiny on those big lips… Lisa was clearly the Take-Care-of-Myself type. Good clothes, too. Girls like that made my life miserable at the old school. I was never put together enough, my clothes were never expensive enough, and I didn't stroll the halls broadcasting to everyone who cared that I was much better than they were.

But we weren't at my old school, and a lot has changed since. Besides, she could be a perfectly nice person. Although somehow I doubted it.

"You shouldn't be doing that," Lisa said, entirely too loudly.

If I poked her, would her magic get even veinier? Was veinier even a word? "I'm looking for Ashlyn," I told her.

"She's dead," Lisa announced and checked the room out of the corner of her eye.

Don't worry, you have everyone's attention.

"Here we go," Brook muttered.

"How do you know that? Did you kill her?" Poke-poke-poke.

Lisa raised her chin. "I know because I spoke to her spirit."

"Her spirit?" I asked.

"Yes, her spirit. Her ghost."

That was nice, but there was no such thing as ghosts. Even

Kate had never run across one. I never saw any ghost magic and I had seen a lot of messed-up things.

"Did her ghost tell you who killed her?" I asked.

"She took her own life," Lisa declared.

Brook pushed her glasses up. "Don't be ridiculous. This whole 'I see spirits' thing is getting old."

Lisa rocked back on her heels. Her face turned serious. "Ashlyn! Show yourself, spirit."

"This is stupid," Barka said.

"Show your presence!" Lisa called.

Yellow-green veins shot through her magic, sparking with flashes of dandelion yellow. Whoa.

The desk shuddered under my fingertips. The chairs around me rattled.

Brook took a step back.

The desk danced, jumping up and down. The two chairs on both sides of me shot to the ceiling, hovered there for a tense second, and crashed down.

Nice.

Lisa leveled her stare at me. "Ashlyn is dead. I don't know who you are, but you should leave. You disturb her."

I laughed.

Lisa turned on her heel and walked out.

"So Lisa is a telekinetic?" I asked.

Brook shrugged. "A little. Nothing like this. The chair-flying thing is new. Usually she has to sweat to push a pen across the desk."

And this new power wouldn't have anything to do with those lovely yellow-green streaks in her magic, would it? Like Ashlyn's apples, yellow-green, but not the same shade. Two weird magic colors in one day. That was a hell of a thing, as Kate would say.

"You're not leaving?" Barka asked me.

"Of course she isn't leaving," Brook told him. "I haven't finished the tour."

"When people tell me to leave, it's the right time to stick around," I told him. "Did Lisa have any problems with Ashlyn?"

"Lisa has problems with everyone," Brook said. "People like her like to pick on you if you have any weakness to make themselves feel better."

"She's a dud," Barka added. "Well, she was a dud, apparently. Her parents are both professors at the Mage Academy. When she was first admitted, she made a big deal out of all this major magic that she supposedly had."

"I remember that." Brook grimaced. "Every time she opened her mouth, it was all 'at the Mage Academy where my father works' or 'when I visited my mother's laboratory at the Mage Academy.' Ugh."

"She claimed to have tons of power," Barka added, "but she couldn't do anything with it, except some minor telekinesis."

"Let me guess, people made fun of her?" I asked.

"She brought a lot of it on herself," Brook told me. "Not everybody here has super-awesome magic."

"Like Sam." Barka shrugged. "If you give him a clear piece of glass, he can etch it with his magic so it looks frosted. It's cool the first time you see it, but it's pretty useless and he can't control it very well either. He doesn't make a big deal out of it."

"It's in Lisa's head that she is super-special," Brook said. "She feels entitled, like we're all peons here and she is a higher being. Nobody likes being treated that way."

"Does she get picked on?" I asked.

Barka shrugged again. "Nothing too bad. She doesn't get invited to hang out. Nobody wants to sit with her at lunch. But that's just pure self-defense, because she doesn't listen to whatever you have to say. She just waits to tell you about her special parents. I guess she finally got her powers."

"Did she get them about the time Ashlyn disappeared?"

"Yeah." Barka grimaced. "Then she started sensing Ashlyn's presence everywhere. Who knows, maybe Ashlyn is really dead."

"Location spell says she is alive. Besides, there is no such thing as ghosts," I told them.

"And you're an authority on ghosts?" Brook asked.

"Trust me on this."

Ghosts might be better. I had this sick little feeling in my stomach that said this was something bad. Something really bad.

I could call Kate and ask her what would cause the magic of two different colors to show up. The colors weren't blended or flowing into one another the way Kate's colors did. They were distinct. Separate. Together but not mixing.

Ehhh. There was some sort of answer at the end of that thought, but I couldn't figure it out.

Calling Kate wouldn't be happening. This was my little mission and I would get it done on my own.

I tried to think like Kate. She always said that people were the key to any mystery. Someone somehow did something that caused Ashlyn to hide and Lisa really didn't want me to keep looking for her. "Did Ashlyn have a best friend?"

Brook paused. "She and Sheila hung out sometimes, but mostly she kept to herself."

"Can we go talk to Sheila?"

Brook heaved a long-suffering sigh. "Sure."

"You're leaving? In that case, Brook, hold this for me for a second." Barka stuck the pen he'd been rolling between his fingers at Brook. She took it. Bright light sparked and Brook dropped the pen and shook her hand.

Barka guffawed.

"Moron!" Brook's eyes shone with a dangerous glint behind her glasses. She marched out of the class. I followed her.

We went down the hallway toward the staircase.

"He likes you," I said.

"Yeah, sure," Brook growled.

Sheila turned out to be the exact opposite of Ashlyn. Where Ashlyn's picture showed a petite cutesy girly-girl, Sheila was muscular. Not manly, but really cut. We caught her in the locker room, just as she was going out to play volleyball. It's not often you see a girl with a six-pack.

She sat on a wooden bench by the small wooden room inside the locker room that said sauna on it. I wondered what the heck sauna meant. It was a first-class locker room; the floor was tile, three showers, two bathrooms, "sauna," large lockers. The clean tile smelled faintly of pine. Special locker room for special snowflakes.

"I don't know why Ashlyn pulled this stunt." Sheila pulled on her left sock.

"Was she worried about anything?"

"She did seem kind of jumpy."

"Did she have a problem with Lisa?"

Sheila paused with the shoe on one foot. "Lisa the Dud?"

Okay, so I didn't like Lisa. But if they called me that, I'd get pissed off really quick, too. "Lisa who senses Ashlyn's 'presence.'"

"Not really." Sheila shook her head. "One time someone left a paw print on Ashlyn's desk. She got really upset."

"What kind of paw print?"

"Wolf," Brook said. "I remember that. She scrubbed her desk for ten minutes."

"How big was the print and when did this happen?"

"Big," Sheila said. "Like bowl-sized. It was about a week ago or so."

Prints that large could indicate a shapeshifter, a werewolf, possibly a werejackal or a werecoyote.

"If anybody had a problem with her, it would be Yu Fong," Sheila said.

"He is the only eighteen-year-old sophomore we have," Brook said. "He's this odd Chinese guy."

"Odd how?"

"He's an orphan," Sheila said. "His parents were murdered."

"I thought they died in a car accident," Brook said.

"Well, whatever happened, happened," Sheila told me. "For some reason he didn't go to school. I heard he was in prison, but whatever. Anyway, he showed up one day, talked to Master Gendun, and got himself admitted as a student. He tested out of enough credits to start as a sophomore. He's dangerous."

"Very powerful," Brook said.

"Uber-magic," Sheila said. "You can feel it coming off of him sometimes. Makes my skin itch."

Brook nodded. "Not sure exactly what sort of magic he has, but whatever it is, it's significant. There are three other Chinese kids in school and they follow Yu Fong around like bodyguards. You can't even talk to him."

"And Ashlyn had a problem with him?" Somehow I couldn't picture Ashlyn deliberately picking a fight with this guy.

"She was terrified of him," Sheila said. "One time he tried to talk to her and she freaked out and ran off."

Okay, then. Next target—the mysterious Yu Fong.

THE SEARCH FOR THE "ODD CHINESE GUY" TOOK US TO THE cafeteria, where according to Brook, this uber-magic user had second-shift lunch. Brook led the way. I followed her through the double doors and paused. A large skylight poured sunshine into the huge room, filled with round metal tables and ornate chairs. At the far wall, the buffet table stretched, manned by several servers in white. Fancy.

The students picked up their plates and carried them to

different tables. Some sat, talking. To the right, several voices laughed in unison.

To the left, a wide doorway allowed a glimpse of a smaller sunroom. In its center, right under the skylight, grew a small tree with red leaves, all but glowing in the sunshine. A table stood by the tree and a young guy sat in a chair, leaning on the table, reading a book. He was too old to be called a boy, but too young to be called a man, and his face was inhumanly beautiful.

I stood and stared.

I'd seen some handsome guys before. This guy...he was magic. His dark hair was brushed away from his high forehead, falling back without a trace of a curl. His features were flawlessly perfect, his face strong and masculine, with a contoured jaw, a tiny cleft in the chin, full lips, and high cheekbones. His eyebrows, dark and wide, bent to shield his eyes, large, beautiful, and very, very dark. Not black, but solid brown.

I blinked, and my power kicked in. The guy was wrapped in pale blue. Not quite silver, but with enough of it to dilute the color to a shimmering blue gray. Divinity. He was either a priest or an object of worship, and looking at him, I was betting on the latter. Glowing like this, he reminded me of one of those celestial beings of Chinese mythology they made me learn about in my old school. He looked like a god.

"That's him," Brook said. "And his guards."

Two boys sat at a second table a few feet away. "I thought you said there were three," I murmured.

"There are—Hui has algebra right now."

I scanned the two guys sitting next to Yu Fong—plain blue— and let go of my sensate vision. His face was distracting enough. I didn't need the glow.

"I'll go ask him if he'll talk to you," Brook said.

"Why don't we go together?" They took the pecking order really seriously in this place.

Brook compressed her lips. "No, they know me."

She made it about two-thirds of the way and then one of Yu Fong's guards peeled himself from the chair and blocked her way. Brook said something, he shook his head, and she turned around and came back to me.

Of course, it was a no. And now they knew I was coming.

Well, you have to work with what you've got.

I raised my hands and wiggled my fingers at the uber-magic guy. He continued reading his book. I waved again and started toward him, a nice big smile on my face. I've seen Kate do this, and if I didn't screw it up, it would work.

The first guard stepped forward, blocking my path. I gave him my cute smile, looked past him, and pointed to myself, as if I was being summoned over and couldn't believe it. He glanced over his shoulder to check Yu Fong's face. I drove my fist hard into his gut. The boy folded around my fist with a surprised gasp. I slammed my hand onto his head, driving his head down. Face, meet knee. Boom! The impact reverberated through my leg.

I shoved him aside and kept moving. The second bodyguard jumped to his feet. I swiped the nearest chair, swung it, and hit him with it just as he was coming up.

The chair connected to the side of his head with a solid crunch. I let go and he stumbled back with the chair on top of him. I stepped past him and landed in the spare chair at the table.

The uber-guy slowly raised his gaze from his book and looked at me.

Whoa.

There was a kind of serious arrogance in his eyes, a searing intensity and determination. Living on the street gives you a sixth sense about those things. You learn to read people. Reading him was easy: He was powerful and arrogant, and he imposed control on everything he saw, including himself. He had been through life's vicious grinder and had come out stronger for it. He would never let you know what he was thinking and you would always be on thin ice.

I touched the surface of the table with the tip of my finger. "Safe."

There was some scrambling behind me. Yu Fong made a small motion with his hand and the noises stopped. I'd won the right to an audience. Wheee!

He tilted his head and studied me with those dark eyes.

I smelled incense. Yep, definitely incense, a strong, slightly sweet smoke. "I always wondered how would one address an object of worship? Should I call you 'the lord of ten thousand years,' 'the holy one,' or the 'son of heaven'?" Dali, one of the shapeshifters, was teaching me the beginnings of Asian mythologies. Unfortunately, that's as far as we got, since I only just started.

"I am not an object." His voice was slightly accented. "You may call me Yu."

Simple enough.

"Is there something you want?" he asked.

"My name is Julie Lennart." Might as well go with the big gun. Most people didn't know the Beast Lord's last name so if he recognized it, it would be a good indication that he was some sort of magic heavyweight.

"It is a weighty name for someone so small." Yu Fong smiled a nice easy smile. He would smile like that while he watched a cute puppy play with a butterfly or while his flunkies were torturing his enemy. Take your pick. "The Beast Lord commands fifteen hundred shapeshifters."

"More or less." It was more, but he didn't need to know that.

His dark eyes fixed on me. "One day my kingdom will be greater."

Ha-ha! Yeah, right. "I'm here with Master Gendun's knowledge and at his request."

He didn't say anything. The metal table under my fingers felt warm. I rested more of my hand on it. Definitely warm. The cafeteria was air-conditioned and even now, with magic up, the air stayed pretty cool, which meant the metal table should've been cold.

"A girl disappeared. She was a small girl. Shy. Her name is Ashlyn."

No reaction. The table was definitely getting warmer.

"She was scared of you."

"I don't kill little girls."

"What makes you think she was killed? I didn't say anything about her being killed."

He leaned forward slightly. "If I take notice of something that offends me, I choose to ignore it or kill it. I ignored her."

Boy, this dude was conceited. "Why did she offend you?"

"I've never threatened her. She had no reason to cringe in my presence. I don't expect you to understand."

I thought hard on why he would find an obvious display of fear offensive.

"When she cringed, you felt insulted. You had no intention of hurting her, so by showing fear, she implied that your control over your power was imperfect."

Yu's eyes widened slightly.

"I'm the ward of the Beast Lord," I told him. "I spend a lot of time with arrogant control freaks."

The table under my hand was almost too hot to keep touching it. I held on. "Ashlyn annoyed you. You said you ignored her. You didn't say anything about your bodyguards. Did they do something to Ashlyn to make her disappear?"

His face was the picture of disdain, which was just a polite way of saying that he would've liked to sneer at me but it was beneath him. I've seen this precise look on the Beast Lord's face. If he and Curran ever got into the same room, Kate's head would explode.

I waited but he didn't say anything. Apparently Yu decided to not dignify it with an answer.

Thin tendrils of smoke escaped from his book. The table near him must have been much hotter than on my end. That had to be something because the metal was now hurting my fingers.

"If I find out that you hurt Ashlyn, I'll hurt you back," I said.

"I'll keep that in mind."

"Do. Your book is smoking."

He picked it up. I slowly raised my hand, blew on my skin, and got up to leave.

"Why do you care?" he asked.

"Because none of you do. Look around you—a girl is missing. A girl you saw in class every day got so scared by something, she had to hide from it. Nobody is looking for her. All of you are just going on with your business as usual. You have all this power and you didn't lift a finger to help her. You just sit there, reading your book, comfy behind your bodyguards, and demonstrate how awesome your magic is by heating up your table. Somebody has to find her. I decided to be that somebody."

I couldn't tell if any of this was sinking in.

"True strength isn't in killing—or ignoring—your opponent, it's in having the will to shield those who need your protection."

He raised his eyebrows slightly. "Who said that?"

"I did." I walked away.

Brook was staring at me.

"Come on," I told her, loud enough for him to hear the derision in my voice. "We're done here."

IN THE HALLWAY I WALKED TO THE WINDOW AND EXHALED. THE nerve. All that power, all that magic boiling in him, and he just sat there. Didn't do a thing to help Ashlyn. He didn't care.

Brook cleared her throat behind me.

"I just need a minute."

I looked outside at the courtyard, enclosed by the square building of the school. It was a really large courtyard. No place to hide, though: benches, flowers, twisted stone paths. A single tree rose toward the northern end of it, surrounded by a maze of concentric flower beds, spreading from it like one of those little handheld puzzle games where you have to roll the ball into a hole through a plastic labyrinth.

"You're wrong," Brook said behind me. "You know what, we all got problems. Just because I didn't look for Ashlyn doesn't make me a bad person. Do you have any idea how competitive the Mage Academy exams are? Getting the right credit is taking up all my time. And I don't even know you! Why do I have to justify myself to you?"

The flowers were in full bloom. Blue asters, delicate bearded irises, cream and yellow, purplish spiderwort—I had a lot of herbology in my old school. Normal for early June. The tree had tiny little buds just beginning to unfurl into gauzy white and pink petals.

"It's not like I even knew her that well. I don't see why I should be held accountable for whatever problem made her hide. If she'd come to me and said, 'Brook, I'm in trouble,' I would've helped her."

"What is that tree?"

"What?"

"The tree down in the yard." I pointed to it. "What kind of tree is it?"

Brook blinked. "I don't know. It's the dead tree. You can't get to it now anyway, not with the magic up, because the flower garden is warded. Listen, I'm not proud that I didn't look for Ashlyn. All I am saying is that maybe I didn't look for her and I probably should have, but I was busy."

I bet it was an apple tree. Some apple trees bloomed late, but most of them flowered in April and May. It was June now.

"How long has that tree been dead?"

"As long as I can remember. I've been in this school for three years and it was always dead. I don't know why they don't cut it down. Are you listening to me?"

"It's flowering."

Brook blinked. "What?"

"The tree is blooming. Look."

Brook looked at the window. "Huh."

Perfect hundred in botany. Apples in the drawer. Wolf print on the desk. Terrified of a boy who creates heat, because where there is smoke, there is fire. Blooming apple tree that has been dead for years.

It all lined up in my head into a perfect arrow pointing to the tree.

"Can we get down there?"

Brook was staring at the tree. "Yes."

Two minutes later I marched out of the side door into the inner yard and down the curved stone path. I was fifty feet from the tree when I sensed magic in front of me. I stopped and snapped into the sensate vision. A wall of magic rose in front of me, glowing lightly with pale silver. A ward, a defensive spell designed to keep out intruders. Currents of power coursed through it.

Some wards glowed with translucent color, both a barrier and a warning that the barrier existed, and walking into it would hurt. This one was invisible to someone without my vision. And judging by the intensity of the magic, touching it would hurt you bad enough to leave you writhing in pain for a few minutes or knock you out completely.

I turned and walked along the ward, with Brook following me. The spell followed the curved flower bed.

"What's the point of the ward?"

"Nobody knows," Brook said.

"Did you ever ask Gendun?"

"I have, actually. He just smiled."

Great.

Ahead, a two-foot-wide gap severed the circle of the ward. I stopped by it, looked through, and saw another ward. This was a magic maze, with rings inside rings of wards and in the center of it all was the apple tree.

"She's watching us," Brook hissed.

"What?"

"Second-floor window, on the left."

I looked up and saw Lisa looking at us. Our stares connected. Lisa's face had this strange mix of emotions, part realization, part fear. She had figured me out. She understood that I saw the ward somehow and I knew about the apple tree, and she was afraid now. It couldn't be me she was scared of. I wasn't that scary. Was she scared that I would find Ashlyn?

A bright green glow burst from Lisa's back. It snapped into the silhouette of an eight-foot-tall wolf. The beast stared at me with eyes of fire.

My heart fluttered in my chest like a scared little bird. Something ancient looked at me through that fire. Something unimaginably old and selfish.

The wolf jerked and vanished. If I had blinked, I would've missed it.

"Did you see that?"

"See what?" Brook asked.

So I had seen it with my sensate vision.

Lisa turned away and walked off. My forehead felt iced over. I swiped the cold sheen off my forehead and saw sweat on my hand. Ew.

Things were making more and more sense. I turned to Brook. "Do you have a library?"

She gave me a look like I was stupid. "Really? Do you really need to ask that question?"

"Lead the way!"

Brook headed to the door. Just as she reached for it, the door swung open and Barka blocked the way. "Hey!"

Brook pushed past him and marched down the hall, clenching her teeth, looking like she would mow down whoever got into her way. I followed her.

Barka caught up with me. "Where are we all going so fast?"

"To the library."

"Is it on fire and they need us to put it out?"

"No."

Barka must've run out of witty things to say, because he shut up and followed us.

The library occupied a vast room. Shelves lined the walls. With magic coming and going like the tide, the e-readers were no longer reliable, but the library stocked them, too. If you needed to find something in a hurry, the e-readers were your best bet. You just had to wait until the magic ebbed and the technology took over again.

Sadly, the magic showed no signs of ebbing.

I walked through the library, checking labels on the shelves. Philosophy, psychology…

"What are you looking for?" Brook snapped. "I'll find it faster."

"Greek and Roman mythology."

"Two ninety-two." Brook turned and ducked between the bookshelves. "Here."

I scanned the titles. Encyclopedia of Greek and Roman Myths. Score!

Brook's eyes lit up. "Shit! Of course. The apples. It's so plain, I could slap myself for being so stupid."

"You got it." I yanked the book from the shelf and carried it to the nearest desk, flipping the pages to get to the letter E.

"What's going on?" Barka asked.

"She found Ashlyn. She is in a tree," Brook told him.

"Why?"

"Because she is an Epimeliad," I murmured, looking for the right listing.

"She is a what?"

"An apple dryad, you dimwit," Brook growled.

Barka raised his hand. "Easy! Greek and Roman was three semesters ago."

"Epimeliads are the dryads of apple trees and guardians of sheep," I explained.

Barka leaned against the desk. "That's a bit random."

"Their name comes from Greek melas, which means both apples and sheep," Brook said.

"This explains why she's scared of Yu Fong," I said. "He's all about heat and fire. Fire and trees don't play well together."

"And someone left a wolf print on her desk. Wolves are the natural enemies of sheep," Barka said.

"Someone was trying to terrorize her." Brook dropped into the chair, as if suddenly exhausted. "And none of us ever paid attention long enough to see it."

"It was Lisa." I scanned the entry for the dryad. Shy, reclusive, blah-blah-blah… No natural enemies. No mention of any mythological wolves.

"How do you know?"

"She has a wolf inside her. I saw it. That's why her powers are stronger. I think she made a deal with something and I think that something wants Ashlyn."

They looked at each other.

"Just what kind of magic do you have, exactly?" Barka asked.

"The right kind." I pulled a chair out and sat down next to Brook. "If Lisa had made a deal with a three-headed demon or some sort of chimera, I could narrow it down, but a wolf, that could be…"

"Anything," Brook finished. "Almost any mythology with a forest has a canid. It could be French or Celtic or English or Russian or anything."

"Can any of you remember her saying anything about a wolf? Maybe there's a record of books she checked out?"

"I'll find out." Brook got up and made a beeline to the library desk.

I flipped through the book some more. Dryads weren't too well-known. They were just supposed to be these flighty creatures, easily spooked, pretty. Basically sex objects. I guess Ancient Greeks didn't really have a lot of access to porn so it must've been fun to imagine that every tree hid a meek girl with big boobies.

Somehow I had to untangle Ashlyn, and not just from that apple tree, but from this entire situation. I didn't know for sure if Lisa had made some sort of deal with the creature. I could be wrong—it could be forcing her. The only thing I knew for sure was that I alone didn't have the strength to take it on in a fight. My magic wasn't the combat kind and that thing…well, from the intensity of the wolf's magic, it would give even the Pack's fighters a pause.

Sometimes I wished I had been born a shapeshifter. If I was Curran, I'd just bite that wolf's head off.

Curran. Hmm. Now there was a smart thought. I pulled a piece of scratch paper from the stack on the library desk, wrote a note, and read it. He would do it. After I pointed out all of his shortcomings, he would do it just to prove me wrong. I felt all happy with myself.

Brook came back with a disgusted expression on her face. "Apple trees. She checked out books on apple trees."

"That's okay. Barka, can you take this note to Yu Fong?"

He shrugged. "Sure. I like to live dangerously." He took the note out of my fingers. "Later!" He winked at Brook and took off.

"You're going to fight the wolf," Brook said. "You are the stupidest person I've ever met. We need to take this to adults now."

"I think Gendun already knows what's going on. He wouldn't have missed the tree coming to life. He didn't seem frantic about Ashlyn's disappearance and he said that the locating spell indicated she was on the grounds. I think that I'm meant to solve this one myself."

"He would be putting your life in danger." Brook shoved her glasses back up her nose. "And Ashlyn's."

"I can't explain it. I just know that I'm trusted to do this on my own." Maybe it was something only I could do. Maybe Ashlyn would trust another girl her age, but not an adult. Maybe Gendun was just clueless. I had no idea. I just had to get Ashlyn out of that tree.

When I was stuck in my old school, there were times I would've hid in a tree if I could have. I knew Kate and Curran and even Derek, the dimwit, would come to rescue me. But I knew none of my school friends would. Sometimes you just want a kid like you to care. Well, I was that kid.

"I'm coming with you," Brook announced.

"I don't think this is a good idea," I told her.

She pushed her glasses up at me.

"Fine." I grinned. "Get yourself killed."

I WAITED IN THE COURTYARD ON ONE OF THE LITTLE BENCHES ON the edge of the wards, reading my little book in plain view. I'd borrowed it from Brook. It was explaining how the universe started with a giant explosion. I understood about two words in it, and those were *the* and *and*.

The day was dying down. Most students were long gone and those who lived in the dormitory had left campus, too. Strangely, no teachers came up and interrogated me or demanded to know when I was planning on leaving. That only confirmed my suspicion that Gendun knew all along what I was up to. Maybe he had some sort of secret adult reason for handling this problem through me. Maybe it was a test. I didn't really care. I just waited and hoped the magic would hold.

The dusk had arrived on the wings of a night moth, silent and soft. The sky above me darkened to a deep, beautiful purple. Stars glowed high above, and below them, as if inspired by their light, tiny fireflies awoke and crawled from their shelter in the leaves. Late enough.

I put my book on the bench and started toward the wards. The magic still held, and when I focused, using my sensate vision, the glowing walls of the wards shimmered slightly. I walked along the first gap and paused. I was pretty sure I'd be followed. Lisa alone might not be capable of remembering all the gaps in the invisible fence, but a wolf would follow his nose and my scent.

I'd have to ask people in the Pack how to make my scent signature stronger. If I had had dandruff, I'd scratch my head, but I didn't. I dragged my hand through my blond hair anyway and moved on, walking along the next ward to the narrow gap.

I weaved my way through the rings of defensive spells, taking my time, pausing at the gaps, until finally I emerged in the clear space around the tree. Blossoms sheathed the branches. Delicate flowers with white petals blushing with faint pink bloomed between tiny pink buds.

I hoped I was doing the right thing. Sometimes it's really hard to figure out what the right thing is. You do something, and you wish you could go back in time for five seconds and undo it or unsay it, but life doesn't work that way.

Nothing ventured, nothing gained.

I pulled a Red Delicious apple from my pocket. The skin of the fruit was so red, it was almost purple. I crouched and rolled the apple gently to the tree's roots. It came to rest against the trunk.

The bark of the tree shifted, crawled... A bark-sheathed leg separated from the trunk and stepped into the grass around the tree. The toes touched the grass and the bark melted into human skin. A moment, and a short petite girl crouched in the grass. I caught my breath. Ashlyn's hair had gone completely white. Not just blond or platinum. White.

She picked up the apple. "Red Delicious."

"Hi, Ashlyn."

She glanced at me with green eyes. "Hi. So you found me."

"It wasn't very hard."

A spark of magic flared beyond the wards. Ashlyn cringed, her eyes wide. "It's coming!"

"It will be okay."

"No, you don't understand! The wolf is coming."

Lisa walked up to the outer ward.

"She's here!" Ashlyn squeaked. "Go away! You'll get hurt."

"Trust me."

Lisa dashed through the wards, running fast, following my trail. I stepped in front of Ashlyn.

Lisa burst out of the ward maze and stopped. "Thank you for showing me the way."

I kept myself between her and Ashlyn. As long as Lisa concentrated on me, she wouldn't look behind her to see who was following her through the ward. "What is the wolf?"

"You saw him?"

"Yep."

Lisa sighed. "It's a forest spirit. It's called Leshii."

"It's a creature of the forest?" Ashlyn gripped my arm. "But why does it want to hurt me? It's like me."

"It wants your blood," Lisa said. "It's weak, and your blood would make it stronger."

"It wants to eat me?" Ashlyn whispered.

"Pretty much. Look, I never had a problem with you. I'm just tired of being Lisa the Dud."

"How did you make the deal?" I asked her.

"I let it out of the Mage Academy," Lisa said. "My dad

showed it to me. The mages trapped it during the last magic wave and gave it some trees, to keep it alive while they studied it, but the trees weren't enough. It wants a forest and I want people to take me seriously. It's a win-win."

"Except for Ashlyn, who will be eaten alive. No biggie," I said. Bitch.

"What am I supposed to do?" Lisa's voice went up really high and I saw that same fear I glimpsed earlier. Except now it was in her eyes and written all over her face. "I didn't know what it wanted when I took it out. The deal was, I carry it out inside me and it gives me powers. I didn't know it was going to kill her!"

"Are you a total moron? That's the first thing they teach you in any school," I growled. "Never make deals with magic creatures. It's a spirit of the damn forest! Do you know how powerful it is? What the fuck did you think would happen?"

"I'm tired of listening to you," Lisa snarled. "This is over. Nobody asked you to stick your nose where it didn't belong. I told you to leave and you didn't listen. You can't fight it. And now you're both going to die, so who is a moron now, huh?"

"You're a terrible person," Ashlyn told her.

"Whatever…" Lisa's arms snapped up and out, as if she was trying to keep from falling. A scream filled with pain and terror ripped out of her. A phantom wolf burst out of her chest, huge, shaggy, glowing with green magic. It landed on the grass, towering over us. Its fur turned gray. The wolf's cavernous mouth gaped open, suddenly solid. Monstrous fangs rent the air.

"Now!" I yelled.

Yu Fong stepped through the ward into the clearing. His irises glowed with orange and in their depth I saw tiny spirals of flames.

The wolf spun to face him.

Magic unfurled from Yu Fong like petals of a fiery flower. It shone with scarlet and beautiful gold and shaped itself into an outline on a translucent beast. It stood on four muscular, strong legs, arms with huge claws rippling with flames. Scales covered its body. Its head belonged to a meld of Chinese dragon and lion, and long whiskers of pure red streamed on both sides of its jaws. Spikes bristled among its crimson mane and its eyes were pure molten lava. Within this beast Yu Fong smiled, a magic wind tugging at his hair.

Wow. He was a dragon.

The wolf charged, aiming for Lisa. Yu Fong stepped into its path, knocking Lisa out of the way. She fell on the grass. The dragon opened its mouth. Flame burst with a roar, like a tornado. The fire engulfed the wolf, and the shaggy beast screamed, opening its mouth, but no sound came.

The wolf lunged at Yu Fong, biting at the dragon with its enormous teeth. Yu Fong clenched his fists. A wall of towering flames shot out from the dragon and wrapped itself around the wolf.

Heat burned my skin.

The wolf writhed in the cocoon of flame, biting and clawing to get free. Yu Fong's face was serene. He leaned back, laughed softly within the beast, and the fire exploded with pure white heat, singeing my hair.

Ashlyn hid her face in her hands.

The wolf burned, crackling and sparking. I watched it burn until nothing was left except for a pile of ashes.

The dragon melted back into Yu Fong. He stepped to the pile of flames and passed his hand over it, so elegant and beautiful, he seemed unreal. The ashes rose in a flurry of sparks, up into the sky, and rained on the courtyard beyond the wards, settling to the ground like beautiful fireflies.

"Well, that's that," Brook said, at the outer ward. "Ashlyn, I have this blanket here for you."

Yu Fong stepped toward us, and Ashlyn took a step toward the tree.

"Don't be afraid. I won't hurt you," he said, his voice soothing. "Come, let's get you dressed."

Around us, the world clenched. The magic vanished, abruptly, like a flame of the candle being blown out by a sudden draft. The wards disappeared. The garden seemed suddenly mundane.

Well. How about that?

Yu Fong escorted Ashlyn away from the tree, guiding her toward Brook.

Lisa got up. Her legs shook. She shuddered and limped away, into the courtyard. I didn't chase her. What was the point?

Brook draped the blanket over Ashlyn's shoulders and gently led her away. I sat down on the grass and leaned against the trunk of the apple tree. I was suddenly very tired.

Yu Fong walked over and looked at me. "Happy, Julie Lennart?"

"It's Olsen," I told him. "I only pull Lennart out of my pocket for special occasions."

"I see."

"Thank you for saving Ashlyn."

Yu Fong reached for the nearest apple branch and gently pulled it down, studying the fragile blossoms, his inhumanly beautiful face framed by the blooms. Somebody should have taken a picture. It was too pretty.

"Of course, now you owe me a favor," he said.

Jerk. No, you know what, forget it. He wasn't pretty. In fact, I've never seen an uglier guy in my whole life.

"The satisfaction of knowing you saved Ashlyn's life should be enough."

"But I didn't just save her life. I saved yours, too," Yu Fong said.

"I would've handled it."

The look he gave me said loud and clear that he thought I was full of it. "I expect to collect this favor one day."

"Don't hold your breath."

"I imagine I'll have plenty of opportunities, since you will be spending a lot of time here," he said.

"What makes you think I'll be studying here?"

"You've made friends," he said. "You will be worried about them." He let go of the branch and walked away. "I'll see you tomorrow, Julie Olsen."

"Maybe!" I called. "I haven't decided yet!"

He kept walking.

I sat under the apple tree. Somehow leaving Ashlyn and Brook to his tender mercy didn't give me a warm and fuzzy feeling.

I was pretty sure I could get admitted into this school. It wouldn't be that hard.

I was right. Kate had set me up.

But then again, maybe it wasn't such a bad thing.

A QUESTIONABLE CLIENT

The problem with leucrocotta blood is that it stinks to high heaven. It's also impossible to get off your boots, particularly if the leucrocotta condescended to void its anal glands on you right before you chopped its head off.

I sat on the bench in the Mercenary Guild locker room and pondered my noxious footwear. The boots were less than a year old. And I didn't have money to buy a new pair.

"Tomato juice, Kate," one of the mercs offered. "Will take it right out."

Now he'd done it. I braced myself.

A woman in the corner shook her head. "That's for skunks. Try baking soda."

"You have to go scientific about it. Two parts hydrogen peroxide to four parts water."

"A quart of water and a tablespoon of ammonia."

"What you need to do is piss on it..."

Every person in the locker room knew my boots were shot. Unfortunately, stain removal methods was one of those trouble-some subjects somewhere between relationship issues and mysterious car noises. Everybody was an expert, everybody had a cure, and they all fell over themselves to offer their advice.

The electric bulbs blinked and faded. Magic flooded the world in a silent rush, smothering technology. Twisted tubes of feylanterns ignited with pale blue on the walls as the charged air inside them interacted with magic. A nauseating stench, reminiscent of a couple of pounds of shrimp left in the sun for a week, erupted from my boots. There were collective grunts of "Ugh" and "Oh God," and then everybody decided to give me lots of personal space.

We lived in a post-Shift world. One moment magic dominated, fueling spells and giving power to monsters, and the next it vanished as abruptly as it appeared. Cars started, electricity flowed, and mages became easy prey to a punk with a gun. Nobody could predict when magic waves would come or how long they would last. That's why I carried a sword. It always worked.

Mark appeared in the doorway. Mark was the Guild's equivalent of middle management, and he looked the part—his suit was perfectly clean and cost more than I made in three months, his dark hair was professionally trimmed, and his hands showed no calluses. In ·the crowd of working-class thugs, he stood out like a sore thumb and was proud of it, which earned him the rank and file's undying hatred.

Mark's expressionless stare fastened on me. "Daniels, the clerk has a gig ticket for you."

Usually the words "gig ticket" made my eyes light up. I needed money. I always needed money. The Guild zoned the jobs, meaning that each merc had his own territory. If a job fell in your territory, it was legitimately yours. My territory was near Savannah, basically in the sparsely populated middle of nowhere, and good gigs didn't come my way too often. The only reason I ended up in Atlanta this time was that my part-time partner in crime, Jim, needed help clearing a pack of grave-digging leucrocottas from Westview Cemetery. He'd cut me in on his gig.

Under normal circumstances I would've jumped on the chance to earn extra cash, but I had spent most of the last twenty-four hours awake and chasing hyena-sized creatures armed with badgerlike jaws full of extremely sharp teeth. And Jim bailed on me midway through it. Some sort of Pack business. That's what I get for pairing with a werejaguar.

I was tired, dirty, and hungry, and my boots stank.

"I just finished a job."

"It's a blue gig."

Blue gig meant double rate.

Mac, a huge hulk of a man, shook his head, presenting me with a view of his mangled left ear. "Hell, if she doesn't want it, I'll take it."

"No, you won't. She's licensed for bodyguard detail and you aren't."

I bloody hated bodyguard detail. On regular jobs, I had to depend only on myself. But bodyguard detail was a couple's kind of dance. You had to work with the body you guarded, and in my experience, bodies proved uncooperative.

"Why me?"

Mark shrugged. "Because I have no choice. I have Rodriguez and Castor there now, but they just canceled on me. If you don't take the gig, I'll have to track down someone who will. My pain, your gain."

Canceled wasn't good. Rodriguez was a decent mage, and Castor was tough in a fight. They wouldn't bail from a well-paying job unless it went sour.

"I need someone there right now. Go there, babysit the client through the night, and in the morning I'll have a replacement lined up. In or out, Daniels? It's a high-profile client, and I don't like to keep him waiting."

The gig smelled bad. "How much?"

"Three grand."

Someone whistled. Three grand for a night of work. I'd be insane to pass on it. "In."

"Good."

I started to throw my stink-bomb boots into the locker but stopped myself. I had paid a lot for them, and they should have lasted for another year at least; but if I put them into my locker, it would smell forever. Sadly the boots were ruined. I tossed them into the trash, pulled on my old spare pair, grabbed my sword, and headed out of the locker room to get the gig ticket from the clerk.

When I rode into Atlanta, the magic was down, so I had taken Betsi, my old dented Subaru. With a magic wave in full swing, my gasoline-guzzling car was about as mobile as a car-size rock, but since I was technically doing the Guild a favor, the clerk provided me with a spare mount. Her name was Peggy, and judging by the wear on her incisors, she'd started her third decade some years ago. Her muzzle had gone gray, her tail and mane had thinned to stringy tendrils, and she moved with ponderous slowness. I'd ridden her for the first fifteen minutes, listening to her sigh, and then guilt got the better of me and I decided to walk the rest of the way. I didn't have to go far. According to the directions, Champion Heights was only a couple miles away. An extra ten minutes wouldn't make that much difference.

Around me a broken city struggled to shrug off winter, fighting the assault of another cold February night. Husks of once mighty skyscrapers stabbed through the melting snowdrifts encrusted with dark ice. Magic loved to feed on anything technologically complex, but tall office towers proved particularly susceptible to magic-induced erosion. Within a couple of years of the first magic wave they shuddered, crumbled, and fell one by one, like giants on sand legs, spilling mountains of broken glass and twisted guts of metal framework onto the streets.

The city grew around the high-tech corpses. Stalls and small shops took the place of swanky coffee joints and boutiques. Wood-and-brick houses, built by hand and no taller than four floors high, replaced the high-rises. Busy streets, once filled with cars and buses, now channeled a flood of horses, mules, and camels. During rush hour the stench alone put hair on your chest. But now, with the last of the sunset dying slowly above the horizon, the city lay empty. Anyone with a crumb of sense hurried home. The night belonged to monsters, and monsters were always hungry.

The wind picked up, driving dark clouds across the sky and turning my bones into icicles. It would storm soon. Here's hoping Champion Heights, my client's humble abode, had someplace I could hide Peggy from the sleet.

We picked our way through Buckhead, Peggy's hooves making loud clopping noises in the twilight silence of the deserted streets. The night worried me little. I looked too poor and too mean to provide easy pickings, and nobody in his right mind would try to steal Peggy. Unless a gang of soap-making bandits lurked about, we were safe enough. I checked the address again. Smack in the middle of Buckhead. The clerk said I couldn't miss it. Pretty much a guarantee I'd get lost.

I turned the corner and stopped.

A high-rise towered over the ruins. It shouldn't have existed, but there it was, a brick-and-concrete tower silhouetted against the purple sky. At least fifteen floors, maybe more. Pale tendrils of haze clung to it. It was so tall that the top floor of it still reflected the sunset, while the rest of the city lay steeped in shadow.

"Pinch me, Peggy."

Peggy sighed, mourning the fact that she was paired with me.

I petted her gray muzzle. "Ten to one that's Champion Heights. Why isn't it laying in shambles?"

Peggy snorted.

"You're right. We need a closer look."

We wound through the labyrinth of streets, closing in on the tower. My paper said the client's name was Saiman. No indication if it was his last or first name. Perhaps he was like Batman, one of a kind. Of course, Batman wouldn't have to hire bodyguards.

"You have to ask yourself, Peggy, who would pay three grand for a night of work and why. I bet living in that tower isn't cheap, so Saiman has money. Contrary to popular opinion, people who have money refuse to part with it, unless they absolutely have to do it. Three grand means he's in big trouble and we're walking into something nasty."

Finally we landed in a vast parking lot, empty save for a row of cars near the front. Gray Volvo, black Cadillac, even a sleek gunmetal Lamborghini. Most vehicles sported a bloated hood—built to accommodate a charged water engine. The water-engine cars functioned during magic waves by using magic-infused water instead of gasoline. Unfortunately, they took a good fifteen minutes of hard chanting to start, and when they did spring into action, they attained a maximum speed of forty-five miles per hour while growling, snarling, and thundering loud enough to force a deaf man to file a noise complaint.

A large white sign waited past the cars. A black arrow pointed to the right. Above the arrow in black letters was written, "Please stable your mounts." I looked to the right and saw a large stable and a small guardhouse next to it.

It took me a full five minutes to convince the guards I wasn't a serial killer in disguise, but finally Peggy relaxed in a comfortable stall, and I climbed the stone stairs to Champion Heights. As I looked, the concrete-and-brick wall of the high-rise swam out of focus, shimmered, and turned into a granite crag.

Whoa.

I squinted at the wall and saw the faint outline of bricks within the granite. Interesting.

The stairs brought me to the glass-and-steel front of the building. The same haze that cloaked the building clouded the glass, but not enough to obscure a thick metal grate barring the vestibule. Beyond the grate, a guard sat behind a round counter, between an Uzi and a crossbow. The Uzi looked well maintained. The crossbow bore the Hawkeye logo on its stock—a round bird-of-prey eye with a golden iris—which meant its prong was steel and not cheap aluminum. Probably upward of two hundred pounds of draw weight. At this distance, it would take out a rhino, let alone me.

The guard gave me an evil eye. I leaned to the narrow metal grille and tried to broadcast "trustworthy."

"I'm here for one fifty-eight." I pulled out my merc card and held it to the glass.

"Code, please."

Code? What code? "Nobody said anything about a code."

The guard leveled a crossbow at me.

"Very scary," I told him. "One small problem—you shoot me and the tenant in one fifty-eight won't live through the night. I'm not a threat to you. I'm a bodyguard on the job from the Mercenary Guild. If you call to one fifty-eight and check, they'll tell you they're expecting me."

The guard rose and disappeared into a hallway to the right. A long minute passed. Finally he emerged, looking sour, and pushed a button. The metal grate slid aside.

I walked in. The floor and walls were polished red granite. The air smelled of expensive perfume.

"Fifteenth floor," the guard said, nodding at the elevator in the back of the room.

"The magic is up." The elevator was likely dead.

"Fifteenth floor."

Oy. I walked up to the elevator and pushed the Up button. The metal doors slid open. I got in and selected the fifteenth floor, the elevator closed, and a moment later a faint purring announced the cabin rising. It's good to be rich.

The elevator spat me out into a hallway lined with a luxurious green carpet. I plodded through it past the door marked 158 to the end of the hallway to the door marked with the EXIT sign and opened it. Stairs. Unfortunately in good repair. The door opened from the inside of the hallway, but it didn't lock. No way to jam it.

The hallway was T-shaped with only one exit, which meant that potential attackers could come either through the elevator shaft or up the stairs.

I went up to 158 and knocked.

The door shot open. Gina Castor's dark eyes glared at me. An AK-47 hung off her shoulder. She held a black duffel in one hand and her sword in the other. "What took you so long?"

"Hello to you, too."

She pushed past me, the thin, slightly stooped Rodriguez following her. "He's all yours."

I caught the door before it clicked shut. "Where is the client?"

"Chained to the bed." They headed to the elevator.

"Why?"

Castor flashed her teeth at me. "You'll figure it out."

The elevator's door slid open, they ducked in, and a moment later I was alone in the hallway, holding the door open like an idiot. Peachy.

I stepped inside and shut the door. A faint spark of magic shot through the metal box of the card-reader lock. I touched it. The lock was a sham. The door was protected by a ward. I pushed harder. My magic crashed against the invisible wall of the spell and ground to a halt. An expensive ward, too. Good. Made my job a hair easier.

I slid the dead bolt shut and turned. I stood in a huge living room, big enough to contain most of my house. A marble counter ran along the wall on my left, sheltering a bar with glass shelves offering everything from Bombay Sapphire to French wines. A large steel fridge sat behind the bar. White, criminally plush carpet, black walls, steel-and-glass furniture, and beyond it all an enormous floor-to-ceiling window presenting the vista of the ruined city, a deep darkness lit here and there by the pale blue of feylanterns.

I stayed away from the window and trailed the wall, punctuated by three doors. The first opened into a laboratory: flame-retardant table and counters supporting row upon row of equipment. I recognized a magic scanner, a computer, and a spectrograph, but the rest was beyond me. No client.

I tried the second door and found a large room. Gloom pooled in the corners. A huge platform bed occupied most of the hardwood floor. Something lay on the bed, hidden under black sheets.

"Saiman?"

No answer.

Why me?

The wall to the left of the bed was all glass, and beyond the glass, far below, stretched a very hard parking lot, bathed in the glow of feylanterns.

God, fifteen floors was high.

I pulled my saber from the back sheath and padded across the floor to the bed.

The body under the sheets didn't move.

Step.

Another step.

In my head, the creature hiding under the sheets lunged at me, knocking me through the window in an explosion of glass shards to plunge far below… Fatigue was messing with my head.

Another step.

I nudged the sheet with my sword, peeling it back gently.

A man rested on the black pillow. He was bald. His head was lightly tanned, his face neither handsome nor ugly, his features well shaped and pleasant. Perfectly average. His shoulders were nude—he was probably down to his underwear or naked under the sheet.

"Saiman?" I asked softly.

The man's eyelids trembled. Dark eyes stared at me, luminescent with harsh predatory intelligence. A warning siren went off in my head. I took a small step back and saw the outline of several chains under the sheet. You've got to be kidding me. They didn't just chain him to the bed, they wrapped him up like a Christmas present. He couldn't even twitch.

"Good evening," the man said, his voice quiet and cultured.

"Good evening."

"You're my new bodyguard, I presume."

I nodded. "Call me Kate."

"Kate. What a lovely name. Please forgive me. Normally I

would rise to greet a beautiful woman, but I'm afraid I'm indisposed at the moment."

I pulled back a little more of the sheet, revealing an industrial-size steel chain. "I can see that."

"Perhaps I could impose on you to do me the great favor of removing my bonds?"

"Why did Rodriguez and Castor chain you?" And where the hell did they find a chain of this size?

A slight smile touched his lips. "I'd prefer not to answer that question."

"Then we're in trouble. Clients get restrained when they interfere with the bodyguards' ability to keep them safe. Since you won't tell me why the previous team decided to chain you, I can't let you go."

The smile grew wider. "I see your point."

"Does this mean you're ready to enlighten me?"

"I'm afraid not."

I nodded. "I see. Well then, I'll clear the rest of the apartment, and then I'll come back and we'll talk some more."

"Do you prefer brunets or blonds?"

"What?"

The sheet shivered.

"Quickly, Kate. Brunets or blonds? Pick one."

Odd bulges strained the sheet. I grabbed the covers and jerked them back.

Saiman lay naked, his body pinned to the bed by the chain. His stomach distended between two loops, huge and bloated. Flesh bulged and crawled under his skin, as if his body were full of writhing worms.

"Blond, I'd say," Saiman said.

He groaned, his back digging into the sheets. The muscles under his skin boiled. Bones stretched. Ligaments twisted, contorting his limbs. Acid squirted into my throat. I gagged, trying not to vomit.

His body stretched, twisted, and snapped into a new shape: lean, with crisp definition. His jaw widened, his eyes grew larger, his nose gained a sharp cut. Cornsilk blond hair sprouted on his head and reached down to his shoulders. Indigo flooded his irises. A new man looked at me, younger by about five years, taller, leaner, with a face that was heartbreakingly perfect. Above his waist, he was Adonis. Below his ribs, his body degenerated into a bloated stomach. He looked pregnant.

"You wouldn't tell me what you preferred," he said mournfully, his pitch low and husky. "I had to improvise."

"What are you?" I kept my sword between me and him.

"Does it really matter?"

"Yes, it does." When people said shapeshifter, they meant a person afflicted with Lyc-V, the virus that gave its victim the ability to shift into an animal. I'd never seen one who could freely change its human form.

Saiman made a valiant effort to shrug. Hard to shrug with several pounds of chains on your shoulders, but he managed to look nonchalant doing it.

"I am me."

Oh boy. "Stay here."

"Where would I go?"

I left the bedroom and checked the rest of the apartment. The only remaining room contained a large shower stall and a giant bathtub. No kitchen. Perhaps he had food delivered.

Fifteenth floor. At least one guard downstairs, bullet-resistant glass, metal grates. The place was a fortress. Yet he hired bodyguards at exorbitant prices. He expected his castle to be breached.

I headed to the bar, grabbed a glass from under the counter, filled it with water, and took it to Saiman. Changing shape took energy. If he was anything like other shapeshifters, he was dying of thirst and hunger right about now.

Saiman's gaze fastened on the glass. "Delightful."

I let him drink. He drained the glass in long, thirsty swallows.

"How many guards are on duty downstairs?"

"Three."

"Are they employed by the building owners directly?"

Saiman smiled. "Yes. They're experienced and well paid, and they won't hesitate to kill."

So far so good. "When you change shape, do you reproduce internal organs as well?"

"Only if I plan to have intercourse."

Oh goodie. "Are you pregnant?"

Saiman laughed softly.

"I need to know if you're going to go into labor." Because that would just be a cherry on the cake of this job.

"You're a most peculiar woman. No, I'm most definitely not pregnant. I'm male, and while I may construct a vaginal canal and a uterus on occasion, I've never had cause to recreate ovaries. And if I did, I suspect they would be sterile. Unlike the male of the species, women produce all of their gametes during gestation, meaning that when a female infant is born, she will have in her ovaries all of the partially developed eggs she will ever have. The ovaries cannot generate production of new eggs, only the maturation of existing ones. The magic is simply not deep enough for me to overcome this hurdle. Not yet."

Thank Universe for small favors. "Who am I protecting you from, and why?"

"I'm afraid I have to keep that information to myself as well."

Why did I take this job again? Ah yes, a pile of money. "Withholding this information diminishes my ability to guard you."

He tilted his head, looking me over. "I'm willing to take that chance."

"I'm not. It also puts my life at a greater risk."

"You're well compensated for that risk."

I repressed the urge to brain him with something heavy. Too bad there was no kitchen—a cast-iron frying pan would do the job.

"I see why the first team bailed."

"Oh, it was the woman," Saiman said helpfully. "She had difficulty with my metamorphosis. I believe she referred to me as an 'abomination.'"

I rubbed the bridge of my nose. "Let's try simple questions. Do you expect us to be attacked tonight?"

"Yes."

I figured as much. "With magic or brute force?"

"Both."

"Is it a hit for hire?"

Saiman shook his head. "No."

Well, at least something went my way: amateurs were easier to deal with than contract killers.

"It's personal. I can tell you this much: the attackers are part of a religious sect. They will do everything in their power to kill me, including sacrificing their own lives."

And we just drove off a cliff in a runaway buggy. "Are they magically adept?"

"Very."

I leaned back. "So let me summarize. You're a target of magical kamikaze fanatics, you won't tell me who they are, why they're after you, or why you have been restrained?"

"Precisely. Could I trouble you for a sandwich? I'm famished."

Dear God, I had a crackpot for a client. "A sandwich?"

"Prosciutto and Gouda on sourdough bread, please. A tomato and red onion would be quite lovely as well."

"Sounds delicious."

"Feel free to have one."

"I tell you what, since you refuse to reveal anything that might make my job even a smidgeon easier, how about I make a delicious prosciutto sandwich and taunt you with it until you tell me what I want to know?"

Saiman laughed.

An eerie sound came from the living room—a light click, as if something with long sharp claws crawled across metal.

I PUT MY FINGER TO MY LIPS, FREED MY SABER, AND PADDED OUT into the living room.

The room lay empty. No intruders.

I stood very still, trying to fade into the black walls.

Moments dripped by.

A small noise came from the left. It was a hesitant, slow clicking, as if some creature slunk in the distance, slowly putting one foot before the other.

Click.

Definitely a claw.

Click.

I scrutinized the left side of the room. Nothing moved.

Click. Click, click.

Closer this time. Fear skittered down my spine. Fear was good. It would keep me sharp. I kept still. Where are you, you sonovabitch?

Click to the right, and almost immediately a quiet snort to the left. Now we had two invisible intruders. Because one wasn't hard enough.

An odd scent nipped at my nostrils, a thick, slightly bitter herbal odor. I'd smelled it once before, but I had no clue where or when.

Claws scraped to the right and to the left of me now. More than two. A quiet snort to the right. Another in the corner. Come out to play. Come on, beastie.

Claws raked metal directly in front of me. There was nothing there but that huge window and sloping ceiling above it. I looked up. Glowing green eyes peered at me through the grate of the air duct in the ceiling.

Shivers sparked down my back.

The eyes stared at me, heated with madness.

The screws in the air duct cover turned to the left. Righty tighty, lefty loosey. Smart critter.

The grate fell onto the soft carpet. The creature leaned forward slowly, showing me a long conical head. The herbal scent grew stronger now, as if I'd taken a handful of absinthe wormwood and stuck it up my nose.

Long black claws clutched the edge of the air duct. The beast rocked, revealing its shoulders sheathed in shaggy, hunter green fur.

Bingo. An endar. Six legs, each armed with wicked black claws; preternaturally fast; equipped with an outstanding sense of smell and a big mouth, which hid a tongue lined with hundreds of serrated teeth. One lick and it would scrape the flesh off my bones in a very literal way.

The endars were peaceful creatures. The green fur wasn't fur at all; it was moss that grew from their skin. They lived underneath old oaks, rooted to the big trees in a state of quiet hibernation, absorbing their nutrients and making rare excursions to the surface to lick the bark and feed on lichens. They stirred from their rest so rarely that pagan Slavs thought they fed on air.

Someone had poured blood under this endar's oak. The creature had absorbed it, and the blood had driven it crazy. It had burrowed to the surface, where it swarmed with its fellows. Then the same someone, armed with a hell of a lot of magic, had herded this endar and its buddies to this high-rise and released them into the ventilation system so they would find Saiman and rip him apart. They couldn't be frightened off. They couldn't be stopped. They would kill anything with a pulse to get to their target, and when the target was dead, they would have to be eliminated. There was no going back from endar madness.

Only a handful of people knew how to control endars.

Saiman had managed to piss off the Russians. It's never good to piss off the Russians. That was just basic common sense. My father was Russian, but I doubted they would cut me any slack just because I could understand their curses.

The endar gaped at me with its glowing eyes. Yep, mad as a hatter. I'd have to kill every last one of them.

"Well, come on. Bring it."

The endar's mouth gaped. It let out a piercing screech, like a circular saw biting into the wood, and charged.

I swung Slayer. The saber's blade sliced into flesh and the beast crashed to the floor. Thick green blood stained Saiman's white carpet.

The three other duct covers fell one by one. A stream of green bodies charged toward me. I swung my sword, cleaving the first body in two. It was going to be a long night.

THE LAST OF THE ENDARS WAS ON THE SMALLER SIDE. LITTLE bigger than a cat. I grabbed it by the scruff of the neck and took it back into the bedroom.

Saiman smiled at my approach. "I take it everything went well?"

"I redecorated."

He arched his eyebrow again. Definitely mimicking me. "Oh?"

"Your new carpet is a lovely emerald color."

"I can assure you that carpet is the least of my worries."

"You're right." I brought the endar closer. The creature saw Saiman and jerked spasmodically. Six legs whipped the air, claws out, ready to rend and tear. The beast's mouth gaped, releasing a wide tongue studded with rows and rows of conical teeth.

"You provoked the volkhvi." It was that or the Russian witches. I bet on the volkhvi. The witches would've cursed us by now.

"Indeed."

"The volkhvi are bad news for a number of reasons. They serve pagan Slavic gods, and they have thousands of years of magic tradition to draw on. They're at least as powerful as Druids, but unlike Druids, who are afraid to sneeze the wrong way or someone might accuse them of bringing back human sacrifices, the volkhvi don't give a damn. They won't stop, either. They don't like using the endars, because the endars nourish the forest with their magic. Whatever you did really pissed them off."

Saiman pondered me as if I were some curious bug. "I wasn't aware that the Guild employed anyone with an education."

"I'll hear it. All of it."

"No." He shook his head. "I do admire your diligence and expertise. I don't want you to think it's gone unnoticed."

I dropped the endar onto Saiman's stomach. The beast clawed at the sheet. Saiman screamed. I grabbed the creature and jerked it up. The beast dragged the sheet with it, tearing it to shreds. Small red scratches marked Saiman's blob of a stomach.

"I'll ask again. What did you do to infuriate the Russians? Consider your answer carefully, because next time I drop this guy, I'll be slower picking him back up."

Saiman's face quivered with rage. "You're my bodyguard."

"You can file a complaint, if you survive. You're putting both of us in danger by withholding information. See, if I walk, I just miss out on some money; you lose your life. I have no problem with leaving you here, and the Guild can stick its thumb up its ass and twirl for all I care. The only thing that keeps me protecting you is professional pride. I hate body-guard detail, but I'm good at it, and I don't like to lose a body. It's in your best interests to help me do my job. Now, I'll count to three. On three I drop Fluffy here and let it go to town on your gut. He really wants whatever you're hiding in there."

Saiman stared at me.

"One. Two. Th—"

"Very well."

I reached into my backpack and pulled out a piece of wire. Normally I used it for trip traps, but it would make a decent leash. Two minutes later, the endar was secured to the dresser and I perched on the corner of Saiman's bed.

"Are you familiar with the legend of Booyan Island?"

I nodded. "It's a mythical island far in the Ocean, behind the Hvalynskii Sea. It's a place of deep magic where a number of legendary creatures and items are located: Alatyr, the father of all stones; the fiery pillar; the Drevo-Doob, the World Oak; the cave where the legendary sword Kladenets is hidden; the Raven prophet; and so on. It's the discount warehouse of Russian legends. Any time the folkloric heroes needed a magic object, they made a trip to it."

"Let's concentrate on the tree," Saiman said.

I knew Slavic mythology well enough, but I hadn't had to use it for a while and I was a bit rusty. "It's a symbol of nature. Creature of the earth at its roots, the serpent, the frog, and so on. There is a raven with a prophet gift in the branches. Some myths say that there are iron chains wrapped around the tree's trunk. A black cat walks the chain, telling stories and fables…"

Saiman nodded.

Oh crap. "It's that damn cat, isn't it?"

"The oak produces an acorn once every seven years. Seven months, seven days, and seven hours after the acorn falls from the tree, it will crack and grow into the World Oak. In effect, the tree manifests at the location of the acorn for the period of seven minutes."

I frowned. "Let me guess. You stole the acorn from the Russians and swallowed it."

Saiman nodded.

"Why? Are you eager to hear a bedtime story?"

"The cat possesses infinite knowledge. Seven minutes is time enough to ask and hear an answer to one question. Only the owner of the acorn can ask the question."

I shook my head. "Saiman, nothing is free. You have to pay for everything, knowledge included. What will it cost you to ask a question?"

"The price is irrelevant if I get an answer." Saiman smiled.

I sighed. "Answer my question: Why do smart people tend to be stupid?"

"Because we think we know better. We think that our intellect affords us special privileges and lets us beat the odds. That's why talented mathematicians try to defraud casinos and young brilliant mages make bargains with forces beyond their control."

Well, he answered the question.

"When is the acorn due for its big kaboom?"

"In four hours and forty-seven minutes."

"The volkhvi will tear this high-rise apart stone by stone to get it back, and I'm your last line of defense?"

"That's an accurate assessment. I did ask for the best person available."

I sighed. "Still want that sandwich?"

"Very much."

I headed to the door.

"Kate?"

"Yes?"

"The endar?"

I turned to him. "Why were you chained?"

Saiman grimaced. "The acorn makes it difficult to control

my magic. It forces me to continuously change shape. Most of the time I'm able to keep the changes subtle, but once in a while the acorn causes contortions. Gina Castor walked in on me during such a moment. I'm afraid I was convulsing, so my recollection may be somewhat murky, but I do believe I had at least one partially formed breast and three arms. She overreacted. Odd, considering her profile."

"Her profile?"

"I studied my bodyguards very carefully," Saiman said. "I handpicked three teams. The first refused to take the job, the second was out due to injuries. Castor and Rodriguez were my third choice."

I went back to the bed and ducked under it. They'd chained him with a small padlock. Lock picking wasn't my strong suit. I looked around and saw the small key on the dresser. It took me a good five minutes to unwrap him.

"Thank you." He rose, rubbing his chest, marked by red pressure lines. "May I ask why?"

"Nobody should die chained to the bed."

Saiman stretched. His body swelled, twisted, growing larger, gaining breadth and muscle. I made a valiant effort to not vomit.

Saiman's body snapped. A large, perfectly sculpted male looked at me. Soft brown hair framed a masculine face. He would make any bodybuilder gym proud. Except for the bloated gut.

"Is he preferable to the previous attempt?" Saiman asked.

"There is more of you to guard now. Other than that, it makes no difference to me."

I headed into the living room. He followed me, swiping a luxurious robe off a chair.

We stepped into the living room. Saiman stopped.

The corpses of endars had melted into puddles of green.

Thin stalks of emerald green moss sprouted from the puddles, next to curly green shoots of ferns and tiny young herbs.

"The endars nourish the forest," I told him.

He indicated the completely green carpet with his hand. "How many were there?"

"A few. I lost count."

Saiman's sharp eyes regarded my face. "You're lying. You know the exact number."

"Thirty-seven."

I zeroed in on the fridge. No telling when the next attack would come, and I was starving. You can do without sleep or without food, but not without both and sleep wasn't an option.

Saiman trailed me, taking the seat on the outer side of the counter. "Do you prefer women?"

"No."

He frowned, belting the robe. "It's the stomach, isn't it?"

I raided the fridge. He had enough deli meat to feed an army. I spread it out on the bar's counter. "What do you do for a living, Saiman?"

"I collect information and use it to further my interests."

"It seems to pay well." I nodded to indicate the apartment.

"It does. I also possess an exhaustive knowledge of various magic phenomena. I consult various parties. My fee varies between thirty-six hundred and thirty-nine hundred dollars, depending on the job and the client."

"Thirty-six hundred dollars per job?" I bit into my sandwich. Mmm, salami.

"Per hour."

I choked on my food. He looked at me with obvious amusement.

"The term 'highway robbery' comes to mind," I managed finally.

"Oh, but I'm exceptionally good at what I do. Besides, the

victims of highway robbery have no choice in the matter. I assure you, I don't coerce my clients, Kate."

"I'm sure. How did we even get to this point? The stratospheric fee ruined my train of thought."

"You stated that you prefer men to women."

I nodded. "Suppose you get a particularly sensitive piece of information. Let's say a business tip. If you act on the tip, you could make some money. If you sell it, you could make more money. If both you and your buyer act on the tip, you both would make money, but the return for each of you would be significantly diminished. Your move?"

"Either sell the information or act on it. Not both."

"Why?"

Saiman shrugged. "The value of the information increases with its exclusivity. A client buying such knowledge has an expectation of such exclusivity. It would be unethical to undermine it."

"It would be unethical for me to respond to your sexual overtures. For the duration of the job, you're a collection of arms and legs which I have to keep safe. I'm most effective if I'm not emotionally involved with you on any level. To be blunt, I'm doing my best to regard you as a precious piece of porcelain I have to keep out of harm's way."

"But you do find this shape sexually attractive?"

"I'm not going to answer this question. If you pester me, I will chain you back to the bed."

Saiman raised his arm, flexing a spectacular biceps. "This shape has a lot of muscle mass."

I nodded. "In a bench-pressing contest you would probably win. But we're not bench pressing. You might be stronger, but I'm well trained. If you do want to try me, you're welcome to it. Just as long as we agree that once your battered body is chained safely in your bed, I get to say, 'I told you so.'"

Saiman arched his eyebrows. "Try it?"

"And stop that."

"Stop what?"

"Stop mimicking my gestures."

He laughed. "You're a most peculiar person, Kate. I find myself oddly fascinated. You have obvious skill." He indicated the budding forest in his living room. "And knowledge to back it up. Why aren't you among the Guild's top performers?"

Because being in top anything means greater risk of discovery. I was hiding in plain sight and doing a fairly good job of it. But he didn't need to know that. "I don't spend much time in Atlanta. My territory is in the Lowcountry. Nothing much happens there, except for an occasional sea serpent eating shrimp out of the fishing nets."

Saiman's sharp eyes narrowed. "So why not move up to the city? Better jobs, better money, more recognition?"

"I like my house where it is."

Something bumped behind the front door. I swiped Slayer off the counter. "Bedroom. Now."

"Can I watch?"

I pointed with the sword to the bedroom.

Saiman gave an exaggerated sigh. "Very well."

He went to the bedroom. I padded to the door and leaned against it, listening.

Quiet.

I waited, sword raised. Something waited out there in the hallway. I couldn't hear it, but I sensed it. It was there.

A quiet whimper filtered through the steel of the door. A sad, lost, feminine whimper, like an old woman crying quietly in mourning.

I held very still. The apartment felt stifling and crowded in. I would've given anything for a gulp of fresh air right about now.

Something scratched at the door. A low mutter floated through, whispered words unintelligible.

God, what was it with the air in this place? The place was stale and musty, like a tomb.

A feeling of dread flooded me. Something bad was in the apartment. It hid in the shadows under the furniture, in the cabinets, in the fridge. Fear squirmed through me. I pressed my back against the door, holding Slayer in front of me.

The creature behind the door scratched again, claws against the steel.

The walls closed in. I had to get away from this air. Somewhere out in the open. Someplace where the wind blew under an open sky. Somewhere with nothing to crowd me in.

I had to get out.

If I left, I risked Saiman's life. Outside, the volkhvi were waiting. I'd be walking right into their arms.

The shadows under the furniture grew longer, stretching toward me.

Get out. Get out now!

I bit my lip. A quick drop of blood burned on my tongue, the magic in it nipping at me. Clarity returned for a second, and light dawned in my head. Badzula. Of course. The endars failed to rip us apart, so the volkhvi went for plan B. If Muhammad won't go to the mountain, the mountain must come to Muhammad.

Saiman walked out of the bedroom. His eyes were glazed over.

"Saiman!"

"I must go," he said. "Must get out."

"No, you really must not." I sprinted to him.

"I must."

He headed to the giant window.

I kicked the back of his right knee. He folded. I caught him on the way down and spun him so he landed on his stomach. He sprawled among the ankle-tall ferns. I locked his left wrist and leaned on him, grinding all of my weight into his left shoulder.

62

"Badzula," I told him. "Belorussian creature. Looks like a middle-aged woman with droopy breasts, swaddled in a filthy blanket."

"I must get out." He tried to roll over, but I had him pinned.

"Focus, Saiman. Badzula—what's her power?"

"She incites people to vagrancy."

"That's right. And we can't be vagrants, because if we walk out of this building, both of us will be killed. We have to stay put."

"I don't think I can do it."

"Yes, you can. I'm not planning on getting up."

"I believe you're right." A small measure of rational thought crept into his voice. "I suppose the furniture isn't really trying to devour us."

"If it is, I'll chop it with my sword when it gets close."

"You can let me up now," he said.

"I don't think so."

We sat still. The air grew viscous like glue. I had to bite it to get any into my lungs.

Muscles crawled under me. Saiman couldn't get out of my hold, so he decided to shift himself out.

"Do you stock herbs?"

"Yes," he said.

"Do you have water lily?"

"Yes."

"Where?"

"Laboratory, third cabinet."

"Good." I rolled off of him. I'd have only a second to do this, and I had to do it precisely.

Saiman got up to his knees. As he rose, I threw a fast right hook. He never saw it coming and didn't brace himself. My fist landed on his jaw. His head snapped back. His eyes rolled over and he sagged down.

Lucky. I ran to the lab.

It took a hell of a lot of practice to knock someone out. You needed both speed and power to jolt the head enough to rattle the brain inside the skull but not cause permanent damage. Under normal circumstances, I wouldn't even try it, but these weren't normal circumstances. Walls were curving in to eat me.

If I did cause too much damage, he would fix it. Considering what he had done to his body so far, his regeneration would make normal shapeshifters jealous.

Third cabinet. I threw it open and scanned the glass jars. Dread mugged me like a sodden blanket. *Ligularia dentata, Ligularia przewalski...* Latin names, why me? *Lilium pardalinum, Lobelia siphilitica.* Come on, come on... *Nymphaea odorata,* pond lily. Also known to Russians as *odolen-trava,* the mermaid flower, an all-purpose pesticide against all things unclean. That would do.

I dashed to the door, twisting the lid off the jar. A gray powder filled it—ground lily petals, the most potent part of the flower. I slid open the lock. The ward drained down, and I jerked the door ajar.

Empty hallway greeted me. I hurled the jar and the powder into the hall. A woman wailed, smoke rose from thin air, and Badzula materialized in the middle of the carpet. Skinny, flabby, filthy, with breasts dangling to her waist like two empty bags, she tossed back grimy, tangled hair and hissed at me, baring stumps of rotten teeth.

"That's nice. Fuck you, too."

I swung. It was textbook saber slash, diagonal, from left to right. I drew the entirety of the blade through the wound. Badzula's body toppled one way, her head rolled the other.

The weight dropped off my shoulders. Suddenly I could breathe, and the building no longer seemed in imminent danger of collapsing and burying me alive.

I grabbed the head, tossed it into the elevator, dragged the body in there, sent the whole thing to the ground floor, sprinted back inside, and locked the door, reactivating the ward. The whole thing took five seconds.

On the floor, Saiman lay unmoving. I checked his pulse. Breathing. Good. I went back to the island. I deserved some coffee after this, and I bet Saiman stocked the good stuff.

I WAS SITTING BY THE COUNTER, SIPPING THE BEST COFFEE I'D ever tasted, when the big-screen TV on the wall lit up with a fuzzy glow. Which was more than a smidgeon odd, considering that the magic was still up and the TV shouldn't have worked.

I took my coffee and my saber and went to sit on the couch, facing the TV. Saiman still sprawled unconscious on the floor.

The glow flared brighter, faded, flared brighter… In ancient times people used mirrors, but really any somewhat reflective surface would do. The dark TV screen was glossy enough.

The glow blazed and materialized into a blurry male. In his early twenties, dark hair, dark eyes.

The man looked at me. "You're the bodyguard." His voice carried a trace of Russian accent.

I nodded and slipped into Russian. *"Yes."*

"I don't know you. What you do makes no difference to me. We have this place surrounded. We go in in an hour." He made a short chopping motion with his hand. *"You're done."*

"I'm shaking with fear. In fact, I may have to take a minute to get my shivers under control." I drank my coffee.

The man shook his head. *"You tell that* paskuda, *if he let Yulya go, I'll make sure you both walk out alive. You hear that? I don't know what he's got over my wife, but you tell him that. If he wants to live, he has to let her go. I'll be back in thirty minutes. You tell him."*

The screen faded.

And the plot thickens. I sighed and nudged Saiman with my boot. It took a couple of nudges, but finally he groaned and sat up.

"What happened?"

"You fell."

"Really? What did I fall into?"

"My fist."

"That explains the headache." Saiman looked at me. "This will never happen again. I want to be absolutely clear. Attempt this again and you're fired."

I wondered what would happen if I knocked him out again right there, just for kicks.

"Is that my arabica coffee?" he asked.

I nodded. "I will even let you have a cup if you answer my question."

Saiman arched an eyebrow. "Let? It's my coffee."

I saluted him with the mug. "Possession is nine-tenths of the law."

He stared at me incredulously. "Ask."

"Are you holding a woman called Yulya hostage?"

Saiman blinked.

"Her husband is very upset and is offering to let us both go if we can produce Yulya for him. Unfortunately, he's lying and most likely we both would be killed once said Yulya is found. But if you're holding a woman hostage, you must tell me now."

"And if I was?" Saiman rubbed his jaw and sat in the chair opposite me.

"Then you'd have to release her immediately or I would walk. I don't protect kidnappers, and I take a very dim view of violence toward civilians, men or women."

"You're a bewildering woman."

"Saiman, focus. Yulya?"

Saiman leaned back. "I can't produce Yulya. I am Yulya."

I suppose I should've seen that coming. "The man was under the impression he's married to her. What happened to the real Yulya?"

"There was never a real Yulya. I will tell you the whole story, but I must have coffee. And nutrients."

I poured him a cup of coffee. Saiman reached into the fridge and came up with a gallon of milk, a solid block of chocolate, and several bananas.

Chocolate was expensive as hell. I couldn't remember the last time I'd had some. If I survived this job, I'd buy a couple of truffles.

I watched Saiman load bananas and milk into a manual blender and crank the handle, cutting the whole thing into a coarse mess. Not the chocolate, not the chocolate... Yep, threw it in there, too. What a waste.

He poured the concoction into a two-quart jug and began chugging it. Shapeshifters did burn a ton of calories. I sighed, mourning the loss of the chocolate, and sipped my coffee. "Give."

"The man in question is the son of Pavel Semyonov. He's the premier *volkhv* in the Russian community here. The boy's name is Grigorii, and he's completely right, I did marry him, as Yulya, of course. The acorn was very well guarded and I needed a way in."

"Unbelievable."

Saiman smiled. Apparently he thought I'd paid him a compliment. "Are you familiar with the ritual of firing the arrow?"

"It's an archaic folkloric ritual. The shooter is blindfolded and spun around, so he blindly fires. The flight of the arrow foretells the correct direction of the object the person seeks. If a woman picks up the arrow, she and the shooter are fated to be together."

Saiman wiped his mouth. "I picked up the arrow. It took me five months from the arrow to the acorn."

"How long did it take you to con that poor guy into marriage?"

"Three months. The combination of open lust but with-holding of actual sex really works wonders."

I shook my head. "Grigorii is in love with you. He thinks his wife is in danger. He's trying to rescue her."

Saiman shrugged. "I had to obtain the acorn. I could say that he's young and resilient, but really his state of mind is the least of my concerns."

"You're a terrible human being."

"I beg to differ. All people are driven by their primary self-ishness. I'm simply more honest than most. Furthermore, he had the use of a beautiful woman, created to his precise specifi-cations, for two months. I did my research into his sexual prac-tices quite thoroughly, to the point of sleeping with him twice as a prostitute to make sure I knew his preferences."

"If we get out of this, I need to remember never to work for you again."

Saiman smiled. "But you will. If the price is right."

"No."

"Anyone will work for anyone and anyone will sleep with anyone, if the price is right and the partnership is attractive enough. Suppose I invited you to spend a week here with me. Luxurious clothes. Beautiful shoes." He looked at my old boots, which were in danger of falling apart. "Magnificent meals. All the chocolate you could ever want."

So he'd caught me.

"All that for the price of having sex with me. I would even sweeten the deal by assuming a shape preferable to you. Anyone you want. Any shape, any size, any color, any gender. All in total confidentiality. Nobody ever has to know you were here. The offer is on the table." He placed his hand on the counter, palm down. "Right now. I promise you a week of total bliss—assuming we survive. You'll never get another chance to be this pampered. All I need from you is one word."

"No."

He blinked. "Don't you want to think about it?"

"No."

He clamped his mouth shut. Muscles played along his jaw. "Why?"

The TV screen ignited. Grigorii appeared in the glow. Saiman strode to the screen with a scowl on his face. "I'll make it short." His body boiled, twisted, stretched. I shut my eyes. It was that or lose my precious coffee. When I opened them, a petite red-haired woman stood in Saiman's place.

"Does this explain things enough?" Saiman asked. "Or do I need to spell it out, Grigorii?"

"You're her?"

"Yes."

"I don't believe it."

Saiman sighed. "Would you like me to list your preferred positions, in the order you typically enjoy them? Shall we speak of intimate things? I could recite most of our conversations word for word, I do have a very precise memory."

They stared at each other.

"It was all a lie," Grigorii said finally.

"I call it subterfuge, but yes, in essence, the marriage was a sham. You were set up from the beginning. I was Yulya. I was also Siren and Alyssa, so if you decide to visit that particular house of ill repute again, don't look for either."

Oh God.

The glow vanished. Saiman turned to me. "Back to our question. Why?"

"That man loved you enough to risk his own neck to negotiate your release. You just destroyed him, in passing, because you were in a hurry. And you want to know why. If you did that to him, there's no telling what you'd do to me. Sex is about physical attraction, yes, but it's also about trust. I don't trust you. You're completely self-absorbed and egoistic. You offer nothing I want."

"Sex is driven by physical attraction. Given the right stimulus, you will sleep with me. I simply have to present you with a shape you can't resist."

Saiman jerked, as if struck by a whip, and crashed to the floor. His feet drummed the carpet, breaking the herbs and fledgling ferns. Wild convulsions tore at his body. A blink and he was a mess of arms and legs and bodies. My stomach gave up, and I vomited into the sink.

Ordinarily I'd be on top of him, jamming something in his mouth to keep him from biting himself, but given that he changed shapes as if there were no tomorrow, finding his mouth was a bit problematic.

"Saiman? Talk to me."

"The acorn... It's coming. Must... Get... Roof."

Roof? No roof. We were in the apartment, shielded by a ward. On the roof we'd be sitting ducks. "We can't do that."

"Oak... Large... Cave-in."

Oh hell. Would it have killed him to mention that earlier? "I need you to walk. You're too heavy and I can't carry you while you convulse."

Little by little, the shudders died. Saiman staggered to his feet. He was back to the unremarkable man I'd first found in the bedroom. His stomach had grown to ridiculous proportions. If he were pregnant, he'd be twelve months along.

"We'll make a run for it," I told him.

A faint scratch made me spin. An old man hung outside the window, suspended on a rope. Gaunt, his white beard flapping in the wind, he peered through the glass straight at me. In the split second we looked at each other, twelve narrow stalks unfurled from his neck, spreading into a corona around his head, like a nimbus around the face of a Russian icon. A bulb tipped each stock. A hovala. Shit.

I grabbed Saiman and threw him at the door.

The bulbs opened.

Blinding light flooded the apartment, hiding the world in a white haze. The window behind me exploded. I could barely see. "Stay behind me."

Shapes dashed through the haze.

I slashed. Slayer connected, encountering resistance. Sharp ice stabbed my left side. I reversed the strike and slashed again. The shape before me crumpled. The second attacker struck. I dodged left on instinct and stabbed my blade at his side. Bone and muscle. Got him between the lower ribs. A hoarse scream lashed my ears. I twisted the blade, ripping the organs, and withdrew.

The hovala hissed at the window. I was still blind.

Behind me the lock clicked. "No!"

I groped for Saiman and hit my forearm on the open door. He ran. Into the hallway, where he was an easy target. I lost my body. Goddamn it.

I sprinted into the hallway, trying to blink the haze from my eyes. The stairs were to the left. I ran, half-blind, grabbed the door, and dashed up the stairs.

The blinding flare finally cleared. I hit the door, burst onto the roof, and took a kick to the ribs. Bones crunched. I fell left and rolled to my feet. A woman stood by the door, arms held in a trademark tae kwon do cat stance.

To the right, an older man grappled with Saiman. Six others watched.

The woman sprang into a kick. It was a lovely kick, strong with good liftoff. I sidestepped and struck. By the time she landed, I'd cut her twice. She fell in a crumpled heap.

I flicked the blood off my saber and headed for Saiman.

"You're Voron's kid," one of the men said. "We have no problem with you. Pavel's entitled. His son just threw himself off the roof."

Ten to a million the son's name was Grigorii.

I kept coming. The two men ripped at each other, grappling

and snarling like two wild animals. I was five feet away when Pavel head-butted Saiman, jerking his right arm free. A knife flashed; I lunged and saw Pavel slice across Saiman's distended gut. A bloody clump fell, and I caught it with my left hand purely on instinct.

Magic punched my arm. Pale glow erupted from my fist.

Saiman twisted and stabbed something at Pavel's right eye. The volkhv stumbled back, a bloody pencil protruding from his eye socket. For a long moment he stood, huge mouth gaping, and then he toppled like a log. Saiman spun about. The muscles of his stomach collapsed, folding, knitting together, turning into a flat washboard wall.

The whole thing took less than three seconds.

I opened my fist. A small gold acorn lay on my palm.

The golden shell cracked. A sliver of green thrust its way up. The acorn rolled off my hand. The green shoot thickened, twisted, surging higher and higher. The air roared like a tornado. Saiman howled, a sound of pure rage. I grabbed him and dragged him with me to the stairs. On the other side, volkhvi ran for the edge of the roof.

The shoot grew, turning dark, sprouting branches, leaves, and bark. Magic roiled.

"It was supposed to be mine," Saiman snarled. "Mine!"

Light flashed. The roaring ceased.

A colossal oak stood in the middle of the roof, as tall as the building itself, its roots spilling on both sides of the high-rise. Tiny lights fluttered between its branches, each wavy leaf as big as my head. Birds sang in the foliage. A huge metal chain bound the enormous trunk, its links so thick, I could've lain down on it. A feeling of complete peace came over me. All my troubles melted into the distance. My pain dissolved. The air tasted sweet, and I drank it in.

At the other side of the roof, the volkhvi knelt.

Metal clinked. A black creature came walking down the

bottom loop. As big as a horse, its fur long and black, it walked softly, gripping the links with razor-sharp claws. Its head was that of a lynx. Tall tufts of black fur decorated its ears, and a long black beard stretched from its chin. Its eyes glowed, lit from within.

The cat paused and looked at me. The big maw opened, showing me a forest of white teeth, long and sharp like knives.

"Ask."

I blinked.

"You were the last to hold the acorn," Saiman whispered. "You must ask the question or it will kill all of us."

The cat showed me its teeth again.

For anything I asked, there would be a price.

"Ask," the cat said, its voice laced with an unearthly snarl.

"Ask, Kate," Saiman prompted.

"Ask!" one of the volkhvi called out.

I took a deep breath.

The cat leaned forward in anticipation.

"Would you like some milk?"

The cat smiled wider. "Yes."

Saiman groaned.

"I'll be right back."

I dashed down the stairs. Three minutes later, the cat lapped milk from Saiman's crystal punch bowl.

"You could've asked anything," the creature said between laps.

"But you would've taken everything," I told it. "This way all it cost me is a little bit of milk."

In the morning Peters came to relieve me. Not that he had a particularly difficult job. After the oak disappeared, the volkhvi decided that since both Pavel and Grigorii were dead, all accounts were settled and it was time to call it quits. As soon

73

as we returned to the apartment, Saiman locked himself in the bedroom and refused to come out. The loss of the acorn hit him pretty hard. Just as well. I handed my fussy client off to Peters, retrieved Peggy, and headed back to the Guild.

All in all I'd done spectacularly well, I decided. I lost the client for at least two minutes, let him get his stomach ripped open, watched him stab his attacker in the eye, which was definitely something he shouldn't have had to do, and cost him his special acorn and roughly five months of work. The fact that my client turned out to be a scumbag and a sexual deviant really had no bearing on the matter.

Some bodyguard I made. Yay. Whoopee. I got to the Guild, surrendered Peggy, and filled out my paperwork. You win some, you lose some. At least Saiman survived. I wouldn't get paid, but I didn't end the job with a dead client on my hands.

I grabbed my crap and headed for the doors.

"Kate," the clerk called from the counter.

I turned. Nobody remembered the clerk's name. He was just "the clerk."

He waved an envelope at me. "Money."

I turned on my foot. "Money?"

"For the job. Client called. He says he'd like to work exclusively with you from now on. What did the two of you do all night?"

"We argued philosophy." I swiped the envelope and counted the bills. Three grand. What do you know?

I stepped out the doors into an overcast morning. I had been awake for over thirty-six hours. I just wanted to find a quiet spot, curl up, and shut out the world.

A tall, lean man strode to me, tossing waist-long black hair out of the way. He walked like a dancer, and his face would stop traffic. I looked into his blue eyes and saw a familiar smugness in their depths. "Hello, Saiman."

"How did you know?"

I shrugged and headed on my way.

"Perhaps we can work out a deal," he said, matching my steps. "I have no intentions of losing that bet. I will find a form you can't resist."

"Good luck."

"I'm guessing you'll try to avoid me, which would make my victory a bit difficult."

"Bingo."

"That's why I decided to give you an incentive you can't refuse. I'm giving you a sixty percent discount on my services. It's an unbelievable deal."

I laughed. If he thought I'd pay him twenty-six dollars a minute for his time, he was out of luck.

"Laugh now." Saiman smiled. "But sooner or later you'll require my expertise."

He stopped. I kept on walking, into the dreary sunrise. I had three thousand dollars and some chocolate to buy.

RETRIBUTION CLAUSE

Adam Talford closed his eyes and wished he were somewhere else. Somewhere warm. Where cool waves lapped hot yellow sand, where strange flowers bloomed, and birdsong filled the air.

"Take off the watch! Now!" a male voice barked into his ear. "You think I am fucking with you? You think I am playing? I'll rip your flesh off your body and make myself a skin suit."

Adam opened his eyes. The three thugs who pinned him to the brick wall looked half-starved, like mongrel dogs who'd been prowling the alley, feeding on garbage.

He should never have wandered into this side of Philadelphia, not in the evening, and especially not while the magic was up. This was Firefern Road, a place where the refuse of the city hid out among the ruins of the ravaged buildings, gnawed by magic to ugly nubs of brick and concrete. The real predators stalked their prey elsewhere, looking for bigger and meatier scores. Firefern Road sheltered scavengers, desperate and savage, eager to bite, but only when the odds were on their side.

Unfortunately, he had no choice.

"You have the cash," Adam said, keeping his voice low. "Take it and go. It's a cheap watch. You won't get any money for it."

The larger of the thugs pulled him from the wall and slammed him back into the bricks. The man bent over him, folding his six-foot-two frame down to Adam's five feet five inches, so their faces were level, forcing Adam to stare straight into his eyes. Adam looked into their blue depths and glimpsed a spark of vicious glee. It wasn't about the money anymore. It was about domination, humiliation, and inflicting pain. They would beat him just for the fun of it.

"The watch, you little bitch," the thug ordered.

"No," Adam said quietly.

A muscular forearm smashed into his neck, cutting off his air. Bodies pressed against him. He felt fingers prying at the metal band on his narrow wrist. His heart hammered. His chest constricted.

Think of elsewhere. Think of blue waves and yellow sand...

Someone yanked at the band. The world was turning darker —his lungs demanded air. Pain shot through his limbs in sharp, burning spikes.

Blue waves... Azure... Calm... Just need to stay calm...

Cold metal broke his skin. They were trying to cut the watch off his wrist. He jerked and heard the crunch of broken glass. Two tiny watch gears flew before his eyes, sparking with residual traces of magic.

Imbeciles. They'd broken it.

The magic chain that held his body in check vanished. The calming visions of the ocean vanished, swept away by an avalanche of fury. His magic roared inside him, ancient, primal, and cold as a glacier. Frost clamped his eyebrows, falling off in tiny snowflakes. The short blond hairs rained down from his head, and pale blue strands grew in their place, falling down to his shoulders. His body surged, up and out, stretching, spilling out into its natural shape. His outer clothes tore under the pressure as his new form stretched the thick spandex suit he wore underneath to its limit. His feet ripped the cheap cloth Converse sneakers. The three small humans in front of him froze like frightened rabbits.

With a guttural roar, Adam grasped the leader by his shoulder and yanked him up. The man's fragile collarbone broke under the pressure of his pale fingers, and the man screamed, kicking his feet. Adam brought him close, their eyes once again level. The thug trembled and fell silent, his face a terrified rigid mask. Adam knew exactly what he saw: a creature, an eight-foot-tall giant in the shape of a man, with a mane of blue hair and eyes like submerged ice.

Inside him, the rational, human part of Adam Talbot sighed and faded. Only cold and rage drove him now.

"Do you know why I wear the watch?" he snarled into the man's face.

The thug shook his head.

"I wear it so I can keep my body in my tracking form. Because when I'm small, I don't draw attention. I can go anywhere. Nobody pays me any notice. I've been tracking a man for nine days. His trail led me here. I was so close, I could smell his sweat, and the three of you ruined it for me. I can't follow him now, can I?" He shook the man like a wet rag. "I told you to walk away. No. You didn't listen."

"I'll listen," the thug promised. "I'll listen now."

"Too late. You wanted to feel big and bad. Now I'll show you what big and bad is."

Adam hurled the human across the alley. The thug flew. Before he crashed into a brick ruin with a bone-snapping crunch, his two sidekicks turned and fled, running full speed. Adam vaulted over a garbage Dumpster to his right and gave chase.

Ten minutes later, he returned to the alley, crouched, dug through the refuse with bloody fingers, and fished out his watch. The glass and the top plate were gone, displaying the delicate innards of gears and magic. Hopelessly mangled. Just like the thug who still sagged motionless against the ruin.

The alley reeked with the scavenger stench: fear, sweat, a hint of urine, garbage. Adam rose, stretching to his full height, and raised his face to the wind. The hint of Morowitz's scent teased him, slightly sweet and distant. The chase was over.

Dean Morowitz was a thief, and, like all thieves, he would do anything for the right price. He'd stolen a priceless necklace in a feat of outrageous luck, but he didn't do it on his own. No, someone had hired him, and Adam was interested in the buyer much more than in the tool he had used. Breaking Morowitz's legs would probably shed some light on his employment arrangements, but it would inevitably alarm the buyer, who'd vanish into thin air. Following the thief was a much better course of action.

Adam sighed. He had failed. Tracking the thief now would be like carrying a neon sign above his head that read, pom insurance adjuster. He'd have to give Morowitz a day or two to cool off, then arrange for a replacement watch to hide his true form before trying to find the man again.

A mild headache scraped at the inside of Adam's head, insistent, like a knock on his door.

He concentrated, sending a focused thought in its direction. "Yes?"

"You're needed at the office, Mr. Talford," a familiar female voice murmured directly into his mind.

"I'll be right there," he promised, rose to his full height, and began to jog, breaking into the long-legged distance-devouring gait that thousands of years ago carried his ancestors across the frozen wastes of the old North.

Night was falling. Anyone with a crumb of sense cleared from the streets or hurried to get home, behind the protection of four walls, barred windows, and a sturdy door. The rare passersby scattered out of his way. Even in post-Shift Philadelphia, the sight of an eight-foot-tall human running full speed in skin-tight black spandex wasn't a common occurrence. He drew the eye, Adam reflected, leaping over a ten-foot gap in the asphalt. He pounded up the wooden ramp onto the newly built Pine Bridge, spanning the vast sea of crushed concrete and twisted steel that used to be the downtown.

The bridge turned south, carrying him deeper into the city. Far in the distance, the sunset burned out, couched in long orange clouds. The weak light of the dying sun glinted from the heaps of broken glass that used to be hundreds of windows. The cemetery of human ambition.

Human beings had always believed in apocalypse, but they expected the end of the world to come in a furious flash of nuclear cloud, or in environmental disaster, or perhaps even on a stray rock falling from the universe beyond. Nobody expected the magic. It came during one sunny afternoon, in broad daylight, and raged through the world—pulling planes from the sky, stealing electricity, giving birth to monsters. And three days later, when it vanished, and humanity reeled, thousands were dead. Survivors mourned and breathed a sigh of relief, but two weeks later the magic came again.

It flooded the world in waves now, unpredictable and moody, coming back and disappearing on its own mysterious schedule. Slowly but surely, it tore down the tall buildings, feeding on the carcass of technology and molding humanity in its own image. Adam smiled. He took to it better than most.

The latest magic shift took place about half an hour ago, just before he got jumped. While unpredictable, the magic waves rarely lasted less than twelve hours. He was in for a long, magic-filled night.

The bridge split into four different branches. He took the second to the left. It brought him deep into the heart of the city, past the ruins, to the older streets. He cleared the next couple of intersections and turned into the courtyard of a large Georgian-style mansion, a redbrick box, rectangular in shape and three stories high. Anything taller didn't survive in the new Philadelphia unless it was really old. The POM Mansion, as the house came to be known, had been built at the end of the eighteenth century. Its age and the simplicity of its construction afforded it some immunity against magic.

Adam jogged to the doors. Pressure clutched him for a brief moment, then released him—the defensive spell on the building recognizing his right to enter. Adam stepped through the doors and walked into the foyer. Luxurious by any standards, after his run through the ruined city, the inside of the building looked almost surreal. A hand-knotted blue Persian rug rested on the floor of polished marble. Cream-colored walls were adorned by graceful glass bells of fey lanterns, glowing pale blue as the charged air inside their tubes reacted with magic. A marble staircase veered left and up, leading to the second floor.

Adam paused for a moment to admire the rug. He'd once survived in a cave in the woods for half a year. Luxury or poverty made little difference to him. Luxury tended to be cleaner and more comfortable, but that was about it. Still, he liked the rug—it was beautiful.

The secretary sitting behind a massive redwood desk looked up at his approach. She was slender, young, and dark-skinned. Large brown eyes glanced at him from behind the wide lenses of her glasses. Her name was May, and in the three years of his employment with POM, he'd never managed to surprise her.

"Good evening, Mr. Talford."

"Good evening." He could never figure out if she had been there and done that and was too jaded, or if she was simply too well trained.

"Will you require a change of clothes?"

"Yes, please."

May held out a leather file. His reason for being called into

81

the office. He took it. Priority Two. It overrode all of his cases. Interesting. Adam nodded at her and headed up the stairs.

THE HEAVY DOOR OF THE OFFICE SLID OPEN UNDER THE PRESSURE of Adam's hand. When he joined the ranks of POM Insurance Adjusters three years ago, someone asked him how he wanted his office to look. He told him, "Like the cabin of a pirate captain," and that was exactly what he got. Cypress paneling lined every inch of the floor, walls, and ceiling, imitating the inside of a wooden ship. The antique-reproduction desk, bolted to the floor for sheer authenticity, supported a sextant, a chronometer, and a bottle of Bombay Sapphire. Behind the desk, an enormous map drawn in ink on yellowed paper took up most of the wall. To the left, bookshelves stretched, next to a large bed sunken into a sturdy wooden frame, so it looked like it was cut into the wall. The bed's dark blue curtain hung open.

His nostrils caught a hint of faint spice. He inhaled it, savoring the scent. Siroun.

"You smell like blood," Siroun's smooth voice said behind him.

Ah. There she is. He turned slightly and watched her circle him, scrutinizing his body. She moved like a lean panther: silent, flexible, graceful. Deadly. Her hair, cropped short into a ragged, messy halo, framed her face like a pale red cloud. She tilted her head. Two dark eyes looked at him.

"You fought with three people, and you let them break your watch?" Her voice was quiet and soothing, and deep for a woman's. He'd heard her sing once, a strange song of murmured words. It had stayed with him.

"I was tracking Morowitz," he told her.

"Into Firefern?"

"Yes."

"We agreed you would wait for me if his trail led into Firefern."

"I did. I called it in to the office, waited, then followed him."

"The office is about four miles from Firefern."

"Yes."

"How long did you wait?"

He frowned, thinking. "I'd say about two minutes."

"And that struck you as the appropriate length of time?"

He grinned at her. "Yes."

A bright orange sheen rolled over her irises, like fire over coals, and vanished. She clearly failed to see the humor in this situation.

Post-Shift Philadelphia housed many people with something extra in their blood, including shapeshifters, a small, sad pack of humans stuck on the crossroads between man and beast. Occasionally, they went insane and had to be put down, but most persevered through strict discipline. Their eyes glowed just like that.

Adjusters worked in pairs, and he and Siroun had been partnered with each other from the beginning. After all this time together, working with her and observing her, he was sure that Siroun wasn't a shapeshifter. At least not any kind he had ever encountered. When she dropped her mask, he sensed something in her, a faint touch of ancient magic, buried deep, hidden like a fossil under the sediment of civilization. He sensed this same primal magic within himself. Siroun wasn't of his kind, but she was like him, and she drew him like a magnet.

Siroun pulled the leather file out of Adam's fingers and sat on the bed, curling around a large pillow.

Adam was possibly the smartest man she had ever known. And also the biggest idiot. In his mind, big and strong equaled invincible. It would only take one bullet to the head in the right spot, one cut of the right blade in the right place, and none of his regeneration would matter.

He went into Firefern by himself. Didn't wait. Didn't tell her. And by the time she'd found out, it was too late—he was already on his way to the office, so she paced back and forth, like a caged tiger until she heard his steps in the hallway.

Adam sat behind his desk, sinking into an oversized leather chair. It groaned, accepting his weight. He cocked his head to the side and moved the bottle of Bombay Sapphire a quarter of an inch to the left. The bright blue liquid caught the light of the fey lantern on the wall and sparkled with all the fire of the real gem.

She pretended to read the file while watching him through the curtain of her eyelashes. For sixteen years, her life was full of chaos, dominated by violence and desperation. Then came the prison; and then, then there was POM and Adam. In her crazed, blood-drenched world, Adam was a granite island of calm. When the turbulent storms rocked her inner world, until she was no longer sure where reality ended and the hungry madness inside her began, she clung to that island and weathered the storm. He had no idea how much she needed this shelter. The thought of losing it nearly drove her out of her mind, what little was left of it.

Adam frowned. A stack of neatly folded clothes sat on the corner of the desk, delivered moments before he walked through the door, together with a small package now waiting for his attention. She'd looked through it: T-shirt, pants, camo suit, all large enough to accommodate his giant body. Adam checked the clothes and pulled the package close. She'd glanced at it—the return address label had one word: Saiman.

"Who is he?" Siroun asked.

"My cousin. He lives in the South." Adam tore the paper and pulled out a leather-bound book. He chuckled and showed her the cover. Robert E. Howard: *The Frost-Giant's Daughter and Other Stories.*

"Is he like you?" Apparently they both had a twisted sense of humor.

"He has more magic, but he uses it mostly to hide. My original form is still my favorite." Adam leaned back, stretching his enormous shoulders. The customized chair creaked. "He has the ability to assume any form, and he wears every type of body except his own."

"Why?"

"I'm not sure. I think he wants to fit in. He wants to be loved by everyone he meets. It's a way of controlling things around him."

"Your cousin sounds unpleasant."

Siroun leafed through the file. Not like Adam would need it. He had probably read it on the way up. She once witnessed him go through a fifty-page contract in less than a minute, then demand detailed adjustments.

He was looking at her; she could feel his gaze. She raised her head and let a little of the fire raging inside color her irises. *Yes, I'm still mad at you.*

Most people froze when confronted with that orange glow. It whispered of old things, brutal and hungry, waiting just beyond the limits of human consciousness.

Adam smiled.

Idiot.

She looked back at the file.

He opened the top drawer of his desk, took out a small paper box, and set it on the desk. *Now what?*

Adam pried the lid open with his oversized fingers and extracted a small brown cupcake with chocolate frosting. It looked thimble-sized in his thick hands. "I have a cupcake."

He had lost his mind.

Adam tilted the cupcake from side to side, making it dance. "It's chocolate."

She clenched her teeth, speechless.

"It could be your cupcake if you stop—"

She dashed across the room in a blur, leaped, and crouched on the desk in front of him. He blinked. She plucked the cupcake from his huge hand with her slender fingers and pretended to ponder it. "I don't like a lot of people."

"I've noticed," he said. He was still smiling. Truly, he had a death wish.

Siroun examined the cupcake some more. "If you die, I will have to choose a new partner, Adam." She turned and looked at him. "I don't want a new partner."

He nodded in mock seriousness. "In that case, I'll strive to stay alive."

"Thank you."

Knuckles rapped on the door. It swung open, and the narrow-shouldered, thin figure of Chang, their POM coordinator, stepped inside. Chang looked at them for a long moment. His eyes widened. "Am I interrupting?"

Siroun jumped off the desk and moved back to the bed, palming the cupcake. "No."

"I am relieved. I'd hate to be rude." Chang crossed the office, deposited another leather file in front of Adam, and perched in a chair across the room. Lean to the point of delicate, the coordinator had one of those encouraging faces that predisposed people to trust him. He wore a small smile and seemed slightly ill at ease, as if he constantly struggled to overcome his natural shyness. Last year, a man had attacked him outside the POM doors with the intent of robbing him. Chang decapitated him and put his head on a sharpened stick. It sat in front of the office for four days before the stench prevailed, and he took it down. A bit crude, but very persuasive.

"That's a beautiful bottle," Chang said, nodding at the

Bombay. "I've never seen you drink, Adam. Especially dry gin. So why the bottle?"

"He likes the color," Siroun said.

Adam smiled.

Chang glanced at the flat screen in the wall and sighed. "Things are much easier when technology is up. Unfortunately, we'll have to do this the hard way. Please turn to page one in your file."

Siroun opened the file. Page one offered a portrait of a lean man in a business suit, bending forward, looking into the dense torrent of traffic of cars, carts, and riders. A somber man, confident, almost severe. Slick lines, square jaw, elongated shape of the face inviting comparison with a Doberman pinscher, light skin, light blond hair cut very short. Early to mid forties.

"John Sobanto, an attorney with Dorowitz & Sobanto, and your target. Mr. Sobanto made a fortune representing powerful clients, but he's most famous and most hated for representing New Found Hope."

Siroun bared her teeth. Now there was a name everyone in Philly loved to despise.

New Found Hope, a new church born after the Shift, had pushed hard for pure human, no-magic-tolerated membership. So hard, that on Christmas day, sixteen of its parishioners walked into the icy water of the Delaware River and drowned nine of their own children, who had been born with magic. The guilty and the church leaders were charged with first-degree murder. The couples took the fall, but the founder of the church escaped without even a slap on the wrist. John Sobanto was the man who made it happen.

"Mr. Sobanto is worth $4.2 million, not counting his investments in Left Arm Securities, which are projected at 2 million plus," Chang said. "The corporation was unable to obtain a more precise estimate. Please turn to page two."

Siroun flipped the page. Another photograph, this one of a

woman standing on the bank of a lead-colored Delaware River. In the distance, the remains of the Delaware Memorial Bridge jutted sadly from the water. She knew the exact spot this was taken—Penn Treaty Park.

Unlike the man, the woman was aware of being photographed and looked straight into the camera. Pretty in an unremarkable way that came from good breeding and careful attention to one's appearance. Shoulder-length hair, blond, worn loose, standard for an upper-class spouse. Her eyes stared out of the photograph, surprisingly hard. Determined.

"Linda Sobanto," Chang said. "The holder of POM policy number 492776-M. She spent the last three years funneling an obscene portion of Mr. Sobanto's earnings into POM bank accounts to pay for it."

A severe, confident man on one page, an equally severe, determined woman on the other. An ominous combination, Siroun decided.

Adam stirred. "So what did Mr. Sobanto do to warrant our attention?"

"It appears he murdered his wife," Chang said.

Of course.

"Mrs. Sobanto's insurance policy had a retribution clause," the coordinator continued. "In the event of her homicide, we're required to terminate the guilty party."

"How was she killed?" Siroun asked.

"She was strangled."

Personal. Very, very personal.

"Mr. Sobanto's thumbprint was lifted from her throat. He had defensive wounds on his face and neck, and his DNA was found under her fingernails. His lawyers have arranged a voluntary surrender. He is scheduled to come in Thursday morning, less than a day from now."

"Is he expecting us?" Adam asked.

Chang nodded in a slow, measured way. "Most definitely. Please turn to page three."

On page three, an aerial shot showed a monstrously large ranch-style house hugging the top of the hill like a bear. Three rectangular structures sat a short distance from the house, each marked by a red X.

"Guards stationed in a pyramid formation, four shifts. The gun towers are marked on your photograph. The house is trapped and extensively warded. At least two arcane disciplines were utilized in creation of the wards. For all practical purposes, it's a fortress. Page four, please."

Siroun turned the page. A blueprint, showing a large central room with smaller rooms radiating from it in a wheel-and-spokes design.

"We believe Mr. Sobanto has locked himself in this central chamber. He is guarded by spells, traps, and armed men."

Siroun shifted in her chair. "The guards?"

"Red Guard," Chang answered.

Sobanto hired the best.

"Expensive to hire," Adam murmured, plaiting the fingers of his hands together.

"And very expensive to kill," Chang said. "Red Guard lawyers are truly excellent, particularly when negotiating a wrongful death compensation. We don't want additional expenses, so please don't kill more than three. A higher death count would negatively impact the corporation's profit margin. Please turn to page five."

Page five presented another image of John Sobanto, surrounded by men and women in business suits, a thin-stemmed glass in his hand. A cowled figure stood in the shadow of the column, watching over him.

Siroun leaned forward. *No, the image is too murky.*

"His reaction time suggests that he is not human. A shapeshifter operative on our staff had an opportunity to sample his scent. He found it disturbing. We don't know what he is," Chang said. "But we do know that John Sobanto made a lot of people unhappy with his latest settlement. There have been two attempts on his life, and this bodyguard kept Sobanto breathing."

Siroun smiled quietly.

"You have eleven hours to kill Mr. Sobanto." Chang closed the file. "After that, he has arranged to surrender into the custody of Philadelphia's Finest. Sniping people in police custody is bad for business. Will you require a priest for your final rites?"

Adam glanced at Siroun. She gave a barely perceptible shake of her head.

"That won't be necessary."

"Good luck. Break a leg, preferably not your own." Chang smiled and headed for the door. "Remember, no more than three Red Guardsmen."

The door closed behind him with a click.

Siroun slipped off the bed. "Disable the guards, break into a fortress, shatter the wards, disarm the traps, bust into the central chamber, kill a preternaturally fast bodyguard, and eliminate the target. Shall I drive?"

"Sounds like a plan." Adam headed for the door.

ADAM SAT ON THE FLOOR OF THE BLACK POM VAN AND WATCHED Siroun drive. She guided the car along the ruined, crumbling highway with almost surgical precision. She had only two modes of operation: complete control or complete insanity. Considering how tightly she clenched herself now, he was in for a hell of a night.

The magic smothered gas engines; the converted POM van ran on enchanted water. The water vehicles were slow, barely topping fifty miles an hour at the best, and they made an outrageous amount of noise. They'd have to park the car some distance from the house and approach on foot.

Adam stretched. They had had to take all of the seats, except for the driver's, out of the van to accommodate him. From where he sat, Adam could see a wispy lock of red hair and Siroun's profile. Her face, etched against the darkness of the night, almost seemed to glow.

Some things can come to pass, he reminded himself. Some things are improbable, and some are impossible.

He had to stop imagining impossible things.

Siroun stirred. "What would drive a man to kill his own wife? Two people live together, love each other, make a safe haven for themselves."

"I saw a play once," Adam said. "It was about a man and a woman: They were in love a long time ago, but as years passed, they ended up spending their time torturing each other. The man had told the woman, 'Here is the key to my soul. Take it, beloved. Take the poisoned dagger.' Those we love know us the best. They know all the right places to strike."

She shook her head.

"If we were lovers, and I betrayed you, you would kill me." Why did he have to go there? Like playing with fire.

She didn't look at him. "What makes you say that?"

"Love and hate are both means of emotional control to which we subject ourselves. Once you were done with me, you'd want to be free of the pain of betrayal. Absolutely free."

No comment, Siroun? No, not even a glance.

He looked out the window. They had exited the highway onto a narrow country road that wound its way between huge trees. The same magic that devoured skyscrapers fed the forests. Moonlight spilled from the sky like a gauzy silvery curtain, catching on massive branches of enormous hemlocks and white pines. The woods encroached onto asphalt weakened by the magic's assault, the trees leaning toward the van like grim sentries intent on barring their passage.

Fifty years ago, this might have been a cultivated field or a small town. But then, fifty years ago, he wouldn't have existed, Adam reflected. Magic fed the ancient power in his blood. Without it, he would be just a man.

Fifty years ago, nobody would've purchased an insurance policy with a retribution clause, which assured that one's murderer would be punished. An eye for an eye, a tooth for a tooth. It had been a gentler, more civilized time.

"Strangulation contains death," Siroun said. "There's no release. It's deeply personal. He wanted to see her eyes as he squeezed the life out of her second by second. To drink it in. He must've hated her."

"The question is why," Adam said. "He was a skilled lawyer. I've looked through the file some more. He seems to have a remarkable talent when it comes to jury selection. In every case, he manages to pick a precise mix of people to favor his case, which suggests he's an excellent judge of human nature, but all of his arguments are very precise and emotionless. People have passions. He is dispassionate. He would have to be at the brink of his mind to strangle someone. Especially his wife. It doesn't add up."

"Still waters run deep," she murmured, and made a right turn. The vehicle rolled off the road, careening over roots. "We're here."

THEY STEPPED FROM THE CAR ONTO A FOREST FLOOR THICK WITH five centuries of autumn. Adam stretched, testing his pixilated camo suit. It was loose enough to let him move quickly. The huge trees watched him in silence. He wished it were colder. He would be faster in the cold.

Siroun raised her head and drew the air into her nostrils,

tasting it on her tongue. "Woodsmoke."

Adam slid the short needle-rifle into its holster on his belt. It was made specifically for him, a modern version of a blowgun made to operate during magic. Siroun stretched her arms next to him, like a lean cat. Her camo suit hugged her, clenched at the waist by a belt carrying two curved, brutal blades. She pulled a dark mask over the lower half of her face and raised her hood. She looked tiny.

Anxiety nipped at him.

"Stay safe," he said.

She turned to him. "Adam?"

Shit. He had to recover. "We're only allowed three kills. You look on edge. Stay in the safe zone."

"This isn't my first time."

She looked up, high above, where the rough column of a tree trunk erupted into thick branches, blocking the moonlight. For a moment, she tensed, the smooth muscles coiling like springs beneath the fabric, and burst forward, across the soft carpet of pine needles and fallen twigs. Siroun leaped, scrambled up the trunk in a brown-and-green blur, and vanished into the branches as if dissolved into the greenery.

Adam locked the van and dropped the keys behind the right-front wheel. The forest waited for him.

He headed uphill at a brisk trot, guided by traces of woodsmoke and some imperceptible instinct he couldn't explain. Stay safe. He was beginning to lose it. *Remember what you are. Remember who she is.* She would never see him as anything more than a partner. To step closer, she would have to risk something. To open herself to possible injury, to give up a drop of her freedom. She would never do it, and if he slipped again and showed her that he had stepped over the line, she would sever what few fragile ties bound them.

The old trees spread their branches wide, greedily hoarding the moonlight, and the undergrowth was scarce. A few times a magic-addled vine cascading from an occasional trunk made a grab for his limbs. When it did manage to snag him, he simply ripped through it and kept jogging.

Forty-five minutes later, Adam stepped over an electrified trip wire strung across the greenery at what for most people would've been a mid-thigh level and for him was just below the knee. With the magic up, the current was dead, but he took care not to touch it all the same. Beyond the wire, the trees ended abruptly, as if sliced by the blade of a giant's knife. The gaps between the tree trunks offered glimpses of the electric fence, sitting out in the open, and the Sobanto house, a dark shape beyond the metal mesh. He saw no guards, but the Red Guards didn't stroll along the perimeter. They hid.

Adam went to ground. The fragrant cushion of pine needles accepted his weight without protest. He slid forward a few feet and saw the house, sprawling in the middle of the clearing. A gun tower punctuated the roof. Two guards manned it, armed with precision crossbows.

Adam craned his neck. Judging by the moss on the trunks, he was facing west. The west guard tower would be behind the house—he didn't have to worry about it. He was at the southern edge of the house, so the north guard tower wouldn't present too much of an issue either. Adam crawled another three feet and craned his neck to look left. A blocky structure wrapped in a cage of metal bars rose a few dozen yards away—the south guard tower and his biggest problem. The bars glowed with a faint yellow sheen. Warded.

Adam reached into his camo suit and pulled a small spyglass free. He raised it to his eye and focused on the house. The fence slid closer. A standard twelve-foot-high affair, horizontal wires, coils of razor wire guarding the top edge. The space between the wires was uneven. Something was pulling the fence inward, and that something was probably a ward.

The defensive spells came in many varieties. Some were

rooted into the soil, some depended on external markers, rocks, sand, bones, trees… The most powerful ones required blood or a living power source. Judging by the distortion in the fence, this was one hell of a ward, very strong and very potent. Definitely fed by a power source.

Adam craned his neck, looking for the pipeline. He found it twenty-five feet above the ground. A long, green shoot passed through the south guard tower and terminated in a network of thin roots. The roots hung suspended in thin air, dripping magic into the invisible spell. The makers of the ward had found some sort of way to tap into the magic of the forest and channeled it to protect the house.

Adam frowned. The closest route to the house was straight on, through the fence, the ward, and finally through the solid-looking side door on the left end of the mansion. The fence didn't present a problem, but the ward would prevent him from getting inside. His magic was too potent. To take down the ward, he had to sever the roots, but to get to the roots, he would have to take down the ward. A catch-22.

A faint scent floated on the breeze. Siroun. She was on the edge of the woods, to his left, probably right beside the south guard tower. If she took out those guards, she could reach the roots feeding the ward, but to do that she'd have to clear a stretch of open ground in plain view of the crossbows from both the house and the tower. He had to give her a distraction, the kind that would focus both the house and the tower on him.

No guts, no glory.

He put away the spyglass, backed away, and rose to his feet. The woods grew fast, which meant they would have to cut down trees at a steady rate to keep the forest from encroaching onto the property. Adam jogged through the woods, searching. There. A two-foot-wide pine trunk lay on its side, its wide end showing fresh chain-saw marks. Just the right size.

Adam strode to the tip of the tree and pulled out his tactical blade. Two feet long, to him it was conveniently sized, more a knife than a sword. He hacked at the thin section of the trunk. Two cuts, and the narrow crown broke off the tree. That gave him a few branches near the tip. Good enough. Adam returned the blade to the sheath, grasped the trunk about four feet from the bottom, and heaved. Small branches snapped, and the pine left the ground. He shifted it onto his shoulder and strode through the nearest gap between the trees, toward the fence.

A moment, and he was out in the open. The guards on top of the house stared at him, openmouthed. Adam waved at them with his free hand, grasped the tree, and spun. The thirty-foot pine smashed into the fence. Boom!

The effort nearly took him off his feet. The wires snapped under the pressure.

Crossbow bolts whistled through the air. One sprouted from the ground two inches from his foot. The fence was in their way.

Adam pulled the tree upright and brought it down again like a club. Boom!

The second bolt sliced his shoulder, grazing it in a streak of heat.

Boom!

The third bolt singed Adam's neck.

The nearest pole careened with a tortured creak and crashed down, taking the fence with it.

Adam spun, like a hammer thrower, and hurled the tree at the house. It cleared the ward in a flash of blue and smashed into the roof guard post. Boards exploded.

A bolt bit into his thigh, a gift from the south tower.

He was completely exposed now. The next bolt would hit him where it counted. Adam braced himself. He couldn't dodge a bolt, but he could turn into it. Better take one in the shoulder than one in the gut.

The guard tower stood silent and still. No bolts sliced his

flesh. He grasped the shaft of the bolt protruding from his thigh and wrenched it out. It hurt like hell, but it would heal. It always did.

The tower's door slid open, and Siroun emerged. Behind her, a camouflaged figure fell to the floor, its arms slack. Siroun leaped onto the green shoot feeding the ward and dashed along its length as if it were a wide path on solid ground.

So graceful.

Siroun reached the end of the shoot, crouched, and struck in the same smooth movement, slashing the roots. Pale liquid oozed from the cuts. She cut again, lightning fast. The ward trembled and vanished, and she dropped to the ground softly.

Adam sprinted to the house. When he got going, he was impossible to stop. His shoulder smashed into the reinforced door. It flew open with a pitiful screech of snapped bolts and shattered boards. Adam stumbled in, glimpsed the sharp end of the crossbow bolt staring at him from six feet away, and dodged to the left. The bow twanged, and the bolt fell at his feet sliced in half. Siroun leaped forward, swung her curved knives, and the guard's head rolled to the floor. Blood spurted in a thin spray from the stump of the neck, painting the wall crimson. The body took a step forward and tumbled down.

Adam exhaled.

"Death number one," Siroun whispered.

THE HOUSE STANK OF UNCLEAN MAGIC. SIROUN RAN DOWN THE hallway, light on her feet. Adam's hulking form moved next to her. It always amazed her how fast he could move. You'd expect a man of his size to shamble, but he was surprisingly agile, the way giant bears were sometimes surprisingly agile just before their claws caught you.

They had been making their way toward the center of the house, where Chang's blueprint indicated a stairway. They'd run into the guards. Both times, she avoided casualties. Now the bloodlust sang through her, slithering its way through her veins like a starving, enraged serpent. She needed a release.

Somewhere deep within the house, a knot of foul magic smoldered. It brushed against her when she stepped through the door and recoiled, but not fast enough, not before she caught the taint of its magic. It felt old, primitive, and starved, gnawed by the same hunger inside her that longed for blood and severed lives.

A faint red sheen blocked the hallway ahead. Another ward, weaker and simpler than the first. Still, it would take time.

Adam moved toward the ward, casually bumping the fey lantern on the ceiling with his hand. The hallway drowned in darkness.

She ran up to the ward on her toes and swept her palm over its surface, close but never touching. Thin streaks of yellow lightning snaked through the red, trailing the heat of her hand. Past it, down the hall, she saw another translucent red wall.

Three men burst from the side room on their left. Adam barreled into them like a battering ram. The two front guards flew several feet and crashed to the ground in a heap of cracked bones. Siroun snapped a kick, connecting with the third guard's jaw. He went down with a low moan.

Adam bent over the fallen female guard. The woman jerked back when she saw his face. He probed her side. "You have a broken rib," he informed the woman. "Don't move."

She glared at him with remarkably blue eyes. "Go fuck yourself."

Siroun pulled the duct tape from her pack. Six seconds, and the guards lay trussed up on the floor. Adam spun toward the ward. Siroun touched his arm and pointed to the side room. He understood and charged into it. His shoulder hit the wall. The wooden boards exploded, and she followed him into the next room, bypassing the ward.

Another wall, another crash, another ragged hole in the wood. The sheer power he could unleash was shocking.

They broke through the next wall. A foul stench hit her, the lingering, heavy odor of a greasy roast burned by an open flame. Bile rose in a stinging flood in Siroun's throat.

Adam halted.

A barrier rose before them. Flesh-colored and transparent, almost gel-like, it cleaved the room in half, stretching from the left wall to the right. Long, thick veins, pulsing with deep purple, pierced the gel, branching into smaller vessels and finally into hair-thin capillaries. Between the veins, clusters of pale yellow globules formed long membranes, folded and pleated into pockets. A loose network of dark red filaments bound it all into one revolting whole. Adam stared at it in horrified fascination.

Tiny gas bubbles broke free of the capillaries and slid to the surface of the barrier to pop open. Here and there, small spherical vesicles of the yellow substance floated through the lattice of the filaments and veins, pushed by the invisible currents, bending and swiveling when they came to an obstacle.

It lived. It was a very primitive kind of life, but a life.

Her gaze traveled to the far left, drawn to the source of the vesicles, and found a gross, misshapen thickening of the yellow membranes, a bulging sack, tinged with carmine filaments. Globules of yellow matter detached from the surface of the sack and fluttered away one by one. She focused on it and found an outline of a human hand within the sack, complete with outstretched fingers. Another vesicle slid from the sack's top, allowing for a glimpse of a swollen blue-black thumb. As Adam watched, the nail broke free from the bloated digit and spun away, caught by a current.

Adam gagged and retched, spilling sour vomit onto the expensive rug.

Siroun took a step forward. She knew this intimately well.

This was witch magic: not the balanced, measured magic of the regular covens, but a darker, twisted kind, born of complete subjugation to the primal things. Most witches withdrew at the first hint of their presence. This witch had embraced it, and it had gifted her with this ward.

The foul magic hissed and boiled around her, sparking off her skin. *That's right. Look but do not touch.*

Siroun thrust her hand into the barrier.

The filaments trembled.

The yellow membranes shivered as if in anticipation. Folds slid and unfolded, streaming toward Siroun's hand.

Adam moved, probably determined to pull her from the thing before it stripped the flesh from her bones.

She let the thing inside her off the chain. Blue fire burst from her skin. The pink gel around her hand shriveled and melted in a plume of acrid smoke. Adam coughed. The fire grew brighter, biting chunks from the barrier in a greedy fury. The membranes tried to sliver away, the filaments collapsed and curled, but the fire chased them, farther and farther, until nothing was left. A swollen, blue corpse crashed to the floor, one arm stretched upward. Its stomach ruptured and a thick brown liquid drenched the rug. The stench of decomposition flooded the room.

The last glowing droplets of the gel dissipated. The blue fire calmed to mere lambency, clothing her hand like a glove. She turned her hand back and forth, watching the glow. Funny how the mind tends to trick you. She never forgot that she was cursed. The constant bloodlust that burned inside her would never let her delude herself. But most of the time she managed to put that knowledge aside, skirt it somehow in the deep recesses of her mind, until she stood there with her hand on fire. Adam was looking at her, and she didn't want to look back, not sure what she would find on his face.

Siroun blew on the flames. The fire vanished.

She stepped through the ward. Pale glyphs ignited on the floor, wheels of strange arcane signs. Siroun glanced back at Adam over her shoulder. She knew blood-red fire filled her eyes, but Adam didn't flinch. For that she was grateful.

"Witch magic?" he asked.

"Yes and no. Sometimes, when a witch is very troubled, she breaks away from the coven and begins to worship on her own. She becomes a priestess of the old gods. This thing was very old, Adam. Older than your blood."

"Why is it here?"

"Because this house has been hexed. But I can tell you that it wasn't meant for us." She pointed at the door at the end of the room. The door stood ajar, betraying a hint of the stairs going down. "It was meant to keep in whoever came up these stairs."

"It sealed Sobanto underground?"

She nodded and padded to the stairs. "Don't step on the glyphs."

The stairs brought them to another door. Siroun paused, listening. Heartbeats, one, two, three, four. She raised four fingers. Adam pulled a small cloth bag from one of his pockets. The spicy scent of herbs filled the air. A sleep bomb, very small, with a tiny radius of impact. Once released, the magic inside it would explode the herbs, and anything that breathed within the room would instantly fall asleep.

Adam passed her the bag. Siroun held her breath.

Three, two...

He smashed his fist into the door, knocking a melon-sized hole in the wood. She tossed the sleep bomb into the opening, and both of them sprinted upstairs.

A muffled cough, followed by a weak scream, echoed from the room. The sound of running feet, a dull thud, a throat-scraping hack, and everything fell silent. They sat together on the stairs, waiting for the power to dissipate. One minute. Two.

"Do you think our client was a witch?" Adam asked.

"That seems the only likely explanation." Siroun leaned forward, looking down the stairs. The less he saw of her face, the better.

"I thought witches didn't work on their own."

"They don't. Being in a coven is like being…in a place where you belong. It's like being with your family. The other witches might judge you, they might fight with you, and you might even dislike some of them, but they will be there when you need them most."

Unless they betray you. Allie's face swung into her mind's view. "I'm your sister," the phantom voice murmured from her memories. "Don't be afraid. I would never do anything to hurt you." But she did. They all did.

"If you're a witch with power, you become aware of things," she said, choosing her words carefully. "Do you know the history of the shifts?"

Adam nodded. "Thousands of years ago, magic and technology existed in a balance. Then humans used magic to lift themselves from barbarism. Extensive use of magic created an imbalance, causing the first shift, when technology began flooding the world in waves. This began the technological age that lasted roughly for six thousand years. Now we have overdeveloped technology, and the world seesawed again—the magic has returned and wiped out our civilization once again."

Siroun nodded. "Before the shifts, before the imbalance, humans worshipped things. If it frightened them, and they couldn't kill it, they called it a god. Faith has a lot of power, Adam. Their faith influenced these entities, nurturing them, granting them powers. They are very simple creatures because the people who worshipped them were simple. Now the magic has awakened, and these things are waking up with it. Witches stand closer to nature than most magic users. They seek balance, and sometimes they come across an old presence. These old ones, they are hungry. We molded them into gods, and they want their meal of magic and lives. For whatever reason, Linda Sobanto broke away from her coven and became a priestess to one of those things."

"What drove her, do you think?"

"Anger." That was what drove her. Anger at being violated, anger at the ultimate betrayal. "The glyphs on the floor upstairs. They are a prayer."

"To whom?"

Siroun shook her head. "I don't know. But I know that what she asked of it cost her. Dealing with gods, even simple gods, never comes without a price tag. Never. They don't gift. They barter."

"How do you know all this?" he asked.

Because my sister did the same, and I paid the price. "I've seen a hex like this before," she said, choosing the words very carefully. "I once handled the case of a child. A girl. She was ten years old."

She wished she hadn't started this, but now it was too late.

"What happened to the little girl?" Adam asked.

"Her sister was a witch. Their coven was inexperienced but powerful. They came across an old god, and they tried to barter for more power. The god needed a flesh form to exist, so during a really strong magic wave, they gave the little girl to the god. The symbols used were nearly identical." She kept talking, holding the memories at bay, keeping her voice flat. "The child proved to be more gifted than anticipated. She fought the god off until technology came and ripped it out of her body for good."

"But she was never the same," Adam murmured.

"No."

Siroun read concern in his eyes. Not for Sobanto, for herself. That was the last thing she wanted.

Siroun pushed to her feet. "Time is up."

They trotted down the stairs. Adam kicked the door, splintering it. Four Red Guards lay on the carpet. She only heard three hearts beating. "Damn it."

Adam turned the closest man over, picked him up, and gently lowered him on the couch. "Dead."

"How?"

"Probably an allergic reaction. It happens occasionally."

She gritted her teeth.

"There is nothing to be done about it now."

Pointless fury boiled inside her. He wasn't supposed to die. Why the hell did he die? So stupid…

"We move on," Adam said.

She snarled. He took a step toward her.

"We move on," Adam repeated.

She spun on her foot, walked out of the room, and stopped. The floor of the hallway was filled with glowing glyphs.

Adam watched Siroun as she crouched, hugging the floor. Her face had this odd look, a disturbing mix of sadness, almost sympathy, as if she were at a funeral, comforting a friend. Around her, arcane patterns on the floor emitted glowing tendrils of vapor. The colored fog stretched upward a couple of feet before gently fading.

"It took her months to do this," she whispered.

The entire length of the hallway floor shimmered with magic. It was oddly beautiful.

Siroun reached out and touched a congealed dark drop on the floor. "Blood," she whispered. Her nostrils fluttered. The orange fire in her irises darkened once again to near red. "Her blood."

She rose and pointed to the middle of the hallway, where red glyphs bloomed, like poppies. "That's where he killed her."

"What's the purpose of all this?" he asked.

"An illusion." The fire in Siroun's eyes died to almost nothing. Her voice held profound sadness. "Give me your hand, Adam."

He offered her his palm and watched as her slender fingers were swallowed by his huge hand. Siroun reached out with her other hand. Her thumbnail flicked across her index finger. A single drop of blood dropped from her hand into the glyphs. The glow vanished like a snuffed-out candle. The hallways went completely dark. A single tiny spark flared at the far end and expanded into a figure of a small boy. He stood on a stool, barefoot, large eyes opened wide. A chain hung from his throat. His mouth opened, and the high voice of a young child echoed through the hallway. "Please let me go, Mommy. Please let me go. I'll be good…"

The stool shot out from under the boy's feet, as if knocked aside by someone's brutal kick. The child hung, on the chain, choking, his eyes bulging.

Adam lunged forward and stopped, pulled back by Siroun's hand.

"It's not real," she told him. "It's only an illusion."

The child struggled. They watched him kick and die. Slowly, one by one, the glyphs ignited. The body, the chain, and the stool faded.

Adam remembered to breathe. His chest refused to expand, as if someone had dropped an anvil on it.

"She made her husband think she had killed their son," Siroun said. "And then he killed her. She sacrificed herself. Whatever dark thing she prayed to now inhabits her body. She made a bargain, you see? Her body for revenge on her husband."

"Why?"

"I don't know. We have to keep going. We'll find answers when we find Sobanto." She pulled him gently, and he followed.

. . .

THE LAST DOOR LOOMED IN FRONT OF ADAM. WOOD REINFORCED with steel. No matter. He crashed into it, and it burst open, unlocked. Adam stumbled forward, into the huge chamber. He had barely enough time to take in the domed ceiling, half-lost in the gloom, the bare walls, and the lonely figure sitting motionless under a column of blue light; and then heat seared his left hip. He saw nothing, felt nothing save for that brief fiery slice, but his leg gave, and he crashed to the floor, catching himself on his bent arms and rolling onto his side to diminish the impact.

A dark stain spread across the leg of his pants. He still felt no pain. Adam pulled back the sliced fabric, revealing a slash across his muscle. The edges of the wound fit so tightly together, it might have been made by a razor blade.

Numbness claimed his hip. He took a deep breath, and, suddenly, he couldn't feel his legs.

Poison. He was cut by a poisoned blade, coated with some sort of paralyzing agent, probably containing anticoagulant. Adam froze. His body regenerated at an accelerated rate. It would overcome most poisons, given time. But time was in short supply. The less he moved, the faster he'd heal, but prone like this, he presented too good a target.

Come on. Take a shot. I'll snap your neck like a toothpick.

Adam scanned the chamber.

Nothing. Only the gloom and a man seated in a metal chair. John Sobanto, wearing the slack expression of a man caught in some sort of spell. A ring of small pale stones surrounded his chair. He knew this spell. If he could remove the stones, the ward would disappear.

A hint of movement made him glance right. Siroun stood next to him. Her eyes glowed like two rubies.

Her lips parted. "I see you, sirrah," she whispered, her hiss carrying to the farthest heights of the chamber.

A blur struck at her from the gloom. The cloaked bodyguard

attacked. She parried, blades clanging together, and the body-guard withdrew. A shred of dark fabric fluttered to the floor.

Siroun laughed, an eerie sound that shot ice down Adam's spine. "I'm coming, sirrah. Face me!"

The blur landed on the floor at the far wall, solidifying into a cloaked man. Soundless like a phantom, he pulled off his cloak and dropped it onto the floor. Chiseled, each muscle cut to perfection, he stood nude, save for muay thai shorts. His bare feet gripped the floor, his toes bore curved yellow claws. Colored tattoos blossomed across his legs, stomach, and chest, muted against the faint green tint of his skin. A striking cobra on one arm, a crouching monkey king on the other, tortoise on the abdomen, elephant on the chest, iguana under the right collarbone, tiger under the left. Faint outlines of scales, tattooed or real, shielded his shaved skull. His eyes were yellow like amber, luminescent with cold intensity, reptilian in their lack of feeling.

The bodyguard raised a knife with a yellow blade that looked as if it were carved from an old bone.

Siroun looked at him. "You need to turn now."

He leaped across the room. They clashed and danced across the chamber, preternaturally fast, slashing, parrying, kicking, and finding purchase on the sheer walls.

Pain clenched Adam's thigh, ripping a deep, guttural moan from him. His body had finally overcome the poison. The cut was deep—the blade had grazed the bone.

Adam began dragging himself toward the spell shielding Sobanto. Fifty feet. He pulled, gripping the slick floor with his fingers, ignoring the jolts of acute pain rocking his thigh.

For the space of a breath, Siroun landed on the floor next to him, barely long enough for him to register a bloody gash across her forearm, and leaped away again, sailing across the chamber. He crawled by the drops of her blood, fixated on the blue beam of light.

Only fifteen feet.

Fourteen.

He saw the tattooed bodyguard loom before him. The man's skin burst, and a monstrosity exploded out, huge, scaled, armed with enormous crocodilian jaws and a massive reptilian tail.

A werereptile. That was impossible. Reptiles were cold-blooded. No shapeshifter could overcome that.

The werecrocodile laughed at him, the feral grin of a predator displaying nightmarish fangs. And then Siroun crashed into the bodyguard. The yellow knife struck twice, biting deep into her side. They broke free and halted six feet apart.

The shapeshifter's yellow eyes focused on crimson drenching Siroun's side. "You're finished," he said, his voice a deep roar disfigured by his jaws.

Siroun smiled. A pale red flush crept on her cheeks and spread, flooding her neck, diving under her clothes, reaching all the way to her fingertips. Heat bathed Adam. "Not yet," she whispered, and charged, sweeping the bodyguard from the floor like a gale.

Adam focused on the blue beam. His entire side was on fire, and he clenched his teeth, clutching on to consciousness. He could feel the soft welcoming darkness hovering on the edge of his senses, ready to swallow him whole.

His fingers touched the stone. A burning pain laced his skin, as if he'd stuck his hand into boiling water. Adam clenched the stone.

The room swayed. He was losing it.

He snarled and fed his magic into his hand. Ice sleeked his skin, welcoming, soothing. Adam strained, using every bit of his strength, and yanked the stone free.

The ward blinked and vanished.

A hoarse scream ripped through the chamber. Across the floor, a body fell from the ceiling, but Siroun was faster still, and she landed a fraction of a heartbeat before it hit the ground, in time to catch the falling man. The body in her arms boiled and collapsed back into its human form.

Gingerly, she carried the prone form, as if he were a child, and lowered the bodyguard by Adam's feet. The shapeshifter's face lost its feral edge. His tattoos bled colored ink in dark rivulets, the images draining slowly from his skin.

Siroun kissed her fingertips and touched the man's forehead. Her eyes were luminescent and warm. Not a trace of bloodlust remained.

"You fought well," she whispered.

In the chair, John Sobanto drew a long, shuddering breath. His eyelashes trembled. Sobanto's eyes snapped open. "You turned off the field and broke the wards," he said. "She is coming."

THE LAWYER WAS LOOKING AT ADAM. SHE LOOKED, TOO. HE WAS bleeding. His big hands trembled. Breaking the ward had taken too much magic. His body didn't have enough strength to regenerate. She had to get him out of there.

"Who's coming?" Adam said. "Your wife?"

"She isn't my wife anymore," Sobanto whispered.

A sharp shriek rolled through the silence. Siroun felt the knot of foul magic at the far end of the house rip apart. A presence spilled out, the force of its fury lashing her like a splash of boiling lead. Siroun recoiled, snarling.

The entity moved toward them, slicing through the walls and doors, churning with magic and malevolence so dark she had to fight to keep clear. There was nothing they could do to stop it.

She spun to Adam. "We don't have much time. Kill him now."

"We can't. We don't know if he is guilty."

They had to follow the protocol. The case was no longer cut-and-dried. She had to buy them time. Siroun swallowed. "Hurry, Adam."

He turned to Sobanto.

She thrust her mind into the path of the entity and struck. Her blow did little damage, but it was too enraged to ignore her. Siroun fled, zigzagging back and forth, and the presence followed, chasing the shadow of her mind.

"What did you see in the hallway?" Adam asked.

Sobanto swallowed. "Our son. I saw her hang our son."

"Did you attack her?"

"Yes. I grabbed her by her throat. I tried... I meant to pull her off him. I didn't know. She died. I killed her. I found a note. It said she sacrificed herself and her body would now belong to a god. It said I would pay for everything."

The entity lashed at Siroun. She barely avoided it. "Why?" she snarled. "Why does she hate you?"

"I don't know. We had a good marriage, considering the circumstances."

"The circumstances?"

"Hurry, Adam." She forced the words out. "I cannot elude her much longer."

Sobanto hesitated.

"We have little time," Adam told him.

The lawyer closed his eyes. "I bought her. From the Blessings of the Night coven."

The wraith bit into Siroun's defenses. Sharp needles of pain stabbed her lungs; for a moment, she could not breathe. She ripped herself free.

"You bought her?" Adam asked.

"They needed a lawyer. They were facing criminal charges, and they had no money. I needed somebody to analyze the behavioral patterns of the jury and my opponents. We made a deal."

"Why did you marry her?"

"I wanted my children to have what she had. I'm deficient. I don't relate to people, not the way she could. And she was beautiful."

He had bought her, like a purebred dog.

"She chose the juries for you," Adam said. "She monitored them through the trial, and you claimed the credit."

"I didn't abuse her!" Desperation rang in Sobanto's voice. "I denied her nothing. Best clothes, best jewelry, the best of everything."

"Why didn't she just leave?" Adam asked.

"She was bound to me by the coven."

The entity clamped her. Pain ripped through Siroun. Emotions twisted her into a knot, echoes of a woman lost. At once she was lonely, longing, caught between the need to please and revulsion, bitter, empty, watching life passing by, unable to escape, growing tired, growing old, growing stupid, knowing she was not loved, would never be loved, would never be free...

She cried out and tore herself free again. She could barely stand. "He's telling the truth," she said.

"Why does she hate him?"

"Because he did not love her. He is a sociopath, Adam. He's incapable of giving her what she wanted. She thought when their son was born, he would feel something, but he doesn't. End it. We must kill him, or the thing that has her body will rip him to pieces. It's almost here."

"Kill me," Sobanto said suddenly. "I want to die. I just don't want her to have me."

Adam raised his chin, his face, blanched of all blood, strangely proud, almost regal. "We have no claim on this man. He served as an instrument in his wife's suicide. On behalf of the POM Insurance, I, Adjuster Adam Talbot, resign all rights to retribution, as specified by Part 23, paragraph 7 of the POM policy manual."

Sobanto's face finally showed emotion: stark, all-consuming fear.

The creature that used to be Linda Sobanto burst through the doorway, a boiling cloud of black, streaked with violent scarlet. The cloud churned, and a woman's face congealed from its depth. She opened her mouth. Sobanto took a step back, his hands raised before him. The cloud lunged…

And howled in fury.

Siroun twisted her knife, turning it all the way around Sobanto's neck. The resistance against her blade was so slight, she barely felt it.

A thick stream of blood slid across the blade to drip on the floor. Sobanto opened his mouth. Blood gushed. Siroun withdrew the blade. He stayed upright for another moment and crumpled to the floor.

The entity screamed. The crimson within her flared and streaked apart, ripping the darkness into pieces. The darkness folded on itself, sucked into a tiny point, and vanished. Quiet reigned.

Adam crashed to the floor.

She crouched by him and brushed the blue hair from his face.

"We had no claim," he murmured.

"I know," she said, and wiped a smudge of blood from his lips. "Rest now. Let your body heal. Once the wound closes, I will get you out of here."

"Why did you kill him?"

"Linda made a bargain: her body for the life of her husband. The transfer would not be complete until the creature that took her form killed Sobanto. If it took his life, it would no longer be a cloud, Adam. It would be an old god made flesh. It wouldn't harm me because of what I am. But it would kill you."

She leaned over him and kissed him gently on the forehead. "I couldn't let it kill you." *After all, you're all I have.*

OF SWINE AND ROSES

Alena took a deep breath. "I'm not going on a date with Chad Thurman."

A deafening silence descended on the dining room. Mother's face assumed a thoughtful expression. No doubt she was already stringing persuasive and weighty logical arguments in her head in favor of the date. To Mother "no" was simply a "yes" that hadn't had a chance to hear her out.

Next to Mother, Aunt Ksenia looked aghast. No surprise there. Aunt Ksenia was all about duty to the family. There was no support to be had in her corner.

Behind Ksenia's chair, Cousin Boris checked his mother's face and carefully arranged his own into a mask of patronizing disapproval. If he ever did manage to formulate his own thought, it would likely knock him senseless.

Alena glanced across the table. Her older sister Liz looked troubled; her bottom lip caught between her teeth. Her husband Vik must've found the situation highly amusing, because the corners of his mouth crept upward in a half-realized smile. Alena mentally steeled herself and looked to Father leaning against the wall. Alexander Koronov's eyes plainly said that he was not amused. Like staring straight into a storm.

"You—" Ksenia began, but Mother raised her hand.

"Why not?" she asked calmly.

Alena knew exactly what would come next: all of her protests would be dismantled into pieces like an old clock taken apart gear by gear, but she had no choice. She had to at least try to put up a fight. "I don't like him."

Mother rose, took a soup plate from the cabinet, filled it with water, and set it on the table. She touched the surface of the water with her fingertip and murmured a single sharp word. The water surged up and blossomed into an image of Chad in all his glory.

"Could you be more specific?" Mother said. "What exactly don't you like about him?"

Looking at him, Alena had to admit that physically there was nothing wrong with Chad. There was a lot of right about him even. He stood tall, his shoulders wide and thick, and his build muscular. He looked strong and sturdy. Capable. His red hair was cropped very short, and he somehow managed to escape the really sensitive skin of most natural redheads. Taken by itself, free of his expression, his face might even be considered handsome, but there was something about Chad, something in the eyes and in the set of his stubborn jaw, that telegraphed "thug" louder than any words.

The city, and Old Town in particular, had long been divided into territories between the prominent magic families. It was customary that young men from local families banded together to defend their combined neighborhood from outsiders before moving on to real business ventures. Most boys participated. It was a rite of passage, but Chad really took the job seriously.

"He's..." Alena paused. Chad wasn't exactly stupid. On the contrary, he was quite shrewd at times. Just last week he and his guys trapped some unfortunate kid from a rival family's territory. They could've beaten the guy and left it at that, but no, Chad had Marky, his chief flunkie, conjure up some rabid-looking mutts and used them to chase the guy into the burned out warehouse down on River Street. The guy didn't have enough magic to see through the illusion, but he did manage a panicked sending back to his family yelling that he was being attacked by a pack of wild animals. Chad and his flunkies sat there until the guy's friends came to rescue him and then claimed it was an invasion of Thurman territory. The rival family had to pay restitution.

Chad wasn't dumb and he would do quite well for himself; he just had no interest in whatever she would have to say and she had no interest in whatever he had to do. "He's cruel and dangerous," she said.

"You're a Koronov," her father said. "Thurmans respect us. He won't lay a finger on you without your permission. And if he does, you have my permission to do what's necessary."

Not having permission wouldn't exactly stop her, but pointing that out didn't seem like the smartest move at the moment.

"You grew up together," Mother said.

"That's exactly the problem! You're making me go out with a guy I've known since he was seven and I was four. I've seen him wipe his snot on a smaller kid's hair. When I was five, he broke my sleigh going down the stone staircase on Butcher Street and I hit him over the head with it."

"So you don't want to go out with him because he broke your sleigh twelve years ago?" Mother said slowly.

Alena unclenched her teeth. "No, Mother, I don't want to go out with him, because he's a thug. And his family is full of thugs. What would we even talk about? He barely finished high school. We have nothing in common!"

"You're both young and attractive," Mother said.

Alena drew back. "So you want me to prostitute myself, is that it?"

Mother arched her eyebrows. "There is no need to be so melodramatic. He's a handsome boy." She nodded at the watery image. "It's natural that there might be some attraction between the two of you. In fact, I think you do protest too much."

Alena nearly choked. "Attracted to what? Mom, he carries brass knuckles in both pockets!"

"You will go," Father said.

Mother shot him a warning glance. "Do you recall how we discussed the purchase of a car last Monday and you told me that it's time you were treated as an adult?"

Alena hesitated. The sudden turn threw her off balance. "Yes?"

Mother smiled. "Do you know what separates adults from children? Self-discipline. We don't want to go to work, we don't want to do our chores, and we don't want to make unpleasant decisions, but we do all those things because we're aware of the consequences which will follow if we don't. Now, I will treat you as an adult, since you are seventeen, and I'll be very blunt. Our family was never rich, as you know. However, your grandfather was a very respected man. Many families owed him a favor. He had a certain influence. When he died, part of that influence died with him."

That part Alena already knew. In the neighborhood, weddings and funerals were an excuse for the adults to gather and talk business. They'd sit for hours, sipping their drinks and writing contracts and formulas on the dinner napkins long after the meal was over. When Grandfather died, almost three hundred people showed up at his wake. Most didn't linger. They paid their respects, said a couple of words to her parents, and hurried off. The loss of family influence was so plain, even she had noticed it.

Mother continued. "Your father was your grandfather's

advisor. That's why the family invested so much in his education. He was never groomed to be your grandfather's successor. That role belonged to Uncle Rufus; however, he also died."

Mother threw an apologetic glance at Aunt Ksenia and kept going. "The other families in the area are aware of this. Even now, they're moving in on our business interests, in particular on our investments in the water communications. To avoid financial ruin, we need a large loan, which would offset the costs of your grandfather's funeral and let us settle various smaller debts, making us appear strong and financially secure. All of our business accounts are housed through SunShine Bank. Do you know who owns the controlling interest in that bank?"

Alena shook her head.

Mother's voice held no mercy. "The Thurmans. Now, you can go on this date with Chad Thurman, with no obligation, I might add, or you can refuse this invitation, insult the Thurmans, and destroy our chances of obtaining the loan. Nobody here will force you. We'll leave the choice entirely up to you."

All arguments died in Alena's throat. She swallowed. Every cell in her body rebelled against going but now refusing would make her look like a spoiled selfish brat. If it meant that much... The future of her family hung in the balance. She would do everything she could to keep it from falling off a cliff.

"I'll go," she said softly.

"Thank you," Mother said.

It was all Dennis's fault, Alena reflected, rummaging through the clothes in her closet. She had been seeing Dennis Mallot for about a year, always in public. They hadn't done anything physical like kissing or holding hands. They just met, strolled along River Street, traded gossip, and told each other how badly their parents treated them. They were friends. She was a nerd, a smart girl, and he was an odd, quiet guy.

Their families didn't mind. Koronovs and Mallots stood close on the social ladder, both solid families with roots in Old Town, both magically adept. With the exception of Grandfather and Uncle Rufus, all Koronovs had graduated well and went on to academies, while most Mallots made their living in the field of medical magic.

All was going nicely and then Father had the bright idea to send her off to boarding school for the year to "challenge" her. Squeezing two hundred teenagers into a campus and blocking access to the outside world made for some heavy social drama. After almost a year of watching stormy breakups and broken hearts followed by clouds of endless gossip, Alena was ready for a real boyfriend. Not a sort-of-boyfriend, like Dennis, but the actual, real, head-over-heels love. As soon as she got home, she bought a dress the color of dark red wine that left absolutely no doubt that she was female. She curled her dark hair, she put on her makeup, she slipped on criminally high heels, and headed to her old school to catch up with her friends.

Dennis had nearly fainted. Even now, she grinned at the memory: him standing against the wall, his eyes bulging, his mouth slack. It had been the most satisfying moment of her life, a triumph. Everything about her had said, "Yeah, so I'm a nerd, but I clean up nice. See what you've been missing?"

Dennis had called the next morning, inviting her to May Ball, a huge outdoor celebration when recent and old graduates came out for a night-time party. There would be food, bands, and magic shows. Everybody would be there. She agreed.

Then the night of the party came. Perfect hair? Check. Makeup? Check. Same red dress? Check. Spiked heels? Check. Dennis…?

Dennis didn't show. She kept walking out on to the balcony, wondering why he was late, thinking she would see him down the street. That's when Chad Thurman had seen her. He was passing by, glanced up, and nearly took a dive onto the pavement. Guess she took him by surprise.

Dennis never did show. The gossip vine said he had gotten drunk with his friend Jeremy instead. She'd felt so stupid and hollow in her perfect makeup and killer dress. So very stupid and pathetic.

The Mallots were told in no uncertain terms that the insult to the family wouldn't be forgotten and that Dennis was no longer welcome. But now Chad Thurman had come to cash in on her misfortune, and the family was only too happy to push her out the door into his arms. And the problem was that if Chad did like her, nobody else would date her either. Chad had the kind of reputation that made rivals run for cover. Still, she would do it. The family needed the loan.

Alena picked out a nice jean skirt, not too short, not too long, a white peasant blouse and new blue shoes that were only a hair shorter than that red pair. She put the outfit on and looked at herself in the mirror: favorite blouse, favorite skirt, brand new shoes. The date would suck enough. At least she could feel comfortable in her favorite clothes.

THE DOORBELL RANG AND THEN MOTHER'S VOICE CALLED, "Alena!"

She sighed and emerged into the foyer. Chad had arrived with two dozen blood-red roses in one hand and a bottle of expensive vodka in the other. The flowers went to her mother, while the vodka went to her father. Thurmans were an Old Town family, after all. They did things properly.

"You have fun," Mother said pleasantly.

A sinking feeling claimed Alena's stomach. She didn't get premonitions often but in that moment she realized with absolute certainty that this date wouldn't end well.

Outside Chad paused for moment, his face deadly serious. She'd seen that look before, usually when he plotted some sort of battle strategy. "You look very nice," he said quietly, his gaze pausing on her breasts.

"Thank you." Alena smiled. "You too."

He did look nice in jeans and a black T-shirt.

They stared awkwardly each other.

"I thought we'd go and see a movie," he said.

"That sounds great. What kind of a movie?"

"It's fighting flick from Kitai Empire. *Gonzo the Spear Carrier*." Chad glanced at her as if expecting a hysterical fit.

"I love historical dramas," she said. At least the movie promised to be good.

"Good." He offered her his elbow.

Alena rested her hands on his forearm and realized that it was the first time she actually touched a guy on a date. The thought almost made her sigh in regret, but she killed the sigh before it had a chance to start. She said she would go. No use moaning about it now.

They strode down the street heading toward the theater. Chad stared straight ahead, his jaw set.

After about five minutes, the silence had become strained. "So what books have you read lately?" she asked to say something.

"Don't read much," Chad said.

"Movies?"

"I liked *Marauder III*," he said. "Good movie."

Like pulling teeth. "What did you like about it?"

"Not sure," Chad said.

Chad Thurman—not a great talker.

"Hold on a second." Chad stepped away from her and barked at a guy across the street, "Hey! Hey, who the hell are you?"

The guy stopped. "I'm here to deliver a package to my uncle. Who the hell are you?"

Chad strode across the street. "Who's your uncle?"

It took them a good five minutes to straighten out who was who and who had a right to be where. For the first minute Alena had looked at her feet, then she looked at the sky, then she counted the fence posts on the long iron fence that guarded the slope of the hills. The whole city was one hill after another with River Street at the bottom of it all.

Chad trotted up. "Don't worry," he said. "We won't be late."

She just nodded. The sooner they got done, the better.

They didn't speak on the way to the theater.

Just before they reached the old theater building, they were stopped again, this time by skinny, dark-eyed Marky. He and Chad spoke in hushed tones, until Chad cut him off. "Screw this shit, I'll do it myself." Marky paled and took off. Chad turned to her as if nothing happened and led her inside. He offered to buy her popcorn and soda, but she declined.

The movie was awful. Long, tedious, odd, and it didn't make a bit of sense. With a name like *Gonzo the Spear Carrier*, she had expected some fights, maybe acrobatics, and Kitai fire magic, but no, the movie followed the story of some medieval Kitai official who was seduced by his boss's wife. Or maybe he seduced her. The movie seemed to consist of one long conversation after another and after a while she got confused.

Chad stared at the screen with a grim expression. He didn't seem to like the movie any more than she did.

After about thirty minutes Alena considered walking out. But then Chad had paid for it. What if he would get offended? She could hear her mother's voice droning on in her head now: "All you had to do was sit through a two-hour movie, a movie, tickets to which had been purchased for you as a gift. Was it really that difficult?"

No, Mother. Of course, Mother.

It was no use. She was trapped.

Finally the credits rolled on the screen. Alena got up and quietly followed Chad out of the theater.

Outside, Chad's face took on the look of serious concentration again. The movie had been an utter failure and now he had to do some damage control. She wondered what his next move would be.

He steered her toward Lion Park, where marble statues of lions guarded a huge three-tier fountain. Of course. The ice-cream stand. Chad followed the Old Town manual of dating to a T: having done the movie, no matter how awful, he would now buy her ice cream.

They walked in silence.

"That movie sucked," he said.

"Yes."

More silence. This was so not working out.

Chad came to a sudden halt. She glanced in the direction of his stare and saw the ice cream shop. A big CLOSED sign hung up front.

Chad looked almost pained. For a moment she actually felt sorry for him. Chad realized that verbal seduction was quite beyond him and her family name prevented him from simply grabbing her and giving her breasts a squeeze, as he obviously wanted to do. What was more, thirteen years of childhood made for a lot of memories and these memories sat between them like an impenetrable barrier.

"Do you remember a couple of years ago, you pushed me off the pontoon?" she said suddenly.

Chad glanced at her.

"My mother forbade me to go swimming because of the factory dumping waste upstream from the pontoon, but I came anyway. I was wearing a black dress with red and yellow dots on it. You pushed me off the pontoon, and I felt something odd with my foot, but I climbed out. And then you pushed my friend

Sveta in. The blonde? She wore a white T-shirt. You pushed her in, and when she surfaced, a dead body came up behind her."

She vividly remembered a pale body rising through the murky water the color of tea. Sveta had screamed and screamed. Even when the cops wrapped her in a blanket, she still made these tiny squealing noises, like something was broken in her chest.

Light gleamed in Chad's eyes. "I remember that. He was a wizard from the local academy. He'd gotten drunk, tried to swim the river at night, and got cut by a propeller."

Alena nodded. "You probably made me step on the dead body."

Chad smiled.

She stared at his grin in disbelief. He thought it was funny. She had nightmares about it for a month after and he thought it was funny.

That was about enough of that. Alena raised her chin. "Look, the movie was bad, the ice cream didn't happen, and we won't even count the broken sleigh or the dead guy. Thank you for taking me out, but I'd like to go home."

A dark shadow passed over Chad's face. He squared his shoulders. "Okay," he said finally.

They headed down the sloping street toward the river. She did try. She gave it her best shot. No doubt everybody would be very disappointed that she failed to hit it off with Chad. But to sit in the park next to him, while he figured out what would be the fastest way to feel her up really was beyond her. Especially after that self-satisfied smile.

They turned the corner and stepped onto River Street. Three blocks, then up the slope and she would be home.

A hoarse howl of outrage rolled down River Street. Alena stopped.

With a loud squeal something small dashed from behind the

stone warehouse. A second later Marky and Pol, two of Chad's finest, whipped around the corner and chased after it.

The thing veered left and bolted toward them. Alena squinted. A pig! A small brown furry pig. What in the world…

"I'm going to kill that fucker," Chad snarled.

She glared at him, sure she misheard.

He charged at the pig. The little beast dodged right, and Chad collided with Marky. The smaller guy bounced off Chad like dry peas from the wall. Chad whirled around, his face contorted with rage.

Oh God, he really is going to kill the pig.

Oh no. No, you don't. A date was fine, but if he thought she'd stand by and let him murder small animals, he was in for a big surprise. She had to catch that beast before he did.

The pig headed straight for her, all but flying above the asphalt.

Twelve feet.

Ten.

Six.

She lunged for it. The pig swerved left. Her fingertips brushed its bristles and then it was off, running for its life down the street.

There was no way she could catch it in her heels.

New shoes or the life of a little pig? It took her less than a second to decide and then she was running after the beast in her stockings. Behind her heavy thudding of boots announced the three guys giving chase.

Three blocks flew by. The pig made a rough left turn and charged into the old soccer field being remodeled into a tennis court. Ha! Nowhere to go: a twelve-foot-high chain fence enclosed the field to keep the soccer balls from flying in to the neighboring apartment house. Alena squeezed out a burst of speed and shot out into the soccer field.

Where did it go?

A hint of movement caught her eye. There it was. The beast had scrambled up a pile of red clay the construction crew was using to smooth out the field and perched there, covered in orange dust.

She jogged to the pile on her toes, trying to appear friendly and non-threatening. The pig watched her advance with a wary look. Carefully Alena began to climb the pile.

"Here, little beast." The run had shredded her stockings into nothing, and the powdery red clay smooshed between her toes. "I won't hurt you."

The pig glared at her but stayed put. Almost there. A-a-almost.

She reached for it, moving as slowly as she could manage.

Behind her Chad's deep voice warned, "Easy…"

Easy my foot, he wouldn't be getting his hands on the pig. Alena leaned until she was almost on all fours, her face level with the pig's nose. Sad brown eyes looked at her from the fuzzy muzzle.

"Don't worry," she whispered. "I won't let Chad get you."

She inched forward, hair by hair, her outstretched hands reaching for the small brown body.

The beast squeaked and darted down the pile.

"Shoot!" Alena straightened in a sharp jerk. The momentum pitched her off balance. She teetered on the apex of a pile, waving her arms like an overgrown stork about to take flight.

Clay crumbled under her feet. She clawed the air, trying to hold on to something, but the sky rolled back, replaced by the view of the apartment house, and Alena plunged, sliding down the slope until the green soccer field grass slapped her face.

The world swam. She shook her head and pulled herself upright. A wide smudge of orange clay marked her side: from the remnants of her stockings across her jean skirt and once-white blouse all the way up to her hairline.

Out of the corner of her eye she saw Chad and his thugs

skirt the pile and halt, staring at her open-mouthed. She staggered to her feet. Her left side stung. Her right ankle was sore.

In the distance the pig shrieked as it tried to squeeze through a hole in the fence.

Surprise twisted into predatory mask of glee on Chad's face. "He's stuck!"

They charged after it like a pack of ravenous dogs. Alena chased after them. They wanted the pig badly, but she was scared for it, and her fear drove her so hard that she caught up with them at the end of the field.

With a heroic tug, the pig squeezed through the hole, leaving clumps of brown fur on the wire. Chad swore. Pol ran to the fence door and struggled with the piece of wire hooked through the lock to keep it shut.

The pig cleared the path from the soccer field and ran onto the old wooden staircase. The stairs led down, and back to River Street. On the left rose a huge yellow apartment building, and on the right sat a row of old storage sheds, covered in grey waves of fibrocement roof. The top of the stairway was just about level with the storage sheds.

The pig looked left, looked right, backed up a couple of steps, and leaped onto the roofs, its hoofs clacking on fibrocement.

Pol finally worked the door open and they filed out onto the path. The pig backed away from them. It had reached the edge of the roof, and it had nowhere to go.

Chad measured the distance between the stairs and the sheds with his gaze.

"You're too heavy," Marky said. 'The roof will break. Let me…"

Chad was too heavy, but she wasn't. Alena took a running start and jumped. The fibro cracked under her but held. Step by step she began to advance. Out of the corner of her eye, she saw Chad, Marky, and Pol run down the staircase, trailing her.

Step. Another step.

The pig gathered itself into a tight clump. Long red scratches scoured its sides, where the fence had torn off the skin when it tried to escape the soccer field.

"It's okay," she told it. "It's alright. It will be okay." Her feet really hurt from all the barefoot running. A stray thought zinged through her brain: this can't really be happening, can it? She pushed it aside, bent down, and grabbed the pig.

It didn't struggle. It just looked at her with huge dark eyes and she was struck by an oddly sad expression in their depths...

With a thunderous crack, the roof collapsed under her feet.

Alena plunged into darkness, pig pressed securely to her chest. Her damaged feet hit something hard. Suddenly there wasn't enough air. She choked, coughed, and realized she'd landed in a pile of coal stored for the winter.

Outside something crashed and then the door was torn from its hinges. Bright light stabbed into the shed. Chad appeared in the light. He held a switchblade in his hand. "You did good," he said. "Real good."

She rose to her feet shakily, clutching the beast.

"Give me the pig," he said.

Her voice came out dull. "No."

"Give me the damn pig," he snarled.

Something inside her broke, like a glass rod being snapped in two. Magic flooded her, roaring through her veins. Behind Chad, Marky backed away and she knew her eyes had ignited with pale green glow.

"No," she growled. The magic swelled inside her and broke loose.

The shed exploded. Chunks of coal pelted the walls, going right through the soft wood. She took a step forward. Chad lunged at her and fell back, knocked aside like a twig.

That was her talent. She didn't have anything elegant, like her father's ability to precisely pinpoint a location miles away and establish that first tenuous connection which would allow the building of a water communication line. Nor was her magic complex like her mother's ability to reconstruct images with her mind with perfect recall.

No, her power was simple and brutal, like her grandfather's. Alena took another trembling step. Pol pulled out a knife and stabbed at her, trying to penetrate the invisible cocoon of magic. She let the magic tear the knife from his hand. The blade streaked past her and bit into the nearest shed, sinking to the hilt. The magic brushed against Pol, and he went flying across the asphalt.

Such a simple magic, really. If she didn't want an object within six feet of herself, it moved out of her way.

Streaks of silver shot in a continuous tornado of magic around her, bright footprints of her power.

Chad had doubled around her and barred her way up the staircase. "Alena…"

"Move," she said.

He held on for another second, his hands white-knuckled on the rails, and then he moved aside. Limping and shuddering, she climbed up the stairway, up the steep path to the gate of her home's wooden fence. As if in a dream, she opened the door, crossed the path between the rows of rose bushes, and came up three stairs to the porch.

Her own reflection stared at her from the glass of the kitchen window. Orange clay covered her left side. Everything else was black with coal dust. Her hair flared from her head in a tangled filthy mess. Her eyes blazed with green. Even the pig she still held seemed to know better than to offer any resistance. It just sat in her arms, filthy with a mix of clay, coal, and its own blood.

She looked down at her legs. Her stockings were in tatters. Long scrapes marked her bare feet.

By this evening everyone in the neighborhood would know

what happened.

Alena sniffled, reached into her pocket, pulled out a key, and let herself in.

The family had just sat down for dinner. They saw her and froze. She looked at them, from the slack-jawed Aunt Ksenia, to the stunned face of her father, to her mother, petrified in mid-move, a pot of mashed potatoes in one hand and a big wooden spoon in the other, and hobbled past them, to her room.

They watched her go. Nobody said a thing.

Inside, she locked the door, crossed the room to her bathroom, got inside, and slid to the floor. Her magic died. Tears swelled in her eyes.

She released the pig and it backed away from her.

"This was my favorite blouse," she told it and wiped the tears away with the back of her hand. "This mess will never wash out. And I don't even know why they were chasing you."

Alena crawled up onto her knees, picked up the pig, and maneuvered it into the tub. "And you got all scratched up. Look, you're bleeding everywhere. We need to wash that or it might get infected."

She turned on the water and began to gently rinse the clay and coal dust from the pig's sides.

"None of this would've happened, if that damn idiot hadn't stood me up. That stupid sonovabitch. Do you know how awful that felt? I felt this small." She held up two fingers with barely any space between them before picking up the soap and building it into lather on the pig's back. "And it's not like Dennis even was a decent boyfriend. He didn't even noticed I was a girl. It's not like I wanted him to be all over me all the time or shower me with flowers. Just some small acknowledgment that I was pretty or at least female would've been nice. So what do I get? I get Chad Thurman who stares at my chest and tries to slaughter small animals. How is that fair?"

She rinsed the pig off and examined the scrapes running

down the pig's sides. Not too bad. The little beast had gotten off with mostly scratches.

"You're one lucky pig. All of your battle scars are shallow." She sniffled, blinking back the tears that kept wanting to break through her defenses into a full-blown deluge. "After I'm done, we'll put some nice poultice on your hide to keep you healthy. And you know, I perfectly understand that you can't understand a word I'm saying. I never thought I'd end up in my bathroom looking like this pouring my problems onto a pig."

She paused and stared at it helplessly. "It's just that I have nobody to talk to. And if I don't talk, I think I'll fall apart to pieces. And I don't want to do that, because then my family will pity me."

Alena reached for the towel. "Let me tell you about Chad. You should at least know who you ran away from. It all started with a sleigh…"

Fifteen minutes later, after the pig's wounds were treated with cinnamon-smelling poultice and Alena had ran out of words, she set the pig on the bathroom floor and began to strip her own clothes off. "I think we'll have keep you in protective custody," she said, climbing into the tub. "Until Chad gives up on his pig-killing dreams. I can probably guilt Father into building some kind of sty."

She picked up the shower head and turned on the water. "So I—"

The pig jerked. Its brown hide boiled, expanded, twisted, like a rapidly inflated balloon, paled, and snapped into a nude man. For a brief moment they stared at each other in total shock. Alena caught a flash of wide shoulders, young face, and dark intense eyes beneath brown eyebrows. The man raised his hand, uttered an incantation, and vanished.

That was too much. Alena dropped the shower head. Her knees buckled. She sat into the bathtub and collapsed into tears.

.   .   .

SOMEONE KNOCKED ON THE DOOR. ALENA PUT HER HEAD DEEPER into her pillow.

Mother swung open the door and brought in a tray. "It's been three days," she said. "I understand you don't want to come down for the family meals, but you have to eat something besides a sandwich a day."

A sandwich a day had been great, Alena thought. That way she didn't have to field questions from Boris and her sister.

Mother put the tray down and sat next to her on the bed. "Would you like to talk about it?"

Alena shook her head.

Mother pursed her lips. "This isn't what your father and I had in mind. Had we known it would turn out this way, I would've never let you out of the house. If it helps, the story hasn't made the rounds. Everybody is talking about how Thurmans are in a heap of trouble. They've managed to offend one of the patrician families, very powerful. Not sure how in the world they would even have come into contact with them—must've been through their bank. Rumor has it, Thurmans have to pay out an enormous sum to avoid a feud. They're liquidating their investments to raise cash."

Alena looked up. "So the date was completely for nothing?"

"It appears so."

It figured. Maybe she was cursed.

The doorbell rang.

"I'll be right back." Mother pushed the tray toward her. "Eat. Please."

Alena looked at the tray. French fries and a piece of baked chicken. At least it wasn't a pork chop. She wouldn't touch another piece of pork even if she was starving to death.

Mother reappeared in the doorway. "Come." Her voice left no room for negotiation.

Alena sighed and got up. What now?

She followed Mother downstairs to the foyer. The outside

door was open. She saw her father on the porch, wearing a plaintive expression she'd never seen before. Her mother pushed her lightly, propelling her out the door into the sunlight.

"Here she is," she heard Father say and then he brushed past her into the house and shut the door.

Alena blinked against the sunshine and raised her hand to her eyes.

Wide shoulders, dark eyes, and brown hair.

"You!"

He nodded. "Yes."

Heat rushed to her cheeks and she knew she blushed.

He was about twenty and taller than her by half a foot. Even with the loose green T-shirt it was plain that he was muscular, but his wide shoulders and powerful chest slimmed down to narrow hips and long legs that looked very nice in blue jeans and boots. He stood with a natural poise, light on his feet, and somehow elegant, despite his slightly disheveled hair. His skin was tan, and his face made her blush harder. His eyes were very dark, like bitter chocolate, and smart. He wasn't strictly handsome, but he was definitely attractive and very masculine.

And he had seen her naked. After she chased him half across Old Town, clutched him to her breasts and carried him around for good fifteen minutes, and then told him her life story.

"Hi," he said.

"Hi," Alena echoed, wishing she could fall through the porch and vanish.

He dragged his hand through his hair. "This is really more awkward than I thought it would be."

He would get no arguments from her.

He pushed his hand through his hair again. Something gleamed on his hand—a ring. Her shocked brain took three whole seconds to digest the significance of the crest on it. A patrician. Oh God. He belonged to one of the magical heavy-weight families.

"My name is Duncan. Would you like to go on a date with me?" he asked.

Alena recoiled. He felt sorry for her. "I don't need charity."

Duncan took a small step back. "I see. I understand, considering the circumstances. Well, if you do feel charitable, I've left my number with your father…"

"I meant that I don't need you to go on a date with me out of pity," she said and almost fainted from her own bravery.

"Pity?"

"Yes. I told you everything. You probably think I'm some sort of hysterical dimwit to be laughed at. Actually, it's taking all of my willpower to stand here and speak to you and not run away screaming."

"It's taken pretty much all of my willpower to ask you on a date," Duncan said. "I mean, I was a pig. There might be a worse way to be introduced to a beautiful girl, but I can't think of any. If anything, I'm the laughing stock here. I'm a Class II pyro."

Alena blinked. A Class II pyromage. He could incinerate entire city blocks in a matter of moments.

"I have been properly educated. And I've managed to blunder right into a trap set by three punks whom I should be able to take down blindfolded with one hand tied behind my back. It's good the academy is out for the summer, or my desk would be filled with pig ears." He growled low under his breath.

"How did you…?"

"A friend of mine had been chased by a pack of wild dogs into a warehouse in this area," he said. "And then when his family came to get him, they were ambushed. A rabid dog is classified as an imminent danger illusion. It's illegal. I came down to see if any traces of the illusion remained, followed the residual magic to its source, and walked right into a trap. In my defense, it was a very good trap, a military grade short-range transmutation mine. I don't know where the hell Chad and his hangers-on got it, but it's illegal for a civilian to own one. More, while it's not unlawful to defend a family's territory, setting traps and summoning imminent threat illusions is carrying it way too far. Chad knew what he was doing would land him in hot water, and once they discovered me, he told the smaller guy…"

"Marky," Alena supplied.

"Marky, to slit my throat."

She crossed her arms. "He's lost his mind."

"He knew the mine magic would wear off eventually and he hadn't a prayer of taking me on when I was human. It was a lot easier to eliminate me while I was a pig. Lucky for me, neither Marky nor his pal had the balls to do it. Apparently Chad decided to kill me himself, but I decided not to go meekly to the slaughter. And you know the rest. Once the mine's effect wore off, I ported back home and came back with cavalry. The thing about military mines—when they go off, they leave a magic trail that even an idiot could follow. We have Thurmans by the throat. That dumb stunt will cost them their financial security, and if they play very nicely, we might condescend not to bring charges."

Duncan did his hair thing again. "Look, I know we haven't met under the best of circumstances. And nobody more than me wants to forget ever being a pig."

"So why are you here?" And why was her heart beating a mile a minute?

Duncan smiled. He had a dazzling smile—it lit up his whole face, compelling her to smile back at him. "The truth is, I can't get you out of my head. I tried. I told myself, 'What will I say to her, oink-oink? She'll laugh at me.' But I just had to try. So here I am." He spread his arms. "Come on a date with me, Alena. Please?"

What did she have to lose?

Alena took a deep breath. "Okay."

He smiled again and she almost swooned. He reached for her

hand, brought her fingers to his mouth, and kissed them gently. A tiny thrill ran through her.

"Are we going to the movies?" she asked him.

"Hell no."

"Where then?"

"Fishing," he told her.

"Fishing?"

He nodded. "The thing about going to the movies—you can't talk to the other person. We'll sit in my boat, drink soda from a cooler, watch the river and chat. Get to know each other. If you're worried about baiting your hook, I can—"

She snorted. "I've fished in that river since I was seven. You just try to keep up."

He grinned. "Deal. Thank you for saving my life, by the way."

"You're welcome." She stepped close and kissed him on the cheek. She had no idea where she got the gall to do it, she just did.

"What was that for?" he asked softly, his eyes dark and warm, as if lined with velvet.

"For being a very brave little pig," she told him.

GRACE OF SMALL MAGICS

"Never look them in the eye," Uncle Gerald murmured.

Grace nodded. He'd calmed down some when they had boarded the plane, enough to offer her a reassuring smile, but now as they landed, he turned pale. Sweat gathered at his hairline. Gripping his cane, he scanned the human currents of the airport as they entered the terminal building. His fingers shook on the pewter wolf's head handle. She'd seen him take out a couple of men half his age with that cane, but she doubted it would do them any good now.

He cleared his throat, licking his dry lips. "Never contradict. Never ask questions. Don't speak until you're spoken to and then say as little as you can. If you're in trouble, bow. They consider it below them to strike a bowing servant."

Grace nodded again. This was the sixth time he recited the instructions to her. She realized it calmed him down, like a prayer, but his trembling voice ratcheted her own anxiety until it threatened to burst into an overwhelming panic. The airport, the booming announcements spilling from the speaker, the crush of the crowd, all of it blended into a smudged mess of colors and noises. Her mouth tasted bitter.

Deep inside her a small voice protested, "This is just crazy. This can't be real."

"It will be fine," Gerald muttered hoarsely. "It will be fine."

They passed the gates into a long hallway. The bag slipped off her shoulder, and Grace pulled it back on. The simple action crested her panic. She stopped. Her heart hammered, a steady heavy pressure pushing on her chest from inside out. A soft dullness clogged her ears. She heard herself breathing.

Twelve hours ago she woke up four states away, ate her usual breakfast of an egg and a toasted English muffin, and got ready to go to work, just like she had done every day. Then the doorbell rang and Uncle Gerald was on her doorstep with a wild story.

Grace always knew her family was special. They had power. Small magic—insignificant even—but it was more than ordinary people had, and Grace had realized early on she had to hide it. She knew there were other magic users in the world, because her mother had told her so, but she had never met any of them. She'd thought they were like her, armed with minor powers and rare.

According to Gerald, she was wrong. There were many other magic users in the world. Families, whole clans of them. They were dangerous, deadly, and capable of terrible things. And one of these clans had their family in bonded service. They could call upon them at any time, and they had done so for years, demanding her mother's assistance whenever they needed it. Three days ago they requested Grace. Her mother had told her nothing; she simply went in her place. But Clan Dreoch called Gerald. They wanted Grace and only Grace. And so she flew to the Midwest, still dizzy from having her world turned upside down and listening to Gerald's shaky voice as he told stories of terrible magic.

Her instincts screamed to run away, back into the airport filled with people who had no concept of magic. It was just an animal reaction, Grace told herself. The Dreochs had her mother and if she did run, her mother would have to take her place. Grace was twenty-six years old. She knew her responsibilities. She had no doubt her mother wouldn't survive whatever they demanded, otherwise they wouldn't have required her presence. Grace knew what she had to do, but her nerves had been rubbed raw, and she simply stood, unable to move, her muscles locked into a rigid knot. She willed her body to obey, but it refused.

The crowd of people parted. A man stood at the end of the hallway. He seemed too large somehow, too tall, too broad, and emanating power. He loomed, a spot of otherworldly magic among people who stubbornly ignored his existence. She saw him with preternatural clarity, from ash blond hair falling to his shoulders to the pale green eyes, brimming with mournful melancholy like the eyes of a Russian icon. His was the face of a brute: powerful, stubborn, aggressive, almost savage in its severity.

He looked straight at her and in the depths of those green irises she saw an unspoken confirmation: *he knew*. He knew who she was, why she was here, and more, if she were to turn around and dash away, he wouldn't chase her. The choice was hers and he was content to let her decide.

The flow of people blocked him and she reeled, released from the spell of his eyes.

Uncle Gerald thrust into her view. "What is it? You have to come now, we can't keep them waiting, we—"

She looked at him, suddenly calm. Whatever would be would be. Her family owed a debt. Her mother had been paying it for years, carrying the burden alone. It was her turn. "Uncle," she said, holding on to her new-found peace.

"Yes?"

"You have to be quiet now. They're here."

He stared at her, stunned. Grace shouldered her bag and walked on.

They reached the end of the hallway. The man was gone, but Grace didn't worry about it. She headed to the twin slope of escalators. Behind her Gerald mumbled something to himself. They took the escalator down to the baggage claim.

"Grace!" The shot laced her ears. She wheeled about and saw her mother on the escalator rising in the opposite direction. Her mother stared at her, a horrified expression stamped on her face.

"Mom!"

"Grace! What are you doing here?"

Mother turned around and clutched the escalator handrail, trying to head down, but two people in grey blocked her. She pushed against them. "Let me through! Gerald, you old fool, what have you done? I've lived my life, she hasn't! She can't do this. Damn it, let me through!"

The escalators dragged them in opposite directions. Grace spun around to run up the moving steps and saw the man with green eyes blocking her way. He towered behind her uncle, immovable like a mountain. Green eyes greeted her again. Power coursed through them and vanished, a sword shown and thrust back into its scabbard. Uncle Gerald turned, saw him, and went white as a sheet.

They reached the bottom. Three people in grey waited for them, one woman and two men. Grace stepped onto the floor, lightheaded as if in a dream.

"I've done... I've done the best I could..." Gerald muttered. "The best. I—"

"You've done wonderfully," the woman said. "Nikita will escort you back to your plane."

One of the men stepped up and held out his hand, indicating the escalator heading up. "Please."

The green-eyed man stepped past them. His gaze paused on

her face. An unspoken command to follow. Grace clenched her teeth. They both knew she would obey, and they both realized she hated it.

He strode unhurriedly toward the glass doors. Grace matched her stride to his. She supposed she should have bowed and kept her mouth shut until she was spoken to, but she felt too hollow to care. "You robbed me of what might be my last moment with my mother," Grace said softly.

"It couldn't be helped," he answered, his voice quiet and deep.

They stepped into sunshine in unison. A black vehicle waited for them, sleek and stylish. The trunk clicked open. Grace deposited her backpack into it. The man held the rear door open for her. Grace took her seat on the leather.

The man slid next to her, filling the vehicle with his presence. She felt the warmth of his body and the almost imperceptible brush of his magic. That light touch betrayed him. She glimpsed power slumbering inside him, like an enormous bear ready to be roused and enraged in an instant. It sent shivers down her back, and it took all of her will to not wrench the car door open and run for her life. "You're him."

He inclined his head. "Yes."

The car pulled away from the curb, carrying them off. Grace looked out of the window. She had made her choice. She was a servant of Clan Dreoch and there was no turning back.

The scenery rolled by, scrawny shrubs and flat land, its sparseness mirroring her bleak mood. Grace closed her eyes. A whisper of magic tugged on her. It was a polite touch, an equivalent to a bow. She glanced at him. Careful green eyes studied her. "What's your name?" he asked.

"Grace."

"It's a lovely name. You may call me Nassar."

Or Master, she thought and bit the words before they had a chance to escape.

"How much do you know?" he asked.

"I know that my family owes your family a debt. One of you can call on one of us at any time and we must obey. If we break our oath, you'll murder all of us." She wished she had been told about it sooner, not that it would make any difference at the end.

His magic brushed her again and she edged away from it.

"What else?" Nassar asked.

Say as little as possible. "I know what you are."

"What am I?"

"A revenant."

"And what would that be?"

She looked him in the eye. "A man who died and robbed another of his body so he can continue to live." The cursed revenant, Gerald had called him. A body snatcher. An abomination. Monstrously powerful, clouded in vile magic, a beast more than a man.

Nassar showed no reaction, but a small ripple in his magic sent her further away from him. She bumped into the door.

"Any further and you'll fall out of the car," he said.

"Your magic… It's touching me."

"If all goes as planned, you and I will have to spend the next few days in close proximity. I need you to become accustomed to my power. Our survival will depend on it."

She sensed his magic halt a few inches from her, waiting tentatively. She was a servant; he could force her. At least he permitted her an illusion of free will. Grace swallowed and moved within its reach. His magic brushed her. She winced, expecting his power to mug her, but it simply touched her gently, as if her magic and his held hands.

"I won't hurt you," he said. "I know how people in your family see me. Body thief, aberration, murderer. The Cursed

One. What I'm called doesn't concern me. Neither I nor my family will torture, rape, or degrade you in any way. I simply have a specific task I need completed. I need you to want to succeed with me. What would make you want to help me?"

"Freedom," she said. "Let my family go, and I'll do whatever you ask."

He shook his head. "I can't give you permanent freedom. We need your services too much. But I can offer you a temporary reprieve. If you and I succeed, you can go home and I promise not to call on you and yours for six months."

"Ten years."

"A year."

"Eight."

"Five." The resolute tone of his voice told her it was his last offer.

"Deal," she said softly. "What happens if I fail?"

"We'll both die. But, our chances of success will be much better if you stop fearing me."

That was certainly true. "I'm not scared of you."

His lips curved slightly. "You're terrified."

She raised her chin. "The sooner we get done, the faster I can go home. What do you need me to do?"

Nassar reached into his jacket and took out a rolled up piece of paper. "In our world disputes between the clans are resolved through war or by arbitration."

Grace arched her eyebrow. "How many clans are there?"

"Twelve. We're now in dispute with Clan Roar. War is bloody, costly and painful for everyone involved and neither of the families can afford it now. We've chosen arbitration. The issue is pressing and the dispute will be decided through a game."

He unrolled the picture and held it. She would have to move closer to him to see it. Grace sighed and moved another three inches to the right. Their thighs almost touched.

Nassar showed her the paper. It was an aerial photograph of a city.

"Milligan City," Nassar said. "Squarely in the middle of the rust belt. A couple of decades ago it was a busy town, a blue-collar haven. Good life, family values."

"Defined future," she said.

He nodded. "Yes. Then the conglomerates shifted their operations overseas. The jobs dried up, the real estate values plummeted, and the residents fled. Now Milligan's population is down forty-two percent. It's a ghost city, with all the requisite ghost city problems: abandoned houses, squatters, fires and so on." He tapped the paper. "This particular neighborhood is completely deserted. The city council's getting desperate. They've relocated the last of the stragglers to the center of the city and condemned this neighborhood. In nine days it will be bulldozed down to make way for a park. The arbitration will take place here."

"When I think of arbitration, I think of lawyers," Grace said. "Both sides present their case and argue to a third party."

"Unfortunately this case isn't something that can be settled through litigation," Nassar answered. "Think of it in this way: instead of having a large war, we decided to have a very small one. The rules are simple. This area of the city was warded off from the rest, hidden in the cocoon of magic and altered. It's been officially condemned, so no others are allowed near it. Those who try are firmly discouraged, but if someone does make it through, to their eyes the area will appear as it always was."

She chewed on that *others*. Normal, non-magical people. He said it in the way one might refer to foreigners.

"Arbitration by game is a big event. By last count, representatives of ten clans have shown up for the fun. Two weeks were allowed to each clan who so wished to dump whatever hazards they could manage into this space. It's full of things that go bump in the night."

"The other clans don't like you," she said.

"None of the clans like each other. We compete for territory and business. We have wars and bloody battles. And it will be up to you and me to help us avoid such a war this time." He touched the photograph. "Somewhere in the zone the arbitraries hid a small flag. Two teams will enter the game zone to retrieve the flag, while the rest of the clansmen will bet on the outcome and enjoy their popcorn. Whoever touches the flag first will win and be ported out of the zone. Whether the flag is retrieved or not, in three days' time the wards will constrict, sweeping anything magic from the area into its center. The pyromancers will destroy it in a preternaturally hot bonfire, while the locals blissfully sleep."

"Are we one of the teams?"

"Yes."

Now she understood. Mother was almost fifty and overweight. She wouldn't be able to move fast enough. They needed someone younger and she fit the bill. "Will the rival team try to kill us?"

Another light smile touched his lips. "Most definitely."

"I don't have any offensive magic."

"I'm sure," he said. "You're entirely too polite for that."

It took her a moment to catch the pun. "I'm a dud. I sense magic and I can do small insignificant things, but I can't foretell the future like my mother and I haven't been trained as a fighter, like Gerald. For all practical purposes, I'm the *other*, a completely ordinary person. I've never fired a gun, I'm not exceptionally athletic, and my strength and reflexes are average."

"I understand."

"Then why do you need—"

Magic stabbed her, cold and sharp, wrenching a startled gasp from her. Her eyes watered from pain.

"Lilian!" Nassar barked.

"Go!" The chauffer mashed a square button on her dashboard.

The roof of the vehicle slid aside. A dark sheath coated Nassar.

The pain pierced Grace's ribs, slicing its way inside.

Nassar jerked her to him. She collided with the hard wall of his chest, unable to breathe.

The dark sheath flared from him, filling the vehicle in long protrusions, shaping into a multitude of pale feathers.

"Hold on!" Nassar snarled. Grace threw her arms around his neck and they shot straight up, into the sky. Wind rushed at her. The pain vanished. She looked down and almost screamed—the car was far below.

"Don't panic."

The flesh of Nassar's neck crawled under her fingers, growing thicker. She turned to him and saw a sea of feathers and high above huge raptor jaws armed with crocodile teeth. Her arms shook with the strain of her dead weight.

"It's okay," the monster reassured her in Nassar's voice.

Her hold gave. For a precious second, Grace clung to the feathers, but her fingers slipped. She dropped like a stone. Her throat constricted. She cried out and choked as a huge claw snapped closed about her stomach.

"Grace?" The feathered monster bent his neck. A round green eye glared at her.

She sucked the air into her lungs and finally breathed. "Your definition of okay has problems."

The wind muffled her voice.

"What?" he bellowed.

"I said, your definition of okay has problems!"

The ground rolled past them, impossibly far. She clenched

her hands on the enormous scaly talons gripping her. "Is there any chance that this could be a dream?!"

"I'm afraid not!"

Her heart hammered so hard, she was worried it would jump out of her chest. "What was it?"

"Clan Roar—our opponents in the game. Or one of their agents, to be exact. They're not dumb enough to attack you directly. Once the game is scheduled, all hostilities between the participants must cease. Interference of this sort is forbidden."

"What about Lilian?"

"She can take care of herself."

Grace shivered. "Why would they be attacking me in the first place?"

"You're my defense. If they kill you, I'll have to withdraw from the game."

"That sounds ridiculous! You're the revenant and I can't even defend myself."

"I'll explain everything later. We're beyond their range now and we'll arrive soon. Try to relax!"

She was clutched in the talons of a monstrous creature, who was really a man trying to rescue her from a magical attack by flying hundreds of feet above solid ground. *Relax.* Right. "I serve a madman," she muttered.

Far beyond the fields, an empty piece of the horizon shimmered and drained down, revealing a dark spire. Tower Dreoch, Uncle Gerald had called it. He'd said the Dreochs lived in a castle. She thought he'd exaggerated.

Nassar careened, turning, and headed to the tower.

THEY CIRCLED THE TOWER ONCE, BEFORE NASSAR DIVED TO A balcony and dropped her into a waiting group of people below. Hands caught her and she was gently lowered to the ground.

In the overcast sky, Nassar swung upward and swooped

down. The group parted. A dark-skinned woman grasped Grace by her waist and pulled her aside with the ease one picked up a child.

Nassar dove down. His huge talons skidded on the balcony and he tumbled into the room beyond. Feathers swirled. He staggered up. "Leave us."

People fled past her. In a moment the room was empty.

Grace hugged herself. Up there, in the evening sky, the cold air had chilled her so thoroughly, even her bones felt iced over. Her teeth still chattered. She stepped to the double doors and shut them, blocking off the balcony and the draft with it.

The large rectangular room was simply but elegantly furnished: a table with some chairs, a wide bed with a gauzy blue canopy, a bookcase, some old, solidly built chairs before the fireplace. A couple of electric table lamps radiated soft yellow light. An oriental silk rug covered the floor.

Nassar slumped in front of the fireplace. Bright orange flames threw highlights on his feathers, making them almost golden in the front. His feathers seemed shorter. His jaws no longer protruded quite as much.

Grace crossed the carpet and stood before the fire, soaking in the warmth. It all seemed so dream-like. Unreal.

"This will be your room for the next couple of days," he said.

"You have no idea how strange this is to me," she murmured.

His smart eyes studied her. "Tell me about it?"

"In my world people don't turn into...into this." She indicated him with her hand. His feathers definitely were shorter now. He'd shrunk a little. "People don't fly unless they have a glider or some sort of metal contraption with an engine designed to help them. Nobody tries to murder someone through magic. Nobody has mysterious castles masquerading as empty fields."

A careful knock interrupted her.

"It's your room," Nassar murmured.

"Come in," she called.

A man entered, pushing a small trolley with a teakettle, two cups, a dish of sugar, a ewer of cream, and a platter with assorted cookies. As he passed her, she saw a short sword in a sheath at his waist. "Your sister suggested tea, sir."

"Very thoughtful of her."

The man left the trolley, smiled at her, and departed.

Grace poured two cups of tea.

"I suppose in your world people don't drink tea either?" he asked.

"We drink tea," she said with a sigh. "We just don't always have servants armed with swords to bring it. Cream?"

"Sugar and lemon, please." Nassar had returned to his normal size. The feathers were mere fur now, and his face was bare and completely human.

"What's happening with your feathers?"

"I'm consuming them to replenish some of my energy. Transformations such as this are difficult even for me." He sank into a chair, took a cup from her with furry fingers, and sipped from it. "Perfect. Thank you."

"I live to serve."

His lips curved into a familiar half-smile. "Somehow I deeply doubt it."

Grace sat into the other chair and sipped shockingly hot tea, liberally whitened by cream. Liquid heat flowed through her. His magic brushed her again, but she had flown over miles bathed in it and she accepted his touch without protest. She was so very tired. "This is a dream. I'll wake up, and all of this will be gone. And I'll go back to my quiet little job."

"What is it you do?"

Grace shrugged. He knew, of course. His clan had been keeping tabs on their family for years. When you own something, you want to pay attention to its maintenance. He probably knew what size underwear she wore and how she preferred her steak. "Why don't you tell me?"

"You're a headhunter. You find jobs for others. Do you like it?"

"Yes. It's boring at times and stressful, but I get to help people."

"You didn't know about your family's debt, did you?" he asked.

"No." She refilled her cup.

"When did you find out?"

"Three days ago."

"Was it sudden?"

"Yes," she admitted. "I always knew about magic. I was born able to feel it. At first I was told I was a very sensitive child, and then, once I was old enough to realize I needed to keep it to myself, more complicated explanations followed. I live in a world of very small magics. I can sense if I'll miss the bus. In school, I could usually foretell my grade on tests, but I could never predict anything else accurately. If I concentrate very hard, I can scare animals. A dog once tried to chase me, and I was frightened and sent it running."

She drank again. "Small things, mostly useless. I thought that all magic users were like me. Working their little powers in secret. I never imagined people could fly in the open. Or walk through crowded airports without being seen. My mother is a fabric buyer. My uncle's a mechanic who really likes weapons. My dad's normal in every way. My mother and he divorced when I was eighteen. He runs a shift at a tire repair plant."

Grace drank more tea. Her head was fuzzy. She was so comfortable and warm in the soft chair. "When Uncle Gerald told me this half-baked story about blood debt, I didn't believe him at first."

"What convinced you?"

"He was terrified. Uncle Gerald is like a rock in the storm:

always cool under pressure. I've never seen him so off-balance." She yawned. She was so drowsy. "I think my mother hoped I would never have to do this."

"I can see why," Nassar said softly. "We live in constant danger. I would think any mother would want to shield her child from us."

"I would." Drowsiness overtook her. Grace set the cup down and curled into a ball in the chair. "Even though your world is so…"

She vaguely saw him rise from his chair. He picked her up, his magic cloaking about her. She should have been alarmed, but she had no resolve left.

"So?"

"So magical."

He drew the canopy aside and lowered her onto the bed. Her head touched the pillow and reality faded.

NASSAR STEPPED OUT OF THE ROOM, GENTLY CLOSING THE DOOR behind him. Alasdair waited in the hallway, a lean sharp shadow, with a robe draped over his arm. Nassar took it from him and shrugged it on, absorbing the last of his feathers. His whole body hurt from too much magic expended too quickly. Walking was like stepping on crushed glass.

"Is she asleep?" Alasdair asked.

Nassar nodded. They walked down the hall together.

"She's pretty. Chestnut hair and chocolate eyes—a nice combination."

She was also calm under pressure, smart, and willful. When she looked at him with those dark eyes, Nassar felt the urge to say something intelligent and deeply impressive. Unfortunately, nothing of the kind came to mind. It seemed her eyes also had a way of muddling his thoughts. The last time he felt that dumb was about fourteen years ago. He'd been eighteen at the time.

"You like the girl," Alasdair offered.

Nassar leveled a heavy gaze at him.

"Lilian said you tried to be funny in the car. I told her it couldn't possibly be true. The moment you try to make a joke, the sky shall split and the Four Horsemen will ride out, heralding Apocalypse."

"How droll. Did you double the patrols?"

Alasdair nodded his dark head and stopped by the ladder. Nassar walked past him, heading to his rooms.

"Did you?" Alasdair called.

"Did I what?"

"Did you joke with the girl?"

Nassar kept walking.

"Did she laugh?" Alasdair called.

"No."

Nassar entered his room. He hadn't expected her to laugh. He was grateful she didn't collapse in a hysterical heap. Her uncle had been scared to within an inch of his life—fear had rolled off of him in waves. In Gerald's life of some fifty-odd years his services had been requested only twice, but the second time had scarred him for life. In the zone he would be useless.

Grace's mother, Janet, was always meticulous and formal. She took no initiative. Working with her was like being in a presence of an automaton who obeyed his every order while being grimly determined to dislike it. Taking her into the zone, even if he could compensate for her age and health, would be suicide.

He was never comfortable with any of them. He was never comfortable with the whole idea of the bonded servant and took pains to avoid requesting their presence. But this time he had no choice.

Working with Grace presented its own set of difficulties. He could still remember her scent: the light clean fragrance of soap mixing with the faint rosemary from her dark hair. His memory conjured the feel of her body pressed against his and when he'd picked her up to place her on the bed, he hadn't wanted to let go. He wasn't an idiot. There was an attraction there, and he would have to manage it very carefully. The imbalance of power between the two of them was too pronounced: he was the master and she was the servant. *Don't think about it*, he told himself. *Don't imagine what it would be like. Nothing can happen. Nothing is going to happen. She's off-limits.*

Grace followed the servant into a spacious atrium. Morning sun shone through the glass panels in the ceiling. The stone path wound between lush greenery, parallel to a stream lined with smooth river pebbles. Spires of bamboo rose next to ficus and ferns. Delicate orchids in a half a dozen shades dotted the moss-covered ground. Red kafir lilies bloomed along the stream's banks, echoed by paler blossoms of camellia bushes. The air smelled sweet.

The path turned, parting, and Grace saw the origin of the stream: a ten-foot waterfall at the far wall. The water cascaded over huge grey boulders into a tiny lake. Near the shore stood a low coffee table surrounded by benches. A dark-haired man lounged on the bench to the left, sipping tea from a large cup.

Nassar stood next to him, talking softly. He wore blue sweatpants and light grey T-shirt. A towel hung over his shoulder and his pale hair was wet and brushed back from his face. Poised like this, he appeared massive. Muscles bulged on his chest when he moved his arm to underscore a point. His biceps stretched the sleeves of his shirt. His legs were long. Everything about him, from the breadth of his shoulders to the way he carried himself—controlled and aware of his size— communicated raw physical power. His wasn't the static bulk of a power weightlifter, but rather the dangerous, honed build of a man who required muscle to survive. If a genius sculptor were to carve a statue and name it Strength, Nassar would've made a perfect model.

He glanced at her. His green eyes arrested her and Grace halted, suddenly realizing she wanted to know what he would look like naked.

The thought shocked her.

Something in her face must've equally shocked him, because he fell silent.

A torturous second passed.

She forced herself to move. Nassar looked away, resuming his conversation.

I can't be attracted to him. He forced me to come here and risk my life and I don't even know why. I know nothing about him. He's a monster. That last thought sobered her up. She approached the benches.

"Grace," Nassar said. His magic brushed her. "This is Alasdair, my cousin."

Alasdair unfolded himself from the bench. "Charmed."

"Hello." Grace nodded at Alasdair, then turned to Nassar. "You drugged my drink."

"Actually I drugged the cream," he said, "and technically it was my sister who did it."

"Why?"

"You were in shock. I wanted to spare you the breakdown and anxiety when you came out of it."

Grace held herself straight. "I would appreciate it if you didn't do it again. We have a deal. I'll keep my part, but I can't do it if I have to watch what I eat and drink."

Nassar considered it for a long moment. "Agreed."

"A deal?" Alasdair's eyebrows crept up. His was lean and sharp, his movements quick. His stare had an edge. If Nassar was a sword, Alasdair was a dagger.

"I've agreed to do my best to help you, and in return, you'll leave my family alone for five years," Grace said.

Alasdair grimaced at Nassar. "That's incredibly generous, considering what they've done. We owe them nothing."

Nassar shrugged his massive shoulders. "It's worth the reward to have her full cooperation."

Grace took a seat on the bench. "What did we do exactly?"

"You don't know?" Alasdair passed her a plate of scones.

"No."

The dark-haired man glanced at Nassar, who shrugged. "You tell it."

"At the end of the nineteenth century your family and our clan were in dispute," Alasdair said.

Grace was learning to decipher their code. "In other words, we were murdering each other."

"Precisely. The dispute grew out of control and so our families agreed to end it. The peace was to be sealed through a wedding. Jonathan Mailliard of your family was to marry Thea Dreoch."

"He was your great-grandfather's brother," Nassar supplied.

"The wedding went well," Alasdair continued. "There was a very nice reception in one of the Mailliard gathering halls, a beautiful old hotel. Everyone ate, drank, and was merry. The couple went upstairs, to their rooms, where Jonathan pulled out a knife and slit Thea's throat."

Grace froze with a scone halfway to her mouth. She had expected something of this sort. To force her family into indefinite servitude, the crime had to be horrible. But it still shocked her.

"He waited for almost two hours by her cooling corpse," Alasdair continued. "Until the party died down. Then he and several Mailliard men and women went through the hotel door to door. They murdered Thea's sister, her husband, and their twin daughters who were flower girls at the wedding. They killed Thea's parents and her two brothers, both minors, and would've slaughtered the entire party, but they were seen by a

Dreoch retainer, who started screaming. Our offensive magic was always stronger and we were inside your family's defenses. There was a bloodbath. Every member of the Mailliard family was killed, except Thomas Mailliard, who was fourteen at the time. He hid in a closet and wasn't discovered until later in the day, when the butchery had stopped. Because Thomas was a child and hadn't participated in the slaughter, he was given a choice: death or servitude for all of his descendants. And that's why you now serve us."

Grace sat in a sickened silence.

"Anything to say?" Alasdair asked.

"That's very horrible," she said.

"Yes, it is."

"However, I never knew Jonathan Mailliard. I didn't even know his name. I feel awful about the murder and I understand that my family bears responsibility, but *I* never killed anyone. I've never hurt you and neither has my mother, my uncle or my great-grandfather, who hid in the closet." She tried to make her voice sound calm and reasonable. "I've done you no harm, yet you limit my freedom and force me to risk my life because of a crime perpetrated a century ago by someone I've never met. Our family has served yours for over a hundred years. At some point this debt will have been repaid. When do you think will that be?"

"Never," Alasdair said.

It felt like a slap. She looked to Nassar. "So this is how you do things? You dumped all of the blame for a bloody feud onto a fourteen-year-old child who hid in a closet, and because he's failed to stop grown men from killing, you keep his descendants in perpetual servitude?"

"Hardly perpetual," Nassar corrected. "Since I assumed the responsibility for the clan fifteen years ago, I've called on your family only four times."

"But we know we can be called at any point. We have to live

with the knowledge that on a moment's notice we might be required to risk our life for a complete stranger for no reason and we might never see our loved ones again. We can't refuse. The terms are obedience or death. Would you want to live like this?"

"No," Nassar admitted.

"Can you tell me when the debt will be paid?" she asked.

"This arrangement is to our advantage," Nassar said. "It makes no sense for us to release you."

"I see. I'll have to release us then."

"Really?" Alasdair gave a short barking laugh. "How exactly are you planning on doing that?"

"My uncle has no offspring and I'm my mother's only child. To my knowledge, I'm the last of Mailliards. I'll have to make sure that I don't continue the line." She rose. "I think I've seen the washroom on the way here. I really need to splash some water on my face."

"Second door on the right," Nassar told her.

"Excuse me."

Grace walked away. Her knees shook a little in her jeans. Her face burned.

Nassar watched Grace's figure retreat down the winding path.

"Wow," Alasdair offered.

"Yes."

"Think she'll do it?"

"She's a Mailliard."

He'd seen the same steely resolve in her mother's eyes, Nassar reflected. He suspected it was the same will that drove the wedding night atrocities a century ago. It enabled her mother, Janet, to grimly bear her service, and fueled Grace's fight against it. He doubted she would ever go into outright rebellion, not while her mother and Gerald were alive, but he could tell by the way she held herself, by her face and her eyes and her voice, that she would rather give up her future children than bring them into Dreoch's "service."

"You like her," Alasdair said.

"What of it?"

"Why don't you make a move?"

The imbalance of power between them was too great and her antipathy and contempt for Dreoch was painfully obvious. Nassar took the towel off his shoulder and sat on the bench. "Because she can't say no."

When Grace returned, Alasdair was gone. Nassar sat alone. It was easier if she simply admitted it, Grace decided. Sometimes you see another person in passing, your eyes meet, and you know by some instinct that there is something there. She felt that something for Nassar.

It was wrong on so many levels, her head reeled from simply contemplating it. He was a revenant, a creature more than a man. Her great-grandfather's brother slaughtered his relatives. His family held hers in bondage. If he really wanted her, he could simply order her to submit. Maybe it was some sort of twisted version of Stockholm syndrome. Or an animal attraction. He was...not handsome exactly, but very male. Powerful. Masculine. Strong. But there was more to it: the sadness in his eyes, the courteous way he managed himself, the feel of his magic. It pulled her to him and she would have to be very careful to keep her distance.

"You still haven't told me what you need me to do," she said.

He rose. "Walk with me, please."

Grace followed him down the path deeper into the atrium. Nassar led her out through an arched door and into a large round chamber. Bare, it was lit by sunlight spilling through a skylight very high above. A thick metal grate guarded the skylight. Plain concrete made up the floor, showing a complicated geometric pattern with a circle etched into its center. Nassar stood on its edge.

"When a revenant takes a new body, he gains great power but he also inherits the weaknesses of that body. The body I took was cursed. After I transferred into it, I was able to heal the damage and break the curse. But all of my invulnerability to the curse is gone. I've used it all up."

"And the man who was born in this body? What happened to him when you took it?"

"He died," Nassar said.

She'd hoped he wouldn't say that.

A woman entered the chamber through the door in the opposite wall. A pale blonde like Nassar. She smiled at them. Nassar didn't quite smile back, but the melancholy of his face eased slightly.

"This is Elizavetta. My sister."

"Call me Liza," she said. "Everyone does."

"Grace," Grace said simply. "You're the one who drugged the cream."

Liza nodded. "Yes. Alasdair warned me I may have earned your undying hate for it. I sincerely hope we can put it past us. I didn't mean to hurt your feelings in any way."

"Given that I'm a servant, my feelings are hardly relevant, but I appreciate it," Grace said.

Liza blinked. An uncomfortable silence ensued. Nassar cleared his throat. "Liza?"

"Yes, right." Liza stepped inside the design.

"Every revenant has a fatal weakness," Nassar said, his gaze fixed on his sister. "This is mine."

Liza arched her back, spreading her arms. Her hands clawed the air. She spun in place, twisting. Magic pulsed from her and filled the lines etched on the floor with pale yellow light. Liza brought her hands together, cried out, and forced them apart with a pained grimace. A clump of mottled darkness appeared between her fingers. She stepped back.

The clump spun, growing, and ruptured, vomiting a creature into the circle. The beast was three feet long and slender, shaped like a slug or a leech except for the fringe of carmine feathery hairs along its sides. A patina of grey and sickly yellow swirled over its dark hide, like an oil rainbow on the surface of a dark puddle.

The creature shivered. The red fringe trembled and it took to the air, sliding soundlessly a foot off the ground. A cold foul magic emanated from it. It touched Grace. She jerked back and bumped into Nassar.

"What is that?"

He put his hand on her shoulder, steadying her. "A marrow worm. They live in dark places, where there is stagnant water and decay. They feed on small animals, fish, and old magic."

The worm hovered behind the glowing outline of the circle. Its head was blunt and as it rose up, testing the boundaries of its invisible cage, Grace saw a slit of a mouth lined with sharp serrated teeth on its underside.

Liza approached the worm. The creature shied away, sliding as close to the glowing lines as it could.

"Think of them as germs. Most people have a natural resistance to them, an immunity. I don't. To me, they're fatal. We did our best to keep this fact to ourselves, but I have no doubt Roars know it. They would be fools not to. Unfortunately, marrow worms are easy to summon."

He'd stepped behind her and she was painfully sensitive to the presence of his large body only an inch from her back. His magic touched her. Her every nerve shivered, hyper-aware of his movements. She sensed him lean to her and almost jumped when his quiet voice spoke into her ear. "Do you remember when you sent that dog running? I want you to do that again."

Grace swallowed. "I don't remember what I did. It just happened."

His big hand pushed against her back gently, making her take a step toward the circle. "Try."

Grace took a deep breath and stepped over the glowing lines inside the circle. The worm jerked away from her like a wet ribbon. Grace glanced at Nassar.

"That's just normal resistance to humans. Keep trying."

Grace stared at the worm twisting. *Go away,* she thought. *Gone. I want you gone.*

The worm remained where it was.

Grace glanced at Liza. "Any idea what I'm supposed to be doing?"

Nassar's sister shook her blonde head. "None. Dreochs are aggressors. We have few defensive abilities and they're radically different from yours. Mostly our defenses consist of Nassar hacking at things with something large and sharp."

"The magic you're trying to do is called the Barrier," Nassar said. "It's one of the natural Mailliards' magics. Very talented members of your family used it both as defense and as a weapon. Your mother stated that it can't be taught. You simply do it or you don't."

Grace focused on the worm and tried to pretend it was a large, mean-looking German shepherd.

An hour later she sat exhausted on the floor. The worm floated at the edge of the design.

"It's useless." Liza unscrewed a cap from a fresh bottle of water. She had gotten a cooler with drinks, migrated to the wall, and now sat on the floor. "Why Janet didn't practice with Grace is beyond me, but she didn't. We'll have to change the plan. Instead of you and Grace, I'll go with Alasdair."

"No." Steel laced Nassar's voice. He leaned against the wall.

"You're being unreasonable."

Nassar's face was dark like a storm. "Both of you will die. I have resistances and power to counter Roar's attacks. You don't."

"You can't counter this one."

He didn't answer.

"Why don't you just turn into a bird and fly through the zone?" Grace asked.

"Flight is forbidden in the game," Nassar answered.

Liza sighed. "Grace, would you like some water?"

"Yes."

Liza tossed her a new bottle.

"Thank you." Grace caught it. "Why are you fighting Roars anyway? What's this dispute about?"

"It's about children," Nassar said. "And killing me."

"Our aunt married a member of clan Roar," Liza said. "Arthur Roar. He turned out to be a wart on the ass of the human kind. Abusive, violent, cruel. She left after eight years and took their three kids with her."

"Should've left sooner," Nassar said. His green eyes promised violence, the light irises so cold that Grace took a small step back.

"She had her reasons for staying," Liza said. "There was a large dowry involved and she didn't want us to have to pay restitution and interest. But in the end it was just too much. After Arthur broke his son's legs, she grabbed the kids and came home. Now, nine years later, Arthur suddenly wants his children back."

Liza took a drink from her bottle. "He's never shown any interest in them. No calls, no letters, not even a card. He's done nothing to support them. But Aunt Bella signed the wedding agreement that specified equal amount of time with the children for each parent in the event of separation. Arthur claims that since the kids were with her exclusively for nine years, now he has exclusive rights to them."

"He doesn't give a damn about the kids. It's an excuse for the

Roars to test the waters," Nassar said. "They have a couple of strong people and they're thinking of moving in on our interests. Before they do it, they want to weaken us. They knew that if they challenged the clan, I would enter the game, and they believe they have a reasonable chance of killing me. They'll knock out Dreoch's biggest power user and earn respect from other clans for killing a revenant and they will do it all before the war ever starts."

He pushed from the wall. "It's almost time for lunch. Let's take a break."

THE LUNCH WAS LAID OUT ON A LONG TABLE IN A VAST DINING hall. Nassar held out a chair for Grace and she sat down. He took a place to her right, while Liza sat down at her left, next to Alasdair. Other people came into the room—two men and three women. They took their seats, nodded and smiled, started conversations in calm voices. Alastair said something and a woman laughed. They were so at ease and the warmth of their interaction began to thaw Grace's resolve.

The four chairs directly opposite her remained empty. She wondered who would sit there and a couple of minutes later she had her answer. Three children entered the room, followed by a pale woman. Of course. Nassar arranged it so she would spend the meal looking at the faces of the children whose fate would be decided in the game.

They took the seats: the woman with careworn eyes, a young
boy with wild mass of dark hair, and two girls, one slender and
blonde and the other only about ten or so, a kid with short dark

hair and big blue eyes. The youngest girl saw Nassar and came grinning around the table. "Hug?" she asked him seriously.

"Hug," he agreed and put his massive arms around her.

"And no dying," she reminded him.

He let go and nodded.

The girl noticed her. "Hi. I'm Polina."

It was impossible not to smile back. "Hi. I'm Grace."

"You're supposed to protect Nassar," Polina said.

"That's what he tells me."

The child looked at her with her blue eyes. "Please don't let him die," she said softly. "I like him a lot."

"I'll try my best."

Polina went around the table to her seat. Grace leaned to Nassar and whispered, "Laying it on a little thick, don't you think?"

"I didn't put her up to it," he told her. She glanced into his green eyes and believed him.

The lunch went on. Dishes were brought and passed around the table: roast beef and mashed potatoes, green beans, corn, iced tea and lemonade. The food was delicious, but Grace ate little. Mostly she watched the children. The boy leaned to his mother, making sure her cup was filled. The older girl seemed on the verge of tears. She became more and more agitated, until finally, just as peach cobbler made its way past Grace, the girl dropped her fork. Her voice rang out. "What if they win?"

The table fell quiet.

"They won't," Nassar said calmly.

"If Arthur touches us, I'll kill him." Steel vibrated in the boy's voice.

Their mother leaned her elbows on the table and rested her forehead on her hands. "No. You're not strong enough," she told him in a dull voice. "Not yet. You must do whatever it takes to survive."

"That's enough." Nassar's magic surged out, spreading

behind him like invisible wings. It brushed against Grace. Breath caught in her throat. So much power…

Nassar fixed the children with his stare. "You're our kin. You belong to Clan Dreoch. Nobody will take you from us. Anyone who tries will have to go through me."

With his power rising above the table, the prospect of going through him seemed impossible. His magic was staggering. It would take an army.

The anxiety slowly melted from the children's faces.

"Let's try again," Nassar said, as the two of them strode back into the room.

The worm still floated in the circle. Grace stepped inside. It shied from her.

"Why did you tell the children about the curse?"

"I won't lie to them. The possibility of defeat exists and they have to be prepared."

That defeat seemed very likely at the moment.

"But I will fight to the death to keep them safe. And even if I lose, the clan won't surrender them. We will go to war. We won't turn over children to a man who will break their bones."

Neither would she. It didn't matter who they were. A child was a child. She couldn't let them suffer, not after watching them near panic with fear of having to leave their mother. Their family and their home, all would be ripped away if Nassar and she lost.

"Now do you understand why I fight?" he asked her softly.

She nodded.

"I need your help desperately. Please help me, Grace."

"I wish I could," she said, her voice filled with regret.

Nassar watched her for a long moment. "What do you remember about your encounter with the dog? What did you feel?"

Grace frowned. "It was twelve years ago. I remember being scared for myself. And for the dog. He was my friend's dog. I knew that if he bit me, he would be put down."

Nassar strode to her, a determined look on his face.

"What are you doing?"

Nassar kept coming. She realized he was going to cross the line.

"Liza isn't here to save you!"

"No." He gave her the familiar half smile. "Only you can save me now."

Nassar stepped over the line. The worm streaked to him. It skimmed the surface of his magic and clamped onto his shoulder. Nassar's magic shrunk. He staggered and ripped the worm off. Grace cried out.

The worm flipped in the air and slid over him. Nassar tried to knock it off, but it slipped past his hands and leeched onto his side. Nassar gasped. His face went bloodlessly white. He spun, tripping over his feet, pulling at the writhing body, and stumbled to her. The worm slithered from his fingers and swooped down on him. Nassar fell.

Grace lunged forward. She meant to thrust herself in front of it, but instead magic pulsed from her in a controlled, short burst. The worm hurtled back, swept aside.

She pushed harder and the worm convulsed, squeezed between the press of her power and the glowing lines. "Nassar?" She knelt by him. "Nassar, are you okay?"

Nassar's green eyes looked at her. His nose bled. He wiped away his blood with the back of his hand. "Protective instinct," he said. "You've done it."

It felt so right. As if the pressure straining at her from the inside suddenly found an outlet. So that's what she'd been missing. All these years, she had suspected there was something more to the magic coursing through her and now she finally found it.

"I guess I did," she murmured.

"Were you scared for me?"

"Yes. How could you have done that? That was so reckless. What if I couldn't save you?"

"I hoped you could," he said.

The way he looked at her made her want to kiss him.

"Your family is free," he said.

"What?"

"I've let Clan Mailliard go," he said. "I signed the order before lunch."

She sank to the floor. "Why?"

He sat up. "Because I decided that's not what I do. I don't force people to fight our battles. I don't want to be the man who blames children for their parents' mistakes. And I don't want you to be the last of the Mailliards. Whether you have children should be your choice alone. I don't want to take it away from you."

It slowly dawned on her. "So I'm free?"

"Yes."

She stared at him. "You don't even know me. I could just take off right now and leave you here to deal with the game on your own. Do you have any idea how scared I am? I don't want to die."

"Neither do I." He gave her another sad smile.

She hung her head, torn. She was deeply, deeply afraid. But walking away from the children wasn't in her. She wouldn't be able to look herself in the eye. It was as if they stood in the road with a semi hurtling at them at full speed. What kind of person wouldn't push them out of harm's way?

"I should practice more," she said.

"We're going to need another worm then," Nassar said.

She glanced at the beast. It lay dead, sliced in half.

"You killed it," he told her. "Sometimes the Barrier magic can also become a blade."

"But I don't even know how I've done it."

"We don't need to worry about that now," he said. "As long as you can defend me, we should be fine."

THREE DAYS LATER GRACE STOOD IN THE MIDDLE OF THE STREET in Millighan City, hugging herself as the sun set slowly. Nassar loomed next to her. Behind them unfamiliar people moved, their magic shifting with them, their clothes color-coded by their clan: grey and black for Dreoch, green for Roar, red for Madrid. Nassar explained the rest of the colors, but she couldn't recall any of it. The anxiety pulsated through her with every heartbeat.

Ahead a seemingly empty stretch of a suburban street rolled into the sunset. The round, red sun hung low above the horizon, a glowing brand upon the clouds.

Familiar magic brushed her and a heavy hand touched her shoulder gently. Nassar. He wore grey pants tucked into military boots. A long-sleeved shirt hugged his arms and over it he wore a leather vest that wanted very much to be called armor. She wore the same outfit. The leather fitted her loosely enough not to be constricting, but tight enough not to get in the way.

"Don't worry," Nassar said.

Her gaze slid to the large axe strapped to his waist. She touched her own blade, a long narrow combat knife. Gerald had taught her the basics of knife-fighting a long time ago but she'd never been in a real fight.

A male voice rose to the side. "Can he bring a servant into the game?"

It took a moment to sink in. Of course, her status would be public knowledge among them, but it still cut her like a knife. She turned. A group of people stood on the side. Five of them wore dark blue robes. The arbitrators, she remembered from

Nassar's explanations. An older female in the arbitrator robe regarded her with serious grey eyes.

"If you want to withdraw, you may do so now," the woman said.

She could withdraw. She could simply refuse to go in. If she did, Nassar would be doomed. He had already committed to the game and she knew he couldn't simply substitute someone else in his place. He wouldn't.

Overnight, her fears had grown into near panic. Now she could walk away from them.

Grace looked at the gathering of the clansmen. Her family used to be a clan. Her people should have stood right here. Instead the clansmen viewed her as a servant. Pride spiked in her. She had as much right to be here as anybody else. The vague feeling of unease that had eaten at her ever since Nassar had transformed into a bird crystallized and she finally understood it: it was envy. Envy of the magic used freely. Envy of knowledge. Circumstances had jettisoned her out of this world, but she refused to stay locked out.

Grace drew herself to her full height. "Why in the world would I want to withdraw?"

A red-haired man in Roar's green shook his head. "She can't refuse. She isn't even properly trained. She's a servant."

"Not anymore," Nassar said softly behind her.

The gathering suddenly grew quiet.

The arbitrator surveyed them for a long moment. "Nassar, am I to understand that you've released Clan Mailliard from their service?"

"Yes," he answered.

The arbitrator looked at her. "You're here of your own free will?"

"Yes," Grace said.

The arbitrator glanced at the Roar clansman. "There is your

answer. Let the record reflect that Clan Mailliard chose to assist Clan Dreoch. You have our leave to proceed."

They passed her. Grace let out her breath.

"Thank you," Nassar murmured.

"You're welcome."

Two young men in Roar's green came to stand at the other end of the street. Both were lean, strong, hard, as if twisted from leather and twine. Both had long hair bound into horse tails: one red, one black.

Nassar leaned to her. "Conn and Sylvester Roar. Powerful, but they lack experience."

The arbitrators passed between them, blocking her vision. As the blue robes fluttered by, Grace saw Conn Roar turn to her. He grinned, his eyes alight with feral fire, and snapped his teeth.

Alarm dashed down her spine in a rush of cold. She raised her eyebrows. "Someone forgot his muzzle."

"See the pendant around Conn's neck?"

Grace glanced at a small black stone hanging on a long chain.

"That's a summoning stone. They'll use its power to manifest creatures."

Marrow worms. They'd use it to summon the marrow worms. Nassar had warned her that the Roars would try to kill them. Him, specifically. The game as only the opening salvo to the hostilities between the two clans, and Roars wanted to land the first blow by taking out Dreoch's best magic user.

The arbitrators raised their hands. A controlled surge of magic washed over the street. The reality drained down, as if it were a reflection in a melting mirror. A new street opened before them. Green and red lianas hung from the dark, sinister houses. Kudzu vines climbed in and out of windows. To the left a huge clump of yellow foam dripped rancid red juice onto the street. A puddle of brown slime slivered across the asphalt like an amoeba and slipped into the storm drain under the light of street lamps. Ahead something furry dashed across the intersection: a long, shaggy body with too many legs.

Somewhere in that zone a flag waited. Whoever touched the flag would be instantly transported out. They just had to survive long enough to reach it.

The woman arbitrator raised her hand, fist closed. Next to Grace, Nassar tensed.

"Let the game begin!" A white light pulsed from the arbitrator's fingers. The crowd erupted in a ragged cheer.

The two Roar clansmen screamed in unison. Flesh bulged under their skin. Their bodies contorted, their limbs thickened. Black fur sheathed their skin. Horns burst through their manes. Their eyes drowned in golden glow and an extra pair opened beside the first set. As one they raised monstrous faces up, the sharp fangs in their jaws silhouetted against the red sky. Eerie howls tore free from their throats, blending into a haunting song of hunt and murder.

The Roars dashed into the zone on all fours. Nassar watched them go, his face calm. Leaping and growling, they turned the corner and vanished behind the abandoned houses. The echoes of their snarls died. Nassar took his axe from its sheath, rested it on his shoulder, and strode into the zone, unhurried. Grace swallowed and followed in his footsteps.

The street lay quiet. They would be watched by magical means while in the zone, but for now the press of many stares bored directly into her back. Her nerves knotted into a clump.

They reached the intersection.

A hint of movement on the roof of a two-story house made her turn. Grace frowned.

A flat, wide shape leaped off the roof, aiming at her. She caught a glimpse of a fang-studded mouth among bulging veins. Too stunned to move, she simply stared.

Nassar's huge back blocked the mouth. A hot whip of magic

sprung from his hand, cleaving the creature in two. Twin halves of the beast fell to the ground, spilling steaming guts onto the asphalt.

"You're allowed to dodge," Nassar said.

The enormous blue beast bore on them. Grace watched it come. It thundered down the street, its six stumpy legs mashing pot holes in the crumbling pavement.

In the past seven hours, she'd used her magic for defense countless times. Blood splattered her face, some dried to flecks, some still wet. Her side burned where a red furry serpent had bit her before Nassar chopped off both of its heads. A long rip split her left pant leg, exposing the puckered flesh of the calf where a liana stung her with its suckers. It never ended. There was always a new horror waiting to pounce on them from some dark crevice. Grace clenched her teeth and watched the beast charge.

It brushed against a house, sending a shower of broken boards in the air, and kept coming, cavernous mouth gaping wide, the sound of its stomping like a cannon blast salute at a funeral. Boom-boom-boom.

Keep it together. Keep it steady.

Boom-boom-boom.

The beast was almost on her. Two bloodshot eyes glared. The black mouth opened, ready to devour her.

"Now!" Nassar barked.

She slammed her magic into it.

With a surprised roar, the beast rammed the invisible barrier. Her feet slid back from the pressure. The beast's momentum pitched it to the side. The mammoth body fell, paws in the air. Nassar leaped over it, a feral shadow caught in the moonlight. White light sliced like a huge blade from his hand

and Nassar landed by her. Filthy and bloody, he looked demonic.

Behind him the beast lay split open, like a chicken with a cleaved breastbone. The soft, beach-ball-sized sack of its heart palpitated once, twice, and stopped.

Grace stared mutely at the carcass. She had never imagined the night could hide things like it, terrible, awful things. She felt like she had aged a lifetime.

A soft humming filled her skull. She shook her head.

"What is it?" Nassar grasped her face and turned it to him.

"Buzzing."

He raised his head, listened, and grabbed her hand. "Run!"

She'd learned not to ask why. They sprinted, zigzagging through the labyrinthine streets, past overgrown lawns, past an abandoned playground, where small things with round red eyes clutched at the jungle gym with sharp claws, past office buildings, and burst into a park. In the middle of the park lay a pond, bordered by a row of street lamps spilling orange light. The moon slid from the clouds, illuminating the water's surface and the raised concrete basin of a dried fountain in the center.

Nassar pulled her into the water and pointed to the fountain. "Go!"

She swam through the murky water without thinking. Something soft brushed her legs. She shied and squeezed a frantic burst of speed from her exhausted body. Dizziness came and then her hand hit the concrete base. She pulled herself up. Nassar climbed up next to her, grabbed her by her waist and hoisted her up into the seven-foot-wide basin. She fell on dried leaves and dirt.

The buzzing grew louder, steady and ominous like the hum of a giant engine.

An invisible whirlpool of magic built around Nassar. He stood cocooned in its fury, his axe held high. His body trembled under the pressure. The cuts and gashes on his arms reopened and bled.

The buzzing swelled like a tidal wave.

She saw the axe fall in an arch, its tip prickling the pond. The magic sucked itself into the axe handle and burst through its blade into the water. The pond became preternaturally calm, its surface smooth like glass. The buzzing vanished.

Nassar swayed. Grace grabbed his shoulders and pulled him against the lip of the basin, steadying him. His hand squeezed hers. He turned carefully, leaped up, and pulled himself into the basin next to her.

A swarm of insects spilled from the street. Green and segmented, like grasshoppers armed with enormous teeth, they were the size of a large cat. They streamed around the water in a mottled mass, bodies upon bodies, packed but none touching the pond.

"What are they?" Grace whispered hoarsely.

"Akora. The spell keeps them out of the water. As long as nothing disturbs the surface, they can't see or hear us. Don't worry. They can't survive the sun. They'll stay here entranced by the spell until morning." He lay on his back and closed his eyes.

Across the water the green insects crawled over the stone benches, perched on lamp posts, and combed the weeds of the once perfectly cut lawn. They had surrounded the pond. Everywhere Grace looked, long segmented legs rubbed, sharp mandibles gnawed on random refuse, and backs split to flutter pale wings.

There were too many of them.

She felt so hollow. The seven hours she had spent in this place had consumed her: there was nothing left inside her. "We'll die here," Grace whispered.

"No."

"They'll eat us, and I'll never see my mother again." What

was the point of going on? They'd never make it out. She no longer cared if they would.

A warm hand grasped her and pulled her with irresistible strength snug against Nassar's chest. His arms closed about her, shielding her, shocking her cold body with their heat. His cheek rested against her hair. "I won't let you die, Grace," he whispered. "I promise I won't let you die."

She lay rigid against his chest, her face in his neck, listening to his strong, even heartbeat. His lips grazed her cheek. "I must be out of my mind," he whispered and his mouth closed on hers.

He kissed her, at first gently, then harder, as if he tried to breathe his life into her. She felt numb, but he persisted, his kiss passionate and searing. His arms caged her. His large hard body cradled hers, keeping her from slipping off into the empty deadness. His magic wrapped them both. He kissed her again and again, anchoring her, refusing to let her go. Caught on the threshold between complete numbness and painful awareness, Grace teetered, unsure. He pulled her back to life, back to the desperate reality. She didn't want to face it.

A shudder ran through her. She closed her eyes and let him part her lips with his tongue. He drank her in and finally she thawed. She wanted to live, to survive so she could feel this again. She wanted Nassar.

Tears wet her cheeks.

Nassar released her mouth and crushed her to him.

"I want you so much," he whispered, his green eyes looking into the distance. "And I can't have you. I really must be cursed."

She lay in his arms for a long time.

The coal darkness of the sky faded to the pale grey of pre-dawn. Grace stirred. "Why did you do it?" she asked softly. "Why did you become a revenant?"

"I was dying," he answered, his voice hoarse. "We had a feud with the Garveys. They cornered my brother, John, and I went to get him. John didn't want to be taken alive. He didn't think help was coming, and he cursed himself and all those around him with a plague of marrow worms. A suicide curse is very potent. I brought him out of the trap, but the curse had caught me. We were both dying and the family could do nothing to keep us alive. I'd lost consciousness. John knew that if I took his body, I'd gain a temporary boost of power to break the curse. He made the family commence the ritual."

"He sacrificed himself?" she whispered.

"Yes. I remember there was a rush of red, like I was swimming through a sea of blood and drowning, and then I saw this shape floating in the depths. I thought it was my body and I knew if I wanted to survive, I had to get to it. I grabbed it, saw it was John… The pull to live was too strong. I awoke in my brother's body."

She put her arms around his neck and kissed his cheek.

"I killed my brother so I can live," he said. "It doesn't get any worse than that."

She simply held him.

A low growl froze both of them. Grace flipped onto her stomach and glanced over the lip of the basin. In the night, the insects had stopped moving. They lay still now, entranced by the spell, their chitin mirroring the grass and weeds around them so closely that if she didn't know they were there, she would've mistook them for heaps of vegetation.

A lean muscled creature trotted along the edge of the pond. It gripped the ground with four oversized paws armed with sickle claws. Its serpentine tail lashed its dark pelt spotted with flecks of red and yellow. The beast padded down the shore, dragon-like jaws hanging open showing off fangs the size of her fingers. Foamy spit leaked from between its teeth, staining the long tuft of red and yellow fur hanging from its chin. It halted, sniffed the air, and turned to the basin. Four glowing amber eyes glared at her.

"Sylvester Roar," Nassar murmured.

Sylvester sniffed the water. His narrow muzzle wrinkled. He looked like he was grinning at them with his monstrous mouth.

Nassar growled. "No, you young idiot! Can't you see the spell on the water?"

Sylvester snapped his teeth and snarled in a feral glee. An eerie raspy growl came from between his teeth. *"I see you, Nassar. You can't hide from me."*

"Inexperienced fool." Nassar reached for his axe.

"I'm coming, Nassar. I'm coming for you." Sylvester gave a short ragged howl and splashed into the water. Little waves ran over the surface of the pond. Behind Sylvester the akora swarm swelled. Buzzing filled the air. Sylvester turned—

Nassar grabbed her and forced her to the floor of the basin, next to him.

A hoarse scream sliced through the morning, a terrible howl of a creature in impossible agony being torn to pieces. Grace squeezed her eyes shut. Sylvester screamed and screamed, the buzzing of the akora a morbid choir to his shrieks, until finally he fell silent.

Grace lay still, afraid to breathe. Slowly she opened her eyes.

An akora perched on the lip of the basin. It sighted her with dead black eyes. Its back split, releasing a pale gauze of wings.

Sun broke above the horizon. Its rays struck the insect. Tiny cracks split its shiny thorax. The insect shrieked and fled, breaking apart over the water of the pond. Grace rose. All around the pond the insect horde fractured and crumbled under the rays of the sun. The air smelled faintly of smoke. She looked beyond the heaps of melting insects and drew a sharp breath. Past the park, to the right, rose a tall heap of rubble that had been a multi-storied building in its former life. Atop the rubble a small white flag fluttered in the wind.

"The flag!"

Nassar had already seen it and jumped into the water. Together they swam across the pond. As she waded onto the solid ground, Grace passed a human skeleton, stripped bare of all flesh—all that remained of Sylvester.

Nassar moved cautiously along the sidewalk, jogging lightly on his feet, axe at the ready. She followed him, gripping her knife.

He wanted her and she wanted him. He'd forged a connection between them she couldn't ignore. The way he had held her, the way he'd touched her made her want to hold on to him. She had no idea what would come of their connection, but her instinct warned her she wouldn't get an opportunity to find out. Thinking of losing him now, before she had a chance to sort it out, terrified her.

They reached the rock pile. Nassar paused, measuring the height of the rubble with his gaze. It was almost three floors tall. He glanced at her. She saw the confirmation in his green eyes: it was too easy. He expected a trap.

"We go slowly," he said. "We must touch it together."

She nodded.

They climbed the pile of debris, making their way higher and higher. Soon they were level with the first floor of the neighboring buildings, then the second. The flag was so close now, she could see the thread weave of its fabric.

The cold magic slammed her. Grace screamed. A lean shape burst over the top of the pile—a half-man, half-demon, surrounded by marrow worms, the summoning stone on his chest glowing with white. The beast hit Nassar in the chest. Nassar reeled, the refuse slipped under him, and he plunged down, rolling as he fell, the dark worms swirling over him.

Grace ran after them. Below, the beast that was Conn Roar tore at Nassar, all but buried under the black ribbons of worm bodies.

She wouldn't get to him in time. Grace jumped.

For a moment she was airborne and falling and then her feet hit hard concrete midway down the slope. It gave under the impact, pitching her forward. She fell and rolled down, trying to shield her head with her arms, banging against chunks of stone and wood. Pain kicked her stomach: she'd smashed into a section of a wall. Her head swam. Her eyes watered. Grace gasped and jerked upright.

Ten feet away the marrow worms choked Nassar.

Magic surged from her in a sharp wave. The blast ripped the worms clear. They fled.

Nassar lay on his back, his eyes staring unseeing into the sky. *Oh no.*

She killed the panicked urge to run to him, crouched, and picked up his axe from where it had fallen. Her own knife was gone in her fall.

A dark shape launched itself at her from the pile. She whipped about, reacting on instinct. Nightmarish jaws snapped, her power pulsed, and Conn Roar bounced from the shield of her magic, knocked back. His paws barely touched the rubble before he sprung back. This time she was ready and knocked him down again, deliberately.

Conn snarled.

She backed away toward Nassar's body.

"He killed my brother," the demonic beast said. His voice raised the small hairs on her neck. *"Let me have Nassar and I'll let you live."*

"No."

"You can't kill me." Conn circled her. He limped, favoring his left front paw, and a long gash split his side, bleeding. Nassar had got a piece of him before he went down.

"Of course I can kill you," she told him, building up her magic. "I'm a Mailliard."

She only had one shot at this. If she failed, he'd rip her to pieces.

Conn tensed. The muscles in his powerful legs contracted. He leaped at her. She watched his furry body sail through the air, watched his jaws gape in joy when he realized her Barrier wasn't there, and then she sank everything she had into a single devastating pulse. Instead of a wide shield, she squeezed all her power into a narrow blade.

It sliced him in two. His body fell, spraying blood. His head flew by her, its four eyes dimming as it spun.

She didn't give it a second glance.

"Nassar?"

She dropped the axe and pulled him up by his giant shoulders, sheltering a weak flutter of magic emanating from him with her own power. He was covered in blood. Her chest hurt as if she'd been stabbed.

"Come back to me!"

He didn't answer.

No! Grace dropped and put her ear to his chest. A heartbeat. Very weak, faltering, but a heartbeat.

She wiped a streak of blood from her eyes with her grimy hand so she could see. She couldn't help him. She didn't know how. But his family would.

Grace looked at the pile of concrete and rubble, to the very top, where a white flag flailed in the breeze.

Nassar leaned against a tree across the street from a brick office building. Grace was inside. He couldn't sense her, not yet, but he knew she was inside.

He vividly remembered waking up to the familiar vaulted ceiling. He'd whispered her name and Liza's voice answered, "She's alive. She dragged you out, and I released her and her family, like you wanted."

He didn't believe her at first. He knew how much he weighed. No woman could have dragged his dead weight up that heap, but somehow Grace had done it.

She left no note. No letter, no message, nothing to indicate that she didn't hate him for dragging her into the horror of the game. He thought of her every day while he lay in his bed waiting for his body to heal.

It took a month for him to recover. Three days ago he was finally able to walk. Yesterday he was able to make it down the stairs unassisted. Now, as he leaned against an old oak for support, his left arm still in a sling, he wondered what he would say if she told him to leave.

He would say nothing, he decided. He would turn around and go back to the airport and fly back to his life as the cursed revenant of Dreoch Tower. Nobody would ever know what it would cost him.

He wanted to hold her, to take her back with him. To have her in his bed, to taste her lips again, and to see the sly smile hidden in her eyes for him alone.

The door opened. Three women stepped out, but he saw only one.

Grace halted. Nassar held his breath.

She took a small step toward him, and then another, and another, and then she was crossing the street, and coming near. He saw nothing except her face.

Her magic brushed him. She dropped her bag. Her hands went up to his shoulders. Her brown eyes smiled at him.

She kissed him.

CURRAN'S POINT OF VIEW

W e've received numerous requests from our readers asking us what this or that character thought about certain scenes from the books. However, nobody has garnered as many requests as Curran. Finally, in the summer of 2009, Gordon decided to write a scene from the Beast Lord's point of view. Curran's POVs, as these scenes have come to be called, have become a favorite with the fans.

Here they are, in chronological order (we think). Enjoy!

UNICORN LANE
(Magic Bites)

I WAS IN UNICORN LANE AT NIGHT. A BAD TIME TO BE IN A BAD place. Anything can happen here, but it's never something good.

No one was in charge of Unicorn Lane. None of Atlanta's many supernatural factions could claim dominion over it. It was populated by those once human and those who had never been, and they hid in the dark ruins, feeding on each other and making visitors unwelcome. Thus, Unicorn Lane was recognized by all as neutral territory, a no-man's-land you entered at your own risk. The scared hovered at the edge, the stupid died not far from it. I was here to meet someone, and if she made it far enough to find me, I would know she was neither.

I leaned against the wall, feeling the cold stone of the abandoned building against my back. Moonlight seeped through the holes in the roof, illuminating a gap in the wall. She would come through there. The night shadows hid me, so I'd have plenty of time to look her over.

The Unicorn lay quiet. The night is never truly silent, but right now the monsters minded their manners. None of them knew why I was here, but all of them recognized that they didn't want to be the reason for my visit.

What I did know of the merc came from Jim, my chief of security. He'd worked with her in the Mercenary Guild. That gave me pause. Jim was a cat and preferred the solitary hunt. It was rare for him to let anyone outside the Pack watch his back. He said she was fast, for a human, and good with a blade. He also said she had a big mouth and fought when she should run. None of this endeared her to me. Mercs were bottom-feeders. No honor, no integrity, no loyalty. They didn't stand for anything. I wasn't in the habit of personally meeting low-life thugs who wanted to be tough guys. I had people for that.

However, I was willing to take a chance this time since Jim had vouched for her. Jim had seen her come out of situations that should have ended her, and he didn't believe all her cards were on the table. She was likely hiding strong magic, which meant she came with baggage. That was fine if it made her useful. Something was hunting my people, the Free People of Atlanta. We were shapeshifters and we had the best trackers in the City, but we had yet to catch it.

Normally we solved our own problems. We kept it in the family. Humans saw us as freaks, and I saw no need to give them more ammunition. But the murders had been too numerous, and some of the vampires had been destroyed as well. No big loss.

Then the Order of Merciful Aid had gotten involved. The only human I trusted in that organization of fanatics, a Knight Diviner of the Order, had been investigating the case and was killed for it, presumably by the same creature. I have little love and less use for humans, but Greg Feldman had died helping us, and that counted for something. Incredibly, this merc was his estranged ward and had inherited the case along with a temporary position with the Order.

I would find this thing that was murdering my people. I would stand over it and taste its blood as the light faded from its eyes. Nothing would change that. But with the Order's help, I would find it faster. If Greg's ward was looking for revenge, all the better. It meant she would be willing to take risks that could help me get my teeth on this creature's throat.

The night wind brought a mixture of scents to my tongue. Leather—old boots. A touch of sweat, clean and unmistakably feminine. A mix of rosemary, chamomile, lavender—shampoo, an herbal fragrance foreign to this dank and moldy place—nice. A very faint trace of cloves and steel—oil for the sword. She was near and moving closer.

She was nearly soundless, unusually quiet for a human. Interesting. What was she?

Finally the faint sound of a step. Come closer, little mouse, you're almost there.

The night shadows swallowed me. She would come in right across from me—it was the only way in—and I would see her before she saw me, if I choose to let myself be seen. Perhaps if she looked as good as she smelled I would give her that privilege.

A slight scratch of a foot sliding on stone. I leaned forward to get a better look.

Moonlight from gaps in the ceiling illuminated the scene as

she stepped through the gap. She came in sideways, slowly and carefully, carrying a sword. An odd-looking blade, pale. She held it like she knew what she was doing, but her faith in its ability to protect her was misplaced. The tips of my claws, wanting to come out, caused the inside of my skin to itch. She had one sword, but I had ten claws.

She scanned the area, stopped to listen, then moved forward again—stealthily, like a dancer—hiding in the nearest shadow before I caught a glimpse of her face. The draft brought another whiff of her scent. She paused and I knew she was peering into the gloom, trying to find me. I liked the way she moved, balanced and light, neither tiptoeing nor stiff. Nice body. Come to me, mouse, don't be scared.

She took a step forward and I saw her in profile. Exotic, strong features. Not pretty, but I liked what I saw.

I drew my fingers through the dirt, scraping the floor a little.

She pivoted on one foot, turning her sword. Fast. Her head snapped toward me. Dark eyes stared straight at me. I detected no fear. Instead, it was a look of challenge. So not a mouse after all, but something more. This could be interesting. I'd let her dance in the dirt a bit more. She was fun to watch.

She crouched with her hand out. What the hell was she doing...?

"Here, kitty, kitty, kitty."

Oh my God. She was an imbecile, and I was going to kill Jim.

She blinked and stared at me. She'd seen my eyes glow.

I let go, shifting in the dark into my true form. If you want a kitty, little girl, I'll give you one you'll never forget.

I stepped into the moonlight. She froze.

That's right. No sudden moves. I padded toward her slowly and circled her, allowing her take it all in. Do you like the kitty now? I could smell her surprise and fear. Our gazes met. Her eyes went wide, and then she fell on her ass.

Heh. A bow would have been sufficient.

I retreated into the shadows of the corner. I wasn't sure what effect a laughing lion would have on her, and I didn't want her to faint. I reverted to human form and changed into sweats and a tee. Any other time, I might have walked out to her as is, but this was a business meeting. Best to keep it that way.

I gave her a few seconds to recover. She was dusting off her jeans.

"Kitty, kitty?"

She jumped a bit. Smart girl. Most shapeshifters can't switch back and forth like that. I'm not most shapeshifters. I'm the Beast Lord.

"Yeah," she managed weakly. "You caught me unprepared. Next time I'll bring cream and catnip toys."

Toys wouldn't be necessary. "There may not be a next time."

I stepped out and she turned toward me. She seemed almost relieved that I wasn't naked. Most women had the opposite reaction. Her loss.

I hit her with my hard stare. She met my gaze and didn't look away or cringe. Points for her. She was tall for a woman, maybe two or three inches shorter than me. Young, maybe early- or mid-twenties. She looked strong and lithe, like an athlete or martial artist.

"What kind of woman greets the Beast Lord with 'here, kitty kitty'?"

"One of a kind."

She continued to hold my stare. She might not have been as funny as she thought she was, but she wasn't a coward. Good. I could work with brave.

I took a step toward her. "I'm the Lord of the Free People."

FERNANDO'S
(Magic Bites)

I SAT AT A TABLE AT FERNANDO'S. IT WASN'T MY FAVORITE PLACE—
too posh, too public—but Myong liked it. The service was good,
the food was okay, but people didn't really come to Fernando's
to eat. They came to be seen. Most of them were self-important
people indulging themselves. It wasn't my crowd and I didn't
care to be seen by them.

Myong glanced up from her menu. She, on other hand, fit
into Fernando's quite well. She was beautiful and she had that
cultured elegance that went along with wealth and privilege.
Any of the men here would've loved to have her on their arm. It
was almost as if she were one of the rewards of power—a
gorgeous woman suitable for a successful man—and she did
nothing to break that impression. And now I was that guy with
her. I was in a restaurant I didn't like, among people I couldn't
stand, and I was bored.

I surveyed the patrons. Men and women, sitting around
identical tables, murmuring in quiet voices, drinking their wine.
A woman walked between the tables, led by a waiter. She wore a
champagne-colored gown, and something about the way she
moved, perfectly balanced, caught my eye. Most people would
be focusing on the waiter, but she seemed aware of her
surroundings, not anxious but ready, cataloging the possible
dangers and summing people up.

The waiter turned. The woman turned after her, and I saw
her face.

Kate.

Kate Daniels. Here, in Fernando's. I put down my menu.

Where in that really revealing dress was she hiding her sword? Did she have it strapped to her thigh?

Kate kept gliding in her heels. She looked stunning. Her hair was down, framing her face and falling past her shoulders and down her back. The dress fit her well, almost as if had been tailor-made to flatter her lean, strong frame, displaying all the things jeans and those ugly sweatshirts usually concealed. She looked…well, feminine. Long legs. Supple. Bare shoulders. The dress softened her, but she had definition to her arms. Don't see that often in a human woman.

In the short time I had known her, she had struck me as many things—brave, competent, smart-ass—but tonight she looked beautiful. It made me regret that she had declined my earlier offer of joining me in the tank.

The waiter led her to a table where a man sat alone. She was on a date. And the poor fool wasn't even armed. He didn't stand a chance.

Kate circled the table, giving me a lovely view of her back-side. Mm. She stood by a chair that would let her see the door. Ha. I wondered for a moment if she would flip it over and sit cowboy style, with the back of the chair protecting her stomach.

"Is something funny?" Myong asked.

"No."

Kate's date, a handsome man in an expensive dark suit, stared at her, his mouth hanging slightly open. You and me both, brother.

The waiter held the chair for her. Her date didn't even rise. Come on, fancy lad, stand up, say something charming, hold her chair for her. Did they not teach etiquette at Little Lords Academy?

Kate sat. The fancy lad kept staring.

Gods, man, act like you've been out with a lady before.

He finally recovered and said something. She said something back. He smiled. They managed to engage in some small talk.

I glanced across the table at my own date. Myong looked lovely as always, in her perfect little black dress. She caught me looking, and as usual, she looked down demurely. *Yes, yes, I get it, you're not offering me a challenge.* I didn't need a show of submission every time I looked at her. This Beauty and the Beast routine was getting stale.

Where Kate radiated strength and a capacity for violence, Myong's beauty was far more fragile, like an exquisite crystal bird. The contrast was striking. I glanced at Kate again. If I walked over to their table and started trouble, Myong would, despite being a shapeshifter, seek safety rather than risk injury, possibly under the table, clutching a fork as a weapon. She had once confided that she found violence—how had she put it?—"distasteful." I was very frequently distasteful.

Still, she was intelligent and cultured, and I wanted her take on them.

"Glance casually at the couple two tables down and give me your impression of them both, please."

Myong looked surprised but did as asked. She studied them carefully, and after a moment, she spoke softly. "His haircut is in fashion and expensive. The suit is custom made, and the tailoring is impeccable. His shoes are Italian leather. His hands are elegant and well taken care of. I don't think he's a fighter. He has no calluses or scars and his nails are manicured. He seems at ease here, an important man. The waiter seems to know him, so he must be a regular. She is not. The dress is suitable, but seldom worn. The heels are the appropriate height and coordinate well with the dress, but she doesn't like wearing them. If she has to run or fight, she will take them off." Myong paused and allowed herself a small, slightly superior smile. "If something untoward occurs, she might use them as weapons."

A waiter came by our table to refill Myong's water. He took care to stand as far away from me as possible and looked down. Once again, somebody had recognized me, and the appropriate instructions had been issued to the staff. Don't provoke the psychopath in charge of the shapeshifters or he might slaughter us all. The violent animal can't control himself. Ugh.

"Who's that man two tables down?" I asked.

"Dr. Maximillian Crest," the waiter said.

"Medical doctor?"

"I believe he's a plastic surgeon."

The waiter fled, no doubt grateful to escape unharmed.

Crest, Kate's date, was meanwhile droning on, while Kate herself seemed to be only half listening. I couldn't hear him clearly, but I could guess at the gist of it.

"Blah blah blah, I'm handsome, I make a lot of money, this suit is expensive, and my shoes are made of the finest Corinthian leather hand stitched by virgins under the moonlight. Of course, I could have gone into pediatrics, but for someone of my amazing skill, plastic surgery was really the only option. Beauty is so important, don't you think? Oh, Kate, you are nearly as attractive as I, why then should we not be beautiful together?"

The way he looked at her bugged me. As if he was studying her face, searching for tiny flaws that he could correct. Kate could do better.

I pressed Myong further. "What is your impression of them as a couple?"

Without a moment of hesitation, she said, "He could do better."

"Really?" I allowed a slight edge to creep into my voice.

She seemed to shrink into herself and I could tell she regretted the remark. "My lord," she began.

Every time I gave my chain a little slack, she cringed. This was just not working out.

"It's fine. Don't worry about it."

It wasn't Myong's fault that she found him appealing. He was handsome and he was probably a decent human being. I had no reason to dislike him this much, except that he was at the table with Kate. I had offered her a dip in my tank. And she declined so she could go and dress up like that for him.

Crest was wearing a custom-made suit and expensive shoes, while I, on the other hand, was dressed in faded jeans and a comfortable tee. The interesting thing was that Kate looked as out of place as I did, despite her fancy dress and shoes. Hmm. I wondered what would happen if I walked over there and asked her to blow this joint and grab a burger with me. She'd probably laugh. But then again, she seemed to like the spotlight. Maybe she was enjoying being the center of attention at Fernando's. There were enough men looking at her. Her clothes were crap, and from what Jim said, money was tight for her. This must've been her rare opportunity to shine and she'd pounced on it.

Crest finally caught me staring and said something to her. Kate turned. Her eyes widened. *Surprised to see me?*

Her gaze lingered over Myong and slid back to me. I grinned. *Yeah, my date is almost as pretty as yours, baby.*

Kate motioned to the waiter while pretty boy looked at me. He was actually trying to stare me down. I hid a smile. *Dear Doctor, you don't want any of this. Trust me.*

He kept looking. I returned the stare. I was kind of curious if he would have the nerve to come over and do something about it. Then again, who knows, maybe he just was wondering if he could fix my nose. Believe me, Doc, you don't wanna see my other face. I thought about giving him just a quick peek. Just a hint of a fang.

A waiter approached our table, carrying a silver tray with a bowl on it. Now what?

The waiter deposited the bowl in front of me. Milk. Ha!

"Compliments of the lady at that table, sir."

Oh, this was too good. I locked eyes with Kate and picked up the bowl. While she was looking, I raised the dish and drained it. *Salute! Your move, baby.*

She smiled.

Crest was glaring now. He tossed his napkin on the table. Uh-oh. I wondered if I was supposed to faint or flee.

He shifted his gaze and let it linger over Myong. It was meant to provoke me, but instead he just looked at her, caught off guard, as if he'd just realized for the first time that she was there and she was gorgeous. He was wondering what she would look like out of her tight black dress. Your guess is as good as mine, pal. Every time I tried to touch her, she made this face, as if she was going to bravely endure. She didn't have to worry. I would never put my "big rough hands" all over her unless I thought she wanted it. She would consent, but she didn't want me, and that killed it for me.

I realized I didn't really give a damn that another male was openly staring at my date. What did that say about Myong and me, exactly? That our relationship would never go anywhere.

Kate had that look in her eyes that said she was contemplating punching me in the face. Settle down, buttercup. I'm not going to embarrass Dr. Dreamboat in front of you and ruin your chances of entering the upper echelons of society.

I gave Crest a little wink, just to screw with him.

He started and then said something to Kate. She glanced at me, almost with regret, or maybe I was reading too much into it. They rose. Again, didn't hold the chair for her. Seriously?

They walked out. And just when we were starting to get along.

Where the hell were they going? He was probably going to try to impress her with the opera or something. I looked back at Myong. She smiled. Very dutiful.

Kate was leaving with Crest. Possibly she'd spend the night with him. And I was going home alone. I'd drop Myong off and try to salvage what was left of my evening.

SOUP
(Magic Burns)

When I broke through Kate's front door, the first things I smelled were blood and poison. Then smoke and something else, salty, bitter. Like a fish tank. What the hell had happened here?

The little girl was hysterical, crying that Kate was dying. She was almost right. I'd expected it to be bad, but the sight of her stopped me cold. Kate was lying on her stomach in her bathroom, her pale skin in stark contrast to the dark blood that seemed to be everywhere. Her back had been ripped open by something with savage strength. In that moment, I realized I could lose her. I'd seen humans die from less.

The Keep was out of the question. Too far. That's why I'd ordered Doolittle to the Southeast Office before I went to rescue the idiot.

I scooped her up off the floor, told the girl to follow me, and ran downstairs. Kate's skin was on fire. I loaded her into the front seat of the Jeep, stuffed the kid in the back, and drove out of there with one hand on Kate's wrist. Her heartbeat was fading and I had this dumb idea that if I let go of her, she would die. I had to get her to Doolittle.

I burst into the office with Kate in my arms, roaring for Doolittle. There was little need, he was standing by. I lowered her gently onto a waiting gurney and fixed him with a stare.

"Can you save her?"

He took in her condition with a glance. "My lord, her wounds are extensive and her kind are—"

I cut him off. "Try."

He rushed off with her and all I could do was stand there and watch her go.

I found my way to the study, pulled a battered copy of White's *The Once and Future King* off the shelf and ordered a beer to be brought to me. Ten pages in, I knew it was useless. I closed my eyes, leaned back, and waited for the call.

Sometime later the phone rang and Doolittle informed me that she seemed to be stabilizing. He had purged her system of the poison, and her fever was coming down.

Somebody once said it's better to be lucky than good. He or she must have had Kate in mind. With the flare so strong, the good doctor's already considerable medmage powers had been augmented enough to heal the slashes on her back and neutralize the poison coursing through her body. I don't know why, but when he told me she would, in all likelihood, live, I let out a breath I hadn't known I was holding. I should have known she was too stubborn or too stupid to die.

The real question was why had I been so worried? Why did I care so much if this idiot girl lived or died? She wasn't Pack—not quite human, but not one of us either. Whenever she blundered into my life waving that toothpick of hers around, I knew there would be trouble, the kind that usually ended with one or both of us badly wounded. She was arrogant, impulsive, and failed to recognize my authority or respect my position. She challenged me in front of my people. If anyone else ever...

But she was funny, sometimes, and never boring. God, it would almost be worth it to see her face when she realized I had saved her ass again.

Actually it was quite a nice ass, come to think of it. In fact, my memory of the ass and its owner seemed to be remarkably clear. I got up. That way lay dragons.

What I needed was a shower and some shut-eye. I'd be damned if she saw me looking tired or disheveled. When she finally did wake up, feeling like half a mile of bad road, I wanted to stroll in looking fresh and clean, as if I hadn't a care in the world.

· · ·

I NEEDN'T HAVE WORRIED. ALMOST A DAY PASSED BEFORE Doolittle called to tell me his patient seemed to be coming around.

"How will she feel?"

"She'll be in considerable pain and probably—"

"Hungry," I guessed.

"Yes, I should think so. Accelerated healing burns the body's resources. I do believe she will be ravenous."

I smiled. "Doctor, do you think she might enjoy some nice hot chicken soup?"

There was a tiny pause before Doolittle answered. "My lord, I think she would like that very much."

Oh yes, she would sit in bed and eat the soup I had gotten for her like a good little girl. The best thing would be watching her gulp it down, clueless as usual to the consequences of her actions.

As I strode into the room, with one of the cooks behind me carrying the soup on a tray, I caught the tail end of a conversation.

"How did I get here?"

"His Majesty carried you."

"Is he burned to a crisp or sliced in half this time?"

Her concern was touching. "Neither," I answered.

Her eyes grew wide. I can walk quietly if I wish to; I'm a cat, after all. I gestured for the cook to put the soup down. Doolittle bowed and both he and the cook left the room.

I took a moment to look Kate over. I hadn't seen her since bringing her in. Her appearance had improved, but not much. Her face was bloodless. Dark circles puffed under her eyes, and the skin stretched tight over her face. She looked like a ghost of herself. Almost frail.

I wasn't used to seeing her like this and it scared me a little bit.

"You look like shit." Honesty is important in any relationship.

She cleared her throat. "Thanks, I try."

Frail and weak, but still Kate.

I picked up a bowl of soup and thought about what it would mean, here, in this place, if I offered it to her and she accepted. She might not know what it meant, but I would. This was it. Nothing ventured...

I held the bowl out to her so she could smell it. Before I could warn her, she grasped it with both hands and burned herself.

"Idiot." I set the soup in front of her with a spoon.

"Thanks."

She actually thanked me. This was going well. I had half expected her to throw the soup at me.

Kate grabbed the spoon and went at it. That's right, eat it.

"Did you get the surveys? They were..."

"On the dresser. Shut up and eat your soup."

I pulled up Doolittle's chair and watched her while she ate. This was nice, we were together, and so far we hadn't tried to kill each other. If I could just keep her quiet... Maybe if I kept feeding her?

"So that's the secret."

She looked slightly shocked. No witty comeback. Did I scare her? Nah, not the ass-kicker.

"You okay? Gone a bit pale there."

"Secret to what?"

"Secret to shutting you up." I smiled. "All I have to do is beat you till you're half dead, then give you chicken soup, and I get blessed silence."

She made a face and went back to the soup.

"What did you think I meant?"

"I don't know. The ways of the Beast Lord are a mystery to a humble merc like me."

"You don't do humble." Smart-ass was more her speed.

Her bowl was empty, so I handed her another. This time our fingers brushed together. I held still and looked into her eyes. Our faces were very close. Her lips parted slightly. I leaned in toward her and... She grabbed the bowl and pulled away, and it was as if a spell was broken. Funny little mouse.

"Why did you save me?"

"I picked up a phone and there was a hysterical child on the other end, crying that you were dying and that the undead were coming. I thought it might be an interesting conclusion to a boring evening." That and I fucking hate the undead.

She looked puzzled. "How did Julie know to call here?"

"Hit redial from what I understand. Smart kid. You're going to tell me what you've blundered into." I wasn't asking. My people had crawled all over her place, sniffing every inch. There had been three assailants, none human. No bodies, but some evidence of a fire and dents and stains on the wall. The best they could figure out, she'd killed something in the kitchen, set the second attacker on fire, and rammed the third one into the wall. Derek had brought Julie to the Keep. He was working on her, but she was a street kid. She trusted no one and so far hadn't talked.

Dark eyes looked at me from Kate's pale face. "No."

Maybe she'd misunderstood. She'd been through a lot.

"No?" Give her a chance.

"No."

God fucking damn it, not this shit again. I crossed my arms and gave her my displeased look and meant it. She stared back. This was too much.

I leaned back. "You know what I like about you? You have no sense. You sit here in my house, you can barely pick up a spoon, and you're telling me 'no.' You'd pull on Death's whiskers if you could reach them." She didn't know it, but at this moment she was close. Damn close. "I'll ask one more time, what were you doing?"

"I see. I retrieve the surveys the Pack let slip through its fingers, and in return you bring me here against my will, interrogate me, and threaten me with bodily harm. I'm sure the Order will be amused to learn the Pack kidnapped its representative."

"Aha. Who is going to tell them?" Yes, the Pack greatly regrets being unable to save the Order's representative. Her injuries were extensive. It would be so easy. Windpipe and larynx crushed? Like someone strangled her? You don't say.

She looked at me as if to gauge my intent. Would I do it?

I stared back at her. My stare said "Try me." Not that I would ever hurt her, but she didn't know that.

"I guess I'll just have to kick your ass and break out of here."

Ha! Maybe if I had a seizure or a blood vessel burst in my brain.

She shot me her crazy smile.

I showed her the edge of my teeth. "In your dreams."

"We've never had our rematch. I might win."

Yeah, and on that day we'd get together with the People and put on a show in the old barn.

She grimaced. "Bathroom?"

I gestured toward it and she carefully got out of bed, like she wasn't sure if she could stand on her own. I almost felt sorry for her. Then I saw the rest of her and couldn't help smiling.

"What's so funny?" she demanded.

"Your panties have a bow."

She looked down. She wore a little tank top and blue panties with a silky bow. Her face went white, then red. I stifled a laugh.

"What's wrong with bows?"

"Nothing. I just expected barbed wire or something with chains."

She stuck her nose in the air. "I'm secure enough in myself to wear panties with bows on them. Besides, they're comfy and soft."

You don't say. "I bet."

Big eyes again. She hesitated. "I don't suppose you'd mind giving me a bit of privacy for the trip."

And miss the panty parade? "Not a chance."

She made a valiant effort to get out of bed, but her legs betrayed her. I was barely able to catch her before she hit the floor. I held her tightly for a moment, enjoying the closeness. She smelled like Kate. I could get used to her scent.

"Need some help, ass-kicker?"

"I'm fine, thanks." She tensed, and I held her for a moment longer before releasing her. She carefully made her way to the closest door.

"That's the closet," I pointed out helpfully.

She looked like she was going to cry and staggered into the bathroom, leaving me to lean back and plot my next move.

MIDNIGHT GAMES
(Magic Strikes)

NEARLY HALF A DOZEN OF MY BEST PEOPLE HAD GONE ROGUE, among them my Chief of Security, our Head of Medicine, a young wolf, and the alpha male of Clan Bouda. They had broken my first law. They had chosen to participate in the Midnight Games and had refused direct orders to appear before me and explain their actions.

I had never before questioned Jim's loyalty; he was Alpha of Clan Cat and, for all intents and purposes, my Second. Doolittle despised Pack politics and had saved my life more often than I liked to think about. Derek had become a member of the Pack after his father had gone loup and slaughtered his mother and sisters. When that happens, and it happens more often than humans think, SOP used to be to kill male survivors, especially adolescents, as they were believed to have a genetic predisposition to going loup. Jim had been in favor of putting Derek down. I had overruled him, which I rarely do. The kid had been through a lot and I'd decided he deserved a chance. Had I made a mistake? That Raphael was involved in this surprised me not at all. If Bea's little peacock thought I wouldn't mess up his pretty face, he was as dumb as those girls who followed him around like dogs in heat.

What could possibly cause a cat, a wolf, a hyena, and a middle-aged medmage honey badger to risk my wrath? I couldn't figure out the what or the why, but I had a damn good idea of the who. Kate Daniels, professional fuckup. Yeah, she was employed by the Order, humans who happened to despise my kind, and did jobs for the Guild, but I swear her mission in life was to make mine miserable. She defied me publicly, challenged me privately, and God help me, she bounced around inside my head like a bull in a china shop.

As soon as I had gotten wind that something was amiss, I had called her. In her usual charming and diplomatic way, she had both denied any and all knowledge of what was going on as well as politely declined to assist me in any way. Of course, she was in this up to that nice ass of hers. Later, as I started to put the pieces together, she had called to tell me that she and Jim were running off together and even offered me an erotic dinner if I could find them in three days. Kate short-circuits my brain. In my head we always have these clear coherent exchanges, but once we meet, what comes out is "Kate, do what I say or I'll kill you." Her default reply is "Fuck you!" and we go downhill from there.

Even after I shook the idea of naked Kate out of my head, the big picture still made no sense. Jim and Kate had worked together on odd jobs for the Guild, but there had never been a hint of anything more than a friendship built on mutual respect.

I knew for a fact that Jim liked that half-blind vegetarian tiger. Who the hell ever heard of such a thing? To top it off, the cat kept trying to kill herself by driving too fast.

Jim had a high opinion of Kate's abilities, which was a rare thing. Kate was skilled with that sword of hers, almost as good as she thought she was. I kept trying to puzzle it out: even if they had decided to run away together, how did the Games figure into it? I knew Kate would fight for the fun of it or the money. Did they need the money for their new life together? How had they gotten the others involved? Derek worked for Jim and almost worshiped Kate. If they had used him... That I could not forgive.

I also knew that Raphael's mate was Kate's best friend. He would do anything for her or just to piss me off. Perhaps he thought his mommy could intervene on his behalf if he got caught. I almost hoped Bea would interfere and get tangled up in it. After all, she's been a thorn in my paw for as long as I can remember. It would feel good to remove it. Since Mahon wasn't mixed up in this nonsense, I could give him that honor. I knew he would enjoy it and faithfulness should not go unrewarded. None of this, of course, explained Doolittle's involvement. Had they forced him to help? Possibly, but he's a tough old bastard and you don't cross a badger without a good reason.

I had to know, so I tracked Kate to one of Jim's safe houses. She was alone but I could smell the others; they had been there recently. Derek was hurt, I could sense it. That had driven me over the edge, and I had leaped at her without looking. Right into a loup cage.

When I had stopped roaring, Kate explained it all. I now knew about the Wolf Diamond and the Rakshasas. I understood why Kate had felt compelled to do these things. It made sense; she was trying to help her friends and the Pack. What I could not condone or comprehend was the how. Some people go about things in a roundabout way. Kate blows things up and then tries to glue the pieces together with spit. If she had only come to me in the beginning, but now it might be too late.

As I sat at the bottom of the loup cage, waiting for the skin on my palms to heal enough to try the silver bars again, I slowed my breathing and went over my options. None were great. I could wait for them to let me out of this cage or for someone else to find me. No, that was unacceptable. I was the Beast Lord. I wouldn't be crated and let out like a puppy. I could break out of this, but it would hurt, a lot, and in that rage I would slaughter not only Kate and her cohorts, but also anyone who tried to stop me. As angry as I was, I had to admit I didn't want to do that either.

By now they would already be in the Arena. Short of slaughtering the entire Red Guard, I couldn't get in there to stop them before the entire audience of sick fucks saw members of the Pack take part in the Games. After that, too many people would know, and I couldn't let that pass. If they survived, I would have to kill them. By myself in front of the rest of the Pack.

Kate had finished her spiel and left. I forced myself to relax and try to find a way out of this mess. I had assumed I was alone with my thoughts when I heard something move down the hallway. The smell was familiar, but I couldn't place it. Definitely not Kate, but…

Julie. Her kitten. All I had to do was to convince her to let me out.

I closed my eyes and listened to her sneaking through the house. Close by, almost close enough. Here, kitty kitty.

I CLOSED MY EYES AND CONCENTRATED ON THE SOUND OF THE footsteps approaching my cage. They belonged to Julie. She showed potential, moving well for a human child, quiet and careful despite the dim and unfamiliar surroundings. Kate would have stormed into the dark, stabbing at shadows. I wondered briefly where, or from whom, Julie had learned to sneak. She had not survived on the streets by being slow or stupid. Derek seemed fond of her and it was obvious Julie was smitten with him. To her, he was older—but not too old—and good-looking.

Damaged Derek, lying somewhere now with his good-looking young face forever ruined. Would she even look at him the same way?

A fresh wave of rage and grief almost overcame me, and I had to fight the urge to roar in frustration. *No, hold it together.* There would be a time for fur and fury, for the rending of flesh and the taste of blood on the tongue. Not now. *Take a deep breath, keep it together. Don't scare the kitten. Convince her to let you go.*

Come closer, Julie, that's it. You're almost here.

When she was near enough that I could hear her breathing, I called out to her in my best not-crazy voice, "Okay, Kate, you win. I couldn't break out. Let me go and I'll give you that hundred bucks I owe you." Kids like money, right?

Julie walked into the room and sat on the floor. A tiny thing, skin and bones, narrow face, pale hair.

"Nice try. You know I'm not her, and you should know she's gone now where you can't get her."

Smart girl. "Look, kid, I don't want to get anybody. Just let me out of here, please."

"Julie. My name is Julie. Why?"

"Why what, Julie?"

"Why should I let you out?"

"Because I asked you nicely, and it would be better for you and your"—psychotic guardian, terrible role model, bad influence—"Kate, if you release me."

"Why do you do that?"

Okay, I'd play along, but my patience was growing thin. "Do what, exactly?"

"Bully people. Threaten them in that calm but scary voice. They're all afraid of you."

Ridiculous. "I don't threaten people. I'm nice. I don't yell or scream." Keep going, though, and you'll see how terrifying I can be.

"Bullshit. They're all scared of you. Jim, Derek, even though he looks up to you. Kate, too, and she's not afraid of anything."

That was interesting. "First, watch your mouth, child. Second, what makes you think Kate is scared of me?"

"Screw you. I'm not a child and you aren't the boss of me. She said you broke into her house and stole things."

I crossed my arms on my chest. The last thing I wanted to do was to explain mating rituals to a human girl. "I'm the Beast Lord, not a thief or burglar."

"You took a pie. Why would you do that? Don't you have whatever, servants, who cook for you? Kate doesn't have a lot of money—why would you steal her food?"

"That is adult business; I won't explain myself to a child."

"It was an asshole thing to do."

I choked back a snarl. "I'm not going to warn you again. Don't speak to me like that again—"

"Or what?"

She had me there. As pissed off as I was, there were lines I wouldn't cross. I wouldn't harm a child. Ever.

I had to take a deep breath and step away from the ledge. Persuade her. Be reasonable. I could do reasonable.

"Look, Julie, I'm trying to be a nice guy. I've asked you nicely to release me. I could break out of here, but you wouldn't like that, I promise you. That would be scary and loud, and nobody wants that sort of thing. This is the last time I'm going to ask. Please free me before I become angry and do something we both regret."

"You're doing it right now. I'm not stupid. I know you're

mad and I know if I let you out, you'll hurt me and try to make me tell you where Kate is."

"No. I don't hurt little human kittens. Never have and never will. I give you my word."

She looked at me, thinking about it.

I leaned forward. "I know where Kate is and why, but I don't know why she left me in this cage. I wouldn't hurt her, and she knows that."

I broke into her place, I kissed her, and I've indulged her beyond what any of my people could get away with. Any sane woman at this point would know where we stood. I would never harm Kate. I might roar and threaten, and I might even pounce when occasion called for it, but she knew damn well that no violence would follow.

But then again, we were talking about Kate. Nothing was sane about Kate. That's why I was sitting in a loup cage, trying to reassure a frightened child that I wouldn't rip her to pieces.

Julie drew her knees to her chest. The kid looked like she never ate. A stiff wind might knock her over. "Kate thinks she has to save everybody. Duh."

"Who is she saving by keeping me in here, Julie?"

"Her friends, and you from having to hurt them. She knows you'll feel bad if you do."

"What's that supposed to mean?"

She paused for a moment and then continued slowly, "She knows you're pissed and you'll do your Lion King thing, punishing them for…" She paused, considering her words. "Dis-obeying you. You'll regret it when you calm down, but then it will be too late. Dead is dead."

"Why would she think that I would regret it?" I was actually curious. Also what the hell was my "Lion King thing"?

"'Cause she likes you and believes you're a good guy."

"She said that?" A good guy, huh.

"No, but I can tell. The way she looks when she talks about you."

Getting more interesting by the second. "Looks like what?"

"She looks the way my mom used to when she talked about my dad. And they're dead now."

"I know. I'm sorry."

"Everybody always says that, but it doesn't mean anything. It's like saying hello or something."

"It means something," I told her. "My parents are dead, too, and I was about your age when I lost them."

Julie looked like she was about to cry and waved her arms. "Whatever. Look, I'm not stupid. I know things! Adult things."

"Like what?"

"Like sex. I know about sex."

I just stared at her. I wasn't opening that can of worms.

"The point is, she likes you. She *likes you* likes you. She was going to kill Derek for you if he went loup so you wouldn't have to do it."

Now it was starting to make sense. So that was what all this was about. Derek was Jim's responsibility, and both Jim and Derek had fucked up royally. Now Kate was caught up in this mess. In her mind she was as accountable for the boy as we were. Derek had come to her for help, and she had been unable to refuse. Unfortunately, it had all gone to hell, as things tend to in our world, and the kid had gotten hurt bad. Now she blamed herself, and the only thing she could do was to go all in and hope for the best. She had taken it all on herself, as an alpha would do. I had to give her credit for trying to see this thing through to the end, but it should have been me. It was my job to know what was going on, to save, to protect, and to kill when there was no other way, and I'd dropped the ball.

I couldn't undo the damage, but I could step up and take charge. I could make sure that while there was breath in my body, not another of my people would be harmed. Whether or not she knew it, Kate was mine now and I would save her or die trying. That is what I do, I'm the Beast Lord. I stood and locked eyes with the girl.

"Julie, if you release me, I swear that I will not harm you, Kate, or any of my people."

"Will you help them in the Games?"

"Yes, I will."

"Even Derek?"

"What?" What could I do for him that Doolittle could not?

"He's with them, fighting the creatures who hurt him. He's so brave."

Damn idiot. "Yes, but foolish as well." *I wonder if she knows the whole story?*

Julie grimaced. "Yeah, I know. It's about the girl. I'll take care of her later, but I need you to promise about the others."

"Julie, I give you my word, I will do everything in my power to help our friends and punish our enemies."

She let out a breath she had been holding and smiled finally.

"Okay, deal."

HOT TUB
(Magic Strikes)

MY BACK HURT LIKE HELL. I'D FREED MYSELF FROM KATE'S CAGE and followed her to the Games. As usual, she'd made a complete fucking mess of things, and I was the one who was going to clean it up.

I had to admit I was impressed. She had somehow convinced some of my best people to break my first law. Even Doolittle had fallen for it. So it was kill everyone involved, or join them in the pit and try to keep them alive. Really, it was no choice at all. Knowing all this did not make the slowly closing holes in my back feel any better.

Our first fight had been easy: snake woman, swordsman, and werebison. Dali had cursed, Kate had head-butted her opponent unconscious, and the bison, big and dumb, had tripped over my foot and broken his neck. The second fight hadn't gone as well. Dali had outdone herself. The tiger girl had taken out an ancient vamp. I'm sure later, in private, Jim would express his admiration. I tore apart a troll, then had to save Kate from a golem she'd been taking her time with.

It was a silver golem.

She was bleeding from a wound in her side and looked like she needed some help. When I grabbed him from behind, he filled me with silver spikes, like I was a big gray pincushion. While I held him, she stuck him in the eye with her sword. It was a pretty good thrust.

She hadn't exactly thanked me, but she had cut the silver out of me. It hurt like hell and took a long time. Kate was pissed. And why did I jump on the golem, and she had it under control, and look at the holes in my back. When she was done, she ran off without saying much else. I waited until I knew she was out of earshot and then alternated between snarling and cursing for a good five minutes. I'd probably been hurt worse, but I couldn't remember when.

Now that I was feeling better, it was time to find her and have a little chat. There were things we needed to discuss. Important things.

I started looking for her in the team room. Jim and Dali were gone—their bunks stood empty. I could hear Andrea and Raphael's muffled voices in the other room.

Derek lay on his back in his bunk, his face hidden by an old paperback depicting a man with some serious tattoos. Doolittle sat in a chair, reading *Casino Royale*.

They both looked at me. Derek started to get up.

"Don't bother. What the hell are you reading?"

"Big Jake the Snake and the Viper Commando Squad."

What the hell…

"I tried to get him to read something decent," Doolittle said, "but he's got this trash instead."

"You're reading a novel about an effete British snob," Derek said, clearly trying to get a rise out of Doolittle.

I looked at him for a while. He needed to take his tone down a notch.

He ducked his head. "I apologize."

"It's a classic," Doolittle said.

I left them to it and stepped into the hallway, sorting through the mess of scents. Sweat, blood, more sweat… Kate. The smell was sweet. I inhaled it deeper, making sure I had a good hold on it. Time to go hunting.

The scent floated through the hallway. I followed it and it led me through the doors of the gym, flaring stronger, then getting muddled. She must've stretched here some time ago, but since then morons had walked over it, leaving their own imprints in the air. I crouched for a long second. Ahh. There it was.

The trail cut through the gym, down the hallway, to a door with a man in Red Guard getup by it. There was a small window in the door. I looked through it.

A hot tub. And long dark hair. *Found you.*

She might still be fuming about me getting hurt, so I went into the rec room, found a couple of beers, and snuck in with them.

"Peace offering." Umm, yummy beer, you know you want it.

Kate reached out and took the Corona from my hand. So far, so good.

I had to warn her out of courtesy before I slipped out of my towel and into the hot tub. I didn't want her to faint and drown. Of course, if she did go under, I would be honor bound to pull her out and revive her. That she appeared to not be wearing a top did enter my mind. I'd only peek a little. I was a gentleman, not a saint.

"I'm about to take the towel off and hop in," I said. "Fair warning."

"I've seen you naked."

"Don't want you to run away screaming or anything."

"You flatter yourself."

I took the towel off and got in. She remained conscious and upright. Too bad. I was all set for the rescue.

"How's your back?" she asked.

"It's fine," I lied. "Thanks."

"Don't mention it."

"Does your side hurt?" I knew it must, just as she knew the silver had burned like fire in my chest and back.

"No."

She would no more admit weakness than I would.

"Are you going to sack Jim?" she asked suddenly after taking a huge pull on her beer.

I gave the question some thought. Why did she care? Would she fight me on it?

"No," I answered finally. She was listening. I liked sitting close to her like this, without us brawling. For once she wasn't kicking me or waving her sword in my face. And if I kept talking, she would stay just like this, relaxed, in the hot tub. Topless under the water. "I concede that if I'd been paying attention, I would have nipped this in the bud. It should have never gotten to this point."

"How so?"

"Jim took over security eight months before the Red Stalker appeared. The upir was his first big test. He blew it. We all did. Then there was Bran. Bran stole the surveys three times, waltzed in and out of the Keep, attacked you while you were in our custody and took out a survey crew, Jim included. Jim considers it a personal failure."

The worst thing about Bran was that Kate seemed to like him. He'd had a wink-and-smile bullshit-your-way-out charm. It's easy to be like that when you don't have fifteen hundred shapeshifters in your care and your day isn't scheduled down to the minute. It isn't enough to always be ready to back up your authority with violence, you have to consider what kind of violence, how much violence is too much violence, when to use it, and when to exercise patience. Despite how I was sometimes viewed, I never wanted to be a tyrant, and making sure I didn't turn into one took up most of my time.

Bran was like a kid. The man had experienced three lifetimes of acting like spoiled a teenager, bedding pretty girls, getting into fights, and getting away with it consequence free. If he fucked up, he could run away back to his goddess and his fun camp, or whatever the hell he had there in the mist. Everything I did had consequences, and running away wasn't an option.

If Kate wanted someone like him, it would never work between us. Even if I wanted to be that guy, and there were rare moments when I did, I never could. It wasn't who I was.

I looked at her. She shrugged in the water, raising her shoulders above the water level. Definitely no top.

"The guy teleported. How the hell are you supposed to guard against someone who pops in and out of existence?"

I sank a little deeper into the warm water, the tension easing out of my shoulders.

"Had I known how hard Jim had taken it, I would have pointed that out to him. You remember when he tried to use you as bait?"

She scowled. "I remember wanting to punch him in the mouth."

"It was the first sign of trouble. His priorities had shifted to 'win at any cost.' I thought it odd at the time, but crazy shit kept happening and I let it slide. Then he became paranoid. All security chiefs are paranoid, but Jim took it further than most. He began to obsess about preventing future threats, and when Derek screwed up and got his face bashed in, it pushed Jim over the edge. He couldn't handle being responsible for Derek's death or for my having to kill the kid. He had to fix it at any cost. Basically, there was a problem and I missed it. And he sure as hell didn't bring it up."

I'd known Jim a long time and he was too proud to admit he was afraid of anything, but if the kid had turned loup, it would have broken him. One of us, probably me, would have had to put him down. I wondered if that had happened if Kate would've understood or been able to forgive me.

"I can't keep up with everyone all the time, and Jim's the one who never went nuts on me. It was his time, I guess. So to answer your question fully, there's no reason to demote him. He has a talent for his job and he's doing reasonably well considering what he's up against. If I have to sack him, I'll have to replace him with someone who has less experience and will screw up more. This is a lesson. Three months dragging giant rocks around will help him get the stress out of his system." What I didn't say, didn't need to, was that Jim was my best friend and I trusted him like a brother.

She listened while I explained all this and I realized how nice it was when we just talked. We sat quietly together, enjoying each other's company. Her face lost its edge. I understood the edge—she needed it. If you look like you're ready to fight, you can win most battles without throwing a single punch. But now, with her hair down and her features relaxed, she looked beautiful. I wondered if she knew. No, probably not. "So, you didn't want to see me get hurt?"

"I didn't want you to have to kill Derek," she said, her eyes still closed.

Wait, what? "And if he had gone loup?"

"I would've taken care of it."

She said it like an alpha—no bluster, just matter of fact.

"How exactly did you push Jim aside? He was the highest alpha. The duty was his."

More like horrible responsibility, one that was ours to carry. Would she really have done it? We all knew she cared a great deal about Derek, and it would have hurt her badly to have to kill him. It would've hurt me to kill him.

I decided she would've done it. Maybe she cared enough to want to spare me that pain. Of all the women I'd been with over the years, how many would have done that?

"I pulled rank," she continued. "I declared that since you accepted the Order's assistance, I outranked everybody."

"And they believed you?" It slowly dawned on me that they had obeyed her. Huh.

"Yep. I also glared menacingly for added effect."

She gave them her alpha stare. I tried not to laugh. It was kind of cute. I would've liked to have seen that.

When I was angry, my eyes glowed. I could also do it whenever I wanted, really. And when I stared at someone, they felt it and they wanted very badly for me to stare at someone else. Her hard stare was good, but mine was major league. It was a good tool.

She looked so comfortable leaning like that. I started moving toward her through the water.

"Unfortunately, I can't make my eyes glow the way you do," she said.

"Like this?" I asked, my mouth only a few inches from her ear, my arms on either side of her. She was so close, warm and wet.

Her eyes popped open and I could read the surprise and something else. Could it be an invitation?

"Don't make me break this bottle over your head," she said, her voice soft.

"You won't. You don't want to see me hurt."

I searched her face. Yes or no? Come on, Kate, give me

something to work with.

She moved toward me and I grabbed her. Finally. She wrapped her arms around me. I slid my hands over her body, feeling the strong, smooth muscle. She didn't lay back and wait for me take the lead. She pressed against me, strong, supple. It was exciting. She wanted me. This wasn't passive acceptance, this was active involvement.

I kissed her. I was already hard and this was fuel to the fire. God, I wanted her, more maybe than I'd ever wanted anything. But I had to be sure. You just never know. I didn't want her to regret it. I wanted her to want me.

"Only if you want me to—say no and I'll stop."

"No," she said softly.

Argh. Breathe out, take control, step back. Let her go. I pulled away slowly.

We stared at each other.

"Okay," I told her.

She put her hand on my chest. When she touched me, her fingers warm, something passed between us like a spark of static and my pulse spiked. I took her hand gently and brought it to my lips. *Easy boy, take it slow.*

She pulled her hand free and moved closer. Her lips played upon my throat. She was driving me crazy. I had to have her.

"What are you doing?" I growled, wondering if she was just teasing or if she wanted me too.

"Pulling on Death's whiskers," she breathed out softly.

She kissed me again. I had to let her take the lead. Don't push her, don't scare her off. If we were going further with this, she would have to make the next step.

Her hands moved over my body, chest, and shoulders, down to my biceps. I flexed a little and tried to remember to breathe. Oh, yeah, this was totally happening.

"Is that a yes or no?" I asked.

She slid against me and lightly nipped at my lower lip. *Oh yeah! It's a yes. It's definitely a yes.* "I'll take that as a yes."

I grabbed her and pulled her on top of me. Bare skin. She wasn't wearing *anything.* I kissed her again, my tongue probing her mouth. She put her arms around my neck. Her breasts pressed against my chest. Mmmm. I brushed her hair off her neck with one hand and kissed the delicate curve of her throat, cupped her tight little butt, and pulled her against my body. I was almost painfully aware that she was sitting astride my erection.

Finally—

From beyond the door, Derek's new voice, more of a growl, demanded, "Let me in."

No fucking way, not now. If they don't send him away I might just kill him myself.

My hand was still on Kate's breast, gently rubbing her nipple. I kissed her again. *Don't listen to the voices at the door, Kate.*

Somebody said something and Derek snarled back about being a member of the team. *Not for long if you barge in here.*

"Curran," Kate whispered. "Curran!"

No. I was naked, she was naked, she was sitting on me, we were doing this.

The door started to open. Don't you fucking do it. Don't you walk in here, or I will fucking strangle you. Turn around, keep walking. You don't need to talk to me right now.

Kate hit me with something on the back of the head and I dove under the water.

Five goddamn minutes. They wouldn't let me have five goddamn minutes to myself.

I counted to ten and emerged on the other side of the hot tub. Kate was sitting on her side, looking like nothing had happened. Derek was telling her something about a hand in a box. It was a dead hand. Why the hell did he have to bring it to me right this second? Was it going anywhere?

216

Kate closed her eyes. She looked exasperated.

"Give the hand to the Red Guard," I told him. "There's nothing for us to do about it until tomorrow."

He looked like he wanted to say something. I looked at him. Derek turned and left without another word. Smart kid.

I stared at her from across the hot tub. Where were we?

She stared back, looking defiant. Soft, sweet Kate was gone.

"You missed your chance. I'm not coming anywhere near you, so you might as well turn off your headlights," she said.

Baby, you don't have to come to me. I'll come to you.

I moved toward her.

She stayed completely still. "No."

I stopped. Damn it.

"You wanted me," I said. We both knew it.

"Yes, I did," she admitted.

See, now was that so hard?

She crossed her arms. It wasn't happening, not tonight anyway.

"What happened?" I deserved an explanation, at least.

"I remembered who I am and what you are."

Okay, well that was how it was.

"Who am I?" I demanded, though really the question was who did she think I was. "Enlighten me."

"You're the man who likes to play games and hates losing. And I'm the idiot who keeps forgetting that."

No, I'm the idiot sitting here with a raging hard-on.

"Turn around so I can get out, please."

No. I sat back and relaxed against the wall of the hot tub. She'd seen me naked—fair is fair. If she wanted to rush off in a huff, I could at least enjoy the view.

She glared at me.

Not happening.

Kate exhaled and stood up. She was perfect. Strong but feminine.

Oh, the things I could've done with that body. She had no idea. I realized I groaned and shut up.

"Fine," she said.

Yes, it could have been. It can still be fine, if you get back into the water.

She wrapped a towel around her bare body. It would be so easy to just grab it off her and pull her back into the tub. I could, but I wouldn't. She walked out with her dignity intact and her towel in place.

I needed very badly at that point to find someone and hurt them. I stayed in the hot tub until that urge and others died slowly.

We weren't finished yet, not even close. I could still smell her. I remembered what she felt like. What she tasted like. This wasn't a casual sex thing. This was a mating. I would have Kate as my mate. Whatever it took, no matter how long, she would be with me.

KATE'S ORIGIN
(Between Magic Strikes and Magic Bleeds)

I WAS SITTING IN MY OFFICE, THINKING MY LIFE WAS PRETTY good. The magic was down, and I had a hot cup of coffee and *Great Big Sea* on the old CD player. The last couple of weeks had been awful. Well, that was a bit of an understatement. Members of the Pack had broken my first law and joined Kate in the Midnight Games. Derek had gotten hurt, bad. Kate had almost died, and I have never been that scared, not since my family was murdered. I had felt that same sense of helplessness as I held her limp form. Still, we won, the kid recovered his health, if not his looks, and things had calmed down.

I even managed to put that fucking pervert in his place. Such a waste—instead of reveling in the power of his true form, he hid like a coward behind beautiful masks and played seduction games. Saiman was weak but very vain. I had stung his pride. He would probably retaliate in some way.

I toyed with the idea of telling Jim to get rid of him. It would be easy. Saiman had no friends or family. Who would miss him? Besides, Saiman dealt in knowledge and secrets, and I knew a jaguar who would love to spend some quality time with him and pry some information out of that pretty head.

I drank my coffee from my blue metal mug. When I was a kid, after my parents died, I'd lived in the woods for a while, and once I'd raided a holiday cabin. They had a set of blue metal plates and mugs, the camping dinnerware. I'd stolen it and their instant coffee and drank it by myself that night over my meager fire. That first cup of coffee had tasted like pure heaven. George, Mahon's daughter, had found the same set of dishes and given it to me for Christmas.

A familiar scent and a knock on the door told me my head of security had arrived.

Think of the devil…

"Come in."

Jim strode through the door, carrying a thick leather file. At least an inch thick. Great. This would take forever.

Jim checked the hallway and closed the door behind him. He was wearing his "we need to talk" face, which was quite different from his normal "I'm a badass, don't mess with me" face that Jim believed to be pleasantly neutral. He wasn't just physically imposing; he had the ability to radiate menace. I think most of the time he wasn't even aware of it. He would make a terrible kindergarten teacher, but he was perfect in his position as alpha of Clan Cat and my second-in-command. The rest of the clans didn't necessarily like him, but they respected his power and position.

"We need to talk," he announced without preamble.

And there went my pleasant mood. I braced myself. "How bad is it?" It sure as hell wouldn't be good.

He put an old Polaroid down in front of me. In it a young girl, maybe twelve or thirteen, with a swollen eye and a split lip, stared back at me defiantly. I would know those eyes anywhere.

"Kate," I said. It wasn't a question.

"Yes." Jim sat down in the chair. "The best we can figure, this was taken in Guatemala, over a decade ago. She won a bare-knuckle boxing tournament. The rest were boys, some as old as sixteen."

"Is that a big thing down there now?"

"Yeah. I guess it beats watching roosters tear each other apart."

And humans called us animals. "Why are you showing me this?"

He held up a finger. Apparently there was more. Jim opened the file in his hand, took out another picture, and put it down. Kate was older now, a gladius in her right hand and a bandage on her left shoulder.

"Rio," he announced, "two years later. She fought in and won a citywide sword tourney, sponsored by one of the big gangs. A way of scouting new talent, I suppose. Matches only ended when one of the fighters was crippled or killed. She disabled most of her opponents, but the last guy, twice her size and age, she sliced his throat open in thirty seconds. They called her 'pequena assassina' and still remember her."

The little killer. Kate would love that. So her childhood had been horrific. A lot of people had less-than-perfect childhoods. Why did he feel it was so important? There had to be more.

"I thought she was raised by Greg." Greg was a knight of the Order, a diviner, and an ally. He'd died not that long ago. That's when I'd met Kate. She'd come looking for his murderer.

Jim shook his head. "No, this was before that. But it segues nicely into the next bit."

He pointed at the first and then the second picture. "Look closely. Notice anything?"

It took me a few moments, but I found him, the same man in the crowd, staring at Kate with what might be described as fierce pride or approval on his cruel-looking face. He was big, dwarfing the men around him. Tall, powerful, well-muscled despite being in his late forties or early fifties. His graying hair hung limply down to his broad shoulders. His features, once perhaps handsome, had turned coarse, thickened by scar tissue and time. He looked like an old boxer who'd spent too many days exposed to the sun and wind. Still, he bore no resemblance to the young Kate in the photos.

Jim put another photo down. In this picture, Kate and the man sat in a bar, a bottle of something between them, too out of focus to read the label. Kate looked about fourteen.

"They traveled together," Jim said. "They never stayed anywhere for very long. Every once in a while they would show up, enter some sort of martial contest or take a hard job, win, kill, and leave. This was Cuba. They were spotted once more in Miami, then not seen again. At least not together."

"Do you know who he is?"

"I have a pretty good idea." He pulled a thin manila folder labeled "Voron" out of the leather file and opened it on the desk in front of me.

Inside was a picture of the same man, younger-looking, maybe by a decade or more, in some sort of combat fatigues. He held a black axe in one hand and a man's severed head by the hair in another. His face was demonic, twisted by elation, reveling in violence, like an ancient battle mask. He seemed to be roaring toward the sky. He resembled nothing more than a bloody god of war. Invincible and terrible to behold.

"Why is he dressed like a soldier but holding an axe?"

"Technically it's a tactical tomahawk. It was known to be his weapon of choice once he ran out of bullets. Our information leads us to believe that this picture was taken over fifty years ago. Magic was coming back, but it was still weak and guns were more reliable."

"A pleasant chap," I remarked.

"You have no idea. By all accounts he was a gifted commander but prone to berserker rages. In hand-to-hand combat, he would be overcome by bloodlust and tear into his enemies like an animal."

"Who's holding his chain?" I was pretty sure I already knew.

"Roland."

"The Builder of Towers and Lord of the People."

"Yep."

Fucking shit. Metal groaned in my hand. I put the crushed clump of blue down on my desk and shook the coffee off my hand. Jim said nothing, just waited.

"Now you're going to tell me why Kate was raised by this man and why I should give a damn." Why could nothing with Kate be simple? Why couldn't Jim ever just come by to tell me that he had bowled a perfect game or benched a personal best? Maybe finally asked that weird tiger girl out.

"I like Kate," Jim said. "I've known her for years and we've even saved each other's asses, more than a few times. Back then I didn't care much where she grew up or who she was related to, because it wasn't a safety issue for us. I only cared that she was good with a blade and did what she said she would. She talked a lot of shit, but she could mostly back it up."

Jim leaned back. "At present, everything is different. Personally, I admire her. You could do a lot worse, but it's my job to tell you what you don't want to hear. Now, I'm going to tell you a story and you are going to listen to me because I'm in charge of the Pack's security and I'm your friend."

Fuck you and fuck your story. "Proceed."

"This here is what you call an urban legend or modern-day fairy tale. It involves a very bad man, king of the vamps, and all manner of horrible undead shitheads. People like Ghastek and even this Voron, they flocked to him. He can keep them alive, young. He is old, real old, like he's in the Bible old. According to some, he made the first vampire. For most, he is a legend, like Merlin or Heracles. Real smart people, college-educated types, will tell you that he is a parable or an analogy. Same types will tell you that Cain and Able is about hunter-gatherer cultures being replaced by agriculture and the rise of cities. That Roland represents rulers and their laws imposing order on chaos and anarchy. That he is every fabled builder or city founder. That's all good and well I suppose, but the truth is he exists. We both know that. The rest is not as easy. There are a lot of stories about him, some true, some not. What we do know is that every one of his children have rebelled against him. Some rejected him, some of the less fortunate sought to usurp him. Gilgamesh, for example, left and founded Uruk. Abraham took him on and lost. Everything—"

I interrupted him. "Jim, where did you get this shit?"

"I did some checking. I've got my sources."

"You asked Dali, didn't you?"

He broke into a rare grin. "Yep, she's damn smart. Took her a while, but she dug most of this up."

"Does she know you like her?"

"We aren't talking about me. We are talking about you and your...honey bunny."

"In that case, professor, I'm terribly sorry for interrupting your fascinating lecture on bullshit. Please proceed."

He shrugged. "Thank you, I will. Now, before you interrupted me, I was explaining that Roland has had bad luck with his children. Very tragic. Now, fast-forward to about thirty years ago. The main man has a new consort. She's beautiful and everyone loves her. Especially Roland. He's smitten, and soon his lady is in a family way. At first Roland is overjoyed. It's been centuries since he spawned any little monsters, and he's feeling sentimental. Everybody is happy. Then, out of nowhere, he changes his mind and tries to kill his blushing bride and the child she's carrying. She flees with his warlord. It's like King Arthur, but Lancelot is a butcher and Guinevere is knocked up."

This story was just getting better and better.

Jim kept going. "The two of them take off to parts unknown. Like any man would be, Roland is put out and looks for them. He isn't any man though, and nowhere in the world is safe for them. He finds them and confronts her while Voron flees with the child. Roland kills his wife, but not before she takes out his eye. Grievously wounded and heartbroken, he leaves. Alone. Now Voron, being the sentimental type, raises this child to be as deadly a killer as he can make her. They travel, they train, and he hones her into a living weapon. One he will wield against his former master. He tells her how her father tried to murder her and killed her mother. At some point, he got careless and had to leave the girl with another man. The killers were close when he disappeared. His whereabouts are currently unknown."

"That's a great story, Jim, but what does it have to do with me?" I was daring him to say it.

"You know damn well what it has to do with you. There are more pictures, more testimonies from witnesses, more legends. It's all in there." He pushed the file across the desk, toward me. I kept my eyes locked on his until he looked down.

"I'm sorry," he said. "I didn't want to tell you all this and if you love her, I will stand by you. Both of you. But you have to know. He's going to come for her. He always does."

"Then we will fight him." No man would take what was mine from me.

"Yes, we will, but we might not win."

"Who else knows?"

"Me, you, Doolittle suspects, Mahon knows and likes it not at all. He sees her as a threat to the Pack. He's not wrong. He always hoped you would end up with one of his girls, George maybe." He smiled. "Keep it all in the family, I guess. Kills him a little that you chose Kate."

"He'll get over it." George was like my sister. Kate... I didn't want anyone else. Just Kate.

Jim nodded. "Look—you, Kate, I get it. I just wish it could have been somebody else. If Roland comes... We aren't ready for him yet. Even if we win, most of us won't make it. I hope she's worth it."

"Roland is coming anyway," I said. "Whether Kate is part of the equation or not. She made a third of a demon army kneel. She has power and she will be an asset." And I loved her.

"What if she leaves when her daddy shows up?"

I stared at him. "Kate? We're talking about the same woman, right? When other people are running away, she's heading into the fight."

"Roland's very strong," Jim said. "Look, I don't know that much about how their magic works, but from what Dali said, Kate took that sword to the gut because it was made out of her father's blood. She couldn't control it by just grabbing it. She had to dissolve it into her body. That tells you something."

It told me Kate had a long way to go before she could face her father. She would need help, and I would be that help.

"I'm going to see her in a week," I said. "She's making me dinner."

Jim sighed. "So you decided."

"I've decided."

"Okay." He chewed on that for a while. "Well, it'll make my life easier. I guess my people can stop chasing after you when you go to visit her apartment."

I simply looked at him.

Jim rose and walked to the door. "One thing. If I were Voron, I'd program her to hide who she is. The man wasn't a moron. He would've drilled it into her to hide. Does she trust you enough to tell you who she is? Because if there is no trust, you know this won't work."

"I guess we'll find out."

NAKED DINNER
(Between Magic Strikes and Magic Bleeds)

It took a moment to realize I was awake and that the phone ringing was not just in my dream. It was a good dream. Kate and I were moving to the bed after the naked dinner. The phone kept ringing. Okay, this better be good. Since tech was up, I figured it couldn't be anything too dire.

I rolled over, picked up the phone, and growled into the receiver. "What?"

"You up?" Jim asked.

"I'm talking to you."

"Doesn't mean you're up. Means you're awake, maybe."

"Jim, if you don't tell me what you want, I'll find you and shake it out of you."

"No time for games, grumpy. You got a brunch with Bea."

"You tell me this now?" Nothing good ever came from meeting with the alpha of the Bouda Clan. Being a werehyena, she seemed to take great delight in making my life difficult.

"I'm telling you now, like I told you before."

"I don't remember. Do I have to go?"

"You only remember what you want to remember, and yes, you do."

"Why and what does she want? I have plans for today."

"Because you said you would, and I wouldn't know why she wants to see you."

Bullshit. "Yes, you do. You've got your fingers in everybody's pies."

"Thanks, I think. Anyway, Bea is, as usual, playing things close to the chest, so your guess is as good as mine."

Usually Jim knew about things before they had a chance to happen. But Bea was a special case. She didn't like or trust cats. Really, the boudas didn't much like anybody.

"Whatever the hell it is, it better not involve bribing law enforcement or public orgies or requests for additional funds. It's like the Warren Zevon song: every time she wants to see me, it ends up being 'send lawyers, guns, and money.'"

"How is it you can remember old song lyrics, but I gotta remind you of significant shit all the time?"

"It gives you something to do and makes you feel important. How long and where?"

"One hour, Dillard house. I let you sleep in, but you won't have much time to do your hair."

"Shut up, Jim. You wanna lift weights and spar a little later?"

"Maybe, but do you really want to be tired and beat up for your big panty party?"

"At least I get to see panties. How are you doing in the romance department?"

He didn't say anything.

"You know, if you keep blowing Dali off, she's going to put some sort of Asian voodoo love spell on you."

Jim's tone changed abruptly. "My lord, a car will be ready in half an hour."

The disconnect signal beeped in my ear.

So Dali must be a sore subject, or maybe he just didn't like me knowing one of his secrets. Served him right. He was far too keen on my love life and needed one of his own. I knew he liked her. I could tell from the way he spoke to her, looked at her when he thought no one was watching, and most of all covered for her after the umpteenth expensive car crash. Any other cat, male or female, would have had their arms and legs broken the next time they disobeyed him. Jim didn't enjoy violence, though as alpha of Clan Cat, he was willing to use it as a tool. Pain is an excellent teacher. Besides, we heal fast. What took humans weeks, we could heal in days or even hours.

A quick shower, shave, and brushing of the fangs and I was ready and headed downstairs. Derek, my werewolf bodyguard and driver, was waiting behind the wheel of a Pack jeep.

"My lord," he intoned with a nod.

"Knock it off." He was a good kid but often went overboard with the formality.

"As you wish." Again the almost bow.

"Derek…," I began.

He grinned and held up his hands as if to ward off imaginary blows. "Okay, Curran. Can I ask why you're meeting with the boudas?"

He managed to put a little disdain into the word. Like most wolves, Derek considered the hyenas to be little more than dangerous degenerates. Emphasis on the dangerous. While their sexual appetites were legend, they were also ruthless and deadly fighters. Their numbers compared to other clans were small, but if you fought one bouda, you better be ready to fight them all. To the death—that's how they rolled.

"Are you worried that there'll be trouble?"

He smiled a little. "With them it's always trouble, but I was wondering if we're going to have to fight."

He was right to be uneasy. Jim had trained him to be cautious.

"Maybe, but don't do anything until I say."

"Of course, but if they start shit and there's more than four or five of them, including Ms. Bea, I might not be able to protect you."

Derek worked in my personal guard now and took his job seriously. It was good for him. It would teach him to be observant and to anticipate possible threats. "I appreciate the honesty, but as good as you are, Bea is better. If that shoe drops, you leave her to me and try to fight your way out and get help. It's unlikely, but just in case Bea's teeth and ambitions are bared, be prepared." He missed the reference and I sighed. Kids. "Derek, stick with me and you'll never go hungry again."

He didn't get that one either.

In less than twenty minutes we were pulling up to the long, winding blacktop drive leading to a large stone building at the top of a hill. It was one story and predated the Shift by several decades at least. It was family-style dining and, while not fancy, the food was good, they served meat, and you got a lot of it. That's five stars for shapeshifters.

Bea and her party, three females and her son, Raphael, were waiting outside. Nobody had sat or eaten before the king, and thus far they had offered no insults. So far, so good.

Bea gave me a big sweet smile. She would smile just like that before stabbing someone in the back with her claws. Raphael nodded at me. Bea ran the clan, but her son was the male alpha. We didn't exactly see eye to eye. Usually Raphael avoided meetings. Why was he here?

"Clan Bouda greets the Beast Lord and thanks him for joining us for a meal." Bea and her son inclined their heads briefly. The others held their heads down, eyes fixed on the ground.

Yeah, right. "Please, Bea, it's too early for such formality. Good to see you, Raphael. I didn't think you liked this place, not quite your style."

Bea's little prince favored fancier fare, with more flash and beautiful people making sure they were seen. The scion of Clan Bouda was five inches taller than me and fifty pounds lighter. Where I went for bulk and explosive power, he was lithe and quick, built for speed and deadly with a blade. If it got ugly, he would go through Derek in mere moments and I would then be hard-pressed to handle him and his mother. If there are enough hyenas, they can take down a lion. Well, maybe not *this* lion, but most others.

Raphael kept his face neutral. "Mother likes it and it does have a certain rustic charm."

"Indeed, Bea, it's such a lovely day, why don't we dine on the patio?" It would give me room to move if they were planning on starting anything.

Bea gave me another sweet smile. "An excellent suggestion. It's been reserved for us."

We went inside and were led through to the rear to a large covered porch. A long picnic-type table had already been set, complete with a red-and-white-checkered tablecloth. Two buffet tables sat a short distance away, one with large stainless-steel pans loaded with bacon, scrambled eggs, sausage, pancakes, and my favorite, French toast, the other with an assortment of sliced and chilled fruit. Maybe later, after I had a few passes at the meat.

I didn't know what they were up to, but they had laid out a great spread and I was never one to turn down a free meal. Of course, with Bea, nothing was free. They wanted something and they were very careful to feed me before they asked for it. Whatever it was, I wouldn't like it.

Everybody got plates and sat down to eat. That's one of the things that make us different from humans—when we sit down to eat, we eat. There isn't a lot of small talk or playful banter. We focus almost entirely on the food. From the outside, it probably seems strange, but we all take it for granted. It's actually considered rude to try to carry on a conversation with one of us while we're eating.

After everyone had consumed several large platefuls, it was time to get down to business.

"Thanks for the food, Bea. Now, what can I do for you and your son?"

"You're quite welcome, and what I would like is a favor, an

indulgence if you will, not just as a fellow alpha but as a mother."

Uh-oh. I turned to look at Raphael. What had the little prince stuck his dick into this time?

"You know, of course, of Andrea Nash, the beastkin knight."

Damn it all to hell. I knew that was going to bite me in the ass. No good deed goes unpunished. Nash was a knight in the Order of Merciful Aid, a group of pro-human zealots with whom we had, at best, an uneasy truce. They were not officially law enforcement, but they were well-trained and funded. They saw themselves as humanity's last great hope against monsters, against us. So far we had coexisted in a state of mutual distrust, but someday push would come to shove and they would come to the Keep with swords and burning torches.

As if that weren't enough, Andrea was also beastkin, the extremely rare result of a successful mating between a human who turns into an animal and an animal who turns into a human. Most animal-weres possessed below human intelligence. Few are capable of speech. Some packs kept them as pets, some murdered them.

Normally any child resulting from such a pairing is considered an abomination. Pack law demands they be killed at birth. Somehow Andrea had survived and as a teen had passed herself off as human enough to enroll in and then graduate with honors from the Order's academy. I wasn't sure how she had managed it, but it couldn't have been easy. What I did know of her came from Kate, and she'd hinted that there was a lot of abuse in Andrea's past. I didn't doubt it. We had a saying: a pack's only as good as the alpha and the alpha is only as good as the pack. Some of the smaller packs outside our territory let themselves be run by sadistic assholes.

I had to give it to the Order—they trained their people well. Andrea had fought with us in the Midnight Games and she was damn good with ranged weapons; maybe as good as Kate was with her sword. Andrea was also a potential problem. She was an unaffiliated shapeshifter in my territory, which was against the Pack law. She had to report to the Pack and ask to be admitted to the ranks, leave, or ask for a special dispensation, none of which she had done. Her only saving grace was that her shapeshifter status was secret.

I leaned back. "Andrea Nash is a knight of the Order. How does she concern us, or you?"

"I love her," Raphael responded before Bea could say anything.

"Really?" I couldn't hide my surprise. He'd had a string of lovers, but I'd never heard him say that about any of them.

"Yes."

"Does she know?"

"Yes. She and I are dating."

That's just great. My life had been far too easy lately, and they'd decided to complicate it. "Good for you. I'm still not hearing an answer to my question, so I will ask again. What do you want from me?"

Bea folded her hands on her lap. "We understand that Andrea presents a problem. What we would like, what we humbly request, my lord, is that you do nothing. We simply ask that you overlook this matter and allow us time to resolve it in a manner that will be mutually beneficial."

"I have been very patient up to this point. I have allowed an unaffiliated shapeshifter, a beastkin even, to live within the Pack's territory. Do you know why?"

I paused in case they wanted to say something. They didn't.

"It's because she has no connection to or dealings with us. She's living as a human knight within the Order. She has rejected her shapeshifter heritage. I know her history and have no wish to expose or banish her as long as she remains apart from us. Now, however, you force my hand. If you intend to date her, or even eventually mate with her, the fact that she's a shapeshifter will come out. She will have to be brought in. Moynohan is surely an ass in this world. If he finds out she's dating you, he'll make her life hell. If he finds out she's a shapeshifter, he'll expel her."

"I know that," Raphael said.

"Then you know that she'll have to choose, and soon, because it can't be both. When she's discovered, the Pack will want to know what I knew and when. If I didn't know about her, I'm stupid. If I knew and did nothing, I'm weak. Why should I allow this?"

"I will fight for her if I have to." He held my gaze.

Wow, he had it bad. Was this a challenge or just mating craziness? "Who are you willing to fight? Think a moment before you speak."

"There will be no need for that," Aunt Bea said. "We are making arrangements for Andrea to be brought into the clan. I've been an alpha longer than you've been alive, and I'm not getting any younger. I'm starting to think of slowing down, retiring and watching my grandchildren grow."

Sure. The only thing she cherished almost as much she treasured Raphael was power, and maybe fucking with me.

"Nash is strong and my son loves her. He has since the night Kate brought her to us. He didn't know it yet, but I did. A mother knows. I realize that things have not always been straightforward between us. I have perhaps on occasion even been the proverbial thorn in your paw—"

I held up a hand and interrupted her. "Bea, you oppose me, even when it is not in your best interest to do so, you undermine my authority, albeit subtly, and you have done so since I first became Beast Lord. Now you want a favor from me because your little boy likes a girl from the other side?"

"You're not going to make this easy are you?"

"No. What we obtain too cheap, we esteem too lightly; it is dearness only that gives everything its value," I quoted.

Derek moved behind me and disappeared into the restaurant. Hmmm.

"Bea, the meal was delicious; additionally I'm, myself, on the hunt, and so I'm in a generous and mellow mood. I will grant you this favor, but not without certain concessions on your part."

"Name them."

I had her. Time to find out how much was she willing to concede to indulge her son. I decided to go for broke. "It's actually quite simple, I want only one thing. Honesty."

Bea leaned forward. "Can you be more specific?"

"When I make a decision and you have genuine concerns or reservations, you tell me. If you have doubts, we will discuss them privately. But afterward, publicly, once a decision is made and announced, you will support me unconditionally. No more games, no more snide comments, no more clever jokes. I know your job is tough. So is mine. Being the boss sucks, and sparring with me is fun, but I need you and Mahon both. I need your counsel and wisdom."

I took a swallow of my drink, letting the words sink in. "You want the best for your clan. So do I. I want it for all of us. I know that I can be a bit of a tyrant, and I'm not always right. When you think I'm wrong, tell me, and when I'm right, back me. Agree to this and Nash is yours to do with what you will. That's the offer, take it or leave it."

She was silent a moment. Thinking it over...

Light steps told me Derek was coming back. A moment later he emerged. His face was paler than it used to be. Either his food hadn't agreed with him or something had happened.

Aunt Bea smiled. "You've finally grown up, dear."

"I've been grown for a long time now," I told her. "You just haven't bothered to notice."

"Very well. You shall have honesty and respect as well. All you ever had to do was ask." She smiled again. "Nicely, without all the roaring."

"Thank you, Bea. I'll try to remember that. Now, if you will excuse us."

"Of course, my lord. I understand you have quite an evening planned with the delightful Ms. Daniels."

And how the hell did she know that?

Aunt Bea's smile got wider. "Don't do anything we wouldn't."

I wondered briefly what exactly that might be, but was unable to imagine something that dangerous or depraved.

I waited until we got to the car and well out of the boudas' earshot.

"Well?" I prompted once we were inside.

"Jim called the restaurant while you were negotiating with Aunt Bea. Boris is dead."

"Big Boris? Boris the Boar?"

Derek nodded.

Whoa. "Did a building fall on him?" Boris the Boar was a tough old bastard. If I ever had to fight him, I would be bringing Mahon.

"Murdered. He didn't die easy. Jim says there was a lot of blood at the scene, too much for all of it to be his."

No doubt. There would have had to be a lot of them and I'd bet some hadn't walked out on their own.

Two hours later, I was in Boris's cabin in the woods northwest of the Keep. Two of Jim's people were posted by the door. Others were carefully walking around outside and looking closely at things on the ground. It wasn't a crime scene so much as a nightmare. Blood was everywhere. Walls, ceiling, most of it on the floor. Busted furniture littered the cabin. Almost everything was broken or knocked over. The place looked like a barroom after a brawl, like you see in one of the old cowboy movies. Except this wasn't some "shady dive," this was the home of someone I knew. I'd visited Boris after he'd moved in. His home had been neat and clean. I remember him telling me that he "never could abide a messy domicile." He'd hate it now if he were alive. Which he wasn't, not by a long shot.

I looked at the body in front of me. Or rather what remained of it.

I'd once read a line in a book. It said *"The guy was dead as hell."* It seemed to fit. Boris hadn't just been killed; he'd been ripped apart by someone or something strong. Smart, too. The killer, or killers, had damn near painted the place with wolfs-bane, covering their tracks. Still, if you knew what you were looking for, there were clues. Deep gouges in the log walls and cabin floor testified to the power of the attacker. Somebody big. Clan Nimble and the Rats were right out. The place wasn't big enough to hold the numbers they would have needed to bring Boris down. The Wolves were a possibility. They'd had an issue with Boris before. I could think of one wolf pair that might have had a chance, but it wasn't Daniel and Jennifer. They were concentrating on smoothing out their family life. Besides, if those two were making a comeback, Derek would've heard something and told me or Jim.

Last time I'd seen Boris, he'd been working on a huge oak table, the top at least two inches thick. Now his battered body was lying in the ruins of it. Who was powerful enough to knock him back into the damn thing or slam him through it? Some-body from Clan Heavy, maybe—Eduardo would be strong enough, but some of the marks on the floor said claws, not hooves. Besides, it wasn't his style. He had a short fuse and didn't mind fighting, but when he lost his temper he attacked right away. He wouldn't brood about it, planning and waiting for the right time. Bison don't have to sneak around or stab you in the back. Still, I'd put my money on someone from Heavy, but who was strong and stupid enough to kill their alpha's oldest friend?

"So, what do you think?" a familiar voice asked from over my shoulder.

"He's dead, Jim."

"You're not as funny as you think you are." Jim grimaced. "I know you didn't do it because I saw you yesterday, and you weren't all fucked up."

"Thanks for the vote of confidence. So when do we think it went down?"

Jim shrugged. "Not long ago, couple days at most, judging from the decomposition and insect activity. Even with our accelerated healing, the killer is still going to look like they've been in one hell of a fight. How many people do you know who could have done this?"

"Not too many." It wasn't a loup. They stank and didn't use wolfsbane.

"Lots of bites, but no signs of feeding," Jim said. "Wolfsbane indicates forethought and planning. They knew they might have to kill him, and they knew we'd come sniffing around."

"Derek, look around and tell us what you think." Let's see how much he'd learned.

"Good idea—impress us," Jim said. "Start from outside and walk us through it.

Derek nodded, stepped out for a moment, then entered again. He shook his head. "No scent, no footprints. It's wolfsbane and then tire rubber and car smell. They drove up, parked maybe fifty yards away, and walked up. Carefully, left no trace. Loups don't drive, don't plan. On top of that, the cabin doesn't have their stink."

He sank a little venom into his words. While the wolfsbane would mask the scent of a human or shapeshifter, loups had an unmistakable stench, equal parts hunger and madness. The boy had been a victim and witness to both, as had I, but in a different fashion. I'd seen my father cut down by them. Derek's dad had turned loup, raping, killing, and cannibalizing his mother and sisters.

Derek pointed at the door. "No signs of forced entry. He let them in or maybe they snuck in while he was out and waited for him. Unlikely though; when he came up, he would have picked up their scent and not gone in. Maybe somebody he knew."

"Don't tell us maybe," Jim said. "Read the signs, tell us what the scene and the body say happened."

Derek nodded, paused, and started again. "There was an altercation in this area. Outside, the trees are damaged where Boris marked them as his territory, but those grooves aren't fresh like the ones in here. Claws." He crouched and spread his hand on the deep gouges in the wood floor. "This isn't a wolf. Three deep gouges here." He dug his fingers in the indentations. "Lighter gouges on the sides. Something was on all fours and got pushed back. Hard."

He took two large steps back toward the wall on the side of the door and pointed up at a spot about eight feet up. "Here, blood and hair. Somebody had the back of his head slammed into the wall. With a tremendous amount of force."

He placed his hand on his own head, stood up on his toes, and raised his arm. His fingertips barely brushed the edge of the bloodstain. "I'm six feet. The stain is at least two feet higher. Someone tall."

Stepping away from the wall, he indicated another set of marks on the floor, near the center of the room. "These tracks are different. Deep ruts in the pine floor, made by blunt, rounded toes, consistent with our victim. Boris charged his opponent and was then pushed or pulled back, possibly both, which would indicate multiple assailants. My lord, if you will stand here." He indicated a spot against the wall, under the stain.

I moved where he pointed.

He placed his feet in the marks believed to be made by Boris and went into a sort of martial-arts stance. I looked sideways at Jim, who shrugged slightly. It was the kid's show.

Derek looked over his shoulder. "Jim, could you please stand behind me at the other wall."

Jim moved into place. Now we stood in a line: Derek facing me, with Jim behind him.

"Okay, so I'm Boris." Derek shrugged his shoulders. "Let's go through this in slow motion."

He looked at me. "If you're ready, I'll charge toward you. Can you go into a half squat?"

I did so. He came at me in an exaggerated slow-motion rush.

"We collide, bounce off each other, you stand up, I come at you again and bash you into that wall."

He pushed against me and I pretended to bounce against the wall.

"You hit your head there. We grapple a bit. Now, Jim, you grab me from behind and pull while Curran pushes."

Jim lumbered over with exaggerated slowness and stood behind Derek, holding his hands out like two large paws. Yeah, he was thinking what I was thinking. He hooked his arms under Derek's and put him in a full nelson, slipping his arms under Derek's and clasped his hands together on the back of his head.

"Drag me back."

Jim pulled and I pushed and we half carried him straight back to the remnants of the table and let him go.

"Somehow, mainly brute force, the two of you lift me and smash me through the table. I'm stunned by the force of the impact, so I just lay there for a second or two. You, both of you, start to bite my head and neck. I'm fighting, but I'm on my back and the two of you are on top, ripping into me and clawing. Note the defensive wounds still visible on the hands and arms of the victim. He tried to protect his face. Blood spatter on the wall adjacent to the table is in the classic teardrop shape. The power of blows forced it away from the body. Here on a shard of the table is a bloody handprint, presumably the victim's, as his body started to revert as a result of shock and blood loss. They battered him down and bled him to death until he couldn't fight anymore, and then they finished him."

He was good. I couldn't really find fault with his analysis.

"Jim, is this how you think it happened? It'd be easier if it was vamps."

"Yeah it would, but he's right." Jim looked at Derek. "All right, now that we know the how, tell us who?"

He looked at us both, perhaps afraid to say what we all were thinking. "Bears."

Yeah, it almost had to be. The moment I saw that stain on the wall, I knew it had to be a bear on his hind legs. Nobody else got that large.

"Does Mahon know?" I asked.

"Only if he did it or had it done. Boris's daughter came to check on him, found him like this, and called us," Jim said. "I told her don't touch anything and wait there for us, but she said she had to get home."

"You like her for it?"

"Meaning she did it and then called us so she wouldn't seem like a suspect?" Jim frowned. "Nah, she seemed pretty upset. Husband says she's in shock. Besides, she's not a fighter, strictly civilian. Husband too, but he could be strong. He has a lot of control, as much as any of my people. I think he's got a half form, but he denies it, says nobody taught him and he's too old to learn. That was the deal Boris made with Mahon—he fights, they don't. They're allowed to live their lives pretty much as they want. They're members of the Pack, but they aren't really active."

"And if he were to die? What happens to them?"

"I don't know," Jim said. "Maybe the old bastard never thought he'd die. We'd have to ask Mahon."

Nobody ever does expect to die. He'd put up a damn good

fight though. Maybe it's the best any of us can hope for. "All right. I'll go talk to his daughter and I need to do it now, before the Old Bear hears about this." Mahon and Boris had been friends for a long time. Mahon wouldn't be exactly rational. "Talk to Mahon and buy me some time. We need to see if anyone in Heavy's missing or severely wounded."

"He won't be happy. Boris was his friend and he'll be looking for some payback."

"That's why I said buy me some time. Keep asking questions. He doesn't have to like it, he just has to answer. You're in charge of this investigation. Pull rank if you have to, but keep him contained as long as you can. We don't need him roaring around and crushing people's skulls into blood and bone. He gets a hold of somebody he even thinks did it and they'll disappear. Whoever did this will face Pack justice, not Mahon's fury. While you're having a nice little chat with him, I'll go see the daughter. She may know something."

BUTTERCUP CREEK WAS A QUIET, UPPER-MIDDLE-CLASS SUBURB IN North Cobb. Most of the houses were two-story and brick. Younger couples with money and kids, older couples who had bought the houses back in the day and stayed. Well-manicured lawns, nice cars in the driveways, solid bars on the windows, and reinforced doors. Safe, comfortable houses for people who worked well-paying jobs and folks who had retired from them.

Derek pulled up slowly to the curb in front of the house, and after stopping, we waited a few moments to give everybody a chance to recognize us. I knew Jim had at least five people out of sight but keeping an eye on the house. Whoever or whatever had gone after Boris might decide to take out his family as well. Maybe the attackers had been looking for something at his house, maybe they didn't find it, maybe they did, or maybe they just wanted him dead. Too many maybes. I needed answers. Here was as good a place to start as any.

Paul and Joan Parker's residence was no different from the others on the street, except that it sat next to a fenced-off wooded lot. Still too many neighbors for my taste. The house stood in stark contrast to Boris's simple, isolated cabin. I guess it depended on how you saw people, whether you were a bee or a bear. Some felt safer having others around and felt vulnerable on their own. Bees gathering in a hive. That's what the neighborhood reminded me of, a honeycomb. All the houses were similar. If I knew the layout of one, my own for instance, I was pretty sure I could navigate any of the others in the dark, no problem. Perfect for bees. Bears, on the other hand, were territorial and enjoyed the solitude of their caves. One does not simply walk into a bear's cave. Boris was like a bear, which was why he'd gotten along with Mahon so well. Was his daughter a bee or had she simply married one?

We walked up to the door, Derek a pace behind and scanning the street. Two doors, a screen one and sturdy wooden one with colored glass in its center. I knocked on the screen door.

No answer.

I tried the latch. Unlocked. I opened it and knocked a bit harder on the wooden front door. I knew they were home. If they'd left, I would have been told about it. Part of me wished they had snuck out and I wouldn't have to interrogate a woman who'd lost her father. And hell, it might have even been a clue.

No such luck. I sensed movement and a tall, sandy-haired man opened the door, eyes very blue behind his wire-rim glasses. He stared at me a moment without recognition, and then it hit him.

"My lord." He bowed his head. "Please come in."

I did and shut the door behind me.

"Isn't your friend coming in?" he asked.

"No, he's going to stay outside and watch the car, says in a

242

shady neighborhood like this somebody might steal it." Not sure why I was messing with the guy. Something about him bugged me.

"Are we in danger?" He chose to ignore my joke. Maybe Jim was right about me not being that funny. Naw.

"That's what I'm here to try to figure out, but no, not at the moment. We have people watching the house to keep you safe." And to keep you from sneaking out the back, which I wisely chose not to add.

"Mr. Parker, what was your relationship with your father-in-law like? Did the two of you get along?" No need to be subtle—I hit him with a hard question and gauged his reaction.

Parker made a face like he tasted something sour. "He was a hard man to like. Always told me that he 'had no use for most people.' I guess that included me. He had very specific ideas about what men should know and do, like know how to work with their hands and fight."

"You don't?" I didn't specify whether I meant the knowing or doing.

"No, I've never been a very physical person, but I'm smart. I got an education, I use my brain to feed my family and put a roof over our heads. I need the roof fixed or a patio built, I pay a professional to do it. He never understood that, said I should do it myself instead of having strangers in my house. Other men shouldn't be around my family. His thinking was medieval like that. Doesn't matter that those people have to make a living too, or that I wouldn't know what to do with a circular saw if my life depended on it. That shack of his, he built it himself, did all the work on it. He was so proud of it."

Wow, I guess I'd touched a nerve. "You've been out there to see him?"

"A few times...always with Joanie and the kids. He was a mean son of a bitch, but he loved his grandchildren, I'll give him that. Spoiled them."

"How exactly?"

He waved his hand. "Oh, you know, toys and games. Gave them money. Let the boys run around in the woods like wild animals, hunting, fishing and sleeping outside even. They loved it."

"They're how old?"

"David is fifteen, Daniel's thirteen, both born in June like me. Weird, huh?"

Paul, David, and Daniel? I was sensing a trend here. Maybe they were religious.

"We haven't told them yet. I'm afraid they won't take it well. He's the only grandfather they've ever known. My father died when I was just a little older than they are now. Worked himself to death, Mom used to say, but it wasn't the work, it was the play."

That was interesting. "How do you mean?" Everybody has a story if you listen.

"Dad was a stone mason down in Florida. After the magic came back, a good stoneworker could make a damn fine living. Problem was he spent it faster than he could make it, sometimes before my mom could pay the bills even. He was what is now commonly called a 'high-functioning' alcoholic. Everybody liked him, said he was a funny guy, a great friend. I don't remember that, I remember my mother crying because he'd spent his paycheck at the bar." He took a deep breath, exhaled. He was looking off into space, reliving painful memories. "I don't think Momma liked him much, and I feel like I didn't really know him. When I was sixteen, they found his body in the Corkscrew."

"Is that a bar down there?"

He looked at me and actually smiled a little. "No, it's a swamp, like a preserve, south of Fort Myers. Daddy went there hunting at least once a month. You know." He let it hang there. "He was proud of being a panther, went to see his people, he called them, a small pack in the Everglades. Never took us with him. My mom told me once she thought he had a woman there. Gave her money, our money. So I'll be honest with you, I never liked my dad. I never liked Boris either."

"Sounds like you had it rough." I pointed around to indicate the house. "But you're doing well enough now."

The place was nice, spotless and tastefully decorated with high-quality furniture and expensive paintings on the wall. Nothing to indicate that two teenage boys lived there. It was almost sterile. As a young man, I would have preferred the cabin.

"Yes, we do okay. Like I said, I got my degree and work as a liaison between insurance companies and contractors. Make sure they don't overcharge for the work. Joanie works for lawyers in Buckhead. Her father hated that, said I should make enough for her to stay home. Said a real man acts as head of the household and provides for his family, and the wife should stay home and take care of the kids. He thought we should home-school the kids. Not sure why—they're in an excellent private school."

He really had it in for the old boar. I decided to ask more questions. Maybe he'd tell me something I could use. "What about Boris? Did he go to good schools?"

"I don't know much about his upbringing. Like I said, we weren't close. Joanie could tell you, but she's still pretty upset. Do we really have to do this now?"

I smelled sweat and fear. There's something about fear. It must be the lion in me. I feel it, I smell it, I taste it. It's almost tangible for me, and when I do catch a whiff of it, the world goes crystal clear.

I stared directly into his eyes. I knew my eyes had gone gold and he knew what that gold meant.

He looked at the floor. That's better.

I stepped closer until mere inches separated us and

continued in a low voice, "Yes, Mr. Parker, we do have to talk about it. Someone murdered your wife's father. It wasn't a quick or easy kill. He suffered before he died. The people who killed him wanted something, and we don't know what it was or if they found it. I'm here asking questions because I mean to catch whoever is responsible and bring them to justice. I rule the pack, I make the laws, and I punish those who break them. That's who I am, that's what I do. I appreciate that this is a rough time for your family and you're grieving, but you will answer my questions and you will not hinder this investigation."

His expression changed, his shoulders slumped, and in a quaking voice he said quietly, "She's not here. They have her."

And there it was.

"Please, the boys don't know. They said they'd hurt her if any of your people came around."

"Who?"

"I guess you or men like the ones hiding outside and the boy by the car."

I took a deep breath. I needed him alive and talking. Roaring at him would just make him clam up. "Who has your wife and when did they take her?"

"A little while ago. She went to see him, came home crying, then she got mad. As angry as I've ever seen her. She asked me if I'd done it or had it done. I told her she was crazy, she said it was my fault that I owed them money and that they'd killed her father to get it. It's not true; I tried. I asked him for the money, just a loan. He laughed at me. Called me weak."

"Who took your wife?"

The words kept spilling out of him like marbles out of a torn bag. "Yeah, I told them he had a stash hidden away, but I swear I didn't know they'd murder him. I sort of hoped maybe he'd kill them. After we fought, she went to see them, said she wasn't afraid of their kind. Later they called and said if I wanted to see her again to bring them what I owed. Why would she do that?

Why would she go and confront them? Now they have her and I don't have the money they want."

Enough was enough. "Mr. Parker, if you don't give me a name in the next five seconds, I promise I will personally beat one out of you."

"THE IRVINE BOYS?" MAHON FROWNED. "YEAH, I KNOW THEM. Mick and John, came down from Michigan with their dad after their parents split up. Must be almost twenty years ago now. They were just kids, teenagers, but they were strong and they started working. Now they each have their own business. Mick does floors and John does pretty much everything else or has a guy who can. They do a lot of flood restoration, total renovations. They did some really nice work on Raphael's house, took the carpet off the stairs, you know he hates it, put down wood everywhere. You should see his kitchen. It's all stainless steel appliances, tile floors, and marble countertops. Why, are you thinking about hiring them for some work?"

"No. I was going to ask them to release Joanie Parker and answer for killing her father." I gave him a moment to process that.

Mahon stood perfectly still. I could sense Jim tensing up beside me, unsure of how the big man would react.

"They killed Boris?"

I nodded.

"You sure?"

"Yeah."

"Where are they now?" he said, his voice low and menacing.

"Funny you should ask. I was wondering the same thing. When was the last time you saw them?"

Mahon squared his shoulders. "I'll handle this; it's my clan and my friend that got killed. I'll find them, we'll talk a bit, and if what you say is true, I'll bring you their heads. Good enough?"

"Not this time. They have Boris's daughter and they'll probably kill her if you go barging in there. Plus we don't know where 'there' is. We're going to do this my way. Jim's people are with the son-in-law at his house. When the Irvine boys call, he'll tell them he has the money but that he doesn't feel safe. He wants the exchange to go down somewhere public, with lots of people. They'll come to the Keep, to the southern construction site, and we'll be waiting for them. They're going to stand trial for this, Mahon."

I could tell by his face he didn't like it. "Why air our dirty laundry?"

"Because that's how we do things," I said.

"You think they're stupid, that they won't smell a trap?"

"No, I think they're desperate and need the money to get out of our territory. Look, if they're found guilty, you still get to kill them. Any way you want. Will that work?"

"It will have to. And you're sure it's them?"

"You keep asking that," Jim said.

"I know their father," Mahon grimaced. "Yeah, I mean they've had some troubles. They can be a handful, but murder?"

I nodded to Jim, who stepped forward with a sheet of paper. "Troubles? That's one way to put it. They're out of control. I have no less than nine documented incidents of assault and property damage involving them. There's a pattern: they drink, they get mean, and people get hurt. Not too picky about who they fight either—they've gotten into three fights with the teamsters just this year. If they can't find other people dumb enough to brawl with, they get into it with each other. Last year, Mick stole one of John's guys to work on his crew. Next family gathering, Mick goes after John and they both wind up hospitalized. And then Doolittle kicked their asses out of his med ward because they started shit with other patients. He won't treat them anymore. They're grown-ass men. You need to stop covering for them."

"Or what?" Mahon moved toward Jim.

This was getting out of hand, so I stepped between them. "Or nothing. You know there's only one way this ends, and you're not really mad at Jim. He didn't kill your friend or abduct Boris's daughter. You want to fix this, help us bring them in. Let them tell their side of it. That or we can hunt them down like animals."

Not everyone lives in the Keep. There's always a certain amount of personnel and some living quarters, but it's more of a place to run things, gather for special occasions, and hole up if the shit hits the fan. When that day comes, and it will, I want to be able to fit everybody inside, so as the Pack continues to grow, I'm also perpetually expanding the Keep. I want the walls higher and thicker, another tower here, cut the trees back there, enlarge the kill zone, anything that will make it harder to take. Because I never can stop playing with it, an area south of the Keep is designated as a construction zone and staging area for the supplies, stone, timber, and tools I need to make the place bigger and better. It was there that we arranged for Paul to meet the men who had taken his wife.

Paul told them he'd borrowed the cash from the Pack and would meet them near the Keep so that he felt protected in case things went sour. The idea was that if they attacked him, he could shout out and the noise would bring the guards.

I crouched in the bushes. Mahon sat next to me. The rest of the Pack Council had arranged themselves around us, out of sight but within earshot. We were downwind, but since it was our construction site, it would smell like shapeshifters anyway.

In front of us, Paul paced between the stacks of mortar bags and loads of stone blocks. Pale and haggard, he looked like a man who'd just come out of the tail end of a weekend drinking binge, not sure where he was or why he was here and panicking because nothing seemed familiar.

I had invited alphas and betas, because I wanted everything to be aboveboard. Due process works best when there are witnesses to the proceedings and no appearance of impropriety. All of which was a moot point if the Irving boys didn't show. I figured they would. What choice did they have really? Jim's people had searched the house they still shared and it looked like the Irvings had packed up some things and split. If they were planning to run, they would need money. If they planned to stay, they would need money. And there was only one place they could get it. They'd have to bring Joan and trade her to Paul for the ransom.

If they hadn't taken a hostage, I'd be inclined to let them go and hunt them down at our leisure, but we owed it to Joan to do everything we could to get her back safely. If they showed up soon and things went smoothly, I could still make my dinner with Kate. Sure, I might be a little late, but I intended to make it up to her.

We didn't have to wait long. In less than an hour, the rumble of a powerful engine alerted us to the approach of the Irving brothers. Just as I thought. They had taken the access road to the construction site. I hoped they had Joan with them. If they arrived without her, things would get considerably more complicated. We would have to try to subdue the pair and beat her location out of them. Dead or alive, we needed to know where she was.

Paul faced us and peered into the woods. Don't look at us, you dumbass.

In a few minutes, lights shone through the trees, then they went out, but the noise told me the vehicle was continuing toward us. Idiots. Their engine sounded like a small tornado. I wondered what they'd been thinking. *Hey, Mick, how can we be inconspicuous? Well, John, we'll turn the lights off. Nobody will ever know we're coming.*

Next to me, Mahon rolled his eyes. We weren't dealing with criminal masterminds. The Irving brothers didn't plan. They saw only a few hours ahead, if that. For once, it played to our advantage. They probably hadn't even considered the possibility of a double cross. In their minds, this was a straight line: show up, get the money.

Paul squared his shoulders and hefted the duffel bag that we'd stuffed with coffee packets. When put inside the bag, they looked just like stacks of cash.

The Irvings parked about a hundred yards short of the site and got out. Even in the light of the quarter moon, I could make out two large shapes with a smaller one between them. Oh, good. They'd brought her alive. She seemed to be walking, but they were keeping her between them and I couldn't see her face.

Maybe Mahon was right and they were just good guys who'd gotten caught up in a bad situation.

"Parker, we brought your sow," one of them called out. "You better have the money or we'll gut her in front of you before you die."

Or not.

"Okay." Paul raised the bag. "I have it—let her go, please."

I could sense his fear and tension, but was it for himself or for his wife?

"Throw the money," the other Irving brother said. "If it's all there, you can have her. She ain't hurt. Much. We could've done worse for all the shit you put us through."

"Me?" Paul's voice shook. "You took my wife! For what, money you think I owed you?"

Ah, here it was. If we waited it would all come out.

"Bullshit," the larger brother said. "You told us they would pay. We did the work, you fucking bastard. Did the insurance company pay? No! We built them folks a brand-new goddamned house, tile fucking floors, granite countertops, custom cabinets, new appliances—we had to buy all that shit, and then nothing. We're out of pocket for eighty grand, goddamn it."

"Homeowners can't pay," the smaller brother growled. "We got barely five out of them. We missed a payroll, Dom quit, plumbing guy quit, and our rep is fucked now. Nobody will hire us after that. You owe us, for all of it."

"It's not my fault!" Paul dropped the bag. "The payment was approved and then they went out of business. How was I supposed to know the owner was going to disappear with all the cash and his secretary?"

"You're supposed to know—that's what we paid you for," the larger brother snarled. "It was a good gig, all you had to do was go back and forth with the rep, get the payment approved. You sit in your nice little office running the numbers while we do the real work. We always gave you your cut. You think you're better than us because you never get your hands dirty, you think you can just fuck us and nothing's gonna happen?"

"I said I was sorry. I tried to get the money. I even told you where to get it, but you couldn't even do that right, could you? You were supposed to get the money from the old man, not kill him."

"Well, how the hell did you think we'd get the money, you stupid bastard?" the larger Irving asked. "Did you think the three of us would sit down to tea and then he'd give us the dough?"

I nodded to Derek. The kid moved forward, struck a match, and dropped it into the metal brazier. The fuel inside ignited and flames shot up, illuminating the site, Paul, the Irving brothers, and Joan with a piece of duct tape over her mouth. To the right and left, three more fires surged into life.

I stepped out and in a loud voice asked, "That's what we all wanted to know. Did you plan to kill Boris?"

The big men froze for a moment. Little drama never hurt.

Joan took the chance and broke from them, ripping the tape from her mouth. She had a split lip and a bruise under one eye. They had roughed her up and they'd done it on the way over here, probably just before they got out of the car, because Lyc-V would've healed the injuries otherwise.

Joan ran toward her husband. He opened his arms to embrace her and she slapped him. Hard, right across the face. He staggered back, looking stunned.

She was breathing hard but between breaths managed to squeeze out four words. "I want a divorce."

"Granted," I said. It seemed fair under the circumstances.

Around me, members of Clan Heavy moved from the woods, heading for the Irving brothers.

"Good," she ground out between clenched teeth. A terrifying grin spread on her face as she advanced on her now former husband.

"You did this," she hissed. "You sent them to kill my father. He was right about you—you're just a coward. You knew what they'd done and you let me go see them by myself. What kind of man does that?"

"I provided for you!" Paul barked. "I made a life for you and the boys. You liked it, the nice house, the good neighborhood. What are you going to do, get a little apartment, put the boys in public school? You'll come crawling back, or is one of those lawyers you 'work for' going take care of you?"

"Aaaargh! I make as much as you do, asshole. I have money put away. You think you're so much better than me and the people I work with, but I don't have to cheat people and deal with stupid, violent thugs like those two."

"Hey!" One of the Irvings started to protest. They had been surrounded by several members of Clan Heavy, under the direction of Mahon. They weren't going anywhere.

"Shut up," I suggested. "You'll get your turn."

The happy couple needed to work this out. Years of bitterness and resentment were being dragged out, and it felt a bit voyeuristic to be watching their life together unravel.

"Hell, I did you a favor!" Paul screamed. "Now you'll get his place and his money. Did you think he'd live forever?"

For a moment, Joan said nothing. She just stood perfectly still. Uh-oh.

"Petition for full custody of the children," she finally asked in a loud voice.

"Granted," I said.

He turned toward me. "What, why? They're my kids too. Are you're just going let this slut have them? Let them decide who they want to live with."

Joan's laugh was bitter. "What do you think they'll say, Paul, when they find out that you had their grandfather killed? The man who loved them and took care of them and taught them things. The man who took them camping and fishing. And why did you do it? For a little bit of money. They'll know what kind of man you are, and they'll hate you for it."

"You whore!" Paul Parker's skin split. Fur spilled out, fast, twisting to cover the new bone and muscle. Three of Jim's people were on him. They grabbed him, but suddenly he was in his panther half form, hissing and spitting, and they were struggling to hold him back. This was getting out of hand.

Joan just watched him for a moment and then shrugged. "Fine. If that's how you want it, fine. Let him go."

Jim's people looked at me. I nodded. We waited until she changed, then just stood back to give them room.

Where once had stood a petite blond woman in her late thirties, there was now a huge female razorback. All of us were larger in our beast form than normal animals, but members of Clan Heavy were giants. She had to be over five hundred pounds of hard bone and powerful muscle. Dark grayish fur bristled along her broad back. Her eyes were small and full of malice. She was mad as hell.

Paul took a step forward. Joan outweighed him by nearly two hundred pounds, but Paul in warrior form was still a three-hundred-pound monster, a mass of tightly coiled muscle, sinew, and spotted fur with enormous fangs and claws. And she didn't have her father's tusks.

The werepanther crouched low. His lips trembled and a half snarl, half growl rippled from his mouth. I had the feeling this fight had been a long time coming.

The sow answered the challenge with a deep grunt. She pawed the ground with one enormous hoof and charged. Five hundred pounds of pissed wild sow shot past me like a runaway train. Her head was up. She tried to ram him, but the panther leapt up on liquid joints and landed on her back. He buried his front claws in the sow's shoulders and bit down hard on her snout. Blood poured.

Joan squealed in rage and dove forward into a roll. All her weight crashed down on the cat-man, and she rolled over him like a steamroller flattening the pavement. The werepanther let go of the sow's snout and leapt away. She spun to face him, breathing hard. Deep gouges carved her snout, her face a wet mask of crimson. They stood for a moment, unmoving. Then suddenly she charged again.

This time, instead of meeting her head-on, the big werecat dodged to the side and jumped onto the sow's back, teeth latching down savagely on her neck. Joan dashed around the clearing, sprinting like her life depended on it. It wouldn't help her. He would bleed her dry. Paul clung to her back, ripping into her.

Joan banked sharply, turning, and hurled herself at the stack of huge stone blocks waiting to become a wall. The werepanther screamed as five hundred pounds of razorback moving at thirty miles per hour slammed into stone, with him cushioning her fall. Bone crunched. The sow rolled to her side again and again until finally she rose up, legs shaking, back gushing blood but now unburdened by the panther. Paul sprawled on the ground, his breathing shallow. His ribs looked wrong. He was all busted up inside. Rather than allowing him to recover, Joan ran at him, hooves trampling muscle and bone into wet mush. She dropped down to her knees and brought her large head down onto his chest. His breastbone cracked, and his neck rolled to the side. He was finished. She started to use her huge canine teeth to tear out his throat.

Enough was enough. I let out a roar to get her attention.

"Joan, stop. He's gone."

She eyed me, bloody but unbeaten, and I thought she might charge me. Instead, the huge sow bowed her head. Flesh flowed as she changed back, and once again a small blond woman stood on the grass, but now she was naked, filthy, and bleeding from a dozen deep cuts and serious scratches. A deep gash on her neck was closing.

"Get her to Doolittle and get the body out of here."

Bea stepped out of the ring that had formed around the combatants and put a blanket around Joan. "Come with me, dear. We'll get you all fixed up." Her voice was soft and soothing, but she took an iron grip of Joan's shoulders and started to lead her away.

The widow stopped and turned to me. "What about them?" She gestured to the Irvings, still held tight by Mahon's people. "They killed my father."

"I know, and I'm sorry for your loss. We'll hear them out and then they'll be judged by the Council and punished. Good enough?"

"I want to see."

Bea turned Joan to face her and said in a quiet voice that would move rocks out of her path, "No, dear, you really don't."

For a second they were eye to eye, and then Joan ducked her head. Tears formed in her eyes and slid down her cheeks.

Bea pulled her in close. "You're a right mess. Let's get you cleaned up, why don't we?"

Joan nodded and started to weep. I made eye contact with Bea and nodded toward the Keep. Bea gently led her away, petting her back.

"Crazy bitch!"

It was the smaller of the Irving brothers. Mahon smacked him upside the head and he went down. Hard. The other struggled against his captors, to no avail.

"Let me go, you fuckers, we didn't do nothing. This ain't fair."

"Was it fair when the two of you killed Boris? We're still waiting to hear what happened with that. Please tell us why you shouldn't be held accountable for murdering the old man?"

"It wasn't like that. We just went to talk to him, to ask him for the money. We might have mentioned something about him not wanting anything bad to happen to his pretty daughter and her kids. He went fucking nuts—I swear we never touched him till he turned and pushed me back. He knocked me back into a wall and then Mick grabbed him from behind—you know, just to drag him off me—and he turned on him. Nobody hits my brother. He started it—we didn't mean to kill him, but he gave us no choice. It was self-defense."

"It doesn't work like that. You can't go to an old man's house to rob him and then claim self-defense when he fights back. You threatened the only people he cared about in the world. What did you expect him to do?"

"He shoulda just gave us the money. This is all his fault. Now all y'all are going to gang up on us and it ain't fair, none of it."

He was overly fond of that word. "All right John, what do you think would be fair? You know we can't just let you go, but how should we settle this?"

"One-on-one, I'll fight any one of you. If I win, you let us go. I'll fight anybody, even you—I'm not afraid of any of you."

Really, he should be, but then again they had killed Boris, so maybe he was pretty tough.

"Is that a challenge?" He needed to say it.

"Yes, it is. Come on, just you and me. Promise that if I start winning these bastards won't jump in."

"No one will interfere—this is a fight to the death. If you kill me, I give my word that you and your brother will be given free passage out of the Pack's territory. If I win, though, Mahon gets your brother. Are you sure you want to do this? Women and old men seem more your speed."

"You still yapping? Are you planning to talk me to death or are we going to fight?"

I nodded to Mahon, who gestured for John Irving to be let loose. Without further ado, he burst into his full bear form. He rose up on his hind legs and let out a deafening roar. He was big, no doubt, an adult male grizzly. Derek had been spot-on, he was a fully eight feet of rage and power. Not quite as large as Mahon, but still massive.

People who thought bears were slow and clumsy hadn't fought one before. I had and I knew that if I let him connect with those big paws, he'd take my head off. My best bet was to dart in and out, bleeding him. My warrior form would be best, a good mix of speed and strength, and I could use my training and hope that my skill made up for the size difference.

He dropped heavily to all fours and started to shuffle toward me. We circled each other, each of us wary and neither wanting to make the first move. Suddenly he took a big swing; I dodged the huge paw and threw a quick flurry of my own: overhand left, straight right, left again. I connected with his nose and left deep cuts along it. He backpedaled and began to circle me again, looking for an opening. When he reared up and tried to wrap his big arms around me, I dropped down and out of his grasp. I wasn't going to let him pull me into a bone-crushing hug. On the way down, I raked his chest and belly, but his fur was so thick that it did very little damage. He bore down on me and I rolled out from under him and to the side before he could bring all his weight down, but it was a near thing. If he pinned me down I was screwed. I nipped his ass before darting back out of range.

Frustrated now, he closed on me. It was an odd sort of shamble—he lowered his head and started swinging it back and forth as he lumbered toward me. He was hoping to batter me with it while protecting his vulnerable eyes and nose. I waited until he got within striking range, and sidestepping his charge, I grabbed his left foreleg and bit down hard on his ear. The claws of my right hand were buried in the fur and fat of his hump and his blood was hot and salty on my tongue.

He tried to shake me, but I had a good grip on his back and my jaws were locked on his ear. He swung his head to the side to knock me off, but instead I used the opportunity to swing my legs up and around his neck, squeezing it in a scissor move. Oops, one of us has been studying his jujitsu. He bucked like a bronco trying to throw a cowboy, but I had a really good position and I was using all my weight as well as my leg muscles to constrict his throat. After what seemed like forever, he started to slow and stumble. That's right, big boy, just go to sleep. It's almost over. Well, that wasn't so bad.

Something crashed into me. What the fuck? It hit me again and John and I fell together, and somehow he ended up on top of me. I was holding his dead weight up with my legs, but I didn't know how long I could keep it up. He was starting to come around, and in few moments he would be awake and clawing at my face. Suddenly the weight on my legs seemed to double. Son of a bitch! Mick must have jumped on top of his brother, bringing the combined weight of the two bears down on my legs. The load was too much and sure enough, my legs snapped like twigs. The pain was excruciating. I roared out in pain and rage. As John came down on me, I latched onto his throat with my jaws. My only hope was to crush his windpipe. I held on with all my might and bit down as hard as I could. I was rewarded by the satisfying sound of the thyroid cartilage and hyoid bone crunching between my teeth. John convulsed on top of me then went limp, and I knew he was gone.

Someone was pulling John off me, thank God. Unfortunately, it was Mick. He was standing over me with murder in his eyes. This wasn't good. He started raining blows down on me, and I covered my head and took most of the impact on my arms. My legs were useless; I wouldn't be getting up. I had to end this before he beat me to death. I took a chance, let one of the blows land, and locked my arms on his and pulled him down to me. When he was good and close, I let go of his arm, grabbed the sides of his head, willed my jaws to expand, and clamped down on his nose. It was a good bite and part of his nose came off in my mouth. I spat it at him. That was it for Mick—the shock and pain was too much. He turned and started to run away.

From out of the ring of bodies, Mahon stepped into his path. The two huge bodies crashed into each other. Almost instantly they were standing and had their arms entwined and seemed to be grappling. The larger bear twisted and actually tossed his opponent over his hip and onto the ground. Mick had barely hit before Mahon came down on him. With his left paw, he put his weight on Mick's chest; with his right, he reached way back and then the enormous paw came down hard on the smaller bear's head, smashing it like a ripe melon. It was Mahon's signature move. I'd seen it before, but it was still damn impressive. I didn't think I'd ever have to fight him, but if I did, I was going to stay away from that big claw cannon he was carrying.

"Anytime somebody wants to help me up, that would be

great." The spell cast by the blood and violence seemed to break and Jim and Derek hauled me up between them.

"My lord, that was amazing...you beat them both." Derek was awed.

"Yeah, about that. Who wants to explain why the fuck the other one was able to jump me?"

This time it was Jim. "Well, while we were watching you, we thought he was out. He managed to get free, broke Eduardo's nose, and clawed up George to get loose. Desperate, I guess. I knew you'd be okay."

"Yeah...how about that doesn't happen again? Damn it, get me to Doolittle. I need him to get me fixed up—got a big date tonight. I'm late enough and Kate's gonna be pissed. In this condition, she might be able to take me."

It didn't take long to get to the Keep and then into the med ward. Doolittle looked me up and down, then directed Jim and Derek to set me down on an examination table.

"What sort of foolishness you been up to? Looks like you fought a landslide."

"Bears actually. Two of them."

"Why the hell would you do that?"

"It seemed like a good idea at the time."

"Seems damn foolish to me. Don't you have a lot of big strong killers, like these two?" He nodded his head to indicate Jim and Derek. "Why you feel like you have to fight every damn soul in Atlanta is beyond me."

"If I say you're right, will you heal me? I've got places to be."

Doolittle raised an eyebrow.

"Tonight? You just fought two bears and you've got someplace to be? You do know that both of your legs are broken, don't you?"

"Oh, that's what that sound was. I figured they fell asleep."

"Don't get smart with me. I've always patched you up and I'll do it again, but there's no need for you to be like that."

The world was getting kind of fuzzy. "How about you stop bossing me around and just fix me, damn it."

"What's the hurry?" Doolittle began examining my legs. His voice was coming from far away, as if he was speaking from a bottom of a deep stairwell. "What's so important?"

Words came slowly. "I have to meet a girl."

"Is she special?"

"Yes."

"Then she'll understand."

The world spun, blinked, and then darkness took me into its mouth and bit down.

She would understand. I would explain it.

It would be okay.

CONCLAVE
(Magic Bleeds)

I HAVE BEEN THE BEAST LORD OF ATLANTA FOR HALF MY LIFE. I'm responsible for the lives of several hundred Free People of the Code. Some people will tell you that being in charge means telling other people what to do. That is only a part of it. Leadership means doing what you know is the right thing. In my experience, it rarely involves doing what you want or like.

Tonight was no exception. I was attending a meeting between the Pack Council, the alphas of all the clans, and the People, necromancers who piloted the dead. Bernard's was neutral ground, a sanctuary where all of Atlanta's players came to be seen and feel important.

Violence was strictly forbidden. No problem—we could dress up and play nice with Nataraja's corpse fuckers. For now, there was no need for open conflict between the Pack and the People. But the peace wouldn't last forever, and one day I would watch the light go out of Nataraja's eyes while the Casino burned down around him.

Pushing that pleasant thought aside, I entered the main floor. Jim was waiting there with the other alphas. I nodded to him and he led the group upstairs. I had started to follow them when I detected a familiar scent. It couldn't be. Why would she be here?

She had broken into my place, messed up my weights, and even put catnip into my bed. In retaliation, I had glued that cute butt of hers into her office chair. In short, we were doing the mating dance.

For a while I'd thought I had lost her for good, but in our own fucked up way we had swallowed our pride and reached out to one another. We both knew it would never be easy, but we were willing to try. I knew Kate wasn't universally loved by the Pack, but they owed me. I bled for them, I mediated their petty squabbles. I had given them everything—they would give me this one thing. Or I would break it all apart.

As I reached the top of the stairs, I saw Jim chewing one of his crew a new asshole. What the fuck? Maybe she was here. Kate was trouble and I wondered what she had done to piss Jim off. Maybe tonight wouldn't be completely boring after all. I just hoped that I wouldn't walk into a room full of my alphas with their asses glued to their seats.

I stepped into the room and looked for her. She stood by a table on the left, and for a moment, I think I forgot to breathe. Kate looked amazing, her hair was down, she was wearing makeup, and that dress... It was cut low in the front and fit like it was made for her.

She stood next to Saiman.

She was here with him. She was wearing that dress for him. She looked like that for him.

It was like something hit me in the gut. The rest of the room ceased to exist. There was only me and him and the distance between us. Why him, why here? Did she want to hurt me in the most public way possible?

Jim was at my side, trying to tell me something. I stared at them, trying to make some sense of it. The son of a bitch smiled at me and said something to her that I couldn't make out. I strained and picked his smug voice out of the noise. *"...would mean war. He can't move a finger out of line."*

I almost smiled then. He thought he was safe.

Jim's voice broke my concentration. "Not here."

I knew he was right, but it didn't matter.

"I can make him disappear," Jim said next to me. "No one will ever find him. I can bring him to you in chains, or in chunks. Just wait. Don't do it in front of her. We can do it anytime. We've got nothing but time."

I turned my gaze to her and she stared right back. The look was challenging. No, it was going to be right here and right now. She could try to stop me; hell, they all could, but she was going to watch me tear him apart. I would paint the floors and walls with his blood before he died.

The freak laughed. "We aren't without similarities, Curran and I."

Oh, I had to hear this.

"We both fall prey to lust. We both guard our pride and suffer from jealousy. We both employ our resources to get what we want: I use my wealth and my body, and he uses his position of power. You say I want you only because you refused me. He wants you for the same reason. I remember when he became the Beast Lord. The boy king, the perpetual adolescent, suddenly at the head of the food chain, granted access to hundreds of women who can't say no. Do you think he forces them into his bed? He had to have done it at least a few times."

What? That slimy cocksucker was telling her I was a rapist. The guy who would fuck a snake if he could find someone to hold it still. I never, ever.

Kate, tell him it isn't true. Tell him you don't believe it. Tell him.

She said nothing.

I had wanted her, and I thought she wanted me. I had been good, I'd waited. She'd been in the Keep, weak and wounded, but I'd never touched her. He would say or do anything. He would use her and throw her away when he tired of her. I had almost died during the Games for her.

He leaned toward her.

I could clear the distance between us in three leaps. Two seconds and I could twist his head off his shoulders and throw it at her feet.

He raised his voice. "You're all mine tonight. Kiss me, Kate."

No.

He reached for her. She stepped away.

Something inside me snapped, and then I was moving toward him. He wouldn't leave this place alive. I couldn't make her love me, but she didn't want his hands on her. That sick fuck would never touch her again.

She stepped in front of him. He was so drunk or stupid that he still didn't know what was happening.

"...won't hurt me. Not here."

I was almost there; I could smell the alcohol in his sweat. She swiped a bottle off a nearby table and moved toward me. Nice try, but it wouldn't be enough. Maybe if she had her sword...

"The People greet the Beast Lord."

Nataraja. It took everything I had, but I stopped. If I killed Saiman now, it would be war. In that moment, I would have thrown my life away to feel Saiman's skull snap between my jaws, but he wasn't worth the lives of my alphas. Saiman would never know it, but that bald-headed prick Nataraja had saved his life. For the moment.

I stared at Kate and mouthed a single word. *Later.*

She stared back at me, her eyes clear. *Anytime.*

I took a deep breath, turned my back on her, and in a calm voice called out, "The Beast Lord greets the People."

AWAKE
(End of Magic Bleeds)

I FLOATED FOR ETERNITY IN A SEA OF AGONY. SOMETIMES IF I concentrated and blocked out the pain, I could hear her voice from far away. I focused on the sound, willing myself slowly toward it. Finally, after how long I didn't know, I came around and could even make out a bit of what she was saying. "...seems like a decent guy. Now they're stuck."

He had someone, she had someone, nobody was talking and Kate didn't know what to do. She looked tired and battered. Still, I had never in my life seen someone more beautiful. Nor had I ever been happier to be near them. For some reason, the answer to her dilemma came to me far easier than all the things I really wanted to say.

"Have you tried the Second Chance Law?" I asked softly. Her eyes still did not open...maybe we were sharing a dream. I explained as best I could and hugged her as hard as I was able.

Finally she looked at me.

"You stayed with me," I whispered. She said something I couldn't quite catch, but it didn't matter as much as her being there to say it. I smiled and fell back asleep. Real sleep this time —no red haze, just darkness. I knew she'd be there when I came back to the world. No matter what. Eventually I woke again— something was in my arm and I wanted it out. As I located the source of my irritation, Kate came into the room carrying what smelled like soup. "What is this shit?" I demanded as I pulled the needle out of my arm.

"It kept you alive for eleven days," she informed me.

Almost two weeks! I had lain like that for nearly two

goddamn weeks, and she had stayed with me. It wasn't the IV that had kept me alive. The truth of it stunned me.

She handed me the soup, but I set it aside and pulled her close. We held each other for a time. Soon, however, Derek's familiar knock broke our reverie and short-lived reunion.

"Kate," he inquired quietly, clearly asking permission to cross the threshold.

With an authority in her voice that I had never heard, she instructed him to enter. The once-handsome young man did so and informed her of another wolf who demanded an audience, citing some "emergency."

"…probably another challenge…"

Challenge? For me? Every muscle in my body tensed. Really, were they fucking crazy? I'd almost died and they were queuing up to get a piece of what was left of me. I glanced at Kate and her face said it all. She wore a look of weary resignation, and the fractured pieces fell into place. Not me, they were challenging her. Hell no, this shit was going to stop right now.

Sensing the sudden danger, Derek glanced at me and abruptly fell silent. Before he could recover, I ordered him to send the challenger in but not to inform them that I had awakened. The young wolf closed his mouth, turned, and departed quickly to carry out my command. He'd always been a smart kid.

Kate helped me to stand; I'd be damned if they'd see me lying in bed like a weakling.

"Is today Wednesday?"

"Yes," she said.

Pack Council day. Perfect. I picked up the bowl.

As I sipped the soup she had brought in earlier, Jaime Alicia strode into the room as if he owned it. So eager to harm my mate and take what was mine. One of Clan Wolf's best fighters, a boxer in his youth, he was tall and well built. I had seen him fight; I knew he was strong and fast. I was also sure that Kate could cut him into little pieces before the soup got cold. I would never admit it, but she was damn good with that sword of hers. Not that she would have to—he would be dead before he touched her.

None of them would ever harm her again. I would see them all dead first.

Jaime stared at me, his jaw slack.

I finished my soup and spoke. "Yes?"

The wolf dropped into a crouch and stared at the floor. Had he hesitated for even a second, I would have pulled his lungs out through his chest. Claw, reach in, yank out. It would be easy and I would have enjoyed it immensely. I could smell his fear. I wanted to roar at him.

"Do you have anything to say?"

With his eyes still firmly affixed to the floor, he shook his head no. Now we knew again who was who and what was what. Order needed to be restored and the rest of them needed to be reminded why I was the Beast Lord.

"The Council is due for a meeting in three minutes. Go down there and tell them to wait for me, and I might forget you were ever here." For his sake, I hoped he never forgot how close he'd come to a savage and painful death, because I wouldn't give him a second chance.

After he left, I lost my balance and Kate attempted to steady me, but her leg gave way and we crashed together onto the couch. We were a long way from top form, but it would have to do. Together, even in our current state, we were more than a match for any of my subjects. Well, as far as they knew.

Almost as if she knew what I was thinking, Kate asked, "Are you sure you're ready for a Council meeting?"

I turned to her, willing my face into a mask of determination and menace. "They better be ready for me."

We had to make a show of strength. We could not continue

to be seen as anything less than the Beast Lord and his Mate, undisputed masters of the Pack.

It is the nature of our kind that we value power and violence above all else, ruthlessly exploiting any weakness. Authority must be exercised at all times or else it is lost. They didn't have to love or even like me, but by God, they would obey me. If they had forgotten why I was feared, I would remind them. If I had to kill a few as an example, then so be it.

I made my way to the bathroom, falling at least once, but my strength began to return and a couple of minutes later, I was ready to make it down to the Council room on my own. On our way Barabas, one of the Pack lawyers and one of Bea's favorite troublemakers, fell in behind us and kept pace.

I stopped. "Barabas, have you come to challenge me too?" I knew even as I said it that a challenge from him was unlikely. Barabas was slightly crazy and could be insubordinate at times, but he wasn't stupid.

His usual look of amusement evaporated, replaced by one of complete shock and disbelief. "No, my lord, I'm bound to the Consort."

Apparently the entire place had gone to hell while I was asleep. I turned to Kate and waited for some sort of explanation.

She shrugged. "I made a deal with Bea, and she gave him to me as a sort of adviser. I'll tell you all about it later."

I wasn't sure I wanted to know; Bea never did anything out of altruism alone. She wanted something. I dimly recalled Kate telling me about it, but the details escaped me. Had she assisted Kate in some way? A thought struck me. "Barabas, how many members of the Pack challenged my mate while I slept?"

He paused, clearly attempting to recall, and finally he turned to Kate and asked, "Twenty-two?"

She nodded silently.

"How many alphas?"

"Only the Jackals, my lord. The others were rank and file, not even betas."

Of course—you didn't get to be an alpha by being dumb. After the Jackals had been killed, the others had been content to let their subordinates wear her down. Mahon could have stopped it but had not. He'd never made a secret of his disapproval of Kate, but to stand by and allow her to be injured in my absence? He and I would speak of this later. Perhaps it was time for my adoptive father to retire.

The rest I would deal with in Council shortly. As we approached the door, I could hear them mumbling and whispering inside. Were they bored? Irritated? I could fix all of that. I took a deep breath, opened the door, and roared at my subjects as if I had every intent of ending their lives in the next several seconds. The sudden silence was deafening. Oh yes, Daddy's home and he ain't happy. Playtime was over.

As my alphas sat in stunned silence, I pulled out a chair for my mate and then seated myself at the head of the table. No one spoke. I scanned the table, seeking a challenge. Not one of them had the courage to meet my stare. They all knew that an example would have to be made, and none were eager to be the first.

I leaned forward and, in as calm a tone as I could manage, demanded, "Explain yourselves."

Silence.

"I'm waiting for one of you to tell me why you stood by and did nothing while my mate was assaulted on a daily basis."

Finally, Jim spoke. "She had to prove that she belonged."

"Yes," Mahon said. "Nobody expected that she would be allowed to sit at your side without spilling some blood, my liege."

Yeah, actually I kinda did. Last time I had checked, I was in charge around here. It was time to gently remind them of that.

I leaned forward and repeated, "Allowed?"

I let it sink in.

The realization of it hit them. They had just told me what I was allowed to do. I heard the alpha of the Jackals take a deep breath and hold it.

I stared at them. "I will say this only once. I'm the one who allows. I allow all of you to live and I allow you to rule your own clans as you see fit. Whether or not I continue to do so depends solely upon what you say and do in the next few moments. Be very careful."

It was Aunt Bea who spoke next. "Clan Bouda provided the Consort with both counsel and protection from unlawful challenges. No one who answers to me harmed her." She glanced over at Daniel and his mate. "The same cannot be said of the dogs, however."

Of course. She wouldn't have lifted a finger to stop the wolves from digging their own grave. The hatred between the boudas and the wolves went a long way back. Wolves had greater numbers, but boudas played the game better.

"We broke no laws," Daniel protested. "Everyone knows the alpha of the Bouda Clan cut a deal with the Beast Lord's mate."

Jennifer, his mate, nodded. "Yes, because she wanted special status for her degenerates."

A slow smile crept over Bea's lips. "We all know how much the alpha of the Wolf Clan loves his mate and defers to her. Out of curiosity, how many of his wolves was he willing to sacrifice to indulge her?"

"The human had to prove herself like we all did," Daniel said. "It is the law. It is fair."

"Fair, really?" I asked. "Who among you has faced twenty-two challenges in two weeks?"

None had, of course. Not even Mahon, our Executioner, had killed so many so quickly.

Speaking of law... I addressed Jennifer directly. "If I recall correctly, Daniel, despite being chosen upon the retirement of his predecessors, successfully faced a number of challenges before choosing you as his mate. However, you have never been challenged. Do you know why that is? Because, according to the law the two of you are so fond of quoting, whoever challenges you will also have to fight Daniel. The alphas fight as one. If one of the alphas is injured, it has been an unspoken courtesy among the Pack to wait until both are on their feet before a challenge is issued. It is a matter of honor. If you take another's place, you must win it fairly. You did not afford my mate the same courtesy."

"She killed my sister!" Jennifer screamed.

Good, let's get it all out there. Settle things once and for all. "True, your sister went loup and attacked her. But Kate didn't cause it and killed the one who did. Your anger is misplaced. As a matter of fact, she did you a favor. If you were any kind of alpha, you would know that putting your sister down was your responsibility. It was your burden to carry. You are the next of kin."

Jennifer clenched her teeth. I measured every word carefully. I couldn't challenge her, because the challenge had to come from the lower-ranking Pack member. But if I said enough, she would challenge me.

"My mate assumed your burden, and instead of offering her gratitude, you hate her for it. She is a constant reminder of your weakness. You want to fight her, but you can't. Instead, you goad others into doing what you can't bring yourself to do. It is your greatest failing. However, because I'm merciful and just, I will offer you a chance to atone."

"I will not apologize or bow to her. I'll die first." Jennifer snapped at the air like a mad dog.

Good, let's just see about that then. "Again, you misunderstand. What I offer is a chance at the revenge you seek, but properly this time. Challenge us. Couple to couple, as it was meant to be."

I gave the rest a warning glance. "No one will interfere. Just the two of you against the two of us."

Kate tensed next to me. Under the table, I gave Kate's hand a gentle squeeze to reassure her that I was just bluffing and it would be all right. Well, not really, but I was confident that even as we were, we could take them, and all the rest if need be. As long as they believed we could do it, we wouldn't have to.

As Jennifer began to rise—she really was either stupid or crazy—Daniel grabbed her arm, almost too quickly to see, and yanked her back. She landed in her chair, hard.

She opened her mouth and he gave her a flat stare until she shut her mouth and dropped her gaze. Her face turned red.

So he was unwilling to let her throw away her life or his own.

Daniel bowed his head in a slight nod. "Clan Wolf begs the Consort for her forgiveness. We are sincerely sorry for any offense we may have caused. We wish to express our continued loyalty and obedience to the Beast Lord and his Mate."

Well said. Perhaps there was hope for him after all.

"What about the rest of you?" My gaze lingered for a moment on the alphas of Clan Rat. Thomas and Robert Lonesco shook their heads in unison.

Thomas, the older and larger of the pair, spoke. "We have no dog in this fight." He smiled a little, showing very even, white teeth. "We didn't vote for her because we didn't know enough about her."

Kate leaned in and whispered to me, "After I killed the Jackals, they sent me chocolate."

Good, in truth I actually liked them both and would have regretted killing them. I looked at the aforementioned Jackals' replacements.

The female, Tracy, spoke. "We have no problem with the Consort. We are indebted to her for our current position."

I had expected as much. All that was left was Clan Nimble and Mahon's Heavies. The old bear I would deal with privately. Clan Nimble was a sort of anomaly within shapeshifter society. Its alphas, an older Asian couple, ruled not because they were the strongest but because their age and wisdom was highly respected by their subjects. It didn't hurt, of course, that their devoted betas were a vicious pair that was feared by the rest of the clan and many in the Pack. They kept their elders from harm and it was understood that they themselves would take their place as alphas, when the time came.

The alpha of Clan Nimble stood, drew himself to his full height, and then bowed deeply without his gaze ever leaving me. He held the bow, then straightened, and in a very formal tone proclaimed, "Clan Nimble remembers the understanding His Majesty has shown to us and would never dishonor itself by repaying that kindness with treason or betrayal. The Consort has fought admirably and has earned a place of respect at our lord's side."

Okay, a simple "we got your back" would have sufficed, but if he felt more comfortable with formality, then so be it.

"We respect Clan Nimble and hold its friendship in high esteem." Ahh, that got him; he nearly smiled, bowed once more, and sat again.

Almost done.

"So, it's all settled then. Unless there is anything else, you may depart in peace. Mahon, you stay," I commanded. The rest filed out as quickly as they could while maintaining a semblance of dignity.

Kate turned to me. Her eyes asked me *"Do you want me to stay?"*

Silently I shook my head. "No, you don't want to be here for the next part."

· · ·

I watched the Council of the Pack run from the room with their tails between their legs. One by one, they fled, careful not to look at me or the bear. Finally the last shapeshifters went through the doorway. It was just the two of us.

I looked at Mahon the way an alpha looks at a wayward subject. Mahon crossed his massive arms.

"It comes to this, then."

I didn't answer.

"It's about time. I've been waiting for this, boy. It needs to be sorted out."

Good, we understood each other. "Do you want to settle this here, old man, or do you have some other place in mind?"

Mahon considered it for a long moment. "We're going to need space. This is too small."

"Up on the fourth-floor balcony, then."

The balcony, a flat top of one of the smaller towers, was a stone square, about twenty by fifty yards. In spring and summer, we used it for outdoor dining and gatherings, but in winter it was deserted. It would provide us with plenty of room and give us some privacy as well.

This thing between Mahon and me wasn't going to be an exhibition. It wasn't a fight to the death, either, but if any of the Pack happened to witness it, it would become one. I would have to kill Mahon, and I didn't want to do that. Mahon wasn't my father, but I was his son.

This was between the two of us, and when it was over, we would know once and for all who was the strongest.

I walked through the doorway. He followed. Outside the room, Derek saw me and stepped away from the wall. I glanced at him, said, "Follow me," and kept walking. The kid fell in step behind us. We would need a guard to keep the rest of the Pack from sticking their noses where they didn't belong, and it couldn't be Jim or Kate. Jim was my best friend. He would interfere. Kate... This was something I didn't want Kate to see. Derek would do what he was told and would keep the rest out.

The three of us made our way to the fourth floor. A solid wooden door barred the way to the balcony.

I looked at Derek. "You stand here. Nobody gets on the other side of this door." I held his gaze for another long moment to make sure I had his attention. "No one."

"Yes, m'lord."

I opened the door and Mahon and I walked outside. The cold air hit my lungs.

The door shut behind us.

Darkness had fallen. The sky was black and vast, and the small lights of stars pierced it with cold light. Behind us, the gray towers of the Keep blocked the moon, but it was there, spilling light on the snow-strewn clearing around the Keep. Beyond it, black woods rose.

The balcony stretched before us, covered with untouched white snow. Before this was over, we'd paint it red.

"How do you fancy it?" Mahon asked.

"Not like this, and your half form sucks," I told him. "I want you at your best. You better bear out."

"In that case, you better come at me in your warrior form. It'll give you a better chance."

"No need," I answered.

He laid his hand on my shoulder and said quietly, "My son, if you hesitate or hold back, I will break you."

You'll try. "No more talk."

I let go. Heat flooded me. There was a tremendous warmth. It was like being stretched on a rack while being set on fire. And then everything pulled: bones, tendons, muscles, skin, all stretched tight. The hazy veil I didn't notice fell away and suddenly the world was painfully clear. I smelled it all, the wind from the icy sky, the hint of smoke from the Keep's kitchen, the dry stone, the clean snow, and the fur of a huge bear waiting to break my back.

Bear. Familiar scent. Safe. The same scent I had smelled years ago when I had no place to go and Mahon told me I had a home. He was huge then, big and rough, taller than me by almost a foot. *"You can stay here, boy. We'll treat you like our own. You don't have to call me Dad. Just Mahon will do."*

Across the balcony, the Kodiak shook his head. He was huge, nearly twelve feet tall and weighing almost a ton.

Going toe-to-toe with him was out of the question. I shook, testing the shift. Everything had fallen into place. I wasn't at full power, but that was fine. I was too pissed to take a rain check on this fight.

The shaggy, giant beast reared up onto his hind legs and roared at me. That's right, show me that big soft belly. I opened my mouth and roared back, drowning him out. Bring it, fat boy.

My best bet would be to bleed him. Dart in, bite or claw, then out again before those big paws could connect. Don't let him grab or hold me. If he could, Mahon would pull me into a hug and crush my head between his jaws. And if I was really lucky, he'd come at me just like this, on hind legs, gut out.

I dug into the snow, testing the ground. My paw found ice sheathing the stones. Slick.

Come on, bear. Come at me.

He dropped to all fours and shuffled toward me with his head lowered. Damn it.

If I let him, he would try to muscle me to the ground. In my first real fight I'd killed a similar bear, and it was still one of the hardest battles of my life.

Mahon kept moving, head down, shifting in, rocking from side to side. The bear shamble. It looked clumsy, but it let him use the thick layer of fur and fat that sheathed his forequarters like a shield. And a flank attack wouldn't go unpunished. Shambling or not, he was fast.

We'd never fought, not like this, but I had been watching him kill for the last fifteen years, and I knew he would use that big head like a sledgehammer. Getting head-butted by a bear was like being kicked by a horse. He'd knock me down and then put all that weight on me.

It was time to dance. I let him get within five feet of me. Mahon lunged. I dodged to the side and buried my claws in his head and neck. Mostly what I got was fur and fat, but it hurt him. The bear shook, trying to fling me off. I hung on and took a big bite out of his ear. The familiar taste of blood flooded my mouth.

Mahon bellowed in pain.

Yeah, that's gonna leave a mark.

Suddenly my paws left the ground, and then we were moving. He drove me back, like a hammer drives a nail. God, he was fucking strong.

There was nothing I could do about it except to let go. I released my hold. Too late. The wall slammed my back and the full bulk of the bear smashed into me.

Ouch.

THE WALL SHOOK. ON THE OTHER SIDE OF THAT WALL, CURRAN was getting a beat-down and he'd locked me out and left the boy wonder in position by the door to make sure it stayed shut.

The room was full of shapeshifters. The alphas, the betas, anyone with any sort of rank had shouldered their way in.

Jim loomed over Derek. The boy had grown, but Jim still had about three inches of height on him, and he squeezed everything he could out of them. "Move."

Derek didn't answer.

"It's an Order."

Derek stared straight ahead. The message was clear. Jim would have to kill him before he let that door open.

This was pointless. I pushed my way out of the room and into the hallway. Barabas emerged from the room behind me. I dragged myself down the hallway, away from the crowd. My leg was on fire. For once I wished that I had brought the stupid cane so I could move faster. We turned the corner.

"Is there another way to the balcony?" I whispered.

"Get, no. See, yes."

"Take me there."

"There are stairs," Barabas warned.

"Take me there or I will throw you out the window."

"Right this way, Alpha."

I BIT THE BRIDGE OF MAHON'S NOSE. WELCOME TO THE LION'S jaws.

He snarled in pain and dropped back.

I fell into the snow and retreated, putting some distance between us. My ribs ached. Heat flowed, knitting the fractured bones together. No major damage, but one more like that and I was done.

I had to bleed him. In and out. The Lyc-V would repair the damage, but not before Mahon bled. Enough blood in his eyes, and he'd be a lot easier to handle.

The bear shambled over. I dashed in, claws ready.

FIFTY MILLION FUCKING STAIRS, EACH STEP SHOOTING A BURST OF pain into my hip, until I wanted to claw my leg bloody just to get at the source of it.

Come on, Kate, push. Push.

"Sorry about this," Barabas said.

"Sorry about what?"

He picked me up and dashed up the stairs. Two seconds later and we burst out of a small iron door and onto the tiny stone balcony. We were in one of the side towers, at a ninety-degree angle to the main keep. Two floors below us, an enormous bear and my lion squared off on the bloody snow.

Oh, Curran. You stupid, stupid man.

Barabas lowered me to the floor.

Mahon was breathing hard. His shaggy flanks rose up and down as he expelled clouds of moist vapor through his nose. Blood drenched his sides. Curran limped slightly, favoring his left hind leg.

Curran lunged, a blur. I held my breath. He danced close, sliced at Mahon's face, and withdrew, avoiding a swipe of the colossal bear paw by a hair.

Curran was trying to bleed Mahon out, but the Lyc-V was healing him faster than he could hurt him. Sooner or later Mahon would catch him. And an hour ago Curran had been unconscious on his bed.

"Get me down to that balcony," I ground out.

"I can't," Barabas said. "It's too far."

I couldn't jump the distance, not with my leg. "Throw me."

"There are fifty yards between us and them, not to mention the thirty-foot drop," Barabas said. "Your broken body would land between an enraged bear and a blood-mad lion. It's my duty to assist you in any way I can, but suicide isn't on the menu."

My knee gave out. I sagged onto the stone rail and watched Curran fight. It was all I could do.

He was going to catch me. My side hurt like hell and my vision was a little blurry. Mahon had swatted my head with his paw twice. It had felt like being hit by a car. I couldn't take any more big shots to the head. I had to take him down and end this.

Mahon swiped at me. I snapped at him and backed away.

280

I had to goad him to go into a bear rage. If he rose on his hind legs, I had a chance.

I smelled Kate. She was here. Somehow, she was here. If I took my eyes off Mahon, he'd clobber me. Why couldn't she just do what she was told, one damn time, just one damn time?

Mahon charged.

I dodged left, straight into the wall. He thought he had me and closed in—huge, fast, and unstoppable. I bounced off the wall, flipped, and landed on top of him. Hello, old man. I pierced his hide and sliced through his fur with all four sets of claws, peeling it off him from his head to his big, shaggy ass.

Mahon bellowed in pain.

I leaped free and bit his snout. The bear paw caught my side. I took the hit—it hurt like hell—and swatted at his nose, cutting it. One, two, three. Again. Again.

He charged me again, his head lowered. I veered right, closed my jaws on his injured ear, and bit the rest of it off. The bear roared in pain and fury.

I spat the ear out and knocked it toward him with my paw. No, you can keep it. Doesn't taste that great.

The massive Kodiak bellowed like a foghorn and stood up.

Yep, that did it, now he was good and pissed.

With an earth-shattering roar, he lumbered toward me, all bear, no human thought or strategy now, motivated by pure rage and pain. It would be his undoing or mine.

MAHON ROSE ON HIS HIND LEGS. CURRAN LIMPED AWAY. HIS SIDE was bleeding—a bad sign. The Lyc-V wasn't keeping up with the repairs.

Mahon kept moving. Curran backed to the edge of the balcony. No place to go.

If I lost him here, to this idiotic fight, after I'd fought and guarded him for two weeks, after I'd cried and thought he was dying, I would find him in the afterlife and I would murder him again.

Mahon swung, too wide. Curran ducked under the huge claws, shockingly fast, and dug his own claws into the bear's left hind leg and bit down hard.

I knew how much pressure those jaws could unleash. He bit through the fur and the muscle, and then Mahon's leg folded like a broken toothpick as the huge feline fangs crushed his bones.

Curran twisted and kicked out with his back legs, a move no lion would ever think of without a human brain driving it. His battered body swung and his back crashed into Mahon's uninjured leg. For half a second, the bear remained upright by sheer force of will, and then he crashed, falling backward like a giant with his legs cut.

Oh my god.

Curran rolled out of the way before the enormous bulk could crush him. As Mahon lay on his back, Curran placed his front paws and weight on his chest. The massive leonine head dipped down. Curran opened his mouth. His jaws closed on Mahon's neck and held it, easy, almost gently.

A huge brown paw rose and fell.

It was over. Curran had won.

I LAY IN THE SNOW, EXHAUSTED. MY BODY FLOWED INTO THE familiar human form. Everything hurt. My body felt too hot, like I was burning from the inside out.

"Good fight, boy," Mahon boomed from somewhere to the right. "I'm proud of you."

"Shut up."

The snow was melting around me. The icy liquid felt good on my skin. Well, that's downright pleasant. I could lay here for a while as long as I didn't have to move.

"Still think she's worth it?" Mahon asked quietly.

"Of course. She's my mate."

Mahon sighed. "So you decided then."

"Do you think we'd be laying here bleeding in the snow if I wasn't sure?"

"Good point."

I picked up a handful of snow and put it on my face. Mmmm… That's nice.

"I hoped she would be one of us," Mahon said.

"Well, you can't always get what you hope for. I'd hoped my own people wouldn't try to murder my mate while I lay dying."

"It never came to that," Mahon said. "She's stronger than any of us knew."

"I knew."

"I figured." Mahon sighed again. "She'll never understand us completely."

"It's not always about you. This time it's about me. She understands me and that's enough."

Some sort of commotion was taking place behind the door.

"We're never doing this again," Mahon said.

"That's up to you. Anytime you need me to remind you…"

Mahon chuckled. "I've raised you too well."

The door flew off its hinges and slid across the snow, Derek on it. Well, couldn't say the kid didn't try.

Martha stormed onto the balcony.

"Oh-oh," Mahon murmured.

Mahon's wife stared down at us. Her hands went to her hips. "Which one of you idiots wants to explain to me what the hell is going on?"

With great effort, I raised my arm and pointed in Mahon's general direction. "Him."

Kate appeared in the doorway.

"What did you do to the boy?" Martha demanded.

"What did I do to him? Look at what he did to me!"

Kate knelt by me. I raised my hand and touched her cheek.

"You are an idiot," she told me.

"I know. Martha already pointed that out."

"Is it settled?" Martha demanded. It didn't seem aimed at me, so I didn't answer.

"Yes," Mahon said.

"Good. Get up."

There was some movement and then the two of them shambled off back to the door and the light of the Keep. As they passed us, Mahon dipped his head. "M'lord. M'lady."

Then they were gone. Derek followed them, carrying the door.

"You want to leave?" Kate asked.

"Not yet."

She sat in the snow next to me. I put my arm around her, pulling her close. Derek had put the door back in place. We were all alone. Just us, the snow, and the stars.

"That was a nice move with the jump," she said.

"You saw?"

"I saw."

I smiled. "I kicked his ass."

"Yes, you did. You need help getting to your feet, ass-kicker?"

"That's my line."

She laughed quietly. "I can't carry you, you know."

"Give me another five minutes. I should be able to walk."

We sat in the snow and watched the stars. Tomorrow I'd have to deal with all their shit again. But tonight was ours. We'd earned it.

**Prequel
(Magic Breaks)**

It was moving day. Kate, Julie and me were taking boxes out of the back of a rented truck and carrying them into our new place. Kate had labeled them. "Kitchen, living room, master bedroom," etc. It felt odd to have all these different spaces after living in two rooms for so long. The plan was to get all the boxes in before we started unpacking them.

Once we announced that we were stepping down, we had ninety days to separate from the Pack. We were lucky to find a big three-story house located in a subdivision within riding distance to Cutting Edge and Julie's school. It even had a place in the back for Kate and the kid to ride horses. Which I honestly couldn't care less about, but it made the girls happy.

It's not that I don't like horses. Okay, I really don't like them. I just don't see the point. They're big but terribly fragile. Feed one too much food or the wrong food, and they die, just like that. If they step into a pothole and break a leg, you have to put them down. What other animal do you have to do that for? When I was a kid we had a cat with three legs and half a tail. His name was Casper and he got around just fine. When I was a kid...

Yeah, I didn't think a lot about my childhood probably for a good reason. I couldn't really complain though. It had been great before...it became a lot less so. Better not to think about it.

Kate and Julie were struggling to team-lift a big box of books, so I came over, picked it up, and carried it in one hand like a waiter would with a plate or tray of food.

"Where would you like this, ma'am?"

"Show-off," Kate said. "It says 'Library' on it."

"Oh? I thought that was perhaps the work of some deranged graffiti artist."

"Aha. I asked you if you wanted to label them and you passed."

"I was busy, actually packing. I think I did pretty well for my first time."

"Wait, you never moved before?" Julie asked.

"No, not really. When Mahon found me, I didn't really have a lot. All my crap fit into a backpack. I tried to take only what I needed to survive. If you steal too much, people start to notice. I never stayed in one place too long and needed to be able to move quick and quiet."

"Holy crap," she said. "You were a juvenile delinquent."

Kate shot her a warning look. Julie ignored it.

"That's so cool."

I never thought of it as cool before. Lonely, starving and scared, yes. Cool, not so much.

"Julie," Kate started, "I don't think he wants to talk about it."

"No, it's okay. It wasn't exactly like that. I was twelve and after my parents...after they were gone, I lived alone in the woods for several months. I hunted when I could and tried to stay out of the rain but springs in the Smokies are inconsistent. That's when you get the heaviest snows. One day it's nice and the next there's a blizzard. When I was cold, wet, and hungry enough, I would sneak into unoccupied cabins. Some were really nice."

"You never got caught?"

"Just the once. I was careful and made sure the owners were away. Lots of people, especially before the Shift, had vacation homes in the mountains. Usually Florida people who came up in the summer to get away from the heat and in the fall to watch the leaves turn. Most didn't stay for winter. Some came up only for the holidays in winter but it's not as pretty. Just cold, wet and grey."

"How did you know which ones would have food and stuff?"

"The vacation homes were always bigger and nicer than the houses of people that lived there year round. It's a poor area. Some locals live in little more than rundown shacks. They usually have a lot of guns though. I avoided those."

"That's f...messed up."

"Language," Kate warned.

"I didn't say it," Julie said. "But if I had, it would be true."

"She's right." I added helpfully, "It is pretty fucked up. That area suffers from what we would call an 'income disparity' between the tourists and the locals. They had plenty and it didn't really bother me to take what I needed."

"Damn straight," Julie said.

"Language," Kate warned again.

"What?" she said, "I can say damn, it's in the Bible."

"She's got you there."

Kate squinted at us. "How about the two of you stop standing around and actually carry some of this shi…stuff into the house."

"Ha!" Julie said. "You said shit and you owe me a dollar."

Kate, in an effort to curb Julie's cursing, had adopted a system in which the curser owed a buck for each offense. I didn't know what the tally was but I was guessing they were about even.

"I didn't say the whole word," Kate said. "So I owe you fifty cents."

"Seventy-five!"

"Fine."

"I'm hungry, what's for lunch?" Julie asked.

Kate glanced at her. "You just ate before we left. It's barely been a couple of hours."

"Yeah, but we've been working hard, and I'm hungry."

"Me too," I said. "Will you make us something?"

Kate leaned against the stack of boxes. "If you find the kitchen stuff and unpack it. I can't cook if I don't have pans."

"You drive a hard bargain, dread mistress. We accept your offer. Come on, Julie, the sooner we do it, the sooner we eat."

Later, after we had carried all the boxes with Kitchen marked on them into the actual kitchen, and I brought in the table and the chairs, Kate made us some iced tea and then went to off to unpack bathroom essentials. Julie and I started on the boxes. The sooner we put all the pots and pans into the cabinets, the sooner I would get a meal.

It felt strange but good to be settling into the new house. This was our home now, Kate's, Julie's and mine. It had seemed abstract or theoretical before. The house we considered, the house looked at, the house we bought. Now putting our stuff up made it more real.

Julie asked, "So how did you get caught?"

"What? Why do you want to know?"

"I dunno, everybody knows about how you became the Beast Lord, but nobody talks about what you were before. How come?"

"'Cause it's not a pretty story. I didn't pull a sword from a stone. A giant man didn't come on my birthday to tell me that I was a wizard." Well, Mahon had seemed like a giant to me then.

Julie's eyes got really big. "Tell me."

"It's full of gore and bad things happening," I said.

"I've been through some rough shit."

"I heard that!" Kate yelled from the bathroom.

"I can handle it."

I gave her my flat stare. The one meant to convey that I was done discussing something.

"I told you before that didn't work on me. I know you won't hurt me, so stop pretending."

"I know you have been through a lot, and I'm sorry about that. What happened to you wasn't fair, but sometimes the past is best left, well, in the past."

"That's deep," Julie said. "You read that in a fortune cookie?"

She was getting as bad as Kate with mouthing off when she felt uncomfortable, but unlike Kate, she would correct herself if I waited. Three, two...

"Sorry," she said. "I don't like the stare. I understand. I don't like talking about my mom and," she paused and made a hand gesture, "all that stuff."

Because it still hurt. "It will hurt less with time."

"You're old," she said. "If it still hurts too much to talk about it after all that time, then it will probably never stop hurting for me."

Ouch, she had me there.

Julie knew I told this story to only one person—Kate—and now that we were a family, she wanted to know that she was trusted. We were a family. Family knew things outsiders didn't.

"Alright. But it's a long story."

"I won't interrupt," she said. "And I promise I won't tell anyone."

And so I told her, all of it, the whole ugly story.

"MY FATHER AND MOTHER WERE BOTH IN THE MILITARY. HE WAS in the Marines. She was in the Army. The Marines and Army shared a base and they both took courses at the education center. Once the Shift came, my mother was the first to turn. When my dad saw her transform into a lion, it triggered something and he changed shape, too. They both knew that unless they were willing to become guinea pigs for the military, they had to get out before anyone found out. They resigned.

"They had some connections and they tried joining a pack not too far from the base, but it didn't work. My dad was like me. People saw him as a leader and the alpha saw him as a threat. When he tried to claim my mom as part of his harem, my dad killed him. Easily. Then they wanted him to be their pack leader. He didn't want to do it, but he had agreed because he felt responsible for killing the alpha. When it became clear that he wouldn't be taking on any new mates, one of the tougher females tried to kill my mom who was pregnant. My parents left after that."

"With the money they'd saved up they bought a large log cabin in Appalachians. My dad knew that the area had a reputation for being insular and not particularly welcoming to outsiders. That suited him just fine. After their experience with the pack, they just wanted to be left alone and live on their own terms. Not in charge of anyone else and answerable to only themselves."

"Understandable," Julie said. "But you didn't grow up in a rundown shack?"

"Not at all. It was great. Not as big as this place, but not small or dirty."

"So no outhouse?"

I laughed. "No, I don't think my mother would've stood for it. We had indoor plumbing and electricity. Modern conveniences. This was post-Shift so we had a gas generator for when the power went out. Later, when they stopped repairing the power lines, we mostly used it for the fridge. Like I said, my parents were ex-military. Both had been deployed and spent their fair share of time in the field. They wanted to be comfortable and they wanted something nice for us."

"Us? Who else was there?"

"At first just the three of us, then, when I was about five, my sister Alice was born. I was jealous at first. They paid a lot of attention to her. Later it was nice to have another kid around."

"You were close?"

"Of course, it was just us and our parents. She thought I was awesome. In her eyes I was king of the woods. I showed her where to pick the best berries and where to catch the fattest fish. The best places to hide when she wanted to get out of chores or classes."

"Wait, where did you guys go to school and did you walk uphill both ways?"

"No, that's impossible and I guess we were," what's the term, "homeschooled."

"That's sweet. I wish I could stay home and goof around all day."

"You would start howling at the walls in two weeks," Kate called out.

"We had our lessons. Both my parents were well educated. They taught us to read and write. No books were off limits and they made sure we had plenty of time to read. Literature and history were always easy for me. Math was harder. We had an old laptop and there were games that taught us, using fun cartoon characters."

Julie smiled.

"What?"

"I just can't see you playing little kid games."

"I was a little kid. What I'm trying to say is that we had a pretty nice childhood. When my dad thought I was old enough, he started taking me out with him hunting and fishing. I used to love being out in the woods, alone or just me and him."

"Alice didn't go with you?"

"Oh no. At first she was too young and then she talked too much for hunting. You have to be very still and very quiet to sneak up on something. It sounds bad to say, but she had a really hard time being quiet. I can't remember when she couldn't talk. Even when she was a baby, she babbled nonsense constantly. Sometimes Mom and Dad would got out hunting together and leave me to babysit. I would get so mad that I wouldn't talk to them, and Alice would try to make me laugh. I still miss her."

"I'm sorry," Julie said.

"Me too."

"Did they work? What did you guys do for money?"

"We traded mostly. Meat, some vegetables, corn, potatoes and ginseng that we found in the woods. Sometimes when we got low on money or supplies, my dad would disappear for a while and come back with presents and cash. Then we'd get to

291

go to Gatlinburg for supplies. One time they took us to an amusement park run by a famous country singer. I remember because we all had fun. That was right before…"

"Before what?" Julie asked.

"Before everything changed. Before the loups came."

"Oh shit," Julie said. "You don't have to tell the rest of it if you don't want to."

"No, it's okay. We're family now and I feel like you should know why I am the way I am. I remember reading somewhere that we are the sum total of our experiences. Does that make sense?"

"Yeah. It's like sometimes fucked up shit happens but it makes you who you are. You can't change it."

"Exactly. We should put that on a shirt for Kate."

Julie laughed. "Or business cards that she could hand out."

"We could engrave it on some brass knuckles, so she could punch it into people when she got irritated," I said.

"So what happened with the loups?" Julie asked.

"I was twelve when they came for us. It was my sister's turn to set the table. Mom cooked, one of us kids set or cleared the table, and my dad did the dishes. When my mom called for her and she didn't come, they sent me out to find her. I was annoyed because she had a habit of hiding when we had work to do."

"You found her?"

"Yes, but not before they did. I thought she was napping up in a tree. I called out and when she didn't answer me I was going to climb up and push her out. Instead I walked right into a trap. They strung me up with a silver noose."

"Jesus, that's brutal!"

"It is. That's what loups do, Julie. They don't feel fear or pity; all they know is hunger and desire. They can never really satiate either."

"Is that why you hate them so much?"

"Yes. They took everything from me that day. They didn't kill me but they took my life just the same."

"Your parents?"

"When I didn't come back with Alice, my dad followed my scent to the clearing. They were waiting for him, using me as bait. He was strong. He fought and killed some of them but the rest tore into him and took him down. There were too many and he was just one man. After they were done with him, they went after my mom. She didn't stand a chance. Their madness makes them very fast and strong."

"How did you…" She let it hang there.

Not die, not get raped and eaten by monsters?

"Escape?" I offered.

"Yeah, did Mahon come and save you?"

"No. I wish that was the way it happened. That the big bear had come in time and that he and my dad had fought and killed the loups. I really believe between the two of them they could have."

"Could you? Now I mean."

"Maybe. I used to think about that a lot. If I had been older, stronger. In my daydreams I used to save them. In the nightmares I'm still weak and hang there, helpless, while they tear my father apart."

"Holy shit, do you still have those?"

"Not as much anymore. Right after it happened and I slept in the woods I used to always wake up sure that they were sneaking up on me. Still happens sometimes."

"That's messed up. You need to see somebody."

She was probably right.

"Maybe. It's too late now and I was too mad then. I don't think I could have talked about all of it with a stranger. What would they say? That my family is in a better place now? That it was all part of God's plan?"

"Yeah, I hate that crap. Do you believe in Him?"

"I don't know. I'm not an atheist, I've seen too much weird shit to not believe in anything. I guess I think that if He does exist then He has a hell of a lot to answer for. Kind of makes me more of an angry agnostic."

"Careful, you'll go to hell for that sort of talk."

"L'enfer, c'est les autres."

"What? Is that Irish or something?"

"Hell is other people," I quoted. "No, it's French, actually."

"What is that supposed to mean?"

"I believe it means we create enough pain and suffering here on Earth."

"That's heavy. I didn't know you spoke French."

"A little. My mother taught me. They wanted me to be able to read Sartre and Camus in the original language. My dad was big on the benefits of a 'classical education.' I think he minored in philosophy."

"Hey," she said, "you're avoiding the question."

"What question?" I knew what she was talking about but I hoped she hadn't noticed me steering the conversation away from that.

"How you got away?"

"Oh, really? Like you said, I'm old and I forget things."

"You just don't want to tell me."

"No, it's not that, it's just that I needed some time to work up to it."

"You don't have to."

"I know, but I want to or maybe need to. Where did we leave off?"

"Mahon didn't save you?"

"No, that part comes later. Anyway, so like I said when I crawled up the tree to get Alice, they got me. They slipped a silver wire over my head and wrapped me up in silver netting. Hurt like hell. After they got done with my dad, they went after my mom. I think hearing her cries made me a little crazy. I struggled and the wire must have cut through the branch I was hanging on. Must have taken some time to get free of the mesh because by then my mother wasn't screaming anymore."

"Oh my god," Julie said quietly, "that's horrible."

"I told you. So I ran. They chased me but I knew the area better and they made a lot of noise and gave up when they couldn't find me after a while. It went on like that for a few months. They stayed in our house and I hid and watched them. I knew I couldn't take them all so I waited, hoping to catch one of them on their own."

"Did you? Take them out one by one?"

"No, they were always together. There were only five by then, my dad had killed three, but that was still too much for me. Then," I added. Or now, I thought. If I was really honest with myself I would know that one sane shapeshifter against five loups was potential suicide.

"So you just lived alone in the woods? How did you survive on your own?"

"March is a vicious bitch in the mountains, cold and hard as ice. At first, I watched them as long as I could but I also knew that eventually I needed to find food and shelter if I didn't want to get sick or die from exposure. So I found a place that looked empty and I broke in."

"Was it one of the nice ones?" Julie asked.

"Oh yeah, it seemed wonderful to me, but I hadn't really eaten or slept more than an hour or two in a probably a week. I was starving so I raided the pantry and ate most of the dry cereal and canned goods. We can go for a while without food or sleep, but not both. My body shut down and I stayed there for days dead to the world and only getting up to eat. I had nightmares the loups were outside waiting for me. Most of the time I would wake up and freak out wondering where I was and why my family wasn't there. Then I remembered."

"Did you cry? It's okay if you did. I won't tell anybody."

"No, I wanted to but I couldn't. I never saw my father cry. I promised myself that I wouldn't either until I punished the cowards who murdered him. But it was more than that. I'd never in my life felt as helpless as did I hanging in that tree, watching while he fought for his life, his wife and his son, and lost. Powerless to stop what came after."

"It wasn't your fault. You were just a kid and they would've killed you too."

"Oh, I know that now. But I had to deal with it somehow so I decided then and there that I would never be that weak again and I would never feel that same fear. It was that or give in and let the grief swallow me. It's like a line from an old song that goes, 'When I was young I was so full of fear, I hid behind anger, held back my tears.'"

"Is it that band you like to listen to when you lift weights, *Social Destruction?*"

"*Distortion,*" I corrected. "Yeah, them."

"What's it called, the song I mean?"

"I was wrong."

"Well, then it's definitely not about you." Julie checked my face to see if I was going to snarl. I wasn't.

"That's funny so I'll let it pass."

"So what happened? Did you just you run out of random houses to burglarize?"

"Sort of. One time I woke up and the loups really were outside. I guess they ran out of food and had the same idea as me. Only they didn't care if a place was empty or not. If there were people in a place, it just meant more food and fun for them."

Julie made a face. "That's awful."

"Indeed. I got away, but I realized then that I had to be more careful. I couldn't stay in one place too long or risk them tracking me to a house that was occupied. I learned to wait. I started watching places from really far away and for a long time before approaching them. I didn't just bust the front door open. I looked for unlocked windows that I could climb through."

"Oh yeah," Julie said, "that's what I did. I guess they think that nobody can get in that way but if you're small you can. When we ran out of food or money, Red would send me into places to get food and stuff we could sell. I always looked for a bathroom window first, they almost never lock them. I don't know why."

"I believe it's because most people when they think of thieves, think of adults, grown-ups. Not children hungry or desperate enough to squeeze through a bathroom or upstairs window."

Julie seemed to think about it. Maybe about that time in her life. Finally she spoke. "Happens though."

"It did to us."

Perhaps sensing a lull in the conversation, Kate chose that moment to enter the kitchen.

"Would you two like to eat or do you want to finish?" she asked, her voice quiet. "I can wait on the meal."

"Food," Julie and I said in unison.

"Food it is," Kate said.

"To be continued?" Julie asked.

"If you'd like."

"You cool with steaks?" Kate asked. "I've got three nice ones here."

"Sure, but what are you guys going to eat?"

"I guess we'll just have to make do with a bunch of Texas toast."

"Ah, I could be persuaded to trade a couple of steaks for some of that."

"What did you eat?" Julie asked. "You know, back then."

"Whatever I could find and keep down. I was always hungry.

But when it got warmer, I hunted. I already knew the basics before, and as the days and weeks passed, I got really good at it. When the loups went out, I followed them. It became like a game, seeing how close I could get without them catching me. Again."

"Did you ever go back in your house, like when they were gone, to get some of your stuff or whatever?" Julie asked.

"No, never."

"Why not?"

"Didn't seem right. For many reasons. If they smelled me in there, they would take it as a challenge and start looking for me again. Not just that though. I guess I didn't feel like it belonged to me anymore. They took it away and it was theirs now. It wouldn't be mine until I was strong enough to take it back."

"You know that sounds really weird, right?"

"Does it? Made sense to me at the time." Still did. Made more sense than sneaking into my house like a thief. But it was more than that. I didn't want to smell them in my house, see what they'd done to it. It would have been too much, I left all my pain and grief there, all I kept was my anger. It was enough to keep me going.

The steaks were warm and rare, the toast slightly burned the way I liked it. Julie had spent enough time around shapeshifters to know better than to ask more questions while we ate. When we were done, Julie and I cleared the dishes from the table.

"I'll wash and you can dry. Kate cooked so she's off the hook."

"Will you tell me the rest?" Julie asked.

"After. Let's get the dishes done first. It will give me time to remember. I spent most of my life trying to forget."

"You were doing fine before, what happened? Did they catch you and put you in a hillbilly jail?"

"No. I said after."

"Fine."

"It is fine," Kate said. "Help him with the dishes while I finish unpacking the kitchen. Then he'll tell you the rest. Won't you?"

"I said I would."

I wasn't lying. It'd been twenty-some years ago and at the time I had no idea how long I'd been running around the woods. The days got warmer and then it snowed again. The woods were cold and quiet. I slept a lot, ate what I could catch. It wasn't much. Nothing really happened until after the storm. Yeah, that's where I'd start.

We finished the dishes, while Kate unpacked more kitchen boxes. You never quite know how much stuff you have until you have to move. I thought her house in Savannah had been mostly empty, but it took us a week to pack the damn place.

"We'll work on the living room," I said. "Julie can set up her own bedroom."

"Yeah, I'm not a baby."

"Nobody said you were," Kate murmured. She was staring at some spice jars with a look of intense concentration on her face.

"Come on, Julie. We'll do the rugs and bookcases while I tell you the rest."

"If you'd like," she told me. Funny kid.

"A blizzard? In April?"

"Yes. I told you. It's not uncommon in those parts. This one was a big deal. Snowed nineteen inches in Asheville. They had to send the Army to rescue people."

"Did the Army rescue you?" Julie asked.

"No. The Bear did."

"Mahon," she said. It wasn't a question. "He found you."

"Sort of. I was hunting one morning. Hoping to catch a deer or maybe a hog. A deer would have been better. Hogs have a lot of meat, but they're mean and tough as hell. There was still some snow on the ground, and I was looking for tracks when I smelled smoke. I thought maybe the loups had burned someone's house or barn. I climbed up a tree. It was a campfire. Several men moving around in a clearing making coffee and breakfast. It smelled amazing. My stomach rumbled so hard, I thought they'd hear it."

"Did you go down and ask them for 'more sir?'" Julie asked.

"No, Dodger. That's how you get nicked."

She snickered. She'd watched *Oliver Twist* during tech and decided she liked it. Her one criticism was that Oliver was too much of a wimp and a sharp knife would've greatly improved his lot in life.

"I was hungry," I continued, "but I just watched. I didn't know who they were or what they were looking for. Might have been after me for the break-ins, maybe they were just out hunting like me. There was something strange about them."

"What?"

"They moved different. They were quiet. They hardly spoke to each other. They didn't laugh or joke. Just set up their tents, made food, a lot of food, and ate it without talking."

"You guys eat a lot."

"We need to. That's why I was hungry all the time. I was a teenage lion, but I was cautious. Maybe a little feral. A human child lost in the woods would have just walked into the camp and asked for some of their food."

"But you didn't."

"No, I climbed down and moved a little closer, quiet like my dad taught me."

"They didn't know you were there?"

I laughed.

"Why is that funny?"

"I'll get to that part; you have to wait."

"Okay, it's your story. Tell it how you want."

"Thank you. Where was I? You keep interrupting me and throwing me off."

"You were sneaking up on them, like a shapeshifting ninja."

"Yes. Exactly like that. I got as close as I dared and just watched them for a bit longer. I was hoping they would head out and leave the camp empty."

"You were going to steal their food."

"That was the plan. But they didn't leave. It was like they were waiting for something. That was when the biggest bear I had ever seen ambled out of the woods on the other side of the camp and sat down at the fire."

"Did they freak the fu...fudge out? I said fudge. What did they do?"

"Nothing. Well, they brought the bear some food and one of men squatted down and seemed to talk to it for a bit, real quiet. I couldn't hear what he said."

Julie's voice took on a more pronounced southern drawl. "That right there is what we in the sleuthing business call a clue. You should have known something was up."

"You're not wrong, but what the hell did I know? I thought maybe they had a trained bear. But?"

"But what?"

"I'd seen black bears. I knew their scent and to stay away from them, but he was three times their size and smelled different. The men too. I got a little closer and they smelled strange. Like dogs but not."

"Wolves?" Julie guessed.

"Yes. It was Mahon and he brought some of the werewolves with him. No matter what Rats and Jackals say, Wolves are best trackers."

"He was looking for you?"

I shook my head. "He was looking for the loups. After the storm, some local law enforcement started checking on folks. Found victims. The loups had been careless. Left bodies half-eaten and rotting. Most of the cops thought it was serial killer or a satanic cult. A few recognized it for what it was and quietly contacted Mahon down in Atlanta."

"You mean the Pack? He was the Beast Lord before you, right?"

"No. There wasn't the Pack the way there is now. It was more like a collection of families and individuals, but it wasn't really that organized. Mahon was sort of in charge of the Bears, but others respected him because he was the biggest and the strongest. He had connections with some cops and the Order. He could have started the Pack if he wanted to."

"Why didn't he?" Julie asked.

"I always wondered about that when I was younger. The easy answer is that bears just aren't that social. In the wild they don't live in packs or even family groups. Mainly because they don't need to. They're big and strong enough to hunt and fend for themselves. When they do fight, it's almost always with other bears for food and to mate."

"But he's mostly a man. Yeah, a big scary man, but I've never even seen him turn into a bear."

"I hope you never do."

"How'd you know he wasn't one of..." Julie hesitated.

"One of the loups?" I finished for her.

"Yeah."

"It's hard to explain unless you're a shapeshifter."

"I'm not dumb."

"It's not about that. What do I smell like to you?"

"What does that mean? You smell like a guy, I guess."

"Exactly."

"That's not fair."

"Life rarely is. But I will try."

"Please do."

"Okay, so if you were a young rat, or heaven forbid a bouda..."

Julie made a face. "I wouldn't be that. I'd be a wolf."

"You'd be what one or both of your parents were. Nobody gets to pick. Anyway, if you were one of those, I would smell like a big scary cat. My scent would say 'Danger. Proceed with caution.'"

"I'm not afraid of you."

"That's intellect, not instinct. When we smell loups, it alarms us. They smell like rage and hunger. They smell wrong."

"That's what Derek says. You know he hates them more than you do."

"He has reason to."

"He won't talk to me about it. I know something happened to his family. Something really bad."

"It was terrible."

"Worse than what happened to you?"

"I don't know. Worst thing that ever happened to him. He was pretty fucked up when we found him. I wasn't sure he'd recover."

"Hey!" Kate yelled from the kitchen. "Language."

How had she even heard that? "We are the makers of manners, Kate, and the liberty that follows our places…" I began to quote at her.

"Less talk, more work," Kate called out.

"Let the forfeit be nominated for a pound of your fair flesh."

She appeared in the doorway, holding a can opener. "Curran. Stop showing off and just tell the damn story."

"Yes, of course, dread consort."

"You guys are weird," Julie said.

"You have no idea."

"You can tell me about Derek. I'm old enough."

"It's his story, Julie. Maybe he'll talk about it. Or he won't. Where were we?"

"You were lurking in the woods and waiting to steal food from shapeshifters."

"Ah. After the bear finished eating, the men followed him

back into the woods. I waited a bit more and then made my way into the camp. I was very pleased with myself. I'd avoided them way I had the loups. Then I saw it."

"What?"

"They made me a plate, and there was a note. It said, 'Boy, enjoy the food and find us when you want more. You don't have to steal and you don't need to be afraid of us. We're like you.'"

"They knew you were there?"

"The whole damn time. I felt like an idiot, so I grabbed some of the food, stuffed it in my face, and took off as fast as I could in the opposite direction. I ran as far as I could and found another tree to hide in."

"Were you scared?"

"No, not really. Maybe a little. More shocked, I think. I needed time to, what do they call it now? Process everything? What did they mean they were like me? The only others I knew like me were my parents and sister. The loups sure as hell weren't like me."

"You never met any other shapeshifters?"

"Not that I remember. We were isolated. I knew there were others, I knew my parents had belonged to a pack, but I knew it in the way I knew Mars is the fourth planet from the Sun. But now others like me were real. I'd seen and smelled them."

Julie pretended to write something on an imaginary notepad. "And how did that make you feel?"

"Ha. I was confused. Where were they from and why were they here? I was also a little afraid for them. I was scared the loups would find them. I didn't know at the time that they'd come to hunt the loups. That someone, anyone, would want to find them seemed crazy to me. There were five of them. My dad and mom were the strongest creatures I knew and even they couldn't take all of them at once. My dad killed three of them, but in the end they murdered him and ate him. Mahon only brought four wolves."

"Was that enough?"

"I would have brought more. In his defense, loups rarely travel in groups that large, so for all he knew he was tracking one or two. He probably planned on killing them himself after the wolves chased them down. But loups are stronger than most shapeshifters. Five of them working together would have brought Mahon down. Eventually."

"Did you warn them?"

"I wanted to, but I didn't want to expose myself. I still wasn't sure I could trust them."

"But they left food out for you."

"Did you trust everyone who gave you food or money when you were on the street?"

"No, I'm not stupid."

"Neither was I. I wasn't street smart like you, but I was wary."

The doorbell rang.

"Hold that thought." A familiar mix of scents floated on the draft. "It's Mahon and Martha and they brought honey muffins."

"How do you know that?" she asked.

I touched my nose.

"Oh yeah."

Mahon didn't exactly approve of my leaving the Pack. He didn't take it well. He viewed it as me turning my back on everything we built together. I hadn't seen him for a month. Martha called and told me he would come around. Apparently, she was right.

I opened the door and my second mother gave me a hug.

"We came to help," she said. "Where's Kate?"

"In the kitchen. Do I get one of those?" I nodded at the old-fashioned wicker basket Mahon was carrying. The top was covered with a checkered towel.

Martha smiled. "If you're good. Leave some for the child."

"Hi, Martha," Julie said from behind me.

Martha pushed past me and pulled Julie into a hug, then stood back and seemed to look her over.

"Oh, Julie. You're too skinny. Curran, are you not feeding her enough?"

"I thought so. Are you supposed to feed them every day?"

"Don't listen to him, Martha. We just had steak and Texas toast!" Kate shouted from the kitchen.

"I'm coming to help." Martha turned, snatched the basket out her husband's arms, and headed off towards the sound of Kate's voice.

"Boy." Mahon still stood in the doorway, arms crossed against his massive chest, looking displeased.

"Old bear. Would you like to come in?" I asked.

"That would be nice." Mahon stepped inside and scrutinized the walls. "It's a good house, new but built well."

"Thanks, we like it. It needs some work but nothing major."

"All houses need work. You check the plumbing and the wiring?"

"And the roof."

Mahon grunted and pondered the floor, looking for some sort of flaw in it.

"Curran was telling me how he saved you from loups when he was young," Julie volunteered.

Mahon stared at her and then me, then made a deep rumbling noise somewhere between a roar and a cough. It was his version of a chuckle.

"Was he, now? Would you like to know what really happened?"

"Yes!"

"That's good because you're too old for fairy tales." He turned to me. "Do you have a place to sit down?"

"Do you want me to put a rocking chair on the porch for you?" I offered.

"Do you have one?"

"No."

We stared at each other.

"I'll get you a chair," Julie said and went off into the kitchen.

"I've got this," I told him.

"Clearly, you don't. How much have you told her?" he asked in a low voice.

"You mean about my parents?"

"That."

"Everything, and a little of what happened after."

"Why?"

"She asked. She's family."

Julie came back with a sturdy wooden kitchen chair. Mahon settled into it.

"You want a pillow for your back?" I asked him.

"No. I've got enough padding."

"It's the honey muffins. Not good for a man of your age to eat so many."

Mahon snorted. "You like them more than I do. Do you remember the first time you had one? I've never seen a boy so happy."

"I remember. It was amazing."

"We're getting ahead of ourselves," he told me. "I promised to tell the girl the way I remember it, so I better start with how I got involved."

"Curran said the police contacted you after they found some bodies."

"Park ranger, as I recall. Mike Shelton. A good man. Steady. He helped look for people after the storm. Called me after they started finding folks tore apart."

"How did he know it was loups?" Julie asked.

"Mike's a bobcat," I told her.

Mahon nodded. "He knew I was in down in Atlanta and asked if I could come up take a look. He may have also mentioned that there was another cat bumbling around in the same territory as the loups. Big but young and clumsy. Said he'd tracked him to some empty cabins that had been broken into but didn't think he was the murderer."

"Mike didn't say that," I told him.

Mahon chuckled. "Anyway, I called Francois Ambler, the leader of the wolves, asked if he wanted to help but due to him being a coward, he refused to get involved. Not all of his people were so timid though and a few volunteered to come up with me. You remember Francois?" Mahon asked me.

"I recall him running away when Aldorf went berserk."

"Francois always was a coward. At that time, there was no Pack, only individual clans of shapeshifters, every kind of beast for themselves. The wolves were the most numerous and the least stable. They got a new leader every damn week and Francois was the latest. Word was, he got where he did by stabbing his predecessor in the back, and since then he'd been holding on to the alpha spot by the skin of his teeth. I was doing him a favor, you see. Killing loups is a matter of honor for every shapeshifter. I gave him a chance to do something that would make him look good and he told me to go...he declined."

"Wait, who's Aldorf?" Julie asked.

"That's another story altogether," I told her. "Let him tell this one or we'll never get any of those honey muffins."

"Where did he leave off?" Mahon asked.

Julie sat on the floor in front of him. "Curran was hiding in a tree and trying to decide if he should warn you about the loups. He took some food, read the note, but he wasn't sure about you."

Mahon nodded. "Sounds about right. So, I was wandering around the woods a bit on the first morning, glad to be out of the city. It was a grand thing. Fresh snow on the ground, the forest was clean and quiet. A good place except it reeked of loups. They'd ran back and forth like some crazed idiots, pissed everywhere, and I couldn't make sense of their crazy scent trails, so I went back to the camp to confer with the trackers and for some breakfast. Right away one of the wolves, Dolph, the oldest, comes over and tells me to look up into the trees, but to be subtle about it."

"Why?" Julie asked.

"Because they knew he was there, but he didn't know we knew. The wolves smelled him a mile off. He stank like a cat that had rolled in carrion."

"I was covering my scent," I objected. "Worked on the loups."

"Loups are stupid. Crazy, strong and fast but not smart or persistent. Lucky for you."

"I don't remember feeling lucky at the time."

"Doesn't matter now. Anyway, he was alive and knew enough to not just walk into our camp. Figured I'd let him be for a bit. He'd come down when he was ready. Besides, we had things besides lost children to look for in those woods. So, we left him some food, the note, and went on about finding those bastards. The woods in those parts are thick and dark. Once we were in the thick of it, the wolves turned, and we headed out to one of the houses that had been attacked so the wolves could get the scent to try to sort out how many of them were there. They picked up a trail and we followed it.

"The wolves were faster than me and better trackers, so we took it nice and slow. The plan was to find them, not stumble into them. Wouldn't be good if loups found the trackers, but I was too far back to help."

Mahon leaned back, settling into the chair.

"Up on the ridge the trail split. Two of them turned right, up a mountain, and the third one went south, down off the slope. We followed him to a shallow ravine, coming in downwind, so he wouldn't smell us. He'd caught a hog a couple of days back and hid it in the ravine from the others, so he could eat it himself. When we got close, the wolves fanned out, one on each side and one behind. Most loups would rather fight than run, but I didn't want this one getting away. Once the others were in place, Dolph and I started to move in for the kill. We had the bastard cornered. He was a big one, over seven feet. The thing about loups, they are always shifting. They can't go fully back into a human or an animal, so you never know what sort of mess you're going to get."

"What did you get with that one?" Julie asked.

"A panther of some kind. Very rare for cats to go loup, but when they do, it's a terrible thing. Cats are cruel by nature and loupism makes them do perverted, sick things. So, I came into the ravine, and he got off his kill and started snarling and biting the air. I was backing him up against the rock, with the wolves closing in on both sides. I knew he'd go down hard and I was almost wishing I'd brought more wolves. So, the loup rears up and roars. Teeth like steak knives. Huge claws. Neck the size of a man's thigh."

I rolled my eyes.

Mahon fixed Julie with his gaze. "That's when a skinny, dirty kid dropped out of a tree. He is falling through the air and he turns into something I'd never seen before, big and grey and striped with black. I thought I'd gone crazy. So he falls on top of the son of a bitch and roars, and the sound is like thunder. It was a hell of a thing."

Julie's eyes were wide like saucers.

"Oh, it gets better. The huge grey demon puts its enormous paws on each side of the loup's head, digs his claws in, gives it a good twist and pulls the head clean off. Blood gushes everywhere, bright red on the white snow. Then, he holds the bloody thing out and growls, 'Mine.'"

"He was," I said. "And by the way, none of you knew I was up in that tree. Who sucks in the woods now, old man?"

Mahon ignored me. "One of the wolves snarled at him, more out of surprise than anything. The beast roared again and that sound, it punched right through your body to your bones. I'd never heard anything like that before. Chilled my

310

blood. I may have backed up a step or two. That's when I knew."

"Knew what?" Julie asked.

"That he was a First," Mahon said proudly as if that explained everything.

"That's a big deal, right?"

Mahon turned to me. "You've neglected her education."

"I don't like to brag," I told him.

"Since when?" Kate asked from the kitchen.

Martha laughed.

"Child," Mahon addressed Julie. "It is a very big deal. Firsts are exceptionally rare. Their magic is old and powerful. They are meant to rule the other shapeshifters. When they lead us, they make us stronger. It's in their blood." He paused and looked over at me.

Yeah, yeah, I got the message. Still not coming back to the Pack.

Mahon smiled at Julie. "I went into the woods that day on some bad bloody business and found a diamond in the dirt. Sure, it was a rough and unpolished thing, but it had great potential."

"I'm not sure that analogy works," I told him.

"Sure, it does." Mahon winked at Julie. "He cleaned up good though."

"Thanks, I think. Do you want to tell her the rest or shall I?"

"Hardly worth mentioning. Finding you was the important thing and I'm tired of talking for a bit." He leaned back and closed his eyes, pretending to sleep.

"What happened?" Julie asked me.

"I told them I knew where the others were and would lead them there on one condition: they would let me help. I wanted to watch the loups die. I needed to know they were dead. I couldn't leave before I did. I felt I owed them that."

"Didn't need him to find the rest but it seemed fair after all he'd been through," Mahon added without opening his eyes.

"You weren't scared anymore?" Julie asked.

"No. I was tired of running. Tired of hiding. Tired of being hungry. And mostly I was angry."

"You were that," Mahon agreed. "Not that you didn't have cause."

"I took them back to where we lived. We dug some traps and I lured them out. Like he said, not that exciting."

"Loups chasing you wasn't exciting?"

"Not really. There were six of us and only four of them left. When it was all done, I went with Mahon back to Atlanta. Lived with him and Martha. George too. Slept a lot, ate a lot. Not much left to tell."

"Six months later, he was the Beast Lord of the Pack," Mahon put in.

"How?" Julie asked.

"I killed a really big bear," I told her. "Somebody had to."

Kate and Martha came into the living room with plates and cups.

"Can you get the food?" Kate asked me.

I got up.

"Are you going to show me the kitchen, boy?" Mahon asked.

I knew exactly what was coming. "Sure, follow me."

Mahon lumbered into the kitchen after me. "So, this is it? You're really giving it all up?"

"I already have. Fifteen years is a long time. How long did you think I would do it?"

"I guess I never thought you would want anything else."

"Neither did I. Then I did."

"Would you have stayed if it wasn't for her?"

I thought about it. "Yes. But not for long. I am tired of it. I've been tired of it before she ever came along. Of all of it."

Mahon growled. "It's what you were born to do. You don't abandon your birthright because you're bored."

"I wasn't bored, and I didn't abandon anything. We're still

here. We'll defend the Pack if it comes to that. We just won't be in charge of it. Give Jim a chance. He'll do fine."

"Not worried about him. I'm worried about you, and Kate, and Julie. Can you keep them safe out of the Pack and the Keep?"

"We'll be fine. More and more shapeshifters are moving in. It's a pretty safe neighborhood."

"Exactly."

"What?" I thought I knew what he was talking about but wanted him to say it.

"You're a First. Shapeshifters are drawn to you. Some are already here, and more will come. Atlanta can't have two packs. You're still the king, with or without the crown. Think, boy. Will Jim stand for it?"

"I don't see how he has a choice."

"If not him, there will be others. Do you really believe her daddy won't come here and burn this place down?"

"He can try. Until that time, we will be happy here. Isn't that enough?"

"No, not really. I want you to lead. To stand for something bigger than yourself. But you're a grown man and can make your own decisions. I don't have to like it."

"No, you really don't." I winked at him. "But you're welcome to come by anytime you feel like it and tell me all things I'm doing wrong. And if you ever need someone to go with you to hunt loups on the mountain, you know where I live."

Mahon smiled. "I may take you up on that. Let's go get some tea and honey muffins."

JIM'S POINT OF VIEW

(Magic Breaks)

I poured myself half a glass of Maker's Mark, sat in my office with my feet on my desk and let the fire roll down my throat. Getting drunk when you're a shapeshifter is like trying to carry water in a bucket with a hole at the bottom. You get a buzz for a minute or two and it's over. But it's smooth while it lasts.

We made it. We were alive and for now, life was good. We'd survived d'Ambray's attempt to start a war between the Pack and the People, rescued Kate from her daddy's special prison and she and Curran had even managed to thwart his "claiming" of Atlanta.

To think I knew her when she was lowly merc with little more than smart mouth and a sharp sword. I liked Kate, then and now, and I was glad that she came into her own. Maybe now she and Curran could get back to running the Pack and everybody else could get back to doing their damn jobs. It's hard to be on high alert for too long. It wears you down. What we all needed was some stability and routine. Status Quo.

A knock on the door interrupted my musing. What the fuck? I told Logan to not let anyone get to me until the morning.

The knock again, this time more insistent, and Barabas's scent. Tinted with something, adrenaline? Barabas smelled keyed up. I grabbed a pair of sweatpants and pulled them on.

Dali raised her head from the couch and sat up, the blanket slipping off her. She was wearing my favorite outfit of hers: tank top and panties.

"What is it?"

"It's nothing," I told her. We'd celebrated a little when we got to the Keep and everyone was still in one piece.

The knock persisted. "Coming," I growled.

She pulled the blanket up to her chin and yawned. "Make them go away."

I padded barefoot over to the door. Barabas was knocking nonstop.

"Barabas, if your hand touches that door again, I'm gonna rip it off and make you eat it."

"Open the damn door. This can't wait."

What the hell?

I opened the door to see what was so damn urgent that it couldn't wait until morning.

"Well?" I demanded.

He marched in and handed me a stack of papers. "For you. You need to sit down."

"Who died?"

"It's not like that, Jim. Sit down, read the packet, sign on the two pages where the sticky tape is, and I'll answer your questions."

"Or you could stop dicking around and just tell me what this is all about. What if we did that?"

"Fine. Be an ass about it." He straightened, sighed, and in a formal monotone announced, "The king is dead, long live the king. It's my last official duty as the Pack's council to inform you, James Shrapshire, that the Beast Lord, Curran Lennart has abdicated and chosen you as his successor. You have his blessing. Congratulations, my Lord."

He saluted sharply, executed an about face, and closed the door behind him.

Dali's blanket flew aside. She sprinted to me and took the papers out of my hand. She looked them over for a few moments and with great deliberation rolled them up, touched me lightly with them on each shoulder and made a benediction motion before handing them back to me.

"He wasn't lying. You need to read them. He left you a note."

Damn it all to hell. And there it was, in Curran's barely legible chicken scratch.

Lord Jim.

Couldn't resist, could he?

I know you're probably pretty pissed off at me right now, but I'm done, man. I've been doing this shit half my life and all of my adult life. I've got a shot at being happy and I'm going to take it. You can do this, hell, probably better than I did. It's time for a change. This is your chance to make the Pack yours.

Make Peace with the Rats. I'd put them in charge of security. They're at least as good as you were. They could be powerful allies, and you'll have enough enemies as is. Desandra is new and not ready to challenge you. Yet. Keep an eye on her.

Rafael is solid but if you show too much favor to the wolves, the Boudas will resent it. Play them against each other. You don't want them to have a common enemy.

Mahon is getting old. He likes the status quo, but I've spoken to him and he'll support you if for no other reason than I picked you. I know you'll want your own people but keep him on as Pack Executioner. At least for a while, they respect and, more importantly, fear him. Still, you're going to have to kill someone yourself. They have to know you'll do it. They'll test you, they'll flatter you, and some idiot might even challenge you. My advice, make it quick, clean and very public.

Watch out for Dali, a lot of them see her as weak, but she's smart, smarter than both of us put together. After your position is solid, let them come to her with stuff. They'll see her as more approachable, someone that can intercede with you on their behalf. Use that. You get to be the hardass and she's the good guy.

Be tough but fair. Of course, it's your baby now, and I'm retired. When you're done being mad and you feel like having a beer with an old friend, you'll know where to find me.

Take care of yourself,

Curran

No. You. Fucking. Don't! You don't get to dump this shit on me. "Poor me, I'm tired of being the boss, Jim, you do it, oh and here's how I'd do it, but I don't want to do it anymore. I'm running away to the burbs to play house with my scary blood magic queen. Have fun."

"No goddamn way. If he thinks he can just quit and make me take over… I'm going up there and talk some sense into him."

Dali touched my arm lightly. "No."

I turned to her.

"Jim, he means it. He hasn't been happy in a long time, and I think he's doing it, at least somewhat, for Kate. She can't be the Consort anymore. Did you feel the magic when she claimed the city?"

I felt it. It raised every hair on my body.

"She's something else now," Dali said. "And he won't be without her. Just like I wouldn't be without you. He made his choice. We don't have to like it."

"I don't want the Pack. I never did."

"I know, he knows that too and that's why he chose you. You're angry but in his asshole way he paid you a compliment. Of all the people he picked you, not because you're his best friend but because he believes you can do it. The only question now is will you?

"I don't know, maybe. Do you want me to?

She sank onto the couch. "I like this less than you do. It scares me. People will try to hurt us, and we'll have to hurt them, maybe kill them. I don't want to be the Consort."

"You don't have to be. I know you don't want this. I don't want this either…"

"Yes, you do," she said softly. "You do a little bit, Jim. I've seen you rule while he was gone. You liked it."

I opened my mouth to argue.

She put her fingers on my lips. "I love you and I know you can do it. I can't make that decision for you. I will be at your side, whatever happens. You're my guy. My Jim. But don't you dare use me as an excuse."

I took her in my arms, and we sat for a while like that. Holding each other tight, like we would never let go. We were in for shitstorm of biblical proportions and if I let go I knew it would drag me under. Dali sighed softly and, in that moment, I understood Curran and why he did what he did. Some of the anger and resentment faded. I was still going to punch him the moment I saw him, hard as I could. He had it coming, but I understood. If she asked me, in this moment, to leave with her, God help me I would.

And yet, at that moment the last line of an old poem came to mind. My father used to quote it to my mother when she worried about his research into loupism.

"I could not love thee, dear, half so well,
Loved I not honor more."

Now I finally understood what it meant and wished that I didn't. No, we weren't going to run and hide. We were going to do this together.

A cold resolve began to build in me, replacing the rage or maybe fueled by it. *Yeah, okay. It's my baby now and I am going to raise the hell out of it.*

The reign of the benevolent lion king is over. The Pack belonged to me and Dali now. We'd bend it to our will or break it all apart.

I kissed Dali. We would have to tell them all in the morning, but tonight was ours and ours alone.

GROCERY LISTS

Kate

1 lb sugar

6 apples

1 lb flour

2 steaks 4 steaks... Call Jim. Find out, hypothetically speaking, how much meat that bastard can eat in a single seating.

2 baking potatoes

Brown sugar and sea salt to season the steaks.

Onion...a large one...if he gives me any grief, I can cork his mouth with it

What am I forgetting?

Oh yes, refills for the tool belt, ground rosemary, thyme, angelica. And clove oil for the knives.

Curran

10 lbs of meat
Butter to cook it in

Dali
Rice
1 jar sambal bajack
1 clove garlic
Eggs
shallots
1 head broccoli
tofu — do not buy the one in red wrapper, they put it in the
meat section and it was touching bacon last time
a bag of frozen peas
soy sauce

Jim
3 pints white button mushrooms
shallots
4 cloves garlic
10 sprigs fresh thyme, check the leaf quality
4 lb beef tenderloin, center cut
2 lb proscuitto
1 jar Dijon mustard
Chives
1 lb flour
1 carton of eggs
1 bag fingerling potatoes
1 pound puff pastry
brandy

beef stock

cream

1 lb unsalted butter

1 bottle extra-virgin olive oil

Kosher salt and freshly ground black pepper

Copyright Page

EXCERPT FROM BLOOD HEIR

I tossed a handful of wolfsbane into the air, spun Tulip around, and urged her into a canter. She flew through night-soaked streets like a ghost. Wind tugged at my hair. Even if Desandra chased me, she'd have a hard time catching up, and the wolfsbane would leave her nose-blind for a couple of hours.

Ahead, Lucile Avenue dead-ended into Abernathy Boulevard. We made a right and headed north west.

An eerie howl floated on the night wind. The hair on the back of my neck stood on end, an instinctual reaction coded in my genes when humans were food and we feared being eaten.

It came from the left. If Desandra had chased me and howled, it would've come from the right or behind us. Were there wolves guarding her? She could've brought a team with her. Had I blundered into a trap?

I sent my magic out in a pulse. It splayed out, searching, collided with bodies, and I felt them, wolves, running fast through the ruined houses on my right. One, two…

A second group, on the left, gliding through the overgrown wood that used to be Westview Cemetery. Three more, all larger than a wild wolf had a right to be.

Shit.

Another howl rose, a vicious song of hunt, a promise of sharp fangs and swift death. A second howl answered. The pack was closing in.

Tulip neighed, more outrage than fear, and broke into gallop. We thundered up the deserted street past the husks of abandoned homes. The wolves sang again. Ice rolled down my spine. This wasn't a pretend chase. I was being hunted.

A new presence came in from the right, moving fast on the edge of my magic. It lashed my senses like a knife, emanating power. Not Desandra. Something else. Something savage, something more... Moving way too fast.

Tulip screamed in alarm.

The presence tore through the field of my magic like a dagger.

We had to get clear.

We rounded the curve. Ahead, something blocked the road. The moon peeked through the clouds. An overturned semi, flanked by a bunch of smashed cars.

Wolves burst from the woods behind me.

Forest on the left, semi in front. Turning right, toward East I-20, was my only option. I swung Tulip onto MLK Drive.

The overpass in front of me had crumbled. A hill of debris blocked the road.

A dead end. They'd run me to ground.

I let the reins go slack, so Tulip could stop on her own. She made a wide arc by the rubble, slowing, and I turned her toward the road and the cemetery on the other side, our backs to the overpass. I was done running.

No more howling. It was quiet now. The only sound was Tulip breathing hard.

Shadows congealed from the gloom between the trees on the other side. Slowly, paw over paw, the wolves padded out into the open. Three from the woods, two from the left, coming from Abernathy. Two grey Eurasians, one white Arctic, and the other two grey sprinkled with cinnamon - Timbers. Every single one was over two hundred pounds. Five pairs of glowing eyes stared at me.

Tulip bared her teeth.

The odds weren't in my favor. With the magic up, I could take them, but then the Pack would come after me in force.

A huge shape leaped from the roof of a brick building on the left and landed in front of the pack. Magic screamed a warning in my head.

A beast. A massive grey monster, bigger than any lupine shapeshifter I had ever seen. He was almost as big as Dad and Dad was a fucking prehistoric lion.

Two golden eyes focused on me, their gaze pinning me in place. Suddenly it was hard to breathe. My body locked up, convinced that I was prey. The Alpha stare.

He *dared*.

I stared right back. Holding his gaze was like trying to lift a car.

The moon tore through the clouds, spilling pale light onto the intersection. It slid over the giant wolf's fur, setting it aglow. He wasn't grey. He was silver. Unnaturally silver.

I blinked, bringing my magic vision up. A faint mint green rippled over his coat. Fuck.

The wolf took a step forward, bathed in moonlight.

My hands went cold. A bitter metallic taste coated my tongue. I blinked the magic colors away and reached for my bow, attached to Tulip's saddle.

Step.

Another.

I raised my bow. Everything came into crystal clear focus. My breathing was deep and even. The world shrank down to three things: the wolf, my bow, and the distance between us.

A third step.

I plucked an arrow from the quiver.

His black lips stretched, showing me a forest of fangs.

Keep smiling. You'll look really funny with an arrow sticking out of your mouth.

His silver fur tore. In an instant, bone melted like wax, reshaping itself, muscles stretched, snapping over the new frame, and human skin sheathed the new form. A man with golden eyes stared at me, tall, broad shouldered, corded with muscle. The moonlight played over his face, highlighting the network of thin scars.

Derek.

My heart stopped. It couldn't have, because I would've died, but it felt like it had.

His eyes were ice-cold. He looked at me as if this was his land and I trespassed.

Derek opened his mouth.

I had to run. Now. Before I heard his voice.

I sent a mental scream to Tulip. *Go!*

The magic command whipped Tulip into motion. She reared, pawing the ground. A faint outline of a horn shimmered on her forehead. Tulip spun, surged toward the rubble, leaped, landing on the broken concrete like a gazelle and dashed over the fallen overpass. For a moment we went airborne and then we were galloping down the road at a breakneck speed into the night.

Order BLOOD HEIR at the retailer of your choice!

ALSO BY ILONA ANDREWS

Kate Daniels World

BLOOD HEIR

Kate Daniels Series

MAGIC BITES

MAGIC BLEEDS

MAGIC BURNS

MAGIC STRIKES

MAGIC MOURNS

MAGIC BLEEDS

MAGIC DREAMS

MAGIC SLAYS

GUNMETAL MAGIC

MAGIC GIFTS

MAGIC RISES

MAGIC BREAKS

MAGIC STEALS

MAGIC SHIFTS

MAGIC STARS

MAGIC BINDS

MAGIC TRIUMPHS

The Iron Covenant

IRON AND MAGIC

UNTITLED IRON AND MAGIC #2

Hidden Legacy Series

BURN FOR ME

WHITE HOT

WILDFIRE

DIAMOND FIRE

SAPPHIRE FLAMES

EMERALD BLAZE

RUBY FEVER

Innkeeper Chronicles Series

CLEAN SWEEP

SWEEP IN PEACE

ONE FELL SWEEP

SWEEP OF THE BLADE

SWEEP WITH ME

Kinsmen

SILENT BLADE

SILVER SHARK

THE KINSMEN UNIVERSE (anthology with both SILENT BLADE and SILVER SHARK)

FATED BLADES

The Edge Series

ON THE EDGE

BAYOU MOON

FATE'S EDGE

STEEL'S EDGE

ABOUT THE AUTHOR

Ilona Andrews is the pseudonym for a husband-and-wife writing team. Ilona is a native-born Russian and Gordon is a former communications sergeant in the U.S. Army. Contrary to popular belief, Gordon was never an intelligence officer with a license to kill, and Ilona was never the mysterious Russian spy who seduced him. They met in college, in English Composition 101, where Ilona got a better grade. (Gordon is still sore about that.)

Gordon and Ilona currently reside in Texas with their two children, and many dogs and cats. They have co-authored two series, the bestselling urban fantasy of *Kate Daniels* and romantic urban fantasy of *The Edge*.

Visit Ilona Andrews' website for the latest news, freebies, and other fun things. https://ilona-andrews.com/

CPSIA information can be obtained
at www.ICGtesting.com
Printed in the USA
LVHW011423220723
753178LV00030B/593